"I'm so tired of screwing everything up, Laura," Trent whispered.

"I can't fix what I've done. And I damn sure don't deserve your forgiveness." He lowered his forehead to hers, his palms warm and solid against her skin. "But I'm asking you to help me. Help me reset my normal. Help me learn how to be a dad again. A husband." His eyes burned and he blinked rapidly.

She pressed her lips together, biting back fresh tears. "And what happens when you leave again?" she whispered. "What do I do then?" She sniffed quietly. "You keep breaking my heart." Her voice cracked.

His fingers crooked around her jaw. "I want to stop."

Without giving herself time to think about the consequences, she leaned closer and brushed her lips gently against his. She pulled away before he could deepen the kiss. Fear and awareness and arousal skittered through her veins, making her off balance, like a needful, sensual thing. The faintest brush of lips against lips had sparked something primitive inside her. Something deeper and richer. A long-forgotten need to be touched by a man—by this man...

"A moving story with rich, layered characters and real, heart-felt emotion. Don't miss this fabulous read!"

—Brenda Novak, *New York Times* bestselling author

"Jessica Scott's novels are beautifully written, honestly authentic, and richly emotional."

—JoAnn Ross, *New York Times* bestselling author

ALSO BY JESSICA SCOTT

I'll Be Home For Christmas (ebook)
All for You
It's Always Been You

JESSICA SCOTT

Back to You

FOREVER

NEW YORK   BOSTON

Copyright © 2014 by Jessica Dawson
Excerpt from *All for You* copyright © 2014 by Jessica Dawson
Excerpt from *It's Always Been You* copyright © 2014 by Jessica Dawson

Forever
Hachette Book Group
237 Park Avenue
New York, NY 10017

www.HachetteBookGroup.com

Printed in the United States of America

Originally published as an ebook

First mass-market edition: July 2014
10 9 8 7 6 5 4 3 2 1

OPM

Forever is an imprint of Grand Central Publishing.
The Forever name and logo are trademarks of Hachette Book Group, Inc.

The Hachette Speakers Bureau provides a wide range of authors for speaking events. To find out more, go to www.hachettespeakersbureau.com or call (866) 376-6591.

The publisher is not responsible for websites (or their content) that are not owned by the publisher.

To Fluffy and Hammy
The original escape artists

Acknowledgments

Dear Reader,

This is the most difficult book I've ever written. It's also the one that taught me the value of strong friends to lean on when the going gets really, really rough. I've been working on Laura and Trent's story since 2008 so I'll probably screw this up, but anyway, here goes.

Julie Kenner, you kept me sane through long rewrites and many, many rounds of edits and revisions. You always gave me straight advice and let me call you in absolute panic. Thanks for being a great mentor and friend. Allison Brennan and Roxanne St. Claire, thanks for letting me lean on you when I wanted to quit. Ruthie Knox and Elisabeth Barrett, you are both amazing writers and I am lucky to call you both friend. Not too many folks will come running to a hotel room when there's epic flail going on. Thanks for letting me not have my stuff together all the time. My agent, Donna Bagdasarian, thank you. You know all the thousand reasons why but mostly thanks for believing in me, especially when I don't. And finally to my amazing and talented editor, Michele Bidelspach: Thank you for pushing me to write this book the way it needed to be written and for having the faith in this story that I sometimes lacked.

Back to You

Prologue

⁊

I put your checkbook in the front pocket of your rucksack. Did you find the sleep medication? You'll need to sleep on the plane so that you're rested when you land. And I put your calling card—"

Captain Trent Davila looked up from where he sat on the edge of their bathtub. He held a tiny folded flag in his hands. For a moment, he'd been somewhere else. Sulfur scorched the inside of his nose. The thunder of the fifty cal reverberated off his breastbone.

"What's that?" she asked softly, watching him from the bathroom door.

He held out his palm so she could see the little flag. "Good luck charm. I can't deploy without it."

A thousand questions flickered over her face as her gaze fell onto that tiny flag. She bit her lip and turned away, but not before he saw the naked fear looking back at him.

He moved, stepping in front of his wife and capturing her face in his palms. Her skin was smooth and soft and achingly familiar, and a deep part of his soul missed her already.

But that part of his soul wasn't in control right now. The moment she touched him, his soul recoiled, refusing to let him take even the simplest pleasure in her touch.

He'd cheated death and he knew, *knew* he didn't deserve to be there with his wife when so many of his men had died.

That's why he had to leave. Again. It didn't matter to where. It didn't matter if it was the war in Iraq or a transition team somewhere in the mountains of Afghanistan. He needed to get away. To get back into the fight.

And pray that his wife would understand why he had to go.

"Laura." He whispered her name, capturing her attention.

She tried to look away, to pretend that today was just another day. But Trent knew her too well. He saw the doubt and the fear that she tried to hide. Her eyes, though, her eyes always gave her away. He stroked an errant strand of copper hair away from her forehead, meeting her golden eyes, unable to speak any words of comfort. He knew they'd just be more empty lies.

She offered a watery smile. "I'm terrified of losing you again," she whispered.

"I've deployed since I got hurt. This time is no different."

"You didn't get hurt." She refused to meet his gaze. "You died. Your heart actually stopped beating. And this time is worse. This is the Surge." Her voice broke. "I can't lose you again," she whispered. Her voice cracked as the tears tumbled down her cheeks.

He hated to see her cry. Worse, he knew he could prevent those tears.

He pulled her close and simply held her, wishing he could feel as alive with his wife and family as he did when he was at war. Maybe someday, when the war was over, he could figure out what had broken inside him and how to fix it.

He stroked his thumbs over her cheeks as the kids

shrieked in Ethan's bedroom. The sound sent a spike of anxiety through Trent's heart, but he smiled, hoping to cheer her up. "Sounds like someone just lost a Lego."

"Daddy!"

"He's probably going to beg you for a hamster again," she said. Laura swiped at her eyes, blinking rapidly. "Can't let them see me like this."

He slid from her embrace, regret sealing the walls that four deployments had erected around his heart. Trent tried not to notice how intently Laura watched him, her gaze sweeping over the scars on his body as he finished getting dressed. His dog tags banged against his ribs as he dragged his t-shirt over his head and pulled on the rest of his uniform and then his boots.

"Well, you could get one," Trent said, needing the distraction of simple conversation.

"Or," Laura said with a smile that didn't reach her eyes, "you could promise him one when you get home. It'll give him something to look forward to."

Trent frowned at the odd note in Laura's voice and focused on tying his boots and tucking the laces beneath the cuffs of his pants. "He won't even notice I'm gone. They're both too little."

Trent straightened as Laura approached, placing her palm over the scar on his heart. It burned where she touched him. It took everything he had not to flinch away from the gentleness in that touch. "Keep telling yourself that," she said with a soft kiss. "They miss you when you're gone. We all do."

He sighed quietly and glanced at her, resting his hands gently on her hips. "Laura, you know I have to go."

He couldn't explain it. Didn't have the words to explain the emptiness inside him that consumed every waking moment when he wasn't over there. And worse, he didn't ever want her to see the emptiness he tried so hard to hide from her.

She believed he'd come home. As long as she continued to believe that, his world would continue to exist.

She brushed her thumb over his bottom lip. She blinked rapidly and the sight of her tears almost penetrated the cold empty space where his heart had been. "I just wish it got a little easier waiting for you, that's all." Her fingers wrapped around his dog tags, her thumb sliding along the chain. "But we'll be here when you get back. We always are."

He ran his fingers lightly over her face. The lie he'd told his wife so often sat like a concrete wall between them. She didn't know that he'd volunteered for this deployment, for so many others, and he had no way of killing the lie without killing their marriage. "Don't go getting a deployment boy-friend while I'm gone."

"I don't think you have to worry about that." Laura wrapped her arms around him, nuzzling his neck. They stood for a long moment before Laura eased away.

Trent swallowed and let her go. Again.

Five hours later, Trent kissed his wife good-bye for the fourth time in six years. His four-year-old son and two-year-old daughter were getting antsy, climbing up and down the bleachers nonstop. As he walked away from the gym where he and the rest of his unit had checked in for the deployment, he glanced up at her in the stands. She was steady. Stoic. Trying valiantly not to join the ranks of the wives and children who were crying as their soldiers left them, assault packs and weapons in hand. God but he wished he didn't have to go. That he was man enough to stay home and fix whatever was broken inside him. Wished that he was man enough to need her more than the heady, uncertain terror of war.

"You ready, sir?"

Trent glanced over at First Sarn't Roy Story, a man who'd taught Trent the right way to kick in doors and the difference between knowing when to wipe a nose or whip an ass. The war was lined into Story's leathery face. Fifteen years as an infantryman that had started in Mogadishu and continued with the long slog through Iraq.

"Are we ever really ready for this?" Trent asked, taking one more long look at his wife and kids. And then he turned away, needing to harden his heart for the battles to come.

Outside, Trent climbed aboard the bus that would take them to the airfield. Spouses filed out from the gym along the sidewalk. In the seat behind him, Sergeant Vic Carponti was harassing one of Trent's platoon sergeants, Sergeant First Class Shane Garrison. He almost smiled. With those two around, things would never be dull.

He scanned the crowd, searching for his wife amongst the blurry faces of other people's spouses lining the sidewalk. There. She held her vigil in front of a light pole, a tiny hand in each of hers. Beside her, Ethan stood bravely, tears streaming down his face. He held a tiny salute, his mouth pressed into a flat line as he tried to be a tough little man. Emma waved brightly at the bus, still too little to fully understand that Daddy was leaving for longer than a trip to the grocery store.

He looked away but it was far, far too late. When he closed his eyes, the image of his small family was seared onto his retinas as the bus pulled out of the parking lot and headed for the airfield.

"Never gets any easier, does it?" Story asked quietly, sucking on the end of an unlit cigar while he fiddled with a light on his helmet. There was little love left between Story and his wife. Story deployed to avoid his wife.

But Trent deployed to avoid his *life*. Because life back in the rear was too complicated, too loud, too chaotic. War was simpler.

The scar on his chest ached and he rubbed it, wishing

he could forget the way his family looked as the bus pulled away.

He closed his eyes, trying to put them out of his mind. He didn't want to remember his wife with her cheeks streaked with tears or the raw grief in her eyes. He wanted to remember her face as she slept curled into his side. Or laughing with their kids. He needed to carry those memories into war with him. Because that was all that would steel him against the long hours and bone-crushing fatigue to come.

He had soldiers to command. His family would be there when he came home.

He hoped.

Chapter One

🏵

Fort Irwin, California 2008

One year later...

Trent walked out of the ops tent, needing a few minutes to himself. They'd just sent word that the wife of a kid in one of the companies was in the hospital. She was going into labor while her husband was enjoying the fun and sun of the National Training Center.

At least the kid wasn't deployed. He'd be able to get home quickly. Sure, not as quickly as if he was back at Fort Hood, but still. It beat the hell out of trying to get home from Iraq.

The notification was something simple, and yet it had struck Trent that yet another soldier was going to miss the birth of his child because of the army.

He knew exactly how that felt, and right then a thousand bitter memories rose up, reminding him of everything he'd willingly squandered. The resurrected hurt was so raw, the regret so powerful, he nearly choked on it.

He should have been used to the hurt by now, but lately it seemed to be getting worse. It overwhelmed the dead space inside him, forcing him to feel things he didn't want—and wasn't ready—to feel.

He didn't know *how* to feel them, how to deal with them. So for the moment he sat outside the ops tent and let the raging emotions storm inside him. Until he could get them under control. Until he could function again.

It had been happening more and more this year. The things he'd stuffed away had started having a nasty habit of reappearing when he least expected them.

He was starting to get comfortable with the crazy, but at least now he was starting to recognize the warning signs. Which was why he was sitting outside the ops tent.

"So your BFF Marshall is looking for you." Story walked out of the ops tent, a smirk on his face that only meant bad things for Trent. It was so strange calling him "master sergeant" instead of "first sergeant," but Story wasn't a first sergeant anymore. Just like Trent was no longer a commander.

Trent sat on the hood of a Humvee, smoking a cigar and contemplating his sixth cup of coffee since he'd come on shift twelve hours ago. He pushed his glasses up higher on his nose then glanced over as Story hopped up next to him.

Since they'd both been fired more than a year ago, they'd been hanging out on the staff together, responsible for nothing but PowerPoint slides. Funny how getting fired meant giving up the hard jobs in the army. You still got to stay in the army, but you just weren't trusted with taking care of soldiers anymore. It was a punishment, being put in the easy jobs. Trent would have given anything to get his old job as a company commander back, but that wasn't going to happen so he and Story and Iaconelli kept each other sane and avoided the new commander. Captain James T. Marshall the Third drove everyone fucking crazy.

"Should I be worried?" Trent asked dryly, adjusting his glasses again. He'd long ago given up getting upset when

Marshall attempted to piss in his cornflakes. Marshall had been tapped to take over Trent's company when he'd gotten himself fired and Marshall took great pleasure in reminding everyone that he was fixing all the things that Trent had screwed up. It grated on Trent's last nerve every time the words, "Well sir, I'm still fixing the mess I was left when I took over" came out of Marshall's mouth at staff meetings, but what could Trent say? He *had* gotten fired. It didn't matter why. He supposed part of his penance for being a shitty commander was having to listen to Marshall without knocking his teeth out. He'd leave that for Story and a few of the captains like Ben Teague who were leading the insurgency on the staff. Trent had other things on his mind.

Like his wife. His two kids. The house that was no longer his.

He cleared his throat and tried to listen to Story.

"I don't know," Story said. "Marshall wasn't screaming so I think maybe you should be okay?"

Sergeant First Class Reza Iaconelli, one of Trent's former platoon sergeants, stepped out of the ops tent. "No, you should definitely hide," he said, interrupting the conversation. "He's bitching about having to transport you back to the rear early and he's pretty cranky."

Iaconelli was a big man: broad shoulders and built like an ox. He was steadfast and solid downrange but when they got home? Yeah, that's when things went to shit for Iaconelli. He'd never met a bottle of alcohol that he didn't like. He was lucky he still had a career but the sergeant major liked him. Trent respected his ability in combat enough to overlook any personal failings. Trent was the last one to judge someone's personal failings.

He reined his thoughts back to the present and the feeling that flittered in the dead space around his heart. "I'm getting sent back?"

Iaconelli shrugged. "Maybe they're finally going to court-martial your sorry ass," he said lightly.

Trent flipped him off. "That would be nice, actually. If they'd at least get the damn thing over with. If I never see Lieutenant Jason Randall ever again, it will be too soon."

"He is a special little fuckstick, that is for certain," Iaconelli said, staring at the end of his cigar for a moment.

Iaconelli may or may not have threatened to kill LT Randall downrange. Twice. But all of Randall's interpersonal hostility had been a sideshow, a distraction to keep Trent or anyone else from figuring out that he had been selling sensitive items and funneling the money to bribe the Iraqis to stop blowing their boys up. Randall had finally gotten caught and now was determined to take down Trent and anyone else he could with him. Iaconelli chopped the tip off his cigar and sucked on the end while he tried to light it.

"Too bad I won't be around for his court-martial," Story said.

"Did you get reassigned?" Iaconelli asked Story.

"Yeah. I'm deploying again in about two weeks. As soon as we get back from here," he said.

"Your wife isn't going to be happy," Trent said quietly.

"Actually, she's going to be thrilled. It'll give her a chance to find her some twenty-year-old boy toy to keep her busy while I'm gone." Story spat into the dust.

"So you're still married because . . . ?" Iaconelli sucked on the end of his cigar.

"Because it's too fucking expensive to get divorced," Story said. "I'll take care of it after this next deployment. I'll save up some money first, though."

"Sure you will," Trent said. "You've been saying that since '04."

It was Story's turn to flip Trent off. "At least I'm willing to accept my marriage is over."

Trent rubbed his heart, knowing his first sergeant hadn't meant to score such a direct hit. At least not with malice. "Yeah well, my divorce is complicated."

"These things always are." Iaconelli leaned against the truck. "Which is why I've never gotten married."

Trent snorted and was going to make a crack but Marshall took that opportunity to step into the darkness outside the ops tent. "Davila, you're going back to Fort Hood."

Trent glanced at his watch. "It's four-thirty in the morning."

"And you're going to be on a plane in three hours. Pack your shit." Marshall turned to stalk off, mumbling about pain in the ass captains and not having enough time for this shit.

Iaconelli blew a smoke ring into the darkness. "God but he is such a charmer."

Trent sat there long after Story and Iaconelli went back into the ops tent.

He wanted to go home. But now that it was happening, fear slithered down his spine.

It had started slow. One day he'd wake up, dreaming about Laura. Other times, he'd be in the mess tent and he'd think he heard her laugh. He'd hear a kid giggling on the TV and he'd look up, expecting to see Ethan or Emma.

Always, though, he was alone. He'd wanted it that way for so long. He'd wanted quiet when they'd been running around his feet, shrieking and bickering like kids did. He'd craved silence at the end of the day when someone would get out of bed for a glass of water.

He'd certainly gotten the silence and the solitude.

And the oppressive emptiness of it all ate away at him. He'd thrown himself into work here in the California desert. He'd pulled eighteen hour days gladly. The longer he spent away from the war, the less he felt its siren call, luring him back. And somehow, work wasn't enough anymore. Nothing he did pushed away the aching need to get to the one place he simply didn't belong: home.

He was back in the States but he couldn't go home. Not with an investigation hanging over his head and the potential for a very long jail sentence standing in front of him. And the worst part about the entire court-martial was that his brigade commander was changing command soon. If Colonel Richter left before the case was resolved, Trent would be at the mercy of the new commander—a new man with no loyalty to the soldiers he'd put in leadership positions.

It was not a comfortable place to be. The power plays between the senior officers never ended well for junior officers, and Trent? Trent was caught right now. He had to trust that Colonel Richter would take care of this before he left.

But a year after Trent had been sent home, Trent was running low on trust and patience.

Patience had never been his strong suit. Every other time he'd been home, he'd been prepping to go back to war. This time, the year had stretched in front of him like an unending slog.

It was the longest time he'd spent in the States since he'd gotten shot. It had taken him almost that long to realize just how badly he'd fucked up everything in his life that was supposed to be important.

His marriage. His kids. His family.

If there was a grade lower than an F at being a husband or a dad, he'd earned it. He'd come home from Iraq nearly a year ago—pending a court-martial and a divorce. And since then, nothing had happened. The case had been stuck in investigation mode forever. And the divorce? He just wasn't able to sign the papers. His life had been frozen in carbonite on all counts.

The investigation had moved slower than molasses in winter. And he was glad.

Because standing out here in the California desert, he'd come to a conclusion. He wanted his family back. He wanted his wife back. When she'd slapped him with divorce papers last year, he'd refused to sign them, hoping that the investigation would go away and that he could fix things with her. But that hope had proved futile. The distance between them was too much. The warmth he remembered was gone, but still, he'd been unable to let her go. He couldn't. Sure, they spoke on the phone or when he saw her at the office, but they were a few stolen minutes here, a quick chat about the kids. There was nothing there to give him hope that he could fix things with her.

He'd volunteered to train soldiers anywhere he could so that he didn't have to face the cold emptiness of the reality that he was no longer welcome in his own home. And if he volunteered, someone else wouldn't have to.

Now? Now he sat in the middle of the California desert and thought about the new dad who wouldn't be there for the birth of his child. He looked down at his wedding ring and thought of all the time he'd willingly given up.

He was a goddamned fool. He wanted her back. Damn it, he wanted his *life* back. The life with this woman who had once smiled and laughed with him and wrapped herself around him while she slept. Who was as beautiful changing Emma's diaper as she was dressed up in an evening gown for the Cav ball. This woman who used to ask about his day when he called home at two in the morning, even after she'd been up half the night with one of the kids.

He sobered, his hands trembling at the thought of his children and the tiny family that had grown while he'd been away. The tiny family that overwhelmed him and terrified him and dropped him to his knees with a need so strong, it crushed his lungs until he could not breathe. He didn't know how to feel good, but he knew he'd never figure it out without them.

He had no clue where to start. He had no idea how to be a father to his kids. Or a husband to a wife who could barely look at him.

Trent hopped off the top of the truck. He had a phone call to make.

Because it looked like he was getting exactly what he wanted.

And it was time to figure out how to be the man his family needed him to be.

Fort Hood

"Son of a bi-iscuit!"

"Bad Mommy!"

Laura Davila wrapped her scraped and bleeding knuckles in a paper towel and prayed to the patron saint of army wives for patience. Her six-year-old dishwasher was currently spread in carefully laid out pieces across the kitchen floor and counters. And now the cavernous white interior was splattered with her blood. Awesome.

Her son Ethan looked up at her with disapproval in his dark brown eyes, and Laura flinched. "Sorry, honey. Mommy just hurt herself."

"You said a bad word." This from her daughter, Emma. "Agent Chaos said you're not allowed to say those words."

Laura glared at the fat brown hamster that was clutched in her daughter's hands. Agent Chaos looked up at her with disapproving beady brown eyes. Sitting there, silently judging her.

She had joked with Trent that he should buy the kids a hamster when he returned from his latest deployment. By the time he came back, things between them had already crumbled but he still remembered the damn hamster. He'd bought not one, but two of the stinking, smelly creatures. The hamster cuteness factor did not override the pain in the ass factor of having to clean their cages every other day to keep the smell from overpowering the entire house.

Maybe if Trent had been around more over the last year, she wouldn't have minded them so much. But instead of sitting at Fort Hood and working in an office like any other officer who was under investigation, he'd volunteered for several rotations at the National Training Center in Fort Irwin. He'd spent more time there than at Fort Hood over the last year. He might as well have just moved there.

She took a deep breath and pressed on her throbbing knuckles, focusing on the pain so that she wouldn't feel the tension that squeezed her heart every time she thought about her husband. She regretted sending him the divorce papers. She could admit that now, but she'd done the only thing she could at the time.

She could still remember that stupid flare of hope when he'd stood in her office that day. Hope that maybe, finally, he had come home to her.

But he hadn't.

And as time had ticked by and he'd refused to sign the papers and let her go, she'd moved beyond regret. Now, she wanted to move on with her life. Maybe someday she'd be able to think of Trent without the hurt and frustration that kept reminding her of everything she'd lost.

"You have to pay us each a quarter," Ethan said, stroking the fat orange hamster in his hands. Laura was seriously thinking about buying a cat—that would solve the hamster problem quickly enough. But it would be just one more thing to clean up after.

And she wasn't really up for the trauma of finding a dead hamster under the bed.

She could only imagine the therapy bills.

She pursed her lips and counted to ten...thousand. "Okay guys, why don't you go play in the garage or something? Mommy has too many parts in here, and I don't want you to get hurt."

Or move anything. But she didn't say that out loud, because that would only encourage them to run off with some vital component that would take her three days to identify and two more days to find online and order. A new dishwasher was not in the budget at the moment. Besides, she wanted to see if she could actually fix the thing herself.

She shooed the kids and their accompanying hamsters out of the kitchen and made her way through the master bedroom to the cache of Band-Aids she hid in her bathroom. The kids were all too eager to use every bandage in the house if she let them, which always meant that she couldn't find a Band-Aid when she really needed one. She'd resorted to hiding them like they were some kind of precious commodity. In her house, they were.

Laura pulled down the shoebox that held the first aid kit. She held her breath as she cleaned the cuts on her knuckles with iodine, then wrapped gauze halfway down her fingers, covering the empty space where her wedding and engagement rings had once been.

She paused, staring at her ring finger. Blood pooled on the pale band of skin there, as if her finger refused to forget the rings that had been there since forever.

Her finger might not forget the rings but that didn't mean it was a marriage worth waiting for. No amount of waiting or wishful thinking was going to change that. Trent had seen to that. And broken her heart all over again.

She knew in her heart that they were finished. He had lied to her so many times about his deployments. That alone had destroyed her trust in him. And then there was the rest of it...

She was ready for the pain to stop. Ready for her heart to stop waiting for the phone to ring. Waiting, so desperately for her heart to stop beating for a man who was never coming home.

A spike of melancholy pressed on her lungs. Damn it, what was wrong with her today? She was past mourning the death of her marriage. At least she kept telling herself that. So when was it going to stop hurting?

She briefly considered a shot of vodka to numb the pain, but that wasn't really a good idea since she was alone with the kids. She barely ever had a drink these days. She sighed and glanced wistfully at the discreet box on the top shelf in the bathroom closet. Droughts were not limited to alcohol.

She had gotten used to it, this new normal. While the kids were vibrant chaos, full of life and joy, the married part of her life was...well, it simply was. There was nothing there anymore. No joy. No hatred. Just silence and cold detachment overlying a dull aching sadness.

She simply wanted it to be over. And damn Trent to hell for dragging it out when he wasn't even willing to fight for them. And the silence between them? Between her and the man she'd thought she'd love for the rest of her life?

She sat on the edge of their bed, one finger rubbing absently over the bruised knuckles and her empty ring finger. She could hear the kids shrieking in the garage. One of the hamsters had gotten away. She smiled. She really didn't mind them, not when the kids loved the judgmental little beasts so much. It was a gesture of kindness from a man who couldn't be a father. She knew that.

It didn't make it hurt any less. She'd married him knowing what she was getting into, thinking her love for him was strong enough to withstand whatever the army could throw at them. Knowing that the army was a demanding job, that he'd be gone a lot. But that first deployment had done something to him, something deeper than just the visible scars on his body.

Once she never would have thought the silence would grow too loud or that his empty side of the bed would become too heavy to bear. Once she would have waited forever for him to come home to her.

But forever was a long time.

And her faith in their love had died long ago on some distant battlefield.

Chapter Two

Eight hours and a flight from hell later, Trent left his duffle bag in the operations office before walking down the halls of the Reaper Brigade headquarters. It was late summer in Fort Hood, Texas and it was mid to high nineties every day.

It had been a hot summer and an even hotter fall. The heat, Trent could deal with. He'd been in Kuwait when the temperature had hit one hundred and thirty-two. Ninety was a cold front.

But it was the cold from the office at the end of the hall he feared.

He was glad he'd been called back to Fort Hood. He'd let his mind drift the entire flight home. What would happen if he walked into Laura's office? He hadn't gotten through to her before he'd gotten on the plane home. She didn't know he was here.

It gave him a little more time to figure out what to say. How to ask for a chance. Maybe not to be the father of the year but maybe for a chance just to be a dad. If he could figure that out.

He rubbed his thumb over the smooth edge of his wedding band. Laura was an entirely different challenge.

He'd hurt her. Badly. And he had no idea how to fix it.

Maybe he could start with asking her if he could sleep on the couch. Because if he stayed at Fort Hood for more than a few weeks, he was going to have to find a more permanent place to stay than crashing at Shane and Jen's. The thought of asking Laura if he could come home sent a cold sweat prickling over his skin.

The likelihood of her allowing him through the front door for more than a short visit with the kids was snuggled up between slim and none. He had a better chance of hitting an IED and blowing the hell out of his truck in the middle of Highway 190 in Killeen than he had of getting her to agree to that.

Not that he blamed her.

At least she let him see the kids. And even that was a challenge. He didn't know how to be a father to the two small kids who'd morphed from babies to mindless banshees with needs and wants and an uncanny ability to strike all the right nerves and detonate his patience.

No matter how much he wished things were different, when it came to his family, he'd been a failure—and he was determined to fix things. No matter how much he wanted to be a bigger man and let his wife go, he simply could not bring himself to sign the papers that left him cold and empty. He'd tried. And each time, he'd put them away, choosing to wait just one more day, hoping that someday, he'd find the right words to explain to Laura why he'd had to go. To put the ragged emptiness into some form she could understand. He'd never wanted her to see that part of him, the dead part that walked and talked but felt nothing. He was alive. He should have been grateful.

Instead, the emptiness had swallowed everything, leaving him hollow. Until the only thing that felt right was the war.

He didn't want her to know that side of it. Never wanted

her to see him for what he was—a burned-out warrior who was only good at one thing. God but he didn't want her to see what he'd become.

He glanced at his watch. Right on time for the brilliant end to his career. Shoving aside the worries from home, he walked through the headquarters that had been his sanctuary from the tribulations of real life.

The headquarters was largely empty as most of the rear detachment staff had already left for the day. Apparently the staff were taking the new post commander's directive about being out of the office by five p.m. seriously and since they were the "lucky" ones who'd escaped the National Training Center, they were apparently skipping out of real work, too. That wouldn't last, though. About a week would go by before they all realized they couldn't get anything done when everyone left that early. He turned into a conference room and rapped his knuckles on the doorframe.

Major Patrick MacLean looked up from his laptop screen and nodded at the chair next to him at the conference room table, motioning for Trent to take a seat. Trent sat and waited silently for Patrick to finish writing an e-mail.

Trent had known Patrick for years, since they'd both been lieutenants on another brigade staff a lifetime ago. His friend's dark blue eyes were lined with stress and strain. Patrick often said that being an army lawyer was slowly but surely sucking the life out of him. He only saw the bad parts of the army. He never got to see the Soldier of the Year, except when said Soldier of the Year was being charged with something terrible, like aggravated assault or misuse of his government travel card.

Because there was nothing worse than misuse of the government travel card. He'd seen men killed, subordinates abused, but the fastest way to end a career was to get caught defrauding the government. He pushed his glasses up on the top of his head. He wasn't sure what that said about the organization he'd sacrificed everything for, but it didn't leave a good feeling in the pit of his gut.

Trent wished he was being charged with simple misconduct—simple fraud where he could be sent on his way and avoid the lengthy investigation. Instead, the allegations against him seemed like a cruel twist on reality—and a complex, year-long investigation to boot.

"How was your flight?" Patrick asked as he closed the lid of his laptop.

"Terrible. We sat on the jetway for two hours before we took off." Trent sucked in a hard breath through his nose, pushing down the riot of emotions churning inside him. "What's so important that I had to be yanked off the training mission three days early?" Not that Trent was complaining. But it was fear that filled the emptiness inside him now.

Fear that Laura had really gotten over him and let him go when he'd finally gotten his head out of his ass.

Fear that he'd truly lost everything.

Patrick rocked back in his chair. "First off, you should be at home, spending time with your family instead of volunteering for training mission after training mission, but we'll get to that in a minute."

Trent sighed. "I know."

Patrick lifted a single brow and started to say something. Then he snapped his mouth closed, opened a file, and slid the contents toward Trent. "We're getting ready to start the Article 32 hearing."

"That's the one where they decide if there's enough evidence to go to trial, right?"

"Got it in one. The prosecution at division wants a guilty plea, but I didn't accept it." Patrick slid a second manila folder across the desk. "You're in a world of shit, Trent, but we've got a good chance at beating this thing."

Trent snorted and shook his head quietly. "What makes you say that?"

"The witnesses against you are crap, for starters. Your former lieutenant Randall has very limited credibility, no matter who his daddy is, especially since he married his subordinate."

"Speak English?"

"Your lieutenant says you harassed one of your soldiers. That soldier is corroborating his story but since they got married, it looks like they're just backing up each other's stories instead of independently testifying to true events."

Trent frowned. "So the fact that my lieutenant was sleeping with one of his subordinates ruins his credibility?"

"More or less." Patrick sighed. "Ready for the heavy lifting? I need to go over what you're being charged with."

Trent braced himself. Then nodded once.

"I'll read through the specific violations of the Uniform Code of Military Justice first. We can go into the specifics of each charge after that." He flipped over the first sheet. "In that, on or about Fifteen October 2007, you were derelict in your duties to wit—"

Patrick's voice faded as the memory reached up and took hold, sucking him down into a swirling vortex.

"Sir, I don't understand."

"You're under investigation, Trent." Colonel Richter, the brigade commander himself, had broken the news to Trent. He was a man Trent had admired since they'd first rolled into combat together, six years prior. A man he looked up to.

"Am I being relieved, sir?"

"I'm sorry, son."

A man who was relieving him from command. Taking the responsibility, the honor of being a company commander away from him.

"Sir?"

"You're missing sensitive items that no one can account for. Your company funds have come up short on their audit. You've lost control of your officers and your soldiers. And your parts clerk Adorno has made an allegation of inappropriate conduct against you." Colonel Richter shook his head slowly.

"Adorno, sir? I rarely even see her. She works in the motor pool."

"She was recently pulled up to the company ops?" Colonel Richter asked.

"Yes, because she was having problems in the motor pool."

"And she worked long hours, alone in the company ops with just you."

Trent closed his eyes, seeing how neatly the trap had been sprung around him. He'd never even looked at that soldier funny and yet, simply because he'd been alone with her, the allegations were enough. "Sir—"

"I can't leave you in the job. I've lost faith in your ability to command."

"Sir, this is all bullshit. I accept responsibility for the missing items but you can't take me out of command in the middle of the fight. With Garrison and Carponti being wounded, I've lost two key leaders in my company. Give me time to build the new team. Please, sir. Don't do this."

Colonel Richter held up one hand. "I've made up my decision. You're restricted from any unsecure communications while the investigation is ongoing. Do not attempt to contact Adorno. Do not attempt to contact Lieutenant Randall. Let the investigation run its course."

Panic. Fear. Humiliation.

All of it rose up again now, circling like vultures over the kill as Patrick finished listing the charges against him. He'd waited months for the investigation to be complete.

He'd done what he was told. He hadn't called anyone—not even his wife. He'd let the investigation run its course. But he'd had no idea that in doing so, he'd nailed the coffin of his marriage shut. The letter had come from Laura a few weeks later, ripping out his soul and smashing it into the dusty, dried up desert earth. He'd lost everything in ninety-seven days.

"Are you listening to me?" Patrick asked.

Trent looked up. "Yeah. Sorry. What?"

"I said the only thing they have that has any legs is the inappropriate conduct allegation. Everything else, I've already got enough to rip their case to shreds."

Trent flipped through the documents Patrick handed him. "If the case against me is so flimsy, why are they going to all of this effort? What's the point?"

"You want my honest opinion?"

Patrick leaned forward and rubbed his hands over his face. His blue eyes were sharp and weary. "You're the sacrificial lamb."

"Meaning what?" Trent pushed his glasses to the top of his head.

"Lieutenant Randall is one very well-connected lieutenant. His father is connected to every powerful four-star general officer in the army. If you take the fall for this, Randall gets to continue the family name."

The bitterness roared back and this time, it brought its friends anger and hatred. Oh, but he hated that selfish, lying bastard lieutenant. Trent had been working round the clock to try and keep his boys safe and Randall? Randall had been getting blow jobs in the motor pool from Adorno instead of doing his fucking job.

And yet, Adorno had accused Trent of inappropriate conduct when nothing, *nothing*, even remotely close to inappropriate had happened. Oh the irony; it galled.

"Lieutenant Randall stole weapons and traded them for

cash. That was his crime and his alone. Your crime was your failure as a commander to be aware of your subordinate's actions," Patrick said quietly. "The accusations against you are very serious. And unless we can prove that Randall and his wife are lying—that you didn't know about what he was doing, and weren't a part of it—he's intent on taking you down to lessen his punishment. He pleas down his punishment to testify against you. As the commander, you're a bigger fish."

"So then the inappropriate conduct allegations against me are just icing on the cake?"

"It's an attack on your character. Do you have any proof that Randall and Adorno were already involved during the deployment?"

"Sure. I've got YouTube videos of him and Adorno doing the nasty in a Porta-Potty." He swore viciously and tossed his glasses on the table. "Of course not."

"YouTube videos would probably help. At this point, a grainy cell phone photo might do the trick."

"I don't see how we can fix this," Trent muttered, rubbing his eyes.

"You should have more faith in me than that."

"Yeah, well, my faith is in short supply these days."

Trent scrubbed his hands over his face in frustration. From the moment his commander had called him into the office and told him he was being investigated for dereliction of duty, maltreatment of subordinates, sexual misconduct, and a litany of other really bad things that Trent would have never dreamed of, let alone done, his faith in the very military he'd devoted his life to at the expense of all others had been shaken to the core.

The endless deployments, the constant strain to be everything a leader was supposed to be to his men, seemed somehow empty. Futile.

Pointless.

Patrick leaned forward, his mouth set in a grim line. He slid a business card across the table. "I have a plan."

Trent pushed his glasses on and read the card. "Captain Emily Lindberg. Licensed Clinical Psychiatrist." He looked up at Patrick. "What the hell is this?"

"Tomorrow, you're going to call Emily and schedule an appointment. She's expecting your call."

Trent tossed the card onto the table. It floated a bit before it settled next to the folder. "For what?" The words stuck in his throat, dry and harsh as the desert against his skin.

"You didn't hear the part about the wronged hero to your stressed out villain? I need a doc—an army doc—to give you a clean bill of health before we go to this Article 32 hearing. No unexplained anger. No urge to kick puppies. None of that."

Trent folded his arms across his chest. "So I got a little stressed as a commander. Someone told me once if you're swimming as fast as you can and you're barely keeping your head above water, you're probably contributing to the organization."

Patrick shook his head slowly. "Not in this case. We need to show that you were busy commanding your formation and your lieutenant took advantage of that busyness. Not your poor stress management techniques."

Trent frowned. "What exactly are you getting at?"

"Nothing more than what I've said." Patrick looked away, suddenly fascinated by the folders in front of him. "Call her. This needs to happen sooner rather than later."

Trent said nothing for a long moment. He bounced one leg, wrestling with the hundred thousand questions that burned inside him. "So what about the other allegations?" he finally asked.

Patrick scrubbed both hands over his face before releasing

a harsh breath. "Here's how you have to handle this...you're not going to like it, but hear me out." He paused before speaking again. "I'm going to need you to play nice with your wife."

Trent went utterly still. "What do you mean, play nice?" he whispered. The emotions inside him twisted and swirled violently.

"I need you to pretend like you two aren't getting divorced. That you love each other. That you can't live without her."

Trent shoved away from the table and pushed to his feet. He stared at the photos in the glass case behind him of the last deployment. "I can't put Laura in this position," he said after a moment. "I won't." He paused. "It won't work anyway. Everyone knows she's taken off her wedding rings."

"The officers on the board will be from this brigade but that doesn't mean we can't make this a believable lie. It's them we have to convince. No one else."

Trent rubbed the scar over his heart. It ached where he touched it. A dense fire that fucking *hurt*. If he asked her to do this, he would destroy any chance he had of winning her back.

But goddamn it, he couldn't win her back if he went to jail.

"Listen to me. When this whole nightmare first reared its head, you told me you didn't want to drag her through a court-martial, right?"

Trent turned back to face him and nodded, unease twisting in his belly.

"The only way to keep this from going to court-martial is to stop it at the Article 32 level—before it gets to court. We don't do that by attacking Randall and Adorno. We do that by showing the officers on the board that you're a good soldier, a good officer, and a good husband and father. That you wouldn't dream of cheating on your wife. *That's* how we beat this."

Trent shook his head slowly, holding his breath until his lungs felt like they'd burst. "Patrick, I've known you a long time, and you've never suggested anything half as fucked up as this."

Patrick scrubbed one hand over his mouth. "I know. And I hate that I'm asking you to do it. But if you don't want to watch someone else raising your kids because you're in jail, you and Laura need to start looking like a happy husband and wife. And every single officer sitting in that Article 32 hearing needs to believe that it's true."

There was no way he could ask Laura to do this. He'd lost her ages ago, when the rumors about the missing weapons and Adorno had spiraled out of control. When she'd lost faith in him—in them. Not that he blamed her. But goddamn it, that didn't make it hurt any less. She'd ripped his soul out with those papers. There was too much distance between them now for him to ask her for something like this.

But that wasn't the real reason. He didn't want to do this to her. It would hurt her all over again and he'd done enough of that. There had to be another way.

"You need to figure out another plan," Trent said, keeping his voice low. "I won't ask her to lie for me. I won't risk her future. She's been through enough."

"Laura's job as the family readiness liaison is not at risk here. Believe me, she's valued here. They pretty much got down on their knees and begged her to stay when she tried to quit last year."

"That's not the issue," Trent said quietly. *Please don't ask me to do this to my wife.*

Patrick looked at him, his blue eyes filled with sympathy at Trent's unspoken plea. "I know what I'm asking you, Trent."

"Then you know why I won't do it." He stood abruptly, pushing his glasses down and pinching the bridge of his nose with his thumb and forefinger. "Find another way to keep me out of jail. I won't use Laura like that."

* * *

For a training holiday, the office was ridiculously busy. Normally on training holidays, the only people in the office were her and the commander. Sometimes the sergeant major. There certainly wasn't the constant stream of soldiers and spouses that she'd already seen this morning. They were looking for information on when their family members were due back from NTC. Laura knew that and she was doing the best she could pushing out the information that she had as soon as she had it.

Apparently that wasn't good enough. If one more eighteen-year-old spouse stomped into her office, Laura was liable to lose her furry little mind. Just because the Internet existed did not mean communication was either instantaneous or flawless. But you couldn't tell some people that.

Laura clenched her pencil in both hands and pasted on a calm smile. Maybe if she held it long enough, it would bleed over into her mood and she wouldn't feel as stabby as she felt right then.

Not damn likely. She loved her job as the brigade's family readiness liaison, but sometimes it took everything she had. Some spouses were more trying than others but it was her job to keep the Family Readiness Group running smoothly no matter who the current leadership was. Some days she felt like she made a difference; other days it was absolutely exhausting. But she had a purpose. And she loved it.

Except for moments like this.

When the woman who had accused her husband of inappropriate conduct sat across from her and pretended like it was just another meeting. Like Laura didn't know who the young soldier was.

Laura wanted to break something. To scream and rail at the insanity of the world that would have this young woman sitting across from her. Instead, she smiled. Her expression could have cracked glass.

"PFC Adorno, I can't give you the phone number and I'm not calling the brigade commander over your husband's cat."

"Do you know who my husband works for?"

With that single sentence, Laura's patience inched closer to snapping. She forced her smile wider.

"PFC Adorno, I don't really give a flying leap if your husband is on the brigade commander's personal security detail. A cat having kittens is not a reason to call the brigade commander while they are in the maneuver box at the National Training Center."

One would think that after all this time, years into the war, families and spouses especially would understand how things worked.

PFC Adorno, however, turned a deep shade of pink beneath her too-thick foundation. Laura had half a mind to ask her if her makeup was in accordance with regulation but she managed to keep that comment to herself. Barely. She was supposed to be the mature adult here.

As a soldier, PFC Adorno should know how these things worked. And yet, there she was, sitting in Laura's office, asking about a phone call to her husband because of kittens.

"I'm calling the inspector general. I'll have your job."

Laura didn't even blink. She reached into the stack of cards on her desk and handed one to PFC Adorno. "Here's the number. Please spell my name correctly."

She'd been threatened with the IG one too many times to let this latest addition to the roster upset her too much. Half the time, the threats were empty anyway.

PFC Adorno looked like her head was about to explode. She sucked in an outraged breath, then stalked out of Laura's office.

The air was instantly clearer and Laura inhaled a deep breath. Did that soldier honestly think Laura didn't know who she was? Or did she not realize that Laura was her former commander's wife? Dear God in heaven, Laura needed to rail and scream at the heavens.

Instead, she released a deep sigh and tossed the pencil on her desk. It wasn't nearly as satisfying as say, stabbing something violently and repeatedly, but then again the army as an employer tended to frown on fits of violence. Didn't look good on the performance review.

She rubbed her eyes and wished—not for the first time—that she'd slept better. But she'd gotten used to the fatigue that haunted her, keeping her awake at night and rising with her in the morning.

The stress in her life was not work-related.

She was the Family Readiness Group Liaison for Death Dealer battalion, a job she'd taken before her marriage had gone to hell and before she'd gotten run down by life, the war, and everything else.

She covered her face with her palms and just breathed. She was so goddamned tired. The mistakes she'd made haunted her, reminding her that her current predicament was as much her fault as it was her husband's. She should have been stronger. Should have been able to wait for him until he came home.

She shouldn't have let the war break her.

She glanced at the picture on her desk, the picture of the lie she'd lived for far too long. Her husband, holding their daughter, their son between them. A smile on his face, love in her eyes.

Yes, once she'd been part of a happy family. At least that's what she'd told herself. But the lies and the war had wormed their way into the marriage and destroyed her faith in the man she'd pledged to wait for. She didn't know why she left the picture on her desk when she'd taken her rings off. It wasn't like people didn't know.

But something about that picture made her unable to put it away.

She closed her eyes, wishing she could forget the way

he looked. Wishing she could forget the way he'd made her laugh and feel, once upon a time. He was out at NTC now too but not as someone who would be deploying. The army wouldn't let him leave Fort Hood, at least not until the charges against him were fully investigated.

And since the investigation had been ongoing for the last six months, she was starting to wonder if it was ever going to be finished. Her family—her life—was in limbo.

Her heart? Her heart didn't matter anymore. She'd given up trying to piece it back together. Trent had broken her one too many times.

Running off to war, leaving her alone.

Lying to her about the most important things.

She breathed deeply and focused on three p.m., when she could head out to pick up the kids at Shane and Jen's. She loved Jen, she really did, but especially on days like today when Hayley, Laura's babysitter, called in "sick" when she was clearly anything but so she could spend stolen time with her new husband. Laura would have preferred that Hayley be honest about it, but she couldn't really blame her. She'd just gotten married and even though Laura's newlywed days were a distant memory, she could still remember all the hope and promise of that first year.

"Whoever pissed you off, it's not the keyboard's fault."

Laura looked up as Patrick walked in and sat down. "Hey. How's Natalie?"

"She's good. Getting bigger and bossier every day." Natalie and Ethan were in school together. Natalie wasn't technically Patrick's daughter but she was in every way that mattered. Patrick and her mom were in an on again-off again disaster of a relationship but Sammy had continued to let Patrick be active in Natalie's life.

Patrick was a good man. Sammy didn't know what she was giving up.

Or maybe she did. Sometimes, being a good man simply wasn't enough to keep a relationship together.

"So, to what do I owe the honor of this visit?" she asked, minimizing her e-mail to be able to focus.

"Don't throw me out of the office," he said, trying to keep his voice light. "But I need to talk to you about Trent's case."

Laura leaned back in her chair, folding her arms over her chest, and started counting to ten.

"I know you're having a hard time with him."

Laura sucked on her top lip for a moment before answering. "I wouldn't necessarily call filing for divorce a hard time."

"And that's what I need to talk to you about."

"Patrick..."

"Just hear me out, okay?"

She ground her teeth but after a moment nodded.

"Listen, there's no case against Trent. It's weak at best. With the Article 32 about to start, we have a good chance of getting it stopped here before it goes to court-martial. But I need to plant doubt that the allegations against him are true." He met her gaze. "I need you to do that."

Laura chewed on her bottom lip, playing his words over and over in her head, not understanding what he was asking of her. "What do you mean, you need to plant doubt?"

"The primary witness against your husband, PFC Adorno—"

"Oh, we've met," Laura said dryly.

Patrick's smile was humorless. "Yes, well, that's part of the prosecution's problem. She's alleging that Trent was inappropriate but the problem is that she and Lieutenant Randall were caught in their shenanigans downrange."

Laura frowned. "So you think this is a ploy to get herself out of trouble?"

"Her and her husband. If they were working together to steal the missing weapons systems, then what better way to get out of trouble than to make this stuff up against Trent? Takes the focus off her and her husband completely." Patrick leaned forward, tapping his index finger on the desk. "If I can cast Trent as a sympathetic family man who would never do anything like what she's alleging, this case is all but dismissed. I'm not attacking her. All I have to do is make Trent look better than the story she's telling and we've got a win."

"And you need me to paint on a happy face and be the loving wife."

Patrick shook his head. "No, I need you to be one half of a loving couple. And I need you to do it publicly where everyone can see it—in the PX, in the chow hall, everywhere. I need the officers on this board to believe exactly what I'll be telling them on the day of the hearing."

She looked down at her empty ring finger, absently rubbing the bare skin beneath the bandage. "Everyone knows that we're having problems, Patrick."

"Then make sure everyone knows you've fixed it." He leaned back. "I wouldn't ask you to do this if I didn't think it was our best shot at getting this whole thing thrown out."

She looked up at him. "Why didn't Trent ask me to do this?"

Patrick swallowed and looked away. "He refused to drag you into this," he said quietly. "For what it's worth, I don't in a million years believe the allegations against Trent. I don't think he would ever, ever be unfaithful to you."

Laura pressed her lips together in a flat line. "You're wrong, Patrick. He's been cheating on me for years. It was just with the army instead of another woman."

"Laura—"

"Let me think about it," she said quickly. "I won't say no out of hand but I can't make this decision on a whim."

Patrick leaned across the desk, gripping her hand. "I

know this is hard for you, Laura. I know what I'm asking you to do."

She said nothing for a long moment and he gave her a sympathetic but firm smile. "Give it some thought, okay?"

When she was alone, she sat there, staring at the picture of her family. Wondering how she was going to bring him back into the kids' lives and then rip him out again. What he was asking wasn't fair. He had no idea what this was going to do to her family.

She glanced at the photo on her desk as she typed furiously, trying to get ahead of the flood of e-mails in her inbox.

There was a quiet rap on her office door. "I'm not here," she said quickly, looking up.

Her fingers froze on the keyboard. Her heart stopped in her chest.

Trent stood in the doorway. He had a duffle bag slung over his shoulder. His glasses hid the darkness of his eyes. There was a streak of dirt on his cheek. An assault pack hung limply from his left hand.

A thousand emotions ripped through her all at once, rioting for supremacy as she drank in the sight of her husband.

Ex-husband, she reminded herself. Or at least he was supposed to be.

She wished that this were a normal homecoming. One where she would rush across the small space and crash into him. His arms would come around her and she would inhale the strong spicy scent of his skin. Feel the heat of his touch. Savor that first, wild kiss.

Instead she had this. This empty chasm between them, echoing with loneliness.

And she had no idea how to cross it.

Chapter Three

Her husband stood in her doorway and damn it if her heart didn't act like he was a sight for sore eyes. His shoulders were broader than she remembered, weighed down by the heaviness of the war. There were tired lines around his mouth as though he'd forgotten how to smile. But his face was still the same. Lined more with weariness and too much time in the sun but that did nothing to detract from his looks.

It wasn't his looks that kept her longing for this man. No, it was a deeper, more secret part. The part of her heart that had loved a good man. An honest man. And part of her, the tiny part of her heart that soared when she saw him, still loved him.

She wasn't prepared to deal with this today. She stood as he stepped into her office. She wanted to go to him. To cross that space and feel his arms wrap around her like they had once upon a time. But that would be just another lie. Like when he'd told her that he missed her, that he'd do anything to be home with her and the kids. Like when he'd told her he'd never betray the vows they'd made.

Just like everything between them these days.

She shoved aside the crushing pain that threatened to

break her yet again. In a thousand lifetimes, she would never be able to explain what he'd done to her. His quiet abandonment, the empty place in their lives he'd left unfilled.

He looked tired. She wished she didn't notice. Behind the rims of his thin black glasses his eyes—those gorgeous, almost black eyes—were filled with sadness and regret. There was something more there now. A stark determination she hadn't seen in...she couldn't remember the last time he'd looked like this.

For one moment, the lies and the fear and the sadness were forgotten and she savored the sight of her husband. A man she'd loved for as long as she could remember. But she couldn't do this anymore. Not to herself. Not to their children.

Damn it, she was tired of caring about this man. She'd thought she'd loved him enough for both of them. She'd never been so wrong in her entire life.

"You're home early," she said. Her fingers found the pencil on her desk. It comforted her to have something to do with her hands. He said nothing for a long moment. She could have said hello. Could have been polite. Instead, her voice grated, sounding harsh against her own ears.

"Yeah. I, ah, tried to call you." Trent stuffed his hands in his pockets. She wished she didn't see the fatigue etched into the lines around his mouth. She wished she didn't still care.

"Oh." What could she say to that? What did it mean? "So why did they send you back early?"

"They're ready to start the hearing."

She swallowed the lump in her throat. "Is that good or bad?"

He looked away, the muscle in his jaw pulsing. "I don't know."

Silence stretched between them. Laura didn't know what to say to fill the gap. There was nothing she could say so she focused on the best things to come out of the mess that was their marriage. "The kids will be happy to see you," she said quietly.

A half smile cracked the edge of his mouth. "How are the hamsters?"

"Fluffy escapes once a week at least." If hamsters were what it took to make conversation, she'd take it. Anything was better than the awkward silence that hung heavy and oppressive in the air between them.

"They don't cause you too much trouble?" he asked.

She shrugged. "Not too much."

He looked at her then, his eyes dark behind those glasses that really, really worked for her. She remembered when he'd gotten them. He'd been worried she wouldn't like them. Who knew she'd had a thing for men with glasses?

"Thank you. For letting me get them for the kids."

She tipped her head and cupped her chin in her palm. It had been almost a year since he'd bought those hamsters. "You're welcome." A simple response. The only thing she could say.

Another silence. This one less damning. All because of a couple of fat, fuzzy rodents. She swallowed the nerves that tickled the back of her throat. "Where are you staying?" she asked quietly.

She wanted him to ask to come home. Just once she wanted to remember what it felt like to have him in the house. To have another adult to balance out her life. To hear him in the other room or down the hall.

She knew things between them were over but that didn't stop the longing for just one blessed day of normalcy. Just one memory of the way things had been between them. Before the war had torn away everything that he'd meant to her.

"At Shane and Jen's."

Sergeant First Class Shane Garrison had been home from the war for the last year, recovering from injuries that had landed him in the care of Jen St. James, a nurse at Darnall Army Medical Center at Fort Hood.

A tiny frown drew between her brows. "Aren't you going to be a third wheel? They should be preparing for their wedding, not having a houseguest."

"I know," he said quietly. Trent pushed his glasses higher on his nose, then shoved his hands into his pants pockets. "Shane insisted. Says he needs help with the wedding."

Laura smiled wistfully. "Jen is going to be a beautiful bride."

For a moment, Laura glanced down at her empty ring finger. She'd cried as he slipped the wedding ring onto her finger. His gaze locked with hers. For a brief moment, she was looking at her husband. No fear. No regrets. Just the man she loved looking back at her with the same love in his eyes. She blinked, and then it was gone so fast she wondered if she'd really seen it at all.

Trent looked away, clearing his throat roughly. No, she hadn't been seeing things.

"When is the wedding again?" he asked.

"Four weeks."

"That's going to go by fast," he murmured.

Laura glanced down at her watch. "I need to get the kids," she said quietly, ending the moment before it really began.

Silence filled the gulf between them, a silence that once again felt absolute and unbreakable.

She lowered her gaze and it collided with the ring he still wore on his left finger. She looked away, wishing she hadn't seen it.

But she had. He still wore his ring. He hadn't signed the papers. What was he waiting for? Why couldn't he just let her go?

She looked up then and met his gaze. And what she saw looking back at her shocked her. Ripped away at the bandages that had held her heart together and slashed every protective barrier she'd put in place.

His mouth crooked at the corner. His eyes were dark and hungry, his gaze locked on her, devouring her. Looking at her like she was the most precious thing in the world to him. The man who cherished her, who made her feel loved. Who reminded her of the aching desire she felt for him. For just an instant, the damaged warrior in front of her had slipped away, revealing the man she'd loved. Whole. Determined.

Hers.

But then his expression shuttered closed, leaving the man she'd come to know. The man who was distant and closed off. The speed of it almost gave her whiplash. She'd believed him when he'd told her he had to go, that the army needed him. That he couldn't argue with the powers that be.

All the while, he'd been volunteering for deployment after deployment. Leaving her and the kids willingly time and time again. Leaving her hoping and praying for the day when he would come home to her.

She knew in her heart of hearts that day would never come. Because no matter how much she might wish it, the man who stood before her, tired and beaten down by the war and the weight of his own sins, was not the man she'd married.

"I'm going to be around for the next few weeks," he said. His voice was soft, his words sharp. "I'd like to see the kids." A hesitant pause. "I'd like to see you, too."

She stopped breathing. She searched his eyes, looking for a glimpse of the old Trent, but he was gone. Maybe he'd never been there. Or maybe he'd simply been wish fulfillment. Maybe her husband was really dead and gone and the man in front of her was a shell; nothing more.

That wasn't true. The man in front of her had been forged

in fire and come out steel. He'd been cut from the mold of a warrior, an ancient god of war.

The warrior in front of her had perfected the art of war. He knew his profession. He took pride in it. He'd given it everything he had. She knew that now.

But the warrior had sacrificed for his skill. He'd sacrificed his ability to love, to laugh, to smile. She saw the warrior now for who he was.

Because the man in front of her was not the man she'd married.

He was not the man she loved.

Trent knew fear. In that moment, he knew naked, soul-crushing fear as he waited for his wife's response to his tentative gesture. He refused to think of her as his ex-wife. She wasn't. Not yet.

He had to fix this.

A better man would walk away. Would release her from the purgatory of their sham of a marriage.

But Trent was not a better man. He loved this woman. He'd always loved this woman.

The overwhelming love that he felt for her was there. Like a sleeping thing waking from a long dormancy. It was fragile. Malnourished.

But there, stretching after a long slumber.

He held his breath, waiting for her response. Held it until his lungs burned and his hands shook. Still she didn't respond. She toyed with the pencil in her hand. Rolled it along the edge of her desk calendar.

"The kids will be glad to see you," she whispered finally.

It was a dodge. An obvious one.

He could let her go, let her slip away.

But that's not what he wanted. And he'd seen her gaze flicker to his wedding ring. He hadn't made that up.

She didn't want this either.

But fear was a powerful thing. He recognized the look in her eyes, the stiffness in her posture—it was like looking in a mirror the moment she looked back at him. He deserved that. He'd failed her so many times in so many ways. But right then, gazing at her copper eyes and dark copper hair, what he truly saw was her strength. The strength to love his children, to keep their home together.

To walk away when he hadn't been enough.

Now? Now he needed her strength in a different way. He needed her to be strong enough to stay. To give him one more chance. And if he was going to deserve her, that had to start now.

"I was wondering if I could catch a ride with you?" he said, stepping into the breach and facing the possibility that once more, she would back away.

He didn't know how to just be around her. He wanted to be alone with her. Just to see what it felt like. It had been so long since it had been just her and just him. When he'd come home after getting shot, all he'd wanted, all he'd needed, was time with his wife. But Ethan had been little and needy in the way that toddlers often were.

The kids had needed her more. And after too many late night diaper changes and dirty sheets, he'd stopped vying for her time. He couldn't take any more from her. Not when the kids were taking so much. How could he ask her for more time for himself? But he supposed not wanting to ask for more time was how the distance between them had grown into the impossible chasm that stood between them now.

He had to find a way to get her to need him. To want him. A simple ride alone would be a start. A single step on the journey that would take him a lifetime to manage. If he got that far.

Right now? He was just hoping for a yes. And as the

silence grew, so did his dread that what he would hear would be no.

It felt like forever before she said, "Sure. But where's your truck?"

"I let Carponti take it. He needed to go pick something up for Nicole and didn't want her to see it." A version of the truth. Obi Wan would be proud.

Laura's expression softened when he mentioned Carponti. She had a soft spot for Trent's friend and his wife. Strange jealousy slithered through him. Not of her friendship. No, not that. But of the way her expression softened. She would never look at him that way again, and the loss? That loss hurt, cutting him quick and deep.

He took a tentative step forward.

"Laura?"

She wanted to look away. He could see it in her eyes. But she didn't. She was so close, close enough that he could reach out and stroke an errant strand of hair that had fallen across her cheek.

He looked down at her left hand, clenching the pencil like a lifeline. It was a long moment before she turned off her computer and stood, her face a mask of caution. Her bare ring finger haunted him. It never should have gotten this far.

"I need you to be a happy couple." Patrick's words rang through his head. How could Patrick suggest that Trent ask his wife to lie for him and pretend everything was wonderful in their marriage when he could barely get past an awkward hello?

He wasn't asking her for that. He refused.

He wanted this time with her for its own sake. Nothing more.

There was no way he would ask her to do this for him. He watched as she slipped her wallet into her purse. The elegance of her fingers as they flew over the zipper. Longing punched through him.

Laura stood, shouldering the simple black tote he'd bought for her two Christmases ago. It warmed him to see her using something he'd given her. He'd had this mental image of her throwing away everything even remotely tied to his memory and he held on to the ridiculous pleasure of seeing she still had it.

She shifted the tote to her other shoulder, her hand releasing the strap. She caught him looking at her hand and tried to tuck the injured hand behind her back. He moved quickly, capturing it before she could slip it out of his reach.

It was a mistake, touching her. Heat bolted through him the moment her soft fingers were cradled in his and he hung on to the sensation. Her skin was soft and smooth, a stark comparison to his. He'd dreamed about her hands on his body so many times and touching her sparked a thousand images, some real, some pure fantasy.

With a single finger, he traced the top of her knuckles. He brushed his thumb over her bandaged knuckles and felt her jerk. Chilled by her rejection, he let her go. Never would he have imagined that she'd flinch from his touch.

"What happened?"

"I scraped my knuckles trying to fix the dishwasher." Her voice was thick.

"What's wrong with the dishwasher?"

"It's not cleaning the dishes right. I looked up what was wrong, and there's probably food stuck in the chopper. I was trying to clean it out when the screwdriver slipped and I busted my knuckles."

Trent wanted to be able to smile at his wife's stubborn independence. The first time he'd deployed, she'd filled their small study with bookshelves she'd assembled herself. The second time, she'd landscaped. Each time, she learned some new skill around the house, so that when he came back, he was never faced with the honey-do lists that other soldiers had to wrestle with.

He should have been there to do those things for her. But he hadn't, and she'd made one thing abundantly clear. She didn't need him.

He looked at her then and wanted to beg her to give him another chance. To hell with the court-martial, to hell with the rumors. He wanted her back. Wanted to explain everything that he hadn't been able to say for the last year and the year before that and the year before that.

Lay his sins at her feet and allow her to judge him as harshly as she deemed fit. Anything to keep her from casting him out entirely... *Don't give up on me.* But he kept the words to himself, the gulf between them too wide for a single plea to cross.

"I'm sure you'll figure it out," he said. He wanted to ask if he could help. But the words lodged in his throat. He couldn't.

He met her gaze, unable to walk away, despite everything that said he'd already lost her. "I'd like to see you," he said again.

She bit her lip and looked away, down at where his index finger rested near the edge of her pinky. "I can't, Trent," she whispered.

"Can't?" She lifted her gaze at his single word. "Or won't?"

"You can't come in here and ask me that," she said. There was steel beneath the sadness in her voice. "You have no right."

"You're my wife."

"I was your wife," she said. "And you chose the army over your family."

He heard what she didn't say. *You chose the army over me.*

"I did. You're right." Her mouth opened, then closed

again quickly. Surprise flashed in her eyes at his admission. A simple thing. But so very important. He had so many sins to atone for. She bit her lips hard enough that he winced. "I want to try. Just once more, I want to try and make things right."

She swallowed hard, shaking her head. "You can't. You lost that opportunity."

"I screwed up last year."

"This isn't about last year, Trent." She took a step backward. He felt the loss of her warmth in the air around him. "This is about all those years ago. You died. And you never came back to me. You never planned on coming home, not really. Not to me, not to the kids. So why should I believe you now?" she whispered.

He twisted his wedding ring around his finger. Light bounced off white gold. "I can't give you any good reasons." He lifted his gaze to hers. "Other than I screwed up."

Silence stretched between them, harsh and unforgiving and filled with bitterness, sadness and lies. It was forever before she spoke.

"I can't give you what you want anymore, Trent." Her gaze didn't waiver from his. "Because I don't have anything left. You broke me," she whispered. "You finally broke me."

Chapter Four

❦

Laura supposed she should be used to the awkward silence filling the space between them by now. As she turned down Highway 195, heading toward Jen's out-of-town property, Patrick's words weighed heavily on her soul. She drummed her fingers on the steering wheel, trying to figure out what to do with all the uncertainty twisting inside her.

She thought about turning the radio on then thought against it. The sound would be jarring. Grating. Too harsh.

The silence, at least, was as familiar as it was empty.

Trent kept shifting in the seat, fidgeting with his glasses. There had been a time when they would talk about pointless things. Laugh and share jokes or better—find a place to pull off on the side of the road because they couldn't keep their hands off each other.

Now the distance between them was silent and cold.

She sighed heavily. Might as well get started on the old familiar routine. God, but she wanted to break free of all this. She wanted this resolved. She was so tired of ripping the bandage off the wounds on her heart every time he reappeared in her life.

"Is there something on your mind?" he asked. His voice jolted her out of her thoughts.

She considered her next words carefully, knowing they were going to cause a fight and knowing she could do nothing to avoid it. "So Patrick came and talked to me today," she said quietly.

The silence turned frigid, like shattered ice, frozen and suspended in the air around them. Trent swore loud and long. The force of his reaction momentarily stunned her. He pushed his glasses onto the top of his head and scrubbed his hands over his face. "I'm sorry. I asked him not to."

"I know," she said. He glanced at her. "He told me." She took a deep breath. "Were you even going to give me a choice or just make the decision without talking to me?"

"Laura—"

"You weren't, were you?" She paused, breathing deeply, fighting for control of her temper. "No, you did this just like you do everything. You shut it down, you don't talk to me about it and you don't let me in on the really big fucking decisions that oh, I don't know, impact more than just your life. *Our* life." She gripped the steering wheel so tightly that the leather creased beneath her fingers.

She couldn't do this. Not like this. She needed to move. To get away. To release some of the anger and hurt inside her before she lashed out and did something she could not take back.

Laura slowed the car and steered it to the side of the road, breathing deeply through her nose to keep from losing her temper completely. She needed space, needed to do something with the twisting anger inside her. She knew what most of the charges against him were. Dereliction of duty. Conduct unbecoming an officer and a gentleman. But it was the allegations made by another woman that had nearly crushed her soul.

He leaned forward, keeping his hands over his mouth.

"He thinks that everything hinges on their impression of my integrity. That means it's really important to beat the morality charges…"

It was a long moment before he spoke again. "Laura, they're lies."

She swallowed. His denial echoed in her ears. She opened the door, then got out and slammed it shut with extreme violence. He followed her. "Then where did these allegations come from, Trent? Why would your soldier say these things?"

"I don't know. Because of her husband, because she's as guilty as he is? I don't know." He paused and she fought the urge to turn around. Hated that the sound of his voice drew her to him when she should be walking the other way. "Laura, I've done some horrible things in my life. But not this. Never this."

She turned back and looked at her husband and for a brief moment, felt a deep twinge of sympathy. He looked lost. Formal charges of adultery were not something the army did often, and those charges were usually only filed when the commanders had incontrovertible proof that a violation had occurred. Such charges were almost always tied to other—more serious—charges. She'd seen far too many cases like this in her job as the family readiness liaison for the battalion.

She turned away and started walking down a well-worn path near a small stream. The anger overwhelmed her, clawed at her. Made her *feel* again and that was the absolute last thing she wanted.

She needed a minute to cool down before she could face the kids. She didn't want them to see her like this. This needy, sad thing who still, despite everything, hoped her husband would love her enough to come home. God, she was pathetic. But the day he'd died, she'd lost everything. The foundation of her world had been ripped from beneath her feet.

She rubbed her upper arms against a sudden chill.

The snap of a twig behind her told her she was no longer alone with her thoughts. A brush of air against her neck told her he was closer than he had any right to be. But he made no move to touch her. At least none that she could see or feel.

"I remember when you died," she whispered. She wrapped her arms around her waist, a phantom pain rippling through her belly, the memory etched into her very bones. "Ethan was barely two. I was pregnant with Emma."

"I couldn't hear for a day and a half," he murmured.

"For two whole days I thought I'd lost you. I couldn't move, I couldn't get out of bed. I just stared into the darkness, hoping, praying for five more minutes with you. I would have traded anything." She gripped her upper arms tightly, bracing against the cold inside her, fighting the tears that burned behind her eyes. "And when you called, when I heard your voice...I didn't believe it was you." She bit her lips together, fighting to keep everything inside from breaking free. "I was so...I was so happy. You were alive. I got everything I hoped for. But it was all a lie because I never *really* got you back," she whispered, her voice breaking. Finally she turned to face him. "Why can't you just let me go?" She released a shuddering breath, afraid to look him in the eye. Terrified at what she would see.

"Because I can't," he whispered. "I know I broke us. By not calling, by following that goddamned no-contact order instead of breaking the rules and calling you. I know I did this." He lifted one hand. It trembled near her cheek and she hated herself for yearning for his touch.

She didn't speak until she was confident she could, past the block in her throat. "Trent, you've been closing me off and shutting me out for years. Last year? Last year just solidified the death of our marriage. All the rumors. All the allegations? What was I supposed to believe when I didn't hear anything from you?"

"I will regret following that no-contact order for the rest of my life." His voice cracked.

"Then why did you?"

He closed his eyes. His shoulders rose and fell with a deep breath. Finally he met her gaze again. "Because I still believed the system would work. I still had faith."

"Really?" She searched the deep brown eyes behind the soft reflection of his glasses.

His throat moved as he swallowed and looked away. "Yeah."

"Then why stay? Why not get out of the army and have a nice, nine-to-five civilian job?" She needed to know what made this man who had sacrificed everything for the army turn against it.

"Because it's the only thing I've ever known. It's the only thing I'm good at. Hell, I'm not even very good at it anymore." He paused, letting the silence hang between them. Finally, he spoke. "I'm being court-martialed to placate the father of the lieutenant who stole arms from our unit and sold them for cash. They want me to take the fall. There are men who have done far worse than me in the name of God and country but I'm the one who's been chosen for public crucifixion."

The bitterness in his words struck her forcibly, and a renewed anger washed over her. Only this time, her anger was directed at the army.

"You're serious? After everything you've sacrificed, the army is just going to throw you away?"

"Not the army. My esteemed brigade commander." His gaze did not waver from hers.

She hesitated, her mind racing over the implications of her decision.

"If I do this…" Her voice broke and she fought to keep tears from filling her eyes or her words. "If I do this, it changes nothing between us. You'll sign the papers and leave once it's over."

His nostrils flared slightly, the muscles in his neck tense. "Why would you agree to this?" His voice was harsh.

Because I've lost you too many times. I have to walk away. But she didn't voice the silent cry. She lifted her chin and refused to look away from the dark gaze that held too many secrets and lies. "I don't want our children to have to visit you in jail."

Because he couldn't help himself, Trent reached for her. Terrified that she would pull away, his fist trembled. The barest brush of his knuckles against her cheek. She shifted, a slight movement away from his touch. A sharp bolt of hurt sliced through him.

"Why would you do this?" he asked again, dreading the answer. He had to know if he had a chance, even the most minute chance, of fixing things with her.

Conflict passed over her features. "Because I want this over and done with. I'm tired of hurting. If this ends the court-martial, then so be it."

He heard what she did not say: *This ends our marriage.* Standing there in the fading sunlight, he looked at his wife. At the hurt written on her face. At the stubborn line of her mouth.

He wanted to see her mouth soften. To see her look at him like she used to. He wanted to be that man again: worthy of her.

His sins were legion. He was not a good man. The war had seen to that. But he felt a faint brush of warmth inside him and knew it for what it was: hope. And he reached into the darkness, cupping the light. It was a long time before he spoke. "Thank you, Laura," he whispered.

"This isn't for you," she said softly. She offered him a flat smile that did not meet her eyes. "This is about moving on. You and I ..."

"Laura—"

"Don't." Her eyes flashed and he realized he'd pushed too far. "Don't ask for more than that." She released a deep breath, looking away. "I have to get the kids."

He swallowed and nodded, waiting a full breath before following her back up the hill to the car.

Their children had no idea about the world's dangers. About the pain and suffering he'd seen beaten into younger kids' faces before they could even walk.

His kids were always there in the back of his mind, but he'd needed to lock away his love for them and focus on his mission. Some of the most important years of their lives were memories captured only in photographs and videos. Memories he would never be a part of. Because war and children did not mix. That much he knew from brutal, firsthand experience.

He'd tried so hard to protect them but he'd failed so miserably. He glanced at Laura as he climbed into the passenger's seat. In his head, he nurtured a hesitant, fragile fantasy. A fantasy where he offered a tentative smile and her eyes warmed in return. Where for one aching moment, he saw in her eyes the love that he'd betrayed.

A stronger man could fix this. A better man could capture his wife's love and reclaim her heart. Lay down his weapons and become the husband and father she'd promised to wait for.

The fear was back, tormenting him with doubt and all the ways he'd failed.

It whispered in his ear that he'd already lost her.

He refused to listen to the dark thoughts, the whispered torment. It couldn't be true.

Because if he lost them, he lost everything.

Chapter Five

❦

"Daddy!"

"Daddy?" Emma's tiny, squeaky voice echoed her brother's as both kids barreled toward him as soon as he and Laura walked into the house.

For a brief moment, the noise and chaos of their cries overwhelmed him, and he fought an ingrained reaction to shout for silence. These were his children, not his soldiers, and they were still babies, barely out of diapers.

He knelt and met their full-frontal assault head on.

"Daddy, did Mommy tell you what Fluffy did last night?" Ethan asked, jockeying for position directly in front of him. Emma squawked and elbowed her brother.

"No hitting," Trent said, more sharply than he'd intended.

Emma's tiny black brows furrowed. "Not nice, Daddy," she said, waggling a finger at him. "No shouting."

Trent raised both eyebrows and almost smiled at the serious look on his daughter's face. A look he'd seen on Laura's face once or twice. She was a miniature version of his wife, except her hair was longer and darker, her cheeks rounded with the chubbiness of childhood.

From across the small living room, someone laughed, and

Trent looked away, meeting the eyes of his longtime friend Shane Garrison. "Never thought I'd see the day when a four-year-old would leave you speechless," Shane said.

"Yeah, well, she's her mother's daughter." He glanced down at the kids, unsure of how to extricate himself from their embraces. "Do you guys have any stuff you need to police up?"

Ethan frowned. "Why would we put our toys in jail?"

Behind him, Laura laughed softly. "Daddy means go pick up your toys, guys."

The kids disappeared somewhere, and Laura padded over to the kitchen. Shane leaned against the small couch, bracing his hands behind him, only a hint of stiffness in his movements from the injuries that had taken him out of combat less than a year ago. "Any progress on the court-martial front?"

Trent leaned against the arm of the chair next to him. "Patrick is trying to get the whole court-martial thrown out," he said, answering Shane's unspoken question.

"That's good." He was happy to see Shane up and about. His friend was back to shaving his head and he looked like he'd packed on more than a few extra pounds of solid muscle. "Carponti left your truck here and said thanks."

"How's the wedding planning going?"

"I'd rather not say," Shane said with a grimace, running his hand over his bald head. "We—and by 'we' I mean all of us—are going shopping this weekend. Don't argue. I need your support or I might have to turn in my man card."

Trent grinned, feeling more relaxed than he had all afternoon. "What are we shopping for?"

"Wedding stuff. Apparently, there is a whole lot more that goes into a wedding than a pretty dress and a willing woman." Shane rubbed his hand over the back of his neck, a faint smile teasing his lips. "My first marriage was at the Justice of the Peace on a Saturday afternoon. This is much more complex." He glanced into the kitchen at Jen. Shane was not an overly emotive guy but the smile tugging at the corner of his mouth said more than any words could. "And infinitely more worth it."

Trent had never seen the man more at ease, not once in the more than fifteen years they'd known each other. It showed in the relaxed lines around his mouth, the lack of tension in his shoulders.

He turned slightly to look into the kitchen, where Laura was helping Jen clean up. Watching her talk with her friend, he saw the side of his wife that he loved best. Her quick smile. Her easy laugh. The way her eyes lit up when she was surrounded by people she cared for.

The way she no longer looked at him.

Trent cleared his throat and looked away before she caught him watching her. He glanced at Shane, and realized he'd been caught nonetheless.

"How are things going with Laura?" Shane asked softly.

A shriek from upstairs drifted down to them. *How had the kids even made it up there so quickly?* Trent started for them but a quick glance at Laura told him there was no need to go rushing to the rescue. It was amazing how she knew what was serious and what wasn't.

"About as well as can be expected," Trent said mildly.

"That bad, huh?"

Shane threw a quick glance toward the kitchen then looked back at Trent for an explanation. Trent sighed and jerked his head toward the screened-in porch at the back of Jen's house. When they got outside, he filled Shane in on Patrick's Hail Mary attempt to get the court-martial thrown out. As he spoke, Shane's expression hardened.

"That's a screwed up thing to do," he said quietly.

"I didn't ask her to do it," Trent said.

"But you're not going to stop her." There was judgment in Shane's tone, harsh and unforgiving.

Trent ground his teeth, yanking back his temper. "I don't want to raise my kids from jail."

"But you were fine with attempting to raise them from Iraq and Afghanistan." Shane crossed his arms over his chest, bracing his feet wide like a fighter.

"That's not fair."

"No, what's not fair is letting Laura do this. What's it going to do to the kids? Did you think about them?"

He had, but not how Shane had implied. He'd thought about going home and being in the house with them. About putting them to bed at night. Shane's words hit him like a tank: If he did this—if he granted Laura the divorce—he would be lying to them as well as to the world. And they were too little to understand.

They would hate him.

He shoved his glasses to the top of his head in frustration and scrubbed his hands over his face. "I want my family back. And I don't know how to make that happen."

Shane was quiet for a long moment. He shifted against the support beam then folded his arms over his chest. The massive black tattoos that covered his arms writhed with his movement.

"When I was hurt, Laura came to see me in the hospital." Shane stuffed his hands in his pockets and leaned back against the wall. "It was right after she'd found out you'd been volunteering to go on all these missions. She was wrecked. She asked me why you stayed away. Why you'd volunteered for combat time and time again. Why you told her you loved her and still volunteered to leave your family. I told her I didn't know. I still don't know. You love her. You love your kids. *You*," and Shane pointed a finger at Trent, "came home. That's a gift. And you're wasting that gift, brother." He sighed hard. "I don't like this idea."

"I don't either. It's another lie," Trent said. Added to the ones he'd already told his wife. To the ones he'd told himself when he fell asleep at his desk while double-checking the threat assessment from the knucklehead intelligence officer. Or personally checking on the maintenance of the weapons systems. He hadn't pushed hard enough. He could have done more to stop his boys from dying.

Instead he'd been laid out on a gurney while his boys continued the fight in Sadr City. He should have been out there when Mack and Pete had gotten blown up, when Story had taken their boys back into the fight because Trent had been on his ass. The docs hadn't believed him when he'd said he was fine; he needed to go.

Because he hadn't been fine. But he'd been determined to get back into the fight.

But Mack and Pete were already gone. And the war had gone on without him.

He cleared his throat, yanking himself out of the bitter memory.

"You're right; it would be. It would be using your wife for a chance to gain your freedom. And that's wrong no matter how bullshit the charges against you are. You should fight this court-martial with everything you have." He cleared his throat. "Except Laura."

"I know that," Trent said quietly.

But damn his soul to hell, he wasn't going to stop her. He wanted to go home where officers weren't trying to stab each other in the back to make sure their report card was the best. Where the roads weren't hiding bombs in dead things and debris. Where he could hear all the noise and chaos that the kids made and not worry that a bomb would go off, destroying innocence and lives. It was a façade, a grasping chance at a dream he could never enjoy. It might be a lie but it was still a chance. A chance to be around his wife and his kids without letting the dirt and the grime and the hatred of war into their lives. He could do this, right? Without polluting them with the evil that war made good men do? Here was a chance to prove to himself that he could do this, that he could be more than just a soldier. That he could be a husband and a father.

It was the only chance he had.

"You don't have to help clean up," Jen said, folding a towel in the handle on the stove.

"Of course I do. You've been babysitting my spawn for the last five hours. And you even fixed them a snack." Laura wiped the center island with a paper towel. "Now show me the dress you want to order."

A hesitant smile crept across Jen's lips as she turned over a magazine she'd dog-eared, pulling it open to the marked page. "This is the one."

"Oh honey, I love it," Laura whispered. The gown was a classic A-line, delicate lace over chiffon. Pearls shimmered over the bust. Laura smiled as she imagined her friend in the beautiful gown. "You'll look amazing in this." She glanced up at Jen and was surprised by her wistful expression. "What?"

Jen shrugged her shoulder. "I had to have them alter it. I can't wear a strapless dress."

Laura's throat closed off at the sadness in her friend's voice. Jen had never expected to have the problem of finding a wedding gown. After the surgery that had removed her breast to save her life, she'd been convinced that no man would want her.

She'd never guessed that buying a wedding dress would be in her future.

Laura covered Jen's hand with her own, refusing to allow her friend to sink into sadness. "Do you honestly think Shane is going to care what you're wearing on the day you marry him?" she asked softly.

Jen's smile brightened. "He told me he'd marry me naked if that's what it took to get me down the aisle."

"Sounds like something Carponti would say, not Shane," Laura said.

"They've spent a lot of time together this past year."

Laura grinned. "Carponti's sense of humor hasn't failed him yet."

"Tell that to Shane," Jen said softly. "And while you're at it, tell Carponti there is nothing wrong with red velvet cake."

"Red velvet cake? Seriously? Do you even like red velvet cake?"

Jen smiled. "Shane does, apparently. Carponti insists it was made by the devil."

"Shane does not strike me as the kind of man who has a preference for any kind of cake," Laura said dryly. She glanced over her shoulder at Trent and Shane, who were standing in the screened-in back porch, talking in low voices. She and Trent had had yellow cake with buttercream frosting at their wedding. It had been small but perfect. Just close friends and family. Trent had worn his Dress Green uniform and she remembered how handsome he'd looked. She'd never in a million years have thought that day would lead to this one: the day she'd made a bargain to end her marriage.

"Where'd you go just then?" Jen asked quietly.

"Thinking about the day I married Trent." Laura sighed and leaned on the center island, cupping her chin in her palm. "Trent has a chance to beat the charges against him."

"Oh?"

Laura explained what Patrick had asked her to do. She avoided Jen's eyes while she spoke, unable to face the judgment she was sure to find there.

"Are you going to do it?" Something in Jen's voice made her look up.

Laura nodded slowly. "Yeah, I am."

Jen said nothing and turned to put dishes away. "Can I ask why?" she said after a long moment.

"Because Trent may have done a lot of things wrong, but I don't think I believe..." she stopped and sucked in a deep breath. The rumors might have been something she couldn't ignore but in her heart, she'd never wanted to believe them. And if Patrick thought they were bullshit—maybe—well maybe they were. "I don't want to take the kids to visit daddy in prison on the weekends." A convenient lie. Maybe if she repeated it often enough, she would start to believe it.

"A valid reason but this isn't about the kids. At least not entirely," Jen said quietly. "What about you? This isn't going to be easy."

"I know." Laura looked down at her hands, twisting her fingers together in the towel to keep them from trembling. The empty space on her finger felt heavy. "But it's not about me anymore. Trent and I are over. We're going to put on a happy face for the trial, and whether he beats it or not, he's promised to grant me a divorce."

She looked up to find Jen studying her.

"That's a far cry from the woman who wept the last time he deployed." Jen's voice was a whisper. Laura was sure she hadn't meant the words as judgment; Jen didn't have a mean bone in her body, but Laura felt judged and found lacking anyway.

"Yeah, it is. But I just don't know how to do it anymore. I don't know how to be the dutiful wife to a husband who is never really coming home." Her voice cracked and she blinked rapidly, refusing to cry over him again.

Jen leaned across the island, squeezing Laura's hands. "If he hadn't lied, if he hadn't been volunteering for all those tours, would you still have waited for him?"

Laura's throat closed off and she blinked rapidly. "I don't know," she whispered.

Jen shifted then and pulled her into a hug. "Then do this cautiously, because I don't want to see you hurt any more than you already have been." She paused. "And I'd hate to have to have Shane kick his ass. It might do some damage to their friendship."

Laura gave a strangled laugh and she broke their embrace, swiping at the moisture in her eyes that had nearly leaked out. "Not funny."

"Who's joking?" Jen's smile was wicked. She squeezed Laura's shoulders. "I'm here, okay? Vent, scream, whatever. I'm here for you."

Laura hugged her again. "Thank you." She knew Jen would be there for her but it was still nice to hear. "So let's change the subject to something less depressing. Are we still doing lunch with Nicole tomorrow to figure out the colors and stuff?"

"Oh, yes. You cannot plan a wedding without the queen of makeup in this little club. Nicole is the only reason I will have any cosmetics whatsoever for this little event."

"Oh, come on. Makeup shopping will be fun. And she will ensure you look fabulous for your special day. Add in the bonus of getting to see your dress this weekend." Nicole knew every tip and trick to hide a blemish or make you look like you'd had a full eight hours of sleep after being up all night with a sick child. And she made it all look so effortless. Which was why she was in charge of cosmetics for this wedding.

Jen smiled but Laura didn't miss her nervousness. She'd healed so much from being with Shane but she would always be a little self-conscious when it came to makeup. "We're going to drag the menfolk along this weekend, too. They need to try on their tuxes, and Nicole wants to get Carponti to look at some new furniture at some ridiculously expensive store in Austin."

"That ought to be a blast," Laura said dryly. Any time Carponti was involved there was no telling what would happen, but he would go a long way to filling the awkwardness of Trent and Laura's difficulties. "Explain to me again why the guys aren't just wearing their dress blues?"

Jen smiled. "Because Shane has some strange notions about doing this wedding 'right.'"

"O-kay," Laura said.

She glanced outside where Trent and Shane continued their conversation in the fading Texas light. She was bringing her husband back to the house she'd made into a home without him. Back to the family she'd raised without him. She was terrified about being alone with him. Terrified of the memories that he stroked to life.

She wanted their marriage to be over. She wanted to move on with her life.

Somehow, that goal seemed further out of reach than it had ever been.

And that scared the hell out of her.

The kids were racing around upstairs, their feet pounding across the floor like a herd of baby elephants. He could hear them clearly even though he stood on the porch outside. He rubbed the scar over his chest, fighting the urge to go upstairs and tell them to just sit still. For just a minute. That's all he needed. Just a minute of quiet to pull everything back inside.

But that wasn't happening. Laura seemed immune to the noise. She was talking quietly with Jen, leaning over a magazine. He stopped near the door, still on the patio and hidden in the shadows. Her hair spilled over one cheek, her expression soft and smiling. God but he wanted to see that smile turned toward him. Just once.

The tightness in his chest squeezed tighter and tighter until he couldn't breathe. He turned away, facing out over the field behind Jen's house. Watching the stars twinkle in the black carpet of the night sky. It was safe. There would be no red flares filling the sky tonight. No explosions to jerk him out of sleep. No big voice on the loudspeaker warning about an incoming rocket attack.

He heard the stampede overhead and he just needed it to *stop*. He didn't trust himself. Laura was letting them run so it had to be okay, right?

"Hey, are you okay?"

Laura had slipped onto the back porch and he had been so consumed by the panic clutching at his chest, the pounding need for silence, that he hadn't heard her. He looked down at her, her face cast in shadows. There was worry in her eyes, concern in that simple, loaded question.

"I can't come home tonight."

He couldn't. There was too much twisted and raw inside him, too much that he was afraid to let Laura see. He could go home tomorrow night.

He'd have a better handle on things then.

"Were you going to talk to me about that or just make the decision all by yourself?" Just like that the softness was gone, leaving the familiar disappointment in her eyes.

Would he always let her down?

"I . . . I just figured you could prepare the kids for it tonight and tomorrow would be better. Less crazy?"

When he was ready to face his home and his family and was better prepared. Because everything was rioting inside him and he felt his temper snapping at the leash. He'd done better at keeping it under control but not enough. He couldn't let her see.

So he said none of those things.

"You're doing it again," she whispered. "Making all these decisions on your own. You think you know what's best but you've forgotten one key point, Trent." She paused, looking away out over the field toward the distant tire swing. "You don't know what's best for me or for the kids. You don't know us anymore."

She walked away, her head down, her shoulders slumped. Her words stabbed him violently in the heart even as the anxiety tightened in his throat and threatened to choke him.

He lowered his head to the beam in front of him. He was never going to figure this out. He was losing her all over again. But how could he explain to her what he was? The men he'd lost, the choices he'd made? The war was an ugly, evil thing and it had left its mark on him.

She wanted him to talk to her, to open up, but she was right. He didn't know how. And worse? He didn't want to. He didn't want her to know about the little kids running through the piss and the shit with no shoes on. He didn't want her to know about the people so fucking poor they'd fight over a candy bar or plant a bomb for ten dollars.

She was safe here in the States. Their kids would never know what the war was really like.

And damn it, Trent wasn't going to be the one to bring the fucking war home to them. He couldn't let them see the nightmares and the fear that haunted his sleep. That woke him, angry and scared and shaking in the night or worse, sobbing for a lost friend. He didn't want her to see what he'd become.

And tonight, he was having a hard time hiding it. So he would stay away. Just once more. Tomorrow. He could go home tomorrow.

He'd figure out another way. There had to be another way.

Because the alternative? The alternative was not an option.

Chapter Six

🍃

Trent sat at his desk, dreading the ticking of the clock on the wall. Fifteen more minutes and he'd have to leave for his appointment. And wasn't he in a right old jolly mood to sit down and discuss his feelings with the shrink.

He hadn't slept last night. He'd lain awake in Shane and Jen's guest bedroom, the silence sending him crawling up the walls. He'd considered getting up and getting a beer or six and letting the alcohol coax him to sleep but he didn't think that would have helped.

"Don't you look like you're in a chipper mood." Iaconelli swung around the corner of the cubicle that made Trent's "office" and straddled the chair in front of him. "Rough night?"

Trent frowned, pretty certain that Iaconelli had either just woken up or had never gone to bed. "Not as rough as yours, apparently," Trent said.

"Yeah, well, I at least have no idea what happened last night. You look like you remember every single minute."

"Just about," Trent said. He shifted, pushing his glasses higher on his nose. "What are you up to?"

"Running a range with Captain Montoya. We're going out to do a site recon this morning."

Trent frowned. "I thought we had a burn ban going on and they were limiting ranges." There had been flooding the previous year when they'd all been deployed. This year? Dry. Really dry. The kind of dry where a cigarette could set off a range fire that would burn for days.

"So far, range control has cleared us so we're good to go. Why do you look like someone pissed in your Wheaties?"

Trent pushed his glasses up on top of his head and scrubbed his hand over his face. "I've got to go see a shrink in a little bit."

Iaconelli looked like he'd told him he was going to a proctology exam. "You can keep that shit. Shrinks don't do a damn bit of good. They give the kids with no backbones excuses and they don't help the kids who really need it."

"Strong feelings, much?" Trent said.

Iaconelli scowled. "One in a long list of failures that have jaded my opinion of the army's mental health system. And why are you going to a shrink? Isn't that verboten for an officer?"

Trent shrugged. "My lawyer wants me to have a clean bill of mental health."

"Oh, for your court-martial. Good times. Enjoy yourself," he said with an evil grin.

Trent flipped him off but grinned despite himself. "I'm sure I'll have so much fun discussing how not enough hugs in my childhood scarred me for life."

"Yeah, well, watch what you tell them. It goes into a permanent record so if you tell them the war made you crazy, that shit's going to follow you around."

Trent wanted to ask what had happened to Iaconelli to make him distrust the mental health system but the big man was already gone. And it was time for Trent to face the judge, jury, and executioner: his new shrink.

The drive across post was too short. He even had no trouble finding a parking space, something that *never* happened on Fort Hood. So he had no excuse for being late or stalling or any other way of avoiding the doctor's office.

A physical dread uncurled in his stomach as he walked into the R&R Center. His palms were slicked with sweat and his heart pounded in his ears. He checked in at the front desk, rubbing his hands on his uniform, and waited for the admin assistant to lead him back to Captain Lindberg's office.

It was strange walking through the waiting room. The highest-ranking person was a rugged-looking sergeant who looked battle worn and broken down. There were First Cav combat patches on his right and left shoulders but it was the haunted look in his eyes, the strain that Trent recognized all too well.

He felt a rush of sympathy even as he felt all eyes on him from the myriad of soldiers sitting in the waiting room. It was unusual for an officer to be walking through that waiting room. Mental health was something sought by junior soldiers. Officially, anyone could seek mental health without fear of losing their careers. The reality was that officers simply did not go to the R&R Center. Not for themselves, anyway.

Officers didn't break under the stress of war. If they did, they ended their careers. Maybe not immediately, but their inability to cope with the stress and the pressure was there, hanging over their heads.

Trent was leery about using this as a tool for the court-martial. But Patrick had insisted and Trent had known him too long to question his judgment. If he needed to see the shrink and have her tell them he was fine, well then Trent would play along. He could tell her what she needed to hear then move out and draw fire.

Still, it was a hard thing to walk through the maze of hallways knowing that this was where the army sent its broken and breaking soldiers. With one more wipe of his palms on his pants, Trent pushed his glasses up on the bridge of his nose and knocked on the door.

"Captain Lindberg?" he said.

The captain behind the desk stood and Trent was struck by how prim she looked. Most women looked the same in uniform as most men: just like another soldier. But there was something about this woman's movements that reminded Trent of Jacqueline Onassis. Something about East Coast old money. Something desperately out of place in the army.

But she stood and stuck out her hand, clearly comfortable in her own office.

"Please, call me Emily," she said, sticking out her hand. The handshake was firm, though, shattering his expectations with a single gesture. Guess that's what he got for stereotyping. "Have a seat. Trent, right?"

"Yes, ma'am."

"We're the same rank," she said quietly. "I may not know a whole lot about the army but I do know that captains do not call each other 'sir' or 'ma'am.' "

"Why don't you know a lot about the army?" he asked.

"I've only been in a little over a year. So I've got a lot to learn." She glanced down at the captain's bars on her chest. "A special program brought me in as a captain."

"Just add water and stir and poof, insta captain," Trent said.

"Something like that." She smiled easily. He liked this woman. There was something about her that made him feel...comfortable. Some of the tightness in his chest from walking through the waiting room faded.

"So, how does this go?" he asked.

"Well, you're here for me to evaluate you for the defense. My job is to get a feel for your current state of medical readiness."

"Can you state that in English?" He shifted against the chair, his back protesting the too-soft seat and back. It made him want to relax further. "I was a company commander and I don't understand what you just said."

She smiled quietly, folding her hands in front of her. "We're going to do a mental health eval. It won't hurt a bit, I promise."

Just like that, the strain was back. The pressure built above his heart and the scar throbbed over his breastbone. He breathed in slow and deep and tried to keep the panic at bay.

"It's not nearly as scary as it sounds," she said. She was watching him closely. He felt the walls closing in, like he was under a microscope. All his plans about playing it fast and loose slipped right out of his grasp.

"Sounds terrifying." He tried to make his voice light. He failed.

"Trent." She waited until he met her gaze. "Relax. Nothing I write is going to go in your official file. We're just going to talk, okay?"

He swallowed but his throat was closed off, thick. Finally he nodded.

"Do you want to talk about what's going on with you right now?"

He focused on breathing. In. Out. In. Held it until his lungs burned.

Emily came around the desk and sat in the chair next to him. "Look at me, Trent. Are you listening?"

"Yeah."

"I'm not a betting woman but it looks like you're having a little bit of a problem with anxiety."

"Is that what this is? It feels like a fucking heart attack." The words forced their way past the block in his throat.

"That's actually a very common misunderstanding," she said. "Does this happen a lot?"

Trent leaned forward, pushing his glasses up to the top of his head. He covered his mouth with his hands. "Yeah."

"And how long has it been going on?"

He swallowed, staring into the distance, unable to meet her eyes. "Since I got shot."

"Do certain things set it off? Just happens whenever?"

"When things get too...out of control. When things are going smooth and easy, I'm fine. But the minute I tense up, I have trouble breathing." He finally looked at her. "Please tell me I'm not crazy. I really don't want to be crazy."

She smiled. "Crazy isn't really a clinical term," she said. "Anxiety isn't on the spectrum of crazy, at any rate. It's more of an adjustment issue."

He frowned. "What does that even mean?"

"You said you were shot? What happened?"

Trent breathed deeply as the memories rose up out of the dark, one by one, replaying in front of his eyes in vivid Technicolor. "We were in the middle of a bad fight in Sadr City. A round got between my body armor and my heart. The impact stopped my heart. They thought I died."

"If your heart stopped, technically you were dead," she said. "When did the anxiety first happen?"

He rubbed his hands over his mouth. "The first time I was getting ready to go back out in sector with our boys."

"What did you do?"

"What could I do? I stuffed it down and went out in sector." His skin was slick with sweat. His face felt clammy beneath his hands.

"You've been stuffing things down for a long time, huh?"

"Maybe." He felt a little peevish. It was just one round and he hadn't even gotten evac'd out of theater like Garrison. Garrison was fucking fine after getting the shit blown out of him. Trent had gotten one little bullet wound and his world went to hell. What was wrong with him?

"You don't sleep well, either, I bet."

"Jesus, what are you, a psychic?" He tried to make a joke. Failed badly.

"Not really. But your body language is pretty defensive right now and you're presenting some pretty strong indicators of distress."

"English? Did you just tell me I look like I'm crazy?"

"No, Trent, I did not just tell you you're crazy. But, if you're willing to work on things, I think we can make things better."

He glanced over at her sharply. "You can't fix this. You can't make the memories go away or put feeling back in the dead spot inside of me."

"Maybe we can't fix everything but I think we could do better than you're doing right now."

Better than he was doing now? Better so that he could listen to his kids play and not feel the pressure creeping up on him? Better so that he could maybe, just maybe, find a way to fix things with his wife?

Maybe he could go home and just be still for a moment. Maybe there was a chance he could sit on the couch with Laura and watch a movie. He would never complain about Shane and Jen's hospitality but there was something to be said for sleeping in his own bed, with his wife's body curled next to him. A pulse of longing beat through his veins.

Something so simple. Something so important.

He sucked in a deep breath. Each step into this room had made his chest tighter, his lungs more strained but each question was . . . it was lightening the load. Just a little bit, but the pressure around his lungs lessened. Just a little. "Is this going into my official medical record?"

Her expression softened. "I'll make sure there is nothing put in there that will negatively impact your future military career, should you choose to continue."

He rubbed his hands over his mouth again. What good was a worn down infantryman in the civilian world? There wasn't a lot of use for men with his skill set. And how would he support his family? His kids would need money for college and clothes and God knew what else kids required these days.

He needed to take care of his family. What else could he do beyond the military? He'd given it everything he had. Including apparently, his sanity.

"Okay," he said after a while. "So how does this work?"

"So let's talk about this not sleeping thing," she said. "Not sleeping well is the number one cause of some of these issues. I think if we can address that, everything else, especially the anxiety, will be a lot easier to deal with."

Trent took a deep breath and held it. He'd never thought about avoiding the R&R Center because of how other people would judge him. It was because he'd had work to do. He was a good infantryman, a good soldier. He had tactical skills. He'd needed to be in the fight. It had been the most important thing in the world to him to prove that he hadn't been slacking, that he'd been doing everything he was supposed to be doing.

Because the day he'd gotten shot, his soldiers had died. And while intellectually he knew that wasn't his fault, if he'd been there, if he'd been a little bit faster, a little more prepared...maybe they'd still be alive.

He closed his eyes. But they weren't. And nothing he'd done for the last four deployments had made a damn bit of difference to the army. To the individuals he'd served with? Yeah, that mattered. But to the army?

He'd been ready to sacrifice his entire life to that institution and this is where it left him: sitting in a shrink's office, talking about not sleeping.

He'd lost his marriage because of his choices—because

the army had needed him. Or at least that's what he told himself.

And he'd let Laura slip further and further away.

He glanced over at the doctor, sitting patiently while he waged his own private war. "I have to go home," he whispered. "And it absolutely terrifies me."

Laura opened her e-mail and stared at the words scrawled across the screen, her mind foggy from lack of sleep and too many things at home.

Her phone vibrated on her desk. Laura flipped it over. She didn't feel like talking to Jen. It was nothing against her closest friend, but Jen's love for Shane was still so new and shiny that Laura needed sunglasses to protect herself from the brilliance of it. She would never say that to Jen, though, because it would make her feel bitchy and small.

Two days had passed since Patrick had asked her to put on a happy married face. Two days and Trent had found excuses to not come home.

And each day had reaffirmed her belief that whatever demons he was facing, he was going to face them alone. The way he always had.

Just then, as if her thoughts had somehow summoned him, Trent appeared in the doorway, his shoulders filling the narrow entrance. He gripped his beret tightly in both hands, twisting it like he wanted to strip the color from the black wool.

"Hey."

She stopped typing and looked up, wishing she didn't see the worry, the lack of sleep in his eyes. "Hey."

"Can I talk to you?" he asked. His voice was hoarse, deeper than she remembered. It grated over her skin like a callous and she wondered how often he'd had to shout over smoke and gunfire for it to get this gravelly.

Bracing herself, she swallowed the lump that rose in her throat, squeezing out the air along with her ability to speak. She cleared her throat. "Sure." Wariness in that single word.

He glanced at her desk, then his black gaze met hers. He cleared his throat roughly. "I just wanted to see if you could get away. To be alone for a few minutes? It's early. We can go get coffee…"

She heard what he didn't say. He was asking for her. Just her. A chance to be alone with him. To try and talk to him without a thousand things going on around them at once.

It was a risk. But she could do this. She could have coffee with the man and still stick to her guns about ending things. Couldn't she? She picked up her purse and cell phone. An unfamiliar ache pounded through her and for a moment, she couldn't place it.

She stopped short as she recognized the feeling. A latent desire swirled through her belly. Funny how her body recognized him when her heart refused.

He didn't move as she approached. She stopped, stood close enough to see the corded scar running along his jaw. It ended just beneath his left ear, a hard slash through the shadow of his nearly black stubble.

That had happened almost two years ago. He'd called home to tell her about the injury. If she really thought about it, she realized she hadn't ever seen it up close. He was always in motion whenever he'd been home, before she'd sent him the papers. The few times they'd had sex, the lights had been off. She hadn't seen him close up like this for a long, long time. Curiosity tugged at her.

She lifted her fingers to trace the line on his jaw, her anger fading with the evidence of his pain. God, how it must have hurt. He stayed absolutely still as she traced the smooth, white skin, the edge of his stubble scraping the sides of her finger. He might as well have been made of polished granite.

He loomed over her, larger than she remembered. He was leaner, his body hard, the lines on his face deeper.

Alone with her husband in the solitude of her office, the urge to touch him drove her closer to him than she should have been. But she didn't fight it.

"This didn't heal well," she murmured.

"I thought women liked scars." His lips quirked at the edges.

"I don't like how much this must have hurt you," she said, lowering her hand.

He slipped his hands into his pockets. "It was a long way from my heart."

It was the wrong thing to say. Her gaze dropped to his chest, covered now by the grey of his army uniform. She opened her mouth to speak but no words formed in her throat. She withdrew her touch, retreating away from her fragile hopes. What she wouldn't give for a single space of normalcy, a single moment where she could forget the war, forget all that it had done to her husband, to her family. To her marriage.

They could have all the coffee in the world but until he came home, well and truly came home, not this façade they were putting up to convince the world that their marriage was fine, she could never give him her heart again. She knew that. More than half a decade at war had taught her that. And no amount of wishing in the world could change that essential truth.

Trent watched his wife walk in front of him into the coffee shop in Copperas Cove. He'd deliberately driven them away from Fort Hood and Killeen, away from the Starbucks and the McDonalds to a place where they could get away from the uniforms and the crowds and the prying glances.

He wanted time with her away from the office. Away from the constant demands on her attention. He had only just found the words he needed and they were stuck in his throat.

And she was already wary around him, already tense whenever he managed to be near her.

He didn't blame her. He was struggling to find his bearings, struggling to find the strength to walk in through their front door for that first time. He wanted so badly to be a good dad, but it seemed like everything he did with his family came out twisted and wrong. So he kept avoiding it. Until he no longer could.

He didn't talk until they had ordered their drinks and were seated in a quiet corner, him on an overstuffed chair, her on an old couch that once upon a time had probably been fuzzy faux brown suede. Laura traced one finger around the lip of her mug, avoiding his gaze. The steel resolve he saw in the set of her jaw was nothing compared to the intense emotion he'd glimpsed in her deep golden eyes.

There was a reason for her reticence. He didn't deserve to be here with her right now. But he wanted so badly to fix things between them.

Trent cleared his throat. "So, um, Patrick has me talking to one of the counselors," he said quietly. "He's trying to build an 'I'm not one step away from a psychotic break' case." He swirled his coffee, unable to look at her. "And I was, ah, talking to her about stuff. About how I feel out of control around the kids." He rubbed his hand over his mouth, taking her silence as a cue to continue. He pushed his glasses to the top of his head, rubbing the bridge of his nose, avoiding her gaze. And after his session with Emily, he felt a cautious optimism that he might actually be able to pull it off. He wasn't happy about walking out of there with a prescription for Ambien and a low-dose anti-anxiety medication but Emily had given him her cell phone number and he was supposed to call if he had any questions or concerns.

It was probably the best medical care he'd ever gotten from the army.

But right then, all the doctors in the world didn't have the answers he needed.

"She said it's normal." He looked at her then, seeking any hint of compassion in her eyes. He didn't deserve it but still, he dared to hope that maybe, just maybe she could forgive him. "But it doesn't feel normal, Laura. Everything feels wrong."

Her lips parted just a hint. Her expression softened and he thought for a brief moment that he'd broken through the barriers between them. Then she looked down into her coffee.

"I can't fix your normal, Trent." She lifted her gaze to meet his. "And I won't let you keep doing this to the kids. They don't understand what's going on, why you're back in Killeen but won't come home."

Cold crawled across his skin like spiders with icepicks for feet. He leaned back, grinding his teeth. "I understand," he said roughly.

"I don't think you do." There was no acrimony in her soft words. "I don't think you realize what you're doing to them. Emma cried herself to sleep last night because she doesn't think you love her."

"That's horse shit. Of course I love her."

"Yes, I can hear the devotion in your voice," she said dryly. "Emma is barely four years old. It hurts her when you ignore her. She misses you. They both miss you."

"I know that." He gripped his coffee cup tightly. "I just don't know what to do about it."

"And I don't know how to help you," she said, her words hard and filled with hurt. "Because you won't let me."

Tension wound tight around his heart, squeezing the air from his lungs. "You don't understand," he whispered.

"You're right. I don't. Because every time I try to get close to you, you run off to another war. Another training exercise, another deployment. I don't understand what you've been through because you won't talk to me about it. You never have."

"Maybe I don't like talking about it," he spat. "Talking about it doesn't fix anything."

She looked at him with patience and understanding and unbreakable resolve. He'd meant to try and talk to her about things, to try and open up and even that was turning into an epic clusterfuck.

"And maybe not talking about it is what's causing half the damn problems between us," she said quietly.

"No, the divorce is what's causing the problems between us." His words lashed out at her and she flinched.

"That's not fair and you know it."

"You're right, it's not." Trent set his mug down, scrubbing both hands over his face. "I'm sorry," he whispered.

Silence greeted his admission and it was a long moment before he moved his hands to peer at his wife. Tears had filled her eyes and she blinked rapidly, turning her face toward the door, away from him. "Shit, Laura, don't cry," he whispered.

"I'm so tired of crying over you," she said and her voice broke.

Trent didn't think before he moved. A piece of the tight knot around his heart loosened. He didn't consider whether or not his wife would pull away. He simply moved, sliding onto the small couch to pull her against him. He didn't know what he expected her to do but what she did shocked the hell out of him.

She stiffened the moment his arm slid around her shoulder. But he simply held her. One moment. Then another. And then he felt something he'd been longing for since forever.

She relaxed against him.

For a moment, nothing more, until something, some fleeting sensation unfurled in the dead space inside him. She trembled, then, a violent shudder and he realized she was crying. Deep, silent sobs that threatened to break them both.

He sat there and held her, hating himself for hurting her so badly. Hating the war and the illusions that he'd told himself to justify being gone. Hated the fear that made him hide from his family instead of being there for them.

He held her. Because it was the only thing he could do.

His uniform scraped the edge of her cheek. His body was a solid wall beneath her skin and for a brief moment, she simply let him hold her. His strength wrapped around her, his scent pulled her close, reminding her that somewhere inside this man was the man she'd married. The man she'd loved.

She hadn't meant to cry in front of him. Not again. But the truth had simply slipped free of the chains she'd attempted to bind it with, breaking her resolve until it emptied out of her, tearing free and leaving her drained.

It was a long time until the tears stopped. Her eyes felt swollen.

Now, she rested against Trent and closed her eyes. She simply stopped. Stopped fighting. Stopped arguing. Stopped resisting her stubborn heart that still loved this man no matter how many times he hurt her or lashed out.

His leaving, his anger: He wasn't in control of those things. Not like she'd convinced herself he was in those dark days when the rumors and innuendos had been breeding like a live thing in the silence between them. But there was more at work here than her husband simply walking out on her.

He'd made a huge step by talking to the counselor. And he hadn't needed to tell her about their conversation, but he had. Laura leaned back, refusing to believe the insidious voice in her head that said he was just telling her this out of sheer selfishness.

She lifted her gaze, looking deep into his eyes. She

started to shift and pull away but Trent moved first, cradling her face with his palms. Gently, his thumbs caressed her cheeks, wiping away the tears.

"I'm so tired of screwing everything up, Laura," he whispered. "I want to fix this. Not for the trial. For us."

"It's not that simple."

"Yes, it is." His voice was urgent and harsh. "I can't fix what I've done. And I damn sure don't deserve your forgiveness." He lowered his forehead to hers, his palms warm and solid against her skin. "But I'm asking you to help me. Help me reset my normal. Help me learn how to be a dad again. A husband." He blinked rapidly.

She pressed her lips together, biting back fresh tears. "And what happens when you leave again?" she whispered. "What do I do then?" She sniffed quietly. "You keep breaking my heart." Her voice cracked.

His fingers crooked around her jaw. "I want to stop."

They were tucked away in a quiet corner of the coffee shop. The couch was blocked by a high booth. No one could see them. Laura kept her eyes locked on his. Finally he'd laid his fears, his hopes, his dreams in her lap.

She could crush him so easily. A stronger woman might have walked away, doing to him what he'd done so many times to her. But she was not that woman. She wanted to end the pain between them, not prolong it.

She'd thought divorce was the right answer. Ending the sham their marriage had become, protecting their children from more pain. The kids were her life now and she would not apologize for that. For all intents and purposes, she'd been a single parent for years and that was okay because she knew how to do that. Now fear latched on to her heart. Fear that he would leave her again. That he would once again shatter her into a thousand pieces.

But he was here. At this moment, it was all she had. Without giving herself time to think about the consequences, she leaned closer and brushed her lips gently against his.

She pulled away before he could deepen the kiss. Fear and awareness and arousal skittered through her veins, making her off balance, like a needful, sensual thing. She'd grown accustomed to the hugs of her children, their wet kisses and enthusiastic embraces.

What she craved now was something darker. The faintest brush of lips against lips had sparked something primitive inside her. Something deeper and richer. A long-forgotten need to be touched by a man. But not just any man—by this man. His hands, roughened by combat, sliding up her thighs. The coarse pads of his fingertips caressing her skin.

Memories bombarded her as she attempted to lean away and salvage the remnants of her pride.

But Trent was not operating under the get-some-space battle plan. He reached for her, his eyes rich with dark emotion. His palms scraped against her cheeks, his fingers strong as his lips claimed hers.

His breath was a gasp against her tongue and for a moment, Laura was stunned into stillness, unable to move beneath the assault on her senses. But then her body remembered his taste, her tongue remembered his touch, and a warmth awakened inside her. She opened for him, stroking his tongue with hers, her body folding into his like it was meant for him.

Her every nerve came alive. A cascade of long-denied arousal mixed with bittersweet memories of other homecomings, other farewells. It crashed into them both, driving them under a torrent of emotion.

This was the man she had married. A man who could make her body purr just thinking about him inside her. A man who knew exactly how to kiss her to drive her wild.

This was the man she'd been waiting for. She wanted

nothing more than to crawl into his lap and have that urgent, passion-filled sex of first homecoming.

It was a long moment before the arousal faded and she became aware of the tender, sucking kisses he placed on her lips.

Another moment before he rested his forehead against hers.

An eternity passed before the words she'd never thought she'd ever say again slid past her lips. "I miss you," she whispered.

And for once, he did not pull away.

Chapter Seven

Trent looked out the window of the backseat as Shane and Carponti bickered about the radio station. He grinned and felt a little piece of normal that he hadn't known he'd been missing slip back into place. Funny how being around the guys at work always felt...right. He wanted that rightness with Laura. With the kids.

"We're meeting the womenfolk for lunch, huh?" Carponti drove them off post toward the restaurant later that day. It was no longer strange seeing Carponti driving. Funny how the missing piece of his arm was a side note rather than a major descriptor. He was just Carponti, Trent thought. Not his amputee friend.

Just his friend.

Sometimes it was the little things that struck him. He remembered clearly sitting in his office the night Carponti had been evac'd out of theater. He and First Sarn't Story had simply sat, smoking cigars and remembering all the stupid shit Garrison and Carponti—mostly Carponti—had done. Goddamn but he'd almost broken after those two had gotten hurt.

He'd gone through the motions for weeks and the situation with LT Randall had devolved further and further until

Trent had been called into his battalion commander's office and told he was being sent home.

Stripped of command. Disgraced. A failure.

"You okay back there?" Shane asked.

"Yeah," Trent said. "Just thinking."

"About what?" Carponti asked.

"Just glad you guys made it home, that's all."

Silence hung in the truck for a long moment. Finally Carponti sniffed and swiped his finger beneath his eye. "Damn it, you made me all misty-eyed."

Trent grinned. "Cute."

"So changing the subject to something less depressing, have you been keeping up with the drama back in the company?" Carponti asked.

"No. It's bad form for a commander to go back after he leaves," Trent said. "Or in my case, got fired."

"Yeah, well, screw bad form. Marshall is a raging ass-hole. I thought guys like him were a myth but apparently, Assholicus Officerus is alive and well and has been sighted in the wild."

Trent laughed quietly. "Really? Assholicus Officerus?"

"What?"

Shane shook his head. "Nah, Marshall is just being an asshole to anyone on a medical profile. He gave me a massive ration of shit about being on restricted duty after I got my vasectomy."

"So how's that working out for you?" Carponti grinned. "You firing blanks yet?"

"None of your business," Shane growled.

"Is Jen still upset with you about that?" Trent asked. A few months ago, Shane had gone and gotten all of the information about the vasectomy before he'd found the courage to talk to Jen about it. She'd found the paperwork and they'd had a huge fight.

Somehow, when he'd explained that he was afraid of having to choose between her and a baby if her cancer came back, it had convinced her to agree to his decision. He closed his eyes, remembering the first time Laura had gotten pregnant. They hadn't been planning on it. He remembered walking into the bathroom. She'd been sitting on the toilet seat, holding one of those little stick thingys.

She'd looked up at him with pure terror in her eyes. "Um, I'm a little bit pregnant."

"How are you a little bit pregnant? Either you are or you aren't."

She'd pressed her lips together and he'd seen tears fill her eyes. He'd knelt down in front of her. "Hey. It's going to be okay."

"I'm going to get fat and you're going to leave me."

He'd cupped her face. "You're going to get big boobs and I'm going to love you regardless of how big your butt gets."

She'd laughed and kissed him and when they'd made love, he'd marveled that there was a little life growing inside her. Neither of them had expected the miscarriage that had come three weeks later. Somehow he'd said exactly the right thing at a time when she'd been scared half to death. Why couldn't he manage that anymore?

Why couldn't he tell her the things that scared him?

Carponti patted Shane's shoulder as they pulled into the restaurant parking lot. "You must be in love if you were willing to get your balls rewired on a whim."

"It wasn't a whim," Shane said.

Trent rubbed the scar over his heart. Listening to Shane talk about his future wife was…it was good. It was something simple. Something…yeah, something good.

He wanted that goodness back with his wife. If the fucking pills in his pocket and therapy was a way to get back there, then he was going all in. Because he had a long way to go if he ever wanted a hint of the normal that Shane and Carponti had with Jen and Nicole.

And Laura was worth it. Whatever it took, he was willing to do.

"Beer for lunch is always an indicator that things have gone to shit," Nicole Carponti said as she sank into the booth next to Laura. "You should look happy and instead you both look like you're attending a funeral."

Giving her friend a weak smile, Laura sipped her Heineken. "Yeah, well, it's been somewhat of a banner week, all things considered. We saved you some fries."

Nicole swiped a fry through a pile of ketchup and mayonnaise then sighed dramatically. "Who do I need to arrest?"

Across from them, Jen quirked her eyebrows, raising her beer in a salute. "No one. For now. You missed all the wedding planning fun."

"I know, I tried to break away but work...Here, this ought to cheer you both up," Nicole said, tossing a brightly colored catalogue on the table in front of them.

A brilliant pink penis with a smiling face literally waved up at them from the cover of the magazine.

Jen choked and tossed a napkin over the picture before Laura fully registered that it was a penis wearing a jaunty little pair of Easter bunny ears. "You can't have that in here!" Jen hissed, her voice somewhere between laughter and pure horror.

Nicole pulled the napkin off. "We're in a sports bar for lunch. It's not like there are any children around."

Laura peeked inside and saw something that looked anatomically impossible. "Now where on earth would you put all of...never mind. I really don't want to know." She sighed then sipped her iced tea.

Nicole tapped her finger on the page. "That one looks damn near lifelike." She tipped her head. "It looks real."

"That is creepy in so many ways," Jen said, flushing.

Laura cracked a wry grin. "There is a shortage of real penis in my life." She covered her mouth at Jen's horrified expression. "What. It's true."

"Speaking of real penises, how is having Trent home?" Nicole asked, swiping another fry.

"He still hasn't come home so there was no penis involved in this homecoming," Laura said. The humor in the random penis comment dissipated in the thick mayo. Damn Trent for ruining a good joke and he wasn't even there.

"Are you ready for this?" Jen asked. "You looked pretty upset the other night when you left."

"I have to be, don't I?" Laura said. She rolled the tip of a fry in the mayonnaise. "I'm scared," she said after a moment. She looked up at her friends. "What if I can't do this? What if I can't pretend to love him because..."

"Because you still do?" Nicole finished.

Laura swallowed the lump in her throat. "Yeah."

"Then you do the very best you can and you hope that its enough," Jen said.

"And then we'll have him killed," Nicole said. "Instead of 'Good-bye Earl' it'll be Good-bye Trent."

Laura covered her mouth and laughed. "You're both terrible."

"I still think this whole happy family for the court-martial thing is a bad idea," Jen said quietly.

"I know," she said. "But this is something I need to do."

"Why?" Nicole asked, her voice harsh.

Laura hesitated. "Because Trent told me he would finally sign the papers when it's all over."

"It doesn't sound like that's what you still want," Jen said, twirling a fry in the ketchup.

"I've been waiting for him to let me go for almost a year." Laura shrugged and stared into the green glass of the beer bottle. "It might not be easy, but yes, it's what I want." At least, that's what she thought she wanted. Seeing Trent, knowing he was around, in the building at work... He was right there and yet he might as well have been across the ocean.

She didn't know how to tell them about the kiss that had rocked the foundation of her world all over again.

Despite everything, he was still so far out of reach. "I just wish everything wasn't so difficult."

"Maybe ending your marriage isn't supposed to be easy."

"Ouch." Laura winced as Nicole's words scored a direct hit. "Thanks a lot."

"That's not how I meant it," Nicole said quickly. She closed her hand over Laura's and squeezed gently. "I meant that maybe what you're going through isn't anything other than normal divorce guilt."

"I think it's more than that," Laura said. The words she needed lodged in her throat. She didn't want to admit the thing that kept her awake, worrying about a man she was trying not to love anymore. "There's something wrong," she said after a moment. "He gets really tense around the kids."

"I noticed that the other night," Jen said softly. "And it's actually really common. A lot of soldiers have trouble unwinding after deployments and Trent has been gone a lot."

"Does Shane?"

"Sometimes," Jen said. "Sometimes he just sits and listens to music. And I just sit with him. I don't talk or anything. I'm just there."

"I'd like to be there for Trent," Laura said. "But he's done nothing but shut me out since his first deployment. The distance... the coldness... it's too much."

Nicole took a sip from her beer. "Vic was taking an anti-anxiety med when he first got wounded. It made a big difference in helping him reset." She frowned, absentmindedly tearing at the label on her own beer bottle. "He told me once that things were more complex back home. That sometimes everything here is just overwhelming. The anxiety meds helped quiet some of the noise so that he didn't spend all his time pissed off and snapping at people." She blinked and lifted her gaze to Laura's. "And it worked for him. After a while, after he got used to missing an arm and his new normal, he stopped taking them."

"So maybe it's not that Trent can't be around you guys, maybe it's just that he needs time. Time that he hasn't taken for himself yet." Jen was a nurse. She knew what she was talking about, right?

"That could be true," she said quietly. The truth was, she'd suspected this all along but Trent had never given her a chance to do something as simple as sit with him. Just let him lean on her a little bit. He never gave her the chance to be there for him. She wasn't some fragile snowflake that was going to melt at the first sign of trouble. She wanted to feel . . . needed.

"Did you ever think that maybe he finally gets it?" Jen said. "That maybe he knows he needs to figure out a way to be home? To be a good husband and a father."

"Sure," Laura scoffed quietly. "And maybe we'll have miraculous, earth-shaking sex, the sky will open, there will be white doves and singing, and my life will suddenly be perfect."

"Actually, that's not a bad idea," Nicole said.

"What, the doves or the singing?"

"The sex. Maybe you guys should have sex to see if you can work through this." Nicole smirked. "You know, start with a blow job and work your way into couples therapy."

Laura laughed and some of the pain squeezing her heart loosened. Across the table, Jen snorted and barely managed not to spray liquid all over them.

"If only things were that simple," Laura said when she stopped laughing.

"I think we're supposed to try and convince you to give him another chance." Nicole swiped a French fry. "But I'm not going to push you toward a man who doesn't make you happy. You deserve better than that." Nicole waved at someone over Laura's shoulder and she turned in time to see Trent and Carponti and Shane walking toward them.

Jen quickly flipped the magazine over as the men approached but Carponti caught the movement and leaned over, swiping it without missing a beat as he bent to kiss his wife. "This is what you people do during lunch?" he said, flipping through the catalog. "Seriously?" He held up a centerfold of something called the White Rabbit. "Does this get you horny, baby?"

"You weren't supposed to be here for another forty-five minutes," Nicole said, snatching the magazine away.

Carponti reached for it again, and Nicole burst into giggles. He succeeded in grabbing the magazine and started to flip through it. "Oh, now that's interesting."

"And that's my cue to leave," Jen said with a soft smile up at Shane as she slid out of the booth.

"What, you don't want to try—" Carponti laughed but Nicole elbowed him in the ribs, silencing whatever he'd been about to say. "Ow!"

"I'll call you later," Nicole said as Jen slid from the booth.

After Jen left with Shane, Nicole and Carponti stepped over to the bar, and Laura found herself alone with her husband. If she hadn't known better, she would have sworn it was a conspiracy.

Knowing Nicole and Jen, it probably was.

Laura glanced at her watch, trying to ignore the heat creeping up her neck. There was something both awkward and darkly arousing about being caught with a sex toy magazine by her husband. She bit her bottom lip and reached for her purse. "Day job beckons. I'm going to walk over to Home Depot before I go back to work."

She stood, avoiding Trent's gaze, and made to leave. He stopped her with a simple hand on her arm. She stiffened but didn't pull away—they'd agreed to put on a happy face in public but she didn't know how to do that or what that meant. Too bad it was forced enough that she needed to keep reminding herself of that.

"Need help?" he asked softly.

She lifted her eyes and met his gaze. Behind the glare of his glasses, his eyes were dark and serious. It was such a simple thing he was asking but there were layers of meaning in his words.

She could have said no. She could have brushed past him and kept walking away from him like he'd done to her so many times in the past. Instead, she swallowed the nervous lump in her throat.

And took a chance.

Things were all twisted up inside him and for once, the feelings weren't related to anxiety and stress. It was something new, something he'd forgotten: arousal and fear mixed into a potent, explosive cocktail swirling in his blood.

His wife had been looking at sex toys.

He didn't know what to say to that knowledge. It was something they'd joked about back when they'd still joked. It was something they hadn't talked about or done in a very, very long time, and thinking of his wife touching herself, pleasuring herself . . . the image was powerful and erotic.

He supposed he should be grateful she was looking at magazines instead of hitting up one of the local meat markets that passed for bars and nightclubs in Killeen. Far too many of his soldiers had come home to find that their wives had let a man—sometimes more than one—take their place at home. And Texas law being what it was, if their wives had let someone move in, they had no legal right to force them to move out.

It could be worse. Somehow, that was small consolation as the dark and erotic images took hold of his imagination.

Laura walked a few feet in front of him, her eyes glued to an image on her phone. They'd crossed the parking lot from the sports bar to the home improvement store in a companionable silence that had felt like it was laced with something more profound. Now her head was bowed, her brow knit in concentration as she scanned the shelves looking for some mystery part for the dishwasher.

She still wasn't wearing her rings. He wouldn't bring it up. He could wait. He needed patience if he was going to do this—convince his wife that he could do this, that he was serious about coming home and staying home.

About being there for her when he hadn't been before.

This was the most important thing he'd ever do.

"What are you looking for?" he asked. He stuffed his hands in his pockets. He couldn't stand feeling so useless.

"I'm not sure," she said absently. "I'm looking for a clamp that looks like this but I don't see it." She shifted until he could look over her shoulder at the small image of a white—or maybe it was grey—clamp. He couldn't really tell. He was utterly distracted by the soft golden curl brushing against the gentle slope of her neck.

She stilled then, and silence washed over them like a thick blanket, as if she could feel his gaze on her. She lifted her eyes from the phone and looked at him. For a moment, the world fell away and they were alone, the kind of alone that made him want to reach out and touch her. The kind of alone that a man craved with his wife.

Her lips parted for a moment and he felt the tiny huff of

her breath against his cheek. He swallowed, his mouth dry. "I don't see that part," he said softly, after glancing at the shelves around him. "Maybe we should ask someone?"

She raised both eyebrows, her expression softening. "Sure." Her throat moved as she pressed her lips together and took a step away.

"So how was lunch?" he asked as he followed her to the end of the aisle. "Other than the vibrator shopping and all that."

A slow flush crept up her neck and Trent fought the urge to smile. On one of his first deployments, she had e-mailed him a video of herself. There had been nothing more erotic than watching her fingers slide down her stomach to the sweet juncture of her thighs on that grainy video. Just that once, he'd managed to coax her into doing it.

The memory had stayed with him forever.

"It was fine."

He swallowed, his mouth dry, wondering if the video was still saved in an e-mail file somewhere.

Her cheeks pink, she turned down another aisle, tracking the errant part like a homing missile. He smiled at her back, a feeling of triumph fluttering against his heart. She could pretend all she wanted, but there had been a time when things were simpler between them. A time when they might have joked about vibrators just like Nicole and Carponti did.

A time when he might have spent hours on the phone with her, content just to hear her voice.

"I heard from Rebecca Story the other day," she said as he walked up behind her. He recognized her attempt to change the subject. It did nothing to alleviate the small victory he'd just won. "You didn't mention Story was back in Iraq."

"Yeah, he just left." Trent pushed his glasses higher, feeling that awkward distance spreading between them.

"He went straight from the National Training Center back

to Iraq? Trent, he hasn't been home in months. Rebecca is worried."

"She's probably filling her time with shopping and eating out all the time. She's just pissed that he put her on a budget."

"They fight all the time." Laura looked away. "Why don't they just get divorced?"

"I don't know. Maybe he blames himself for being gone so much." He heard the unspoken accusation in her words. But for once, he opted not to fight. "He's fine, Laura. He needs to be with his boys." The old argument between them stood like stagnant pond water, reeking and stale.

"His wife doesn't count? Maybe they'd get along better if he wasn't gone so much."

Trent breathed in deeply, searching for a way out of this familiar territory. He studied her then, her hair neatly pinned out of her face for work, drifting at the base of her neck. Her eyes were guarded and wary.

He'd hurt her every single time he'd left. Even now he was hurting her by defending Story, another man who'd chosen his "boys" over his family.

He could not make it up to her. He had no way of taking away the hurt he'd inflicted.

But maybe, for once, he could try something different.

He took a single step closer and lifted his hands slowly, afraid that she would step away. But she just cocked her chin, pressing her lips tightly together as he cupped her shoulders in his palms.

He tried to think of a way to put it into words, the compulsion—no, the need—that had sent him back into combat again and again. That burning desire to make a difference, to bring just one more kid home.

He'd yielded to it too often as the war had dragged on with no end in sight. It was only now that he'd fully confronted the reality of what he'd done to his wife, to his family.

Gaining that trust started with a single, whispered truth.

"I can't explain why he needs to go," he whispered, praying she would hear what he could not say. Not because he did not want to but because it was true: He could not explain.

Laura looked up into her husband's eyes as her own filled with unshed tears. No matter how many times she swore she would never cry over this man again, somehow there were always more tears.

With that quiet admission, she knew they were no longer talking about Story and his wife. "It's not right, what he's doing to his family."

She saw the regret ripple across Trent's face, a physical pain, and she knew her comment had struck home. There was no victory in landing that blow. She was tired of all the hurt they kept causing each other.

Trent cleared his throat roughly, lowering his hands. "That's between Rebecca and Story, Laura. You can't interfere."

"Maybe the army should interfere. Stop these guys from running themselves into the ground with exhaustion."

"Maybe the army is too deep in the fight to care," Trent said softly.

They stood for a moment at that unrelenting impasse: an immovable object up against an unstoppable force. She didn't know what to say. The army was supposed to care about the soldiers that fought the war. Wasn't that why she had her job? To help the army reach out to families.

Maybe Trent spoke the truth but that only meant she'd bought into the convenient lie. Wasn't she the family readiness liaison so she could make a difference to one spouse? One soldier downrange who didn't have to worry about his wife back home. Wasn't that why she did her job? Or had she simply bought into the convenient lie, too?

She glanced over Trent's shoulder and spotted the part she was looking for over Trent's shoulder and picked it up, comparing it with the picture on her cell phone. "Found it."

When she glanced up, she found him watching her, his dark eyes intense behind those glasses that she loved so much. When he returned from basic training he'd been wearing what he'd fondly dubbed birth control glasses or BCGs. Thick, black rims and even thicker lenses. On their first day back together, they'd picked him up a pair similar to the ones he was wearing now. Wire rimmed and dead sexy.

Why did she have to remember the good times? It was so much easier to hold onto the hurt and the bitterness. But standing in the middle of Home Depot, for a brief moment, the hurt and the anger were gone and it was just him and just her.

It would be so easy to pretend that today was just another day. That they were on a normal lunch break and things hadn't gone to hell between them.

"What?" she whispered.

His expression softened. His lips parted and his throat moved as he swallowed. "Nothing. Just watching you go through Home Depot on a mission." One side of his mouth twisted upward. "You've done really well while I've been gone."

It was a bitter pill to swallow, hearing him compliment her on an independence that had become necessary because of his own actions. A sharp bite of resentment took the place of the pleasure she'd felt a moment ago. "I've had to," was all she said.

He opened his mouth to say something, then closed it. He dragged his hand through his hair roughly. "I know." He pushed his glasses higher. "I should have been here for you a lot more than I was."

The words were an admission, not quite of guilt, but of something else. A tentative step in a new direction.

Either way, it felt like they were on the same side for the first time in a long, long time.

She didn't quite know what to say. He'd ruined more than their marriage. He'd shattered her trust. And trust, like porcelain, was not easily repaired. Even when it was pieced back together, the cracks still showed. She was so used to fighting.

Instead, she chose the middle ground.

"Thank you for saying that," she said, for once opting to keep the fragile peace between them.

Some dark emotion danced behind his glasses and for a brief moment, she was tempted, so tempted to reach for them and drag them off. To look into the eyes of the man standing in front of her with no barrier between them—to find the man she had married.

For a moment, she saw him. Dark, stoic, and sexy. The man who aroused the deepest love in her. It terrified her how the intensity of that love could be so easily resurrected.

"I'm sorry it took me so long to say it." He swallowed and rubbed the back of his neck. There was so much more they needed to say. But Laura couldn't go down that road with him right now. She took a single step backward, retreating now to save her heart from breaking again.

They walked in silence toward the front of the store. For once the silence was not filled with acrimony and bitter memories.

He walked her to her car.

"Do you think you'll have to work late?"

"Depends. I usually don't. Why?"

"Just wondering." Heat sparked deep inside her, her blood warming at the first interaction between them that wasn't laced with anger and sadness and hurt. It unsettled her. "I'll see you tonight."

This was not steady footing. This was not a place she knew. "Sure."

She watched him walk into the sports bar, where Carponti had promised to wait for him. There was something aching and familiar about watching him go, but for once it was not filled with pain.

This was something new dawning between them.

And it terrified her. Because she had once loved this man more than anything else and she'd lost him.

She couldn't go down this road again with him.

Because she didn't think she could survive losing him again.

Chapter Eight

❦

Trent sat. Outside the house he and Laura had bought years before, he sat and stared at the tiny orange bottle of pills in his hand. Emily had said take as needed. He was afraid a pill would zone him out but he was more terrified of his own reactions without it.

He was going home for the first time in forever. He couldn't screw this up. But the pressure was back on his lungs and he sat there until the door closed and Laura turned on the outside light. The scar over his heart ached.

He looked up as Laura ushered the kids into the house. There was curiosity in her eyes but no judgment.

Damn it, he was not going to live like this. He took a deep breath, then killed the truck and headed into the house they'd bought before the war had broken him and he'd broken his marriage.

They'd closed on the house the day after Laura had found out she was pregnant with Ethan. She'd miscarried a few months before and the new pregnancy terrified them both. It had made both of them see the house in a new light. That night, on an air mattress in their new living room, he'd simply held her, knowing her fear was as real as his.

The house today was so different from the house they'd bought all those years ago. It was the same four walls but it was the little things that Laura had done that made it a home. A wall was decorated with pictures of the kids, some black and white, some snapshots. He listened to the noise of them in the kitchen as he looked at the new pictures. Ethan's first day of kindergarten. Emma in front of the giraffe at the Waco Zoo.

He stopped, though, in front of one picture that made his heart hurt. It was a black and white snapshot of him. He hadn't known she'd taken it. He was sitting on the swing in the backyard, with Emma on his lap, her cheek resting against his chest.

She'd snapped him in a moment when he'd rested his cheek against the top of his little girl's head. He'd forgotten about that day until this moment. Seeing it now was proof that he hadn't always been closed off and distant. That at some point he'd been a good, present father.

If he'd done it before, he could do it again. Right?

"Daddy!" Emma rushed him and he unconsciously stiffened for the impact before she skidded to a halt a foot away. "Fluffy is glad you're home."

Emma held up the fat brown hamster, straining her little arms until he crouched down to her level. The hamster's fluff spilled over the edge of Emma's hand. "Hi, Fluffy. You haven't escaped recently?"

"Last week was the last time she got out. She can open the cage," Emma said seriously.

"Hamsters can't open their cages," Trent said.

Laura leaned out of the kitchen. "She's either figured out how to open the cage or someone forgets to close it."

"I do not, Mommy!" Emma said fiercely.

Trent laughed and stroked his index finger along the hamster's back. It flinched and if he didn't know better, he could have sworn it was trying to bite him. "Cute. Antisocial hamster."

Emma took off, streaking toward her brother's room.

He watched her go, still crouched down. He rubbed his hand over his mouth. He'd laughed. For the first time in as long as he remembered, he'd laughed with one of his kids. Dear God, how screwed up was his life that something as simple as a laugh was a monumental event?

He straightened and tried to latch on to the fleeting, unfamiliar sensation.

Trent padded toward the kitchen, soaking in the details that had changed. He hadn't noticed that she'd painted the walls a pale golden yellow. It was a nice subdued color that made the house feel warm and inviting. For whatever reason, being here tonight felt fresh and good even if he did feel like a piece out of place. It was less than it might have been, though.

He didn't know what he should be doing right now. He didn't know what Laura did, what she needed help with. He didn't even know what questions to ask.

He was a stranger in his own home. It was his own fault, but still. He didn't know how to fit and he was afraid to ask her. Afraid to ruin the tentative truce between them and bring the harsh reality of the court-martial, their divorce and everything else, between them.

He stopped just out of sight. He could see her in the kitchen. She had two lunch boxes open on the counter, baggies next to them. Steam rose out of a pot of water on the stove. She was in constant motion but it was motion with a purpose. She had a system.

Watching her then, the scar over his heart ached. He didn't know when the thing inside him had broken, just that it had. And that break had pushed him away, back toward the war. He'd thought she'd be okay without him.

He'd thought he was protecting her from what the war had done to him.

War wasn't some glorified camping trip. It was violent. It was dirty.

And Trent had lived and breathed in that violence and that dirt for so long, he didn't know how to enjoy the feeling of simply standing in his house. He rubbed the scar absently. He remembered the first time she'd seen it.

She'd cried. He remembered he'd stripped off his shirt and stood there, her fingers dancing up his ribs. She'd tried to touch it but he'd stopped her.

He'd never let her. He never realized that until right then. He'd always turned her hands elsewhere when they'd made love.

He wondered what that said about him. He turned away, taking his bag into the master bathroom. He had no illusions that he would sleep in Laura's bed tonight but short of sharing a bathroom with the kids, he wasn't really loaded with other options for personal hygiene. He figured she wouldn't mind sharing the bathroom even if she wouldn't invite him into their bed.

He had no right to ask her for that, no matter how much he missed her. It went beyond sex into something more. Something that might break through the emptiness inside him.

He dropped his bag inside the closet then stripped off his uniform jacket before heading to the kitchen to see if he could make himself useful.

Laura knew what she risked tonight but that didn't make walking through that front door any easier with him at her back. She'd agreed to put on the happy face for the hearing. She'd agreed to let him come home, to pretend that everything between them was wonderful and fine. But she hadn't been prepared for the strength of her own emotions when he stepped across the threshold of their home.

Suddenly the disarray she'd grown used to stood out in stark relief. Did Trent notice the socks and shoes scattered by the door? Or the *Star Wars* toys lined up in mock combat on the fireplace? Was he thinking about how she'd let the place go because there were tire marks on the baseboards?

The kids' clutter had naturally overtaken their modest home, creeping into the corners, on top of the couch and between the cushions. The carpet was worn in places where Ethan rode his bike through the house. The wide open living room was used daily as a staging area for *Star Wars* battles and pillow fights. The old couch was long past needing to be replaced but Laura refused to buy new furniture until the kids were old enough not to spill food and drinks on it every other weekend.

Plus, she kind of loved that couch. It was one of the first things she and Trent had bought together as a couple. It was older than both kids and they'd spent many a night cuddling on it together.

She glanced at him as he disappeared into their bedroom, wondering how this was impacting him. He hadn't noticed her scrutiny, nor did he seem to care about the mess. He was more focused on studying the kids like they were two little aliens. Strangers who belonged to someone else.

She stopped suddenly. They *were* strangers. She'd been home with them when they learned how to walk, when they said their first words. She'd lived through all of it. He'd only heard about it. The things she knew about them on an instinctive level he simply didn't, and that knowledge could not be gained in a few minutes or days or even weeks.

She needed to be patient with him.

But he was here. The least she could do was allow his children to welcome him home, no matter how awkward it might be. The kids, at least, would not have to pretend they were happy to have him here. Still, that welcome came with a cost.

She knew what she was risking. So why did it feel so over-whelming, like she was teetering on the edge of out of control?

She focused on the things she *could* control. She had to cook dinner, get the kids bathed and in bed, pack their lunches, and then get ready for the next day. There was never enough time to get it all done, but she was used to doing it on her own.

She moved through the kitchen as though today was any other day, doing everything in her power to shut down the maelstrom of emotions that threatened to break her. Trent was really home, really walking toward her from their bedroom.

And they both were trying to pretend that the word "divorce" wasn't standing in the room with them as he searched for and found a beer in the fridge and twisted off the cap.

Trent stood uselessly by as the kids attempted to steal cheese sticks from the refrigerator. "No more snacks. It's almost dinner," Laura said, shooing them out of the kitchen.

A few minutes later, Ethan tore through the living room on his skates and nearly crashed into the TV. Emma squealed as she chased him, demanding a turn. The fight faded as they raced into the garage.

"You let him skate in the house?" Trent asked.

Laura tipped her chin at him. She sucked in a deep breath, biting back the harsh retort that was on the tip of her tongue. He was only asking a question, not criticizing her. "It lets him burn off some energy. He doesn't sleep well if he doesn't play. A lot."

"Mom-my! Ethan's climbing the bookshelves again." Emma's singsong voice rang out from the living room.

"That was fast," Trent mumbled. "He must have gotten those skates off in record time."

Laura raised her voice so it would carry through the house. "Ethan! If I tell you one more time to get down…"

Frustration started to twine its way around her. Trent was home. He could be the bad guy for once. It would do him some good, too. Maybe help him fit back into their lives rather than just standing there looking lost and out of place and ripping her heart apart.

"Will you go make sure Ethan isn't climbing?"

Trent stared at her for a long moment. Silence hung between them as he simply watched her, his eyes partially hidden behind the glare of his glasses. It felt like an eternity before he turned and walked into the living room.

"Holy crap, Ethan, get down!"

He sounded so startled that she set down the cutting board she'd just pulled out and rushed to see him pluck Ethan from about midway up the bookshelves.

"Put him in timeout," she said simply, handing their son off.

"What's that involve?" Trent asked as Ethan howled in protest.

"Fireplace. Five minutes. Timer starts when he stops crying."

Ethan apparently decided that tonight would be the night he would break the sound barrier. On any other night, Ethan would have stopped with a sniffle and been done with it. He threw himself off the fireplace onto the floor, screaming at the top of his lungs.

Normally, she would let him go until he wore himself down. She glanced over at Trent. The muscles in his neck were bunched, his fists tight by his sides. He was breathing hard and looking at Ethan like he was a monster.

"Is this normal?" he asked harshly.

"No," she said gently, "not usually."

He looked over at her like she'd grown two heads. "What's the special occasion?"

"This isn't normal—you're home," she said warily and saw him flinch. She reached out, placing her hand on his upper arm. "I'm not saying it to be mean. But it's true. Their entire routine is being thrown off by having their daddy home."

"Lovely."

Laura took a deep breath, then scooped Ethan up off the floor. "You don't get to stop listening just because Daddy's home," she said to her son as she carried the screaming banshee to his bedroom. "When you decide you want to act like a big boy, you can come out."

That set him off on a whole new tantrum, dialed all the way up to eleven. She closed the door behind her as he kicked and screamed on his bed.

The kitchen was a disaster, too. The water for the spaghetti had boiled over, steaming off the hot stove. Trent yanked his hand away. "Here," she said, handing him a dish towel. "Don't burn yourself."

He shot her an inscrutable look, then lifted the pot so she could wipe the stove before turning down the heat. He moved out of her way as she stirred the pasta and heated the sauce. She wondered if he was going to like it. It was a recipe she'd found from Food Network and she usually made a massive pot once every few months then froze it.

She tried not to see Trent studying the pieces of the dishwasher and felt a creeping sense of failure that she hadn't managed to fix it as easily as she'd hoped. Embarrassment crept up her neck that she had to keep moving parts around to make room for dinner. "Hopefully, I'll have it fixed soon," she mumbled.

She tore open the top of the pasta box and dumped it into the barely boiling water, trying not to be self-conscious. Trent said nothing. He stood near the sink, nursing a beer, looking out of place and uncomfortable.

She wished she hadn't noticed. Wished she hadn't seen the strain in the hard set of his back when Ethan had kicked off into his tantrum. Tantrums were part of life with kids.

But he wouldn't know that because he hadn't been there. A wave of sadness washed over her. There was nothing she could say to make this easier. Nothing to do to turn the screaming in the other room off.

She simply prepared dinner with a stranger in her kitchen and tried to pretend everything was normal when it felt like nothing would be normal again.

"Hey?"

Laura's voice interrupted the violent introspection thrashing around in his brain. He looked up at her from where he'd been studying the beer in his hand. Some tendrils of hair clung to her temples now from the steam. Her cheeks were flushed.

God, but he wanted to see her cheeks flush from his touch instead of something as mundane as cooking dinner. Would he ever have a chance to touch her again? To feel her body move with his?

He cleared his throat, redirecting his thoughts away from the bedroom. "Yeah?"

"Can you go tell the kids dinner is ready?"

He frowned slightly. "Think Ethan will talk to me?"

"I heard Emma go into his room a little bit ago. They're remarkably good at not holding grudges."

Trent glanced toward Ethan's bedroom, a deep unease twisting in his guts. He wasn't sure he could handle another tantrum. The last one had crawled up his spine and attempted to stab him in the brain. "Really?"

She walked over to him and patted him on the shoulder. Funny, how she never tried to touch his chest. He'd done that to her. He'd made a part of himself off limits to her touch. He was such an idiot. He thought he was protecting her from the ugliness of the war. Instead, he'd only managed to cut one more piece of her out of his life.

"He's six. He doesn't bite. Go. Get your children."

A few minutes later, Trent found himself in the middle of an argument over who got to sit on Daddy's lap.

"I want to!" Emma said, standing with her fists on her hips and glaring up at her brother.

"I called it first!" Ethan said.

Trent had no idea how to mediate this one. Who did he pick? How did he stop this fight?

Laura stepped in to save him. "Neither of you will sit on Daddy's lap because Daddy needs to eat, too. Each of you pick a side and eat."

Trent glanced over at Laura, who was focused almost entirely on getting dinner on the table. How had she managed to diffuse that one so easily? Everything felt strange, unfamiliar. He didn't have a battle rhythm for the kids, not like Laura obviously did. But the night was young. Maybe if he kept trying he could get through this. And maybe tomorrow, it would be a little bit easier.

Except for the tense set of his jaw, Trent was doing his best to make them laugh and let them be the center of his world.

He was trying. She had to give him credit for that. But that didn't stop her heart from aching as she watched him carefully divide his attention between the kids. He laughed and talked with them and she had to keep reminding herself that he wasn't going to stay. That this was just a temporary fix until the court-martial was over and he could run off happily back to the war.

Part of her was so angry with him for leaving her to raise them on her own and not giving her a choice. She knew army spouses would argue all day long that she needed to suck it up because they were at war and this was what she'd agreed to when she said "I do" to a military man.

And the sad part was there was another piece of her that was so incredibly, stupidly happy to have him home. When

Laura looked at him, she wished she saw the man she'd loved enough to have two children with. The man she would have waited for as the years came and went, until the war was over.

In that man's place sat a father who did not know his children. A husband who was a stranger to his wife.

Sadness ached behind her eyes at everything they'd lost. She got up and walked to the sink, needing something to do with her hands. They weren't going to stay a family, so longing for the past wasn't going to do her a damn bit of good.

If he beat the charges against him, he would leave again. She harbored no illusions that this brief interlude spent at home would end his relentless need for deployments. She knew without a doubt that Trent would deploy again, and she would have to deal with Ethan crying his eyes out because he wanted his daddy. Or with Emma crying just because Ethan was.

She was doing this for them. Maybe, just maybe, Ethan and Emma would remember this one moment of happiness before Trent left again. She got up and mechanically started putting away the leftovers and finished packing the kids' lunches for the next day.

A chair scraped against the floor and then he was there behind her. He leaned against her to place his plate in the sink, his body hard and lean against hers.

Months of eating crappy chow at the National Training Center had eliminated any shred of softness he had ever had. Months of lonely nights sliced away at any hint of rational thought.

She froze at the first brush of his body against hers. It was a simple embrace. Nothing the kids would have noticed. Before, the space between them had been filled with awkward silence. Now it snapped and hissed like a live wire.

His breath stirred her hair and sent a chill down her spine.

Laura couldn't have moved if she'd tried. A long-ignored need settled between her thighs and tingled over her skin.

In all the years she'd spent alone, she'd never once thought of another man. Never looked at anyone else the way she looked at her husband. Never felt the desire to assuage the deep, abiding longing she carried inside her for him with someone else.

Sex between them had always been good. He'd always made her feel like the most beautiful woman in the world. And damn him, he had no right to do this to her now.

She shifted and pulled free from the embrace a moment before Emma shrieked. The mood disintegrated like a puff of baby powder.

She paused, avoiding his gaze.

"Laura—"

"Don't, Trent." She held up her hand, forcing space between them. "Don't try to make me feel something that isn't there." She swallowed the hard lump of emotion in her throat. "We're going to get through this hearing and then you're going to walk away." *Just like always.* "We're over, Trent. We're just playing the happy family. We'll never be one again."

The sooner he accepted that, the better off they would be.

He gripped the edge of the sink and hung his head like he was in pain. She was sorry for that, really she was.

But all the sex in the world couldn't fix what ailed them.

Trent's body was so tight it hurt. He held his head under the steaming water, willing his cock to soften. Every time he closed his eyes, he felt the heat of her body against his. Frustration clawed at his insides.

He didn't know what had made him lean close enough to feel the warmth of her skin. The soft flesh of her neck had been within reach. A faint wisp of her skin had wrapped around him, urging him closer, and he'd surrendered to the impulse to touch her. Just feeling her body against his had nearly undone him. She'd been soft and warm against him.

He'd almost wrapped his arms around her and pulled her close, just so he could feel her breathing.

But she'd moved before his lips could touch the gentle swell of her ear. And he was paying for it now.

Could a man die from a constant erection? It was one thing to dream about his wife while he was deployed and thousands of miles away from her. But being near her and not being able to touch her? It was hell.

Screw Viagra. Back-to-back deployments were enough to fix erectile dysfunction.

He was so hard he thought he'd tear out of his skin. He could solve that problem easily but he wanted it to be Laura's hand stroking him, not his own. He grasped the nozzle and turned the water from hot to ice.

His flesh puckered, and his dick finally cooperated, a little too well. His balls retreated and tried to climb back inside him. Good. Maybe he could think about something other than laying his wife down on their bed and sinking between her thighs.

He was home. For however long it took the army to finally decide whether or not he would face charges, he was home. Really home, beneath the roof he and Laura had bought together years ago. He just needed to figure out how to make this something more than just a roof over his head.

Toweling off, he walked into the bedroom and pulled out a pair of sweatpants from his duffel bag. He wasn't sure how much of his clothing she'd left out, if any. He wasn't really willing to dive in and ask, either—he was afraid of the answer. He didn't like the idea of her boxing his things up.

He closed his eyes and instantly, the weight was there, pressing against his lungs, refusing to let him get enough air. He pinched the bridge of his nose and focused on breathing. Slowly, the disquiet in his soul eased back as his breathing evened out and he padded over to his duffel bag, pulling out the small orange bottle.

He didn't feel a damn thing as he tossed back the tiny round pill, chasing it with water from the bathroom sink. The anxiety medication would be a little stronger tonight since he was mixing it with alcohol. But maybe it would help him get through the evening relaxed. Maybe he could read a story to his kids without feeling like he couldn't breathe.

He closed his eyes and reminded himself that he was home. He was safe. He was going to wake up tomorrow and have a nice, normal breakfast with his family. And do it all again the next day. And the day after that.

If he kept repeating it, it would be true.

"Hey?"

He turned suddenly, feeling like he'd been caught with his pants down.

"Are you okay?" She nodded toward the bottle in his hand.

Trent swallowed and looked around for his glasses, buying some time while he searched for the right words. She looked at him with cautious expectation in her eyes. No judgment, just curiosity.

He cleared his throat. He watched her, searching for any sign that she was freaked out. There was no movement on her face beyond a single glance at the orange pill bottle. "I don't have PTSD or anything," he said when he could speak. "They're just... Doc said my normal is a little jacked up."

"You've been back in the States for more than a year since your last deployment," Laura said quietly.

"I know." He looked down at his hands, shame twisting inside of him. "I can function okay enough at work and all. I'm used to that stress and everything. I just, ah, have a hard time with anything else." *Like being a husband. Or a father.*

She looked away, biting her lip and pushing her hair off

her forehead. But she didn't speak and her silence hung around them like a heavy, wet blanket. "Oh," she said finally.

"Laura." He felt vulnerable, exposed. Embarrassed that she'd discovered what he hadn't even realized that he'd hidden out of shame. He didn't want her to think he couldn't be around his family without medicating himself into a false state of calm, no matter how close to the truth it skirted. "I just need time to get used to everything back here."

"Okay." He wished he didn't see disappointment shimmer in her eyes a moment before she turned away. "I'm glad you're talking to someone, Trent."

He heard what she did not say. That he wasn't talking to her. That once more, he was cutting her out of some vital part of his life, pushing her to the periphery.

For a brief moment, she'd looked at him with expectation in her eyes, like she'd been waiting for him to open up and start pouring out his fears and nightmares. But it didn't work that way. He didn't want her to see the man who woke in the cold sweat on the off times that he did sleep. Didn't want her to know about the fear that he hadn't done enough, that he could always be doing more.

That no matter what he did, nothing would ever be enough to bring his boys back.

He didn't want her to see that.

But she had.

And he didn't know what to do next.

Chapter Nine

"Good night, sweetheart." Laura leaned down and kissed her daughter on the forehead. Her hair was already starting to poof out all over her head but she smelled clean and warm. Laura paused for a moment and just rested there, her cheek against Emma's head, soaking in the feel of her breath on her neck. Her little girl was growing up so fast.

"Mommy?"

She leaned up as Emma yawned. "Yeah, baby?"

"Is Daddy going to be here in the morning?"

Laura swallowed the sudden lump in her throat. "Yeah, baby, Daddy will be here in the morning."

A pleased smile spread across Emma's face as she snuggled down in her blankets, clutching her stuffed bunny close to her chest. She made a happy little sound as Laura stood and left the room.

Laura closed Emma's bedroom door quietly, relieved that there had been no more major tantrums from either child. She heard movement in the kitchen and found Trent washing the dishes by hand because she still hadn't managed to fix the dishwasher. Maybe she'd get to it that weekend.

She paused in the archway of the kitchen and watched

him move. She'd always joked with her married friends that
the sexiest thing their husbands could do was take out the
trash. He wore a pair of sweatpants and an old grey college
t-shirt that stretched tight across his shoulders.

She did not miss how it hugged the muscles in his back
or how he moved with ease and grace. She supposed it
must be different, being home and not wearing his body
armor all the time. Still, it did something to her insides to
watch him—a man who had been the center of her fantasies
for all of her adult life—do something as sexy as doing the
dishes.

He reached up to put away a plate and caught her standing there. He'd taken his glasses off. His eyes crinkled at the
corners as he offered a hesitant smile. "What?" he asked.

She curled her lips in response. "Nothing." She didn't
want to admit she'd been caught staring.

"Kids asleep?" he asked, drying the plate in his hand.

"Yeah. They were whipped," she said.

"Do they sleep through the night and everything?" he
asked.

The attempt at small talk was awkward at best but he was
making the effort. It was something small but something she
appreciated. Maybe they needed the small talk.

It was better than the silence that had stretched between
them for far too long.

She walked over to the sink, taking over drying duties
while he finished washing. They fell into the rhythm easily.
He washed then handed her the clean dish. She rinsed.

And they both tried to pretend that this was something
normal that they did every night as opposed to an act performed by people who felt like strangers.

"Yeah, they sleep through the night. They're not babies
anymore," she said.

He handed her the last plate. His fingers brushed hers.

A gentle, not accidental, caress. A sweep of soapy fingers across her knuckles.

A simple touch. Nothing more than his fingers capturing hers and lingering over the empty space on her ring finger. One of his fingers slipped down the length of hers, a warm, soapy caress that made her insides twist.

She watched their hands for a moment, mesmerized by the movement of soap and skin. Her blood warmed as he tightened his grip, giving her ideas about impossible things. Things she shouldn't want anymore. Not with him.

But she did. And that wouldn't help anyone.

She slipped her fingers from his, rinsing the soap from her hands. She wished she didn't miss the fluid strength in his arms as he moved, or the patchwork of scars that crisscrossed his hands from too much time at war.

He turned back and she wasn't quick enough to avoid being caught again. He moved, just a little, and he was in her space. His hands were still wet. The water dribbled down her neck as he reached up to cup her cheeks. His thumb was slick as he stroked her skin gently. "I miss you," he whispered.

He hesitated, giving her a chance to pull away. Giving her a chance to break this contact before it happened. But everything was twisting and alive inside him, feelings rushing in where none had treaded in far too long.

He wanted to kiss her. Wanted to feel her mouth move beneath his. Wanted to close his eyes and taste her so that just for one moment, he could remember that once, things had been good between them.

Her breath was a huff against his mouth. A gentle puff of air that brushed against his lips. Her hands rose, colliding with his chest, her palm resting over the scar on his heart. But for once, he didn't care.

He kissed her. That first gentle nudge of lips, that whisper of shared breath. His tongue slid against hers, learning the taste of her all over again. And when her fingers curled into the scar over his heart, he was lost.

This was a mistake. Her brain knew it but her body shut down any protests and leaned in closer to the feel of this man. Her hands tightened, trying to hold on to this fleeting taste of him. It would end, all too soon; it would end and she wanted to savor the feel and touch and taste of him. Her blood hummed through her veins, pounding in her ears until the only thing she could hear was the sound of their breathing over the beating of her heart.

If it was a mistake, it was a good one. One that felt more right than anything she'd done recently. She slid her hands over his powerful chest, threading her fingers through the short hair on the back of his head, and leaned into him. Telling him with her mouth, her lips, her body everything that she could not say.

It was Trent who eased away, nibbling gently on her lips with light, teasing nips. She looked up at him, lost in his beautiful dark eyes, filled tonight with desire, not torment. It would be so easy to take him into the bedroom. To close and lock the door and strip away the hurt and the pain and the loneliness until they were all that was left.

But it would be a mistake. A mistake that would break her heart once more.

His thumb brushed over her cheek. "Do you watch TV or anything?" he asked after an impossible silence.

"Not normally," she said. Her voice sounded off to her own ears. Husky and filled with want.

"Would you tonight?" he asked. She wished she didn't hear the odd note of hope in his words.

Standing there with him this close and for the first time in recent memory, well within reach, she decided to take a chance. Because her heart was going to break anyway, why not take a few moments of pleasure before it did?

"What did you have in mind?"

If Trent was hoping for a second miracle that night, he didn't get one. He'd wanted her to sit close like they used to, hoped she would lean against him and just be. It didn't happen but he couldn't shake the sense of victory that wound through his insides.

She sat at the other end of the couch, her feet buried in the pillows near his hip. Not quite touching but not eagerly seeking distance between them, either. A tentative gesture. One that he would gladly accept.

He was conscious of her warmth, her presence. He wanted to lean closer, to pull her across that space and devour her mouth, kissing her for hours until they both forgot the barriers between them. Instead, he flipped through the channels, trying to find something for them to watch. He didn't want to admit that he had no clue what was currently popular or worse, what Laura would want to see.

He paused on Animal Planet as her phone vibrated on the coffee table. He frowned. "Who on earth is calling at this hour?" he asked quietly.

Before he'd deployed, he'd been in command and his phone rang at all hours of the night from soldiers getting arrested and in trouble. He was no longer a commander but apparently his wife's phone was now filling the role of Annoying Electronic.

She offered an apologetic shrug but her eyes were wary. "Work, most likely." She flipped the phone open. "This is Laura."

Her expression shuttered closed. She pushed away from the couch and rushed into the kitchen, writing furiously on the back of an envelope. "Got it. I'll—" she glanced at Trent. "I'll be right in."

She flipped the phone closed. "We have a casualty. I have to go to work."

He opened his mouth then snapped it closed. They weren't deployed. What the hell had happened that they'd lost a soldier during their time at home station? Soldiers weren't supposed to die in the States. They were supposed be safe here. A thousand questions raced through his mind, but instead he simply asked, "What happened?"

"Fatality at NTC. Kid got hurt on the railhead from someone doing something stupid. And now his nineteen-year-old wife is a widow."

"Hey." The bitterness in her voice surprised him, so much so that he reached for her hand. "Are you okay?"

She looked away, tense beneath his touch. But she didn't retrieve her hand from beneath his, a tacit acknowledgement of this temporary truce between them.

She breathed out quietly. "It's just hard when we lose a soldier to something stupid." She paused. "This whole war is stupid. What's the damn point?"

She pulled her hand away and stood up, her back rigid, her movements stiff. He wanted to comfort her. To pull her against him and tell her that he agreed with her. That the war wasn't worth it.

But admitting what he'd taken too long to realize would mean he'd ruined their marriage for nothing. And he treasured this peace between them far too much to ruin it all over again tonight.

He didn't want to argue with her. And he wasn't ready yet to face the harsh reality of everything he'd done to drive her away.

So instead, he stood with her and watched her write down more information—notes about what she had to do. She rested her head in one hand, her fingers threaded through her hair.

"What do you do with the kids when this happens?" he asked.

Her pen froze in her hand. She turned slowly, her expression telling him that she'd just now realized that for once, she might not have to drag the kids out of bed and to the sitter's house in the middle of the night. But then her eyes flickered with uncertainty. Her doubt in him cut him, harsh and ragged across the already raised scar over his heart, but he said nothing. He deserved her doubt. He'd done nothing to earn her trust.

Maybe that could change. Starting now.

"They can stay with me tonight. You won't be all night, right?"

She tipped her head and studied him quietly. The uncertainty in her eyes shamed him. "Are you up for that?"

"Tonight wasn't too bad." He shrugged and wished he could figure out what to do with his hands. "I mean, I didn't run screaming from the house like a Muppet on acid or anything so we can take that as a win, right?"

She laughed quietly and the sound of her laugh did something warm and fuzzy to his insides. "I shouldn't be gone all night. Couple of hours, tops."

She took a step toward him, until he could see the concern written in her eyes, the worry in the lines around her mouth. Lines he badly wanted to smooth away.

"I can handle it, Laura," he said softly. "They're asleep, right? Easy."

Her lips twitched from that strange smile to something warmer.

Because he couldn't help himself, because the urge was too strong, he reached up and stroked a stray strand of hair from her eyes. "Go. We'll be here when you get home. And I promise I won't catch the house on fire, either."

"Okay," she whispered. Then she did something completely unexpected. She leaned up and kissed him. A soft, gentle kiss, her lips moist against his. "Thank you."

Her phone started buzzing again and then she was gone, leaving him alone and unafraid in their quiet house.

There was a strange silence around him without her in the house. The kids were asleep and the silence surrounded him. He could feel the house sleeping, which was weird because in Iraq, there was never real silence. There was always a hum of a generator or an air conditioner or worse, incoming rounds exploding too close for comfort.

This silence was strange. Not oppressive and heavy. Just…there. Something he noticed. He wondered if he would ever get to the point where the quiet didn't bother him anymore.

He wandered through the house, unable to sit on the couch now that Laura wasn't there with him, and looked at the pictures in the dim light. He'd missed so much. His choice.

His fault.

He rubbed his eyes beneath his glasses then looked up. He was standing in the hall between the kids' rooms. He hesitated; then, because it would have been cowardice to turn away, he quietly opened Ethan's door.

His room was filled with the chaos of a six-year-old boy. Toys were scattered across every available space and he was pretty sure that was a pair of blue undies sticking out from beneath the bed. But it was his son that drew his gaze.

Ethan was sprawled out across the bed. One leg dangled over the edge, his toes brushing the carpet. His son's hair was sticking out everywhere and Trent had the sudden uncomfortable urge to never see his son with a military regulation haircut.

He leaned down, brushing his hair from his face. Ethan's eyes fluttered open.

"Hi Daddy," he whispered. He rolled over and Trent pulled the blanket over his tiny shoulders, his throat tight.

He managed to make it out of the room without tripping over any toys, a fact that was actually quite amazing. He stood outside his son's room for a moment and just...stood. He let the stillness wash over him. Fought the tightness in his chest that for the first time wasn't from anxiety or stress, but simply from too much emotion too fast.

It was like everything inside him had been locked at the bottom of a well and was now geysering through him. So much emotion. So raw. So potent.

It was addictive. Actually feeling again, feeling like he was going to really be able to stay home and be a dad. Yeah, this he could get used to.

He pushed open the door to Emma's room, curious to see how his little girl slept. He smiled when he saw her. She wasn't some neat little princess. She was sprawled across the bed like her brother had been, only flat on her back, her arms cast out to the sides. A stuffed bunny lay near the edge of her bed, hanging on for dear life by an ear tucked beneath her shoulder. Her mouth was open and she was breathing in slow, quiet huffs. He stood there for a minute, taking her in. Absorbing the clean, warm smell in her room.

He tried to cover her up but the blanket was stuck beneath her butt. So he pulled an extra one from the foot of her bed and tucked it around her. She made a sleepy sound and rolled toward the bunny, grabbing it and pulling it close.

He took a deep breath and closed the door, then settled on the couch. He set his glasses on the table and closed his eyes, wondering if maybe he'd be able to get some sleep tonight without resorting to the little white pills that Emily had prescribed.

For the first time in as long as he could remember, he felt sleep pulling at him—and for once, he didn't fight it.

Chapter Ten

❧

Daddy."

Trent heard a little voice from very far away. Then he felt something sharp poke him in the chest, right over the scar on his heart. He frowned and tried to ignore it.

"Daddy!"

He blinked and opened his eyes. Emma stood near his shoulder, her little face bunched up in the shadows, her bottom lip quivering. "Daddy, I peed."

He frowned. If there was a significance to this, he was missing it. "Okay, so wash your hands and go back to bed."

"I can't, Daddy. I peed in my bed." Her voice broke. "I'm sorry, Daddy."

He sat up, reaching for his glasses. "You peed the bed?" he asked.

"Yeah, Daddy." She sounded so sad.

"Okay, so what does Mommy usually do when this happens?" he asked.

"You have to change the sheets. And I have to take a bath."

He glanced at his watch. Just what he wanted to do at four-thirty in the morning: bathe a child.

But okay, he could do this.

It dawned on him that if Emma was coming to get him, Laura must not be home. He wanted to know if she was okay but decided not to bother her at work. He could do something simple like this, right?

"Okay, honey, let's get you in the tub while I take care of the bed. Deal?"

She looked up at him, her eyes wide. "Deal."

She padded toward the bathroom and Trent made a mental note to check on her in a few minutes. She was big enough to wash herself up but he didn't want her unsupervised for long in the bathroom by herself.

He walked into her bedroom, hit immediately by the strong scent of pee. Holding his breath, he stripped off the sheets, balling them up and carrying them directly to the laundry room and dumping them on the floor next to the washer. He managed to find clean sheets then went back into Emma's bedroom to discover that his wife was a genius. There was a thin sheet of plastic on top of the mattress. It looked like a shower curtain liner but whatever it was, it had saved the mattress that night.

He sprayed it down with bleach cleaner then let it air dry before he went to check on Emma.

She was standing in the middle of the tub, both the shower and the bath water running. Soap coursed down her back and over her cute little butt as she attempted to wash her own hair.

"Want some help?" he asked.

She'd scrunched up her eyes to keep from getting soap in them so all she did was nod vigorously. He eased her backward under the shower water and rinsed the soap from her hair then pulled her out of the tub. He wrapped her little body in a massive light blue fuzzy towel then wiped her face gently. She beamed up at him. "Thanks Daddy."

In that moment, he knew how a superhero felt. He brushed the towel over the tip of her nose then urged her toward her bedroom. "Get some clothes on."

It might be a small victory, something Laura might do on any random night, but hey, it was still a victory. Child bathed? Check. Back to bed?

Yeah, not so much. Because Ethan woke up just as he was tucking Emma back to bed and that's when all hell broke loose.

Two hours later, Trent's patience snapped at the end of its leash.

"Mommy doesn't let us have cereal on school days."

Trent looked down at his daughter, the tiny reflection of his wife down to the disapproving glint in her dark eyes, and counted to ten. Then twenty while grinding his teeth and trying to keep his emotions from spiraling out of control.

But nothing eased the tension in his chest.

He slapped the cereal box on the counter hard enough that a spray of Kix burst out of the top. He gripped the edge of the counter and tried to keep his voice neutral. "Mommy isn't here, honey. It's okay to have cereal."

Ethan's eyes got wide and he covered his mouth. Trent wasn't sure if his son was laughing at him or upset that he'd spilled the cereal.

Trent wasn't actually sure he cared either way.

Fresh panic gripped his lungs, tearing at his insides, keeping him from taking a proper breath.

Keeping him from thinking clearly. His thoughts raced as he tried to figure out how to get them dressed and ready to go without having the slightest idea what ready actually looked like.

He could handle things blowing up around him. He could handle soldiers completely losing their shit.

But he apparently could not handle two small children.

"Ethan! I thought I asked you to get dressed."

His son lifted his chin and stomped his foot. "I want to wear my Spiderman t-shirt."

"I don't know where it is. You'll wear the green frog t-shirt that Mommy laid out for you."

"I don't wanna!"

Trent's temper snapped its lead. He slammed his palm down on the counter top, hard enough that the shock reverberated up his arm and into his shoulder. "Ethan!"

But that was nothing compared to the shock on his children's faces.

It was past seven a.m. and Laura had been up all night. She was dead on her feet and she had never seen a casualty notification go more wrong. The soldier who had died had been living with a girlfriend and trying to get divorced from his wife. The girlfriend was listed on the official paperwork but the platoon sergeant had contact information for the wife. They'd tried to figure out who to contact and what to do and the parents got into the mix around midnight.

She felt terrible for all of them but at about two a.m., she'd gotten pissed at the company commander for not having his paperwork together and screwing this up in an epic and unforgettable way.

She opened the front door in time to hear Trent shout from somewhere near Ethan's bedroom. It was already seven o'clock and the kids were well on their way to being late for school.

She rushed into the kitchen, expecting to see the kids finishing their breakfast. Instead, Emma was crawling on the counter top, reaching for a cup in the cabinet and Ethan streaked through the living room like he'd just injected a gallon of fruit punch.

She heard Trent shouting for Ethan from the bedroom.

Then everything exploded in slow motion.

The door to the bedroom slammed violently against the wall. Ethan's red backpack flew across the living room, knocking a picture of Laura and Trent from its nail. Glass shattered across the living room floor.

Ethan dove to the fireplace, picking up the pieces of a now broken dinosaur. Tears ran down his face as he held the shattered remains of his favorite dinosaur from his backpack. His cry rose through the entire house, a slow wail.

Silence crashed over the house. Laura's heart slammed against her ribs. Emma crouched on the counter, her hands over her ears.

Trent stormed into the living room. "Ethan!"

She stepped in front of Trent, pulling his attention away from their crying son. Hands up, fear clutched at her throat. "Whoa! That is enough!"

But she'd be damned if whatever started this was going to continue.

Her husband stood in front of her, his fists bunched at his sides, his chest heaving. His eyes were dark and filled with a thousand angry emotions. Behind her, Ethan's wails dragged down her frayed nerves. "Ethan. Go to your room. Now."

"But Mommy—"

"Now, Ethan." She didn't raise her voice, didn't take her eyes off her husband. Ethan threw the ruined dinosaur on the floor and stormed out of the living room, his bedroom door slamming behind him like a gunshot.

Laura took a deep, shaking breath, her mind racing over how to calm everything down. "Trent," she whispered. Took a tentative step toward him. Placed her hands on his chest and forced him to meet her gaze. He opened his mouth. Snapped it closed. And then a deep shame filled his eyes as the anger rolled back beneath an onslaught of remorse.

He took a single step backward. And disappeared into their bedroom.

She sucked in a trembling breath and looked into the kitchen, where Emma sat at the table now, focused intently on her cereal. Torn between her husband and her son, Laura turned toward Ethan's bedroom.

He was facedown on the bed. She pushed the door open a little farther and moved to sit on his bed. She stroked his back gently and felt his little body shake beneath her touch. "I want Daddy to leave," he said into the pillow.

"Don't say that, honey."

"Why not? It's true."

"No it's not. You're just mad because he threw your backpack."

"Parents aren't supposed to yell," he said, rolling over and sitting up. He crossed his arms angrily over his chest with a huff, a sulk furrowing in his brow.

Laura brushed his hair out of his face, glad to see the anger retreating from his eyes. "Since when?"

He shot her a wry look that looked so much like Trent. Then his expression fell and his bottom lip quivered. "Mommy, he scared me," he whispered.

Laura pulled him into her arms and felt his tears, hot and wet on her blouse. Frustrated tears fell down her cheeks but she didn't care. She simply held on to her son and wished she knew how to hold on to his father. She held him until his little body stopped shaking. But he didn't pull away. He just needed to hold on for a little bit. She knew the feeling.

Too bad there was no one there to hold her right then. She was ragged and raw from the all-nighter and now as the adrenaline washed away, it took with it the strength that was keeping her upright.

So Laura sat there and held him. Because that's what mommies did when the world went to shit around them. Guilt clawed at her. She never should have left him with the kids. Not so soon. Not when he was still unfamiliar with the things that they did to work her nerves and push her buttons. She knew how to navigate around them. He didn't. She'd known leaving Trent with the kids was a bad idea. They weren't bad kids but they were *kids*, which by definition meant a lot to handle.

And as much as it pained her to realize it, they were a handful he had not been prepared to handle.

But Ethan didn't need to hear any of that. She smoothed his hair down as he leaned back, his eyes already clearing up. "I'm sorry I made Daddy yell, Mommy," he said in a small voice.

Laura kissed the top of his head then smoothed his hair out of his face once more. "Tell you what, kiddo. Finish getting dressed and go eat your breakfast with your sister. I'm going to go check on Daddy."

"Is he okay?" In that instant, her son was no longer angry with his father. Concern filled his voice, making him sound older than he was.

She wished she knew. She brushed her palm over his damp cheek, wishing she had more reassurances. But the look she'd seen on his face had terrified her. She honestly didn't know the answer to her son's question. But he didn't need to know that. "I'm going to go find out, okay? Go eat?"

She found Trent in their closet. Leaning against the wall, his glasses thrown on the floor, he'd drawn his knees up to his chest and sat with his head bent onto his folded arms. Her heart broke for him all over again.

She could leave him there. She could rail at him for yelling at their kids. For not being there and then acting like some stereotype out of a bad movie.

But she wasn't going to do either of those things. In the last few days, she'd seen more vulnerability in this man than she'd ever realized existed. He'd been running from their family, from her for so long he honestly didn't know how to be there anymore.

He wanted to be. No matter what she'd thought before—that he was home because of the court-martial, that he would leave again as soon as he got the chance—-the fact was she was no longer certain. He was hurting. Badly.

So she did the only thing she could.

Fear, not unlike the fear of approaching a wild animal, slithered through her veins but she forced it down. Forced herself to face the wicked realization that her husband had completely lost his shit and terrified the living hell out of her children and her as well.

She never thought she'd fear this man but for one brief moment, she had.

But she loved him more and she couldn't leave him. Not like this, shattered and broken on their closet floor.

It took everything she had to kneel next to him, careful to move his glasses. His breathing, ragged and harsh, was the only sound over the beating of her heart. She bumped into the pile of uniforms on the floor near his hip. One of the orange bottles poked out from beneath a sleeve.

She took a deep breath and swallowed. Then she reached for him.

"Hey?" She slid her palm over his forearm. Felt the crisp hair on his arms against her skin. Felt the heat. The strength. The power that had terrified their son.

Here was a man who'd given the army everything, and the fear in a child's eyes had reduced him to this. It was a hard thing she did, simply sitting there with him. There was no excuse for violence; she knew that. But even as his temper had snapped, he hadn't hurt the kids. A little plastic dinosaur hadn't been so lucky. But she could fix that.

She didn't know how to reach him through the tangled guilt and shame radiating off him in palpable waves.

She couldn't leave him there. Not like this. He'd never let her in, never lowered his guard enough to let her fix whatever was eating at him. Maybe, she could see him through this.

Maybe.

He tensed beneath her touch, pulling away to rub his hands over his face, leaving them there. She didn't miss the taint of moisture beneath his eyes. Her heart ached for the pain she saw there. She slid closer, until she could lean against his bent knees. She rested her chin on one, pressing against him.

"Did I ever tell you about the time I broke the window in the kitchen?" she said, breaking the silence the only way she knew how. She shifted again, sitting so that her shoulder rested against his knee. The contact bolstered her flagging courage. "Ethan had just exploded out of his diaper and used it as paint in the hall." The memory raced back, bringing with it the long forgotten anger and frustration. "I'd been up all night with Emma." She released a hard breath. "I just lost it. Something snapped and I threw the entire diaper pail."

He lowered his hands, banging his head back against the wall. She flinched, knowing that had been hard enough for him to see stars.

"Did you see his face, Laura?" His voice was scratchy and raw. "He was terrified of me." She slid her hand up to rest on his knees. He opened his eyes. "I fucking terrified my son."

"Trent, we all have bad days." She squeezed, waiting until he met her gaze, needing him to hear her. "All parents lose their shit sometimes. It's part of raising kids."

He looked away, disgust carved into his face. "I should be better than that."

She scoffed quietly, then reached for him, brushing her fingers over the stubble on his cheek. "Says who? Who says you're supposed to be a perfect father? Trent, none of us is perfect."

He opened his eyes then and she was stunned by the depth of the recrimination and bleak guilt she saw looking back at her. She shifted up to her knees, leaning forward and cupping his face in her hands. His skin was cold, clammy. His nostrils flared slightly at her touch, his body tense.

"I need you to hear me on this." She lifted his chin until his eyes met hers. "You didn't hurt him."

His throat tensed as he swallowed. "I broke a dinosaur." A ragged guilt for something far worse than breaking a child's toy.

"That we can replace for three ninety-nine at Target," she said. "He's fine." She stroked one thumb over his cheek, finding it damp. "Trent, you didn't hurt him."

He didn't look away from her but she saw the doubt, the shame fill his eyes. "All I could think about was getting him to stop yelling and listen," he whispered.

"I know. Believe me, I know." She gentled her fingers, keeping the contact, afraid to let him go lest he shatter there in her arms.

He lifted one hand, covered hers where she held him. "I'm sorry." He pressed his lips together, his throat moving as he swallowed. "I'm so goddamned sorry. I'm a mess. I should be better than this."

She smiled gently. "Yes, you are a mess." His cheeks were stiff with stubble beneath her touch. "But you're home for the first time in a long time. Rough spots are normal." She swiped both thumbs over his cheeks before she let him go. His hand lingered over hers for a moment too long.

"How can you forgive me so easily?"

"Because I've been there, too." Her fingers were hot beneath his touch. "But I know when they're getting to be too much. I can walk away before I let my temper get the best of me. You have to learn those things," she said quietly.

"What if I can't?"

"You can." She leaned down and brushed her lips with his.

He closed his eyes, shifting until he could rest his forehead against hers. "I'm afraid. I'm afraid of how I feel around the kids."

"You've been gone a long time. You have to give yourself time to adjust," she said.

"You're not worried?"

What could she say to that? She had been. She was. But there was something between them now that was more powerful than worry. "I am." A slide of her fingers over his cheek, a soothing caress. "But I have faith in you." Faith she'd lost but faith she'd start to find again. One piece at a time, but it was more than it had been.

And it was enough to keep her there with him as the time ticked past and the kids were late to school. Until the fear and loathing in his eyes faded. Until he looked at her and she saw the man she was coming to know. Not the man she'd married. Someone different.

But someone that she could no longer walk away from.

She slid her hand from his and retrieved his glasses, handing them to him before she stood and offered her outstretched hand. He looked up at her from where he still sat. A thousand emotions flickered across his face. Fear. Uncertainty. Guilt.

But he slipped his hand in hers and pushed to his feet. They stood there for another moment, until he reached for her, cupping her face in his hands and kissing her oh so gently on the mouth. It was meant as an apology, nothing more, but it twisted into something else. Something filled with passion and need and a thousand unsaid things.

It was Laura who eased back this time. "I have to get the kids to school," she whispered.

He rubbed his thumb gently over her bottom lip. "I'd like to apologize to him first."

She smiled up at him, her heart swelling in her chest. Knowing it was stupid and savoring the feeling anyway. "I think that's a good idea."

A spark of understanding passed between them, a hint of common ground. She squeezed his fingers then let him go, knowing he was no longer at risk of breaking in her arms.

For now.

Chapter Eleven

🍃

Trent was late. He hated being late but that's how it went sometimes when one was dealing with Fort Hood traffic. Some jackass had just rear-ended some other jackass at the Clear Creek gate and he'd sat on the bridge over Highway 190 and seethed for forty minutes.

He was supposed to be meeting Shane and Carponti at the Community Events Center to make sure things were on track for the wedding reception. It was going to be a small affair but Shane wanted somewhere small that they could have to themselves.

Carponti had suggested Hooters. Shane had not been impressed.

Trent parked in front of the Events Center next to Carponti's bright red truck at the edge of the parking lot and headed toward the front door. The parking lot was crowded from a bunch of conferences being held in the Events Center all this week. They'd be lucky to see the room at all if the sheer amount of rank walking through the parking lot was any indication as to the madness inside.

Trent stuffed his cell phone in his pocket and reached for the door at the same time as another soldier.

He stopped. His skin went cold.

Lieutenant Jason Randall. The weasley little bastard who'd been a pain in Trent's ass since the day he first arrived in Trent's formation. The hackles on the back of his neck rose and he took a single step forward before he remembered that Randall was with a general officer. One simply did not assault one's former lieutenants in front of general officers.

Trent badly wanted to know what ass Randall had kissed to get an assignment escorting a general around when he was pending many of the same charges as Trent.

Trent stiffened as General Ledbetter looked at him. He felt like a hamster being watched by a feral cat. "So you're Davila."

"Sir?" Trent kept his tone neutral, his body at the position of attention.

"I'm sure you two have lots to talk about." He opened the door and Trent spotted a sign for a Warfighter Commanders' Update Brief.

"Roger, sir." Randall looked like he'd rather eat glass.

Trent waited for the door to close completely before he spoke.

"Nice to see your ass-kissing skills haven't atrophied, LT," Trent said, his voice lighter than it had any business being.

"Fuck you. Sir." Randall's face flushed deep scarlet.

"No, you've already done that," Trent said dryly.

"You deserve whatever happens to you. You gave me nothing but shit from the moment I started working for you." Randall lifted his chin.

"So sue me for expecting more from my officers than skating by on their daddy's name. Your father earned that reputation. You did not," Trent said. He clenched his fists, badly wanting to lay his ass out flat. Just once and he'd get it out of his system.

"Maybe if you were a better commander, you wouldn't be under investigation. The army can't find things if there's nothing to be found."

Trent smiled coldly. "And how exactly are you planning on beating the charges against you? Because, as you said, the army can't find things if there's nothing to be found."

Randall flushed and clenched his fists by his sides. "I'll never get why the troopers followed you so blindly."

Trent took a single step closer. "See, that's the problem with you, LT. You never figured it out."

"Figured what out?"

"That no matter how highly ranked you become, the boys will always see through you." Trent took a single step forward and rubbed the tip of his finger over the black thread that made up the lieutenant rank on Randall's chest. "They'll respect your rank because they have to. But they'll never respect *you*," he whispered. "No matter who your father is."

They stood toe to toe for an eternity. Trent wanted so badly to hurt him that it felt like battery acid burned through his veins.

"Fuck you. You knew what I was doing."

"No, I didn't. And I never would have allowed you to put our boys at risk so you could make some extra money selling weapons parts." Trent stroked his hands over Randall's collar. "But you're still under investigation, too. Tell me, does Daddy know you married one of your subordinates?"

Everything happened all at once. Randall hauled off and swung at Trent just as the doors to the Events Center burst open. Carponti and Shane dragged Randall and Trent apart before the blow could land.

Randall yanked away from Carponti, straightening his uniform. "Still the same undisciplined bunch of roughnecks you've always been," he spat.

"God, it's so nice to see you, LT." Carponti reached forward to flatten the collar of Randall's uniform. Randall slapped his hand away. "Tell me, has your sense of smell changed from having your nose buried up General Ledbetter's ass?"

"Fuck you, Carponti. Shove your fake arm where the sun doesn't shine."

Carponti lifted his prosthetic and studied it for a moment, a wicked gleam in his eyes. "How about I shove it up your ass instead?"

"Carponti!" Shane's sharp reprimand was a long familiar refrain with them, and Trent almost grinned. "LT, get back inside before you get hurt."

Randall turned to head inside then paused. His fingers clenched by his sides for a moment and then he turned back to face them, his eyes zeroing in on Trent. "You're not going to win this one."

Trent rubbed his finger down the side of his nose then adjusted his glasses. "We'll see about that."

"Ta-ta for now," Carponti said from behind him, waving his prosthetic. Trent shot his friend a look as the LT disappeared into the Events Center.

"Why the hell was Randall allowed to be that guy's escort? He's still under investigation." There was real anger in Carponti's voice, a rarity for him.

"Randall's father called in a few more favors, I guess," Trent said. He glanced at Shane. "Let's go make sure this wedding of yours still has a place to party. I need something good to replace the slime that fucker left on my skin."

"So how are things going with the kids?" Emily sat in one of the comfortable chairs perpendicular to Trent.

The office door was closed. His back was to the wall. Still, he felt a level of vulnerability he hadn't felt since his first deployment, when incoming rounds had kept him from sleeping—and when he did, they'd exploded so frequently and so often, he'd only slept bits and pieces at a time.

This was his second session with Emily and already he was unearthing things he didn't want to feel. Things he didn't know how to process. Things he'd run from since he'd gotten hurt.

"They're...tough," he finally admitted. He told her about the other morning and his explosion with Ethan.

"So you're still feeling a lot of anxiety around them?" Emily's voice was calm and quiet. Smooth. She made him want to relax.

"Yeah. And when I get anxious, my temper gets short." He twirled his glasses in his hand, avoiding her gaze. "I feel like I'm failing at everything. Being a husband. Being a father. I can't get ahead back here. The only thing I'm good at is being a soldier."

"I don't think that's true," Emily said. "If it were true, you wouldn't be here, now would you?"

He glanced up sharply. "I guess not," he said. "When is it going to get easier?" he asked. "When is it going to feel normal and not like I'm one egg short of a dozen?"

"It takes time, Trent. You've only been home, really allowed yourself to be home, for a really short period. You can't expect miracles." She tipped her head at him. "This isn't the same thing as preparing for a deployment," she said.

"I know that."

"Do you? This isn't a paint by numbers event, Trent. It's going to take years for you to get your normal back. It's a slow decompression. You've had ten years to wind yourself up, to get used to a certain kind of stress. This is the same thing. New stress. Different stress. Not life-threatening but stressful all the same." She shifted, crossing one leg over the other. "Was there ever a deployment when you came home and things felt more normal than they do now?"

He frowned, staring down at his hands in his lap. He'd deployed so many times. Each time he'd thought he couldn't wait to get home. Each time, he'd rushed back out the door as soon as he could. "Nothing has ever felt right since I got shot," he whispered after a silence that stretched until forever.

"Do you want to tell me about that?" she asked gently.

The memories rose up, sharp and poignant. He could smell the stinking sulfur, hear the screams of his men. The fire that ripped through his skin as the round that had damn near killed him tore him apart.

"I should have died that day," he whispered.

"You did die, Trent." He looked up at her. She tapped his file on her lap. "Your medical records show your heart stopped. You were medically dead." He looked back down at his hands. There was a weight pressing down on him. Like an elephant sitting on his chest. Too much, too many memories. A thousand faces stared back at him, swirling around him, taunting him that he should have been better, faster, smarter. Should have seen the bomb that had taken out their truck.

"Trent?" Her voice penetrated the racing thoughts. He looked up at her. "You came home. But you don't feel like you deserve it, do you?"

Her words settled on his shoulders like a heavy, wet blanket. Thick with recrimination that seeped into his bones. And though he tried, there was simply no way for him to wriggle out of this conversation since she'd laid it so plainly in his lap.

"Maybe I wonder what's the point. Good men go to war. They don't come home." He looked up at her. "I didn't deserve to come home. I'm a shitty husband. A shitty father. There are good men, good fathers, who didn't come home. Why the fuck did I?" Harsh words, ripped from his soul.

"Good men do come home," Emily corrected. "They just don't come back the same as when they went. And you have to accept that war asks good men to do bad things, that death in war isn't something you can control and that punishing yourself isn't doing anyone any good."

"What am I supposed to do?" He stood abruptly, pacing the small office, unable to sit with the disquiet in his thoughts. "How do I wake up in the morning and not see everything that's screwed up around me? Things that I screwed up by leaving. By running. My wife doesn't deserve this. My kids don't."

The strain was back, squeezing around his heart.

"Start with something small," she said quietly.

He looked down at her where he stood. The woman was unflappable. Calm in the face of his frustration. How did she manage that? "Like what?"

"Take the kids. By yourself. Do something with them, just them. Show them you're still their daddy but more importantly, show yourself that you can do this."

"I'm not sure Laura would be comfortable with that." A very real fear. "What if I lose my shit again?" he whispered.

"Then don't freak out. Then walk away for a second. Go into the bathroom, close the door and give yourself a minute. And if that doesn't work? Then you stay in that bathroom until it does."

Trent sucked in a deep breath, the shame from the other morning crashing over him.

"You have to give yourself permission to take things slowly, Trent. You can't come back from being at war for most of the last decade and expect to just miraculously turn things off."

He smiled bitterly. "When you put it like that, it sounds a little silly."

"This isn't silly," she said quietly. "This is the hardest thing you will ever do."

Chapter Twelve

I'll pick the kids up.

Laura looked down at her phone, ashamed that her hand trembled as she set it down. That single text message sent a thousand emotions racing through her, but mostly she hoped that the kids wouldn't try to break him again. Kids were funny that way, always pushing to see what they could get away with.

A little piece of her heart soared when he'd told her he wanted to pick them up. He was still in the fight. Still trying. And it made her heart hurt how happy that little effort on his part made her.

So when she walked in the door to hear the kids shrieking with laughter, she was thrown off balance so much so that she stopped and simply stood there for a moment, taking in the sounds of their joy. This? This sounded like a normal she'd only dreamed about.

"Ethan, get the hamster out of the dishwasher."

"Daddy, she needs a bath."

"The dishwasher is not the place for Fluffy to conduct hamster shower operations."

Laura smiled where she stood just out of sight, listening to the debate between her husband and her son. Trent sounded disgruntled but not on edge.

Emma giggled. "Hamsters don't take showers, Daddy!"

Trent grunted and she heard the scrape of metal on metal. Peering into the kitchen, she saw both kids sitting on the floor next to the open dishwasher, two small rodents crawling around on the space in front of them. Periodically, a set of small hands would scoop up one of the hamsters and move it farther away from its planned route to freedom.

The hamsters did not seem to mind. Stinking little buggers. Probably teaming up to plot their next escape.

"You can't wash hamsters," Emma said wisely. "If you do, they'll catch a cold."

She thought she heard Trent mumble something to the effect of "That's why they smell so bad" but she couldn't be sure. She smiled. He was a man after her heart after all.

"All right, guys. Ready to check it out?"

"Did you really fix the dishwasher, Daddy?" Emma asked.

"Well." He stood and wiped his hands on a towel. "It's either going to turn on or catch on fire. Either way is better than it just sitting here broken, right?"

Ethan frowned. "Why would it be better for it to catch fire than for it to just sit here?"

"Because at least it will be doing something. Action is almost always better than inaction."

Laura stepped into the kitchen and five pairs of eyes settled on her. Well, actually four because one of the hamsters had snuck off around the trash can. The escape was short-lived. "How did you fix it?"

"Home Depot left a message that the part came in. Me and Lieutenant Google got down to business." He straightened, brushing his hands on his thighs. Sweat ringed the neck of his t-shirt, causing the fabric to cling to his torso.

Laura swallowed, her mouth suddenly dry, her gaze drawn to his powerful shoulders.

"Should we test it?"

He shoved his glasses to the top of his head and grinned. "I put a few dirty dishes in it, and I was going to run a test cycle. Hopefully it'll clean the dishes." He crouched down to Emma's level. "Want to push the button?"

Emma nodded. Trent slid his hand over hers and pressed the button with her. The dishwasher churned to life with a familiar swish.

Laura met his smile tentatively as the kids cheered around them. Ethan high-fived his father, clutching his hamster to his chest. Trent stood near the dishwasher and braced his hands on the counter, looking easy and relaxed for the first time since he'd come home.

"All right, guys, it's time for the hamsters to go in their balls for a little while. Fluffy is looking a little . . . fluffy. She needs exercise," Trent said.

Emma rolled her eyes at her dad. "She's a hamster, Daddy. She's supposed to be fluffy." As though it was the most obvious association in the world.

"Scoot," he said.

The kids ran out of the room to go find the hamster balls, leaving Trent and Laura alone without a buffer—separated only by the kitchen island. Trent leaned down, his shoulders flexing as he moved. He brushed his thumb over her healing knuckles.

His expression tightened as he stroked at the pink flesh. "Why didn't you just call someone to do it?" he asked softly.

The ghost of their kisses twisted around them as Trent slipped his index finger over her hand. She shivered, needing more than this hesitant touch.

"Because I like fixing things," she said simply. She glanced over her shoulder at the clock on the microwave. "We've got to get dinner started."

She started to straighten but he caught her fingers gently between his. His palm surrounded hers. "Can I help?"

She frowned then, wanting badly to ask how he had become so calm. Whether this mood had come out of a little orange bottle of pills. But the comfort between them was so new, so fresh, she did not dare broach the subject.

And honestly, she didn't care if the calm was from the bottle or not. It was working. If it had helped Trent have a normal afternoon with his children, then damn it, she refused to judge. He'd been through something extraordinary. "I'd like that," she said quietly.

A distant buzzing interrupted them, refusing to be ignored. "I don't suppose you're going to let that go?" she whispered. Too many nights during his time as a commander, his cell phone had pulled him from bed, only to keep him up for hours afterward. But those days were long gone.

She didn't want that same stress coming back into his life now. Not even for an instant. He was working too hard at being here, at being normal. She closed her eyes and wished she could shut out the war, shut out the world, and just keep him there until he knew what normal felt like. Until he was ready for the world again.

But he was already gone, pulling the phone out of his pocket and stepping onto the back porch. Not before she heard him say Story's name.

And just like that, the war slipped back between them.

"Hey, Top, how's it going?" An odd thing to say to a man in a war zone but then again, Trent had always hated the questions about how often he was getting blown up or shot at. Trent sat on the back porch of their home, listening to the static on the cell phone line, waiting for the call to come back in.

"You there?" Story's voice sounded gritty and far away.

"Yeah, I'm here." Trent leaned forward, cupping his fore-head in his palm. "How are things?"

"Bad." Story paused, no doubt to spit into the dirt. The man had an expensive chewing tobacco habit. It was a won-der it didn't break the bank every month. "This is the worst I've seen it."

Fear curled in Trent's guts, twisting with fresh guilt that he wasn't there with Story. That he'd let him go downrange without him. He glanced toward the house, where Laura and his children were waiting for him. The fear remained but the guilt flittered away. He was where he needed to be. The war would get him again if he stayed in. He'd spent too much time chasing the adrenaline and not enough time being a dad. Still, he wished Story wasn't there without him. "What can I do?"

"Can you send me about seventeen boxes of Copenha-gen? The PX is out of my flavor and this generic shit they've got tastes like balls."

Trent grinned, glad it was something simple. Something he could handle. There was silence on the line and Trent thought for a moment that he'd lost his old friend. "Yeah, I can do that for you. Is that why you're calling? Not to tell me you love me?"

Story scoffed. Trent could hear the derision in his tone. "Not likely. Nah, I was just…had a shit day. I need a god-damned cigar. Where's Carponti when I need someone to yell at to unwind?"

Trent stilled. "We can do that when you get home. You're only on a ninety-day stint this time, right?"

"Hope so. I've never seen things this fucked up. They have platoons holding sectors that used to be run by full companies."

That meant the troops were stretched thin. That was never a good thing. "Story…"

"Look, just…promise me that if something happens,

you'll look out for Rebecca. Don't let some scumbag take advantage of her when she gets all the money from me dying. She's going to run off and get a boob job before she buries me. Just, don't let someone fuck her over, okay?"

"That's a fucked up thing to say, man," Trent said, wishing he could make some kind of smart-ass joke like Carponti would to ease the soul-crushing fear that rose up to squeeze his heart tightly. It pushed away the happiness from earlier.

Left the too familiar cold and emptiness once again.

"So look, there's maybe a different reason I'm calling." Story's voice took on that tone that Trent knew too well. He was about to give him some really bad news. Trent hoped it didn't ruin the rest of his night, not when things were this close to going really right with Laura.

Story cleared his throat on the line. "Maybe Randall had the right idea. Maybe paying the bastards off wasn't such a bad call."

Trent stilled, his mind screaming in denial at what Story's words meant. "What are you getting at, Top?" he finally asked.

He heard the sigh over the static. "Look, we had our damn hands full. We were getting blown up every goddamned time we ran outside the wire, we were losing guys left and right. I was willing to try anything." Another pause. "I'm sorry you got caught up in all this. I knew Randall was a shit, but not this bad."

Trent was speechless. He searched the darkness for something, anything to say. "Top…"

"Look, I've sent a sworn statement to Major MacLean. I knew about this. Randall somehow kept me off the list of witnesses but I've fixed that now."

Anger, cold and violent, surged through Trent's veins. "You knew? Top, you fucking knew he was selling sensitive items and you didn't fucking tell me?"

"I thought it was best if you didn't know," Story said quietly.

"Jesus." He fought to find anything to say but the words were locked in his throat. Anger. Betrayal. A man he'd trusted had stabbed him in the back.

For what?

For fucking what?

The line went dead, leaving Trent alone with the bitter anger of his thoughts. Story, a man he trusted, a man whose advice he'd taken, whose counsel he'd sought, had known what Randall was doing. He'd known and he'd said nothing to Trent.

He'd lied.

And that single admission knocked Trent's whole world off its axis.

The back door opened and Laura stepped into the shadows. He wasn't ready to face her yet, hadn't put all the wrong emotions back in the box and pulled the right ones out again.

He tossed the cell phone on the bench next to him and scrubbed his hands through his hair.

And fought for control. He looked up at his wife—his beautiful, patient wife—who was looking at him with expectation and something else that was a little too close to fear. It settled in his stomach like something fetid and vile.

"Are you okay?" she asked quietly, leaning against the door.

"No." He scoffed harshly, then looked up. He shouldn't have. The sharp worry in her eyes had crossed the line, snuggling up to full-blown fear.

"I'm not crazy, Laura. I don't have PTSD and you can stop looking at me like I do." His words were sharp, meant to wound, and he instantly regretted them.

But he could not take them back. Goddamn it. He buried his face in his hands. He just needed a few minutes to pull all the violent emotions back inside him. But he couldn't push her away right now.

What he did right now, in these next few minutes, mattered. More than anything else. He fought the pain, fought the anger. And did everything he knew how to put it away to avoid lashing out at her.

Because she didn't deserve that.

"I didn't say that you did."

He leaned back, resting his head on the brick. Keep talking. Keep letting things out, one thing at a time. It was better than bottling it up, stuffing it down. "I feel like you keep waiting for me to snap."

"I'm worried about you," she whispered. "I don't think that's unreasonable."

He opened his eyes, looking up at her. Willed himself to stay calm. He was pissed at Story, not her. Then she did something unexpected and changed everything. She took a single step toward him. Crossed the tiny distance and sat next to him on the bench. "You said something the first night you were home. You said your normal was screwed up."

Her palm came to rest over the scar on his heart, his pulse pounding against her hand. She seared him with that gentle touch. His body tightened; the scar ached beneath her palm.

"I think you never gave yourself the chance to reset. And I'm sorry if that's hard for me to deal with." The admission was crushing in its simplicity. The fingers of her free hand danced against his neck. "I'm afraid," she whispered, refusing to meet his gaze.

He lifted one hand, stroking her cheek until she met his eyes. "Of me." It wasn't a question.

She nodded, her eyes filling.

He lowered his forehead to hers, their noses brushing together. For a long moment, Trent simply sat with her. The world was not as chaotic here with her. Everything was calm. Everything was quiet.

Real.

Even her admission, as painful as it was to hear, was real. And that was something he held on to as he lifted his other hand to trace the line of her cheek. "I'm not going to hurt you again, Laura."

"I'm trying to believe that," she whispered.

Something snapped and broke inside him. All restraints ripped from their tethers.

"Believe this," he growled. He held nothing back in this kiss. The kisses they'd shared in the coffee shop had been a tender question. This was violence and pain, hurt and hell all wrapped into one intense embrace. It was an outlet, a release valve that he'd never allowed because he *had* been afraid of hurting her. He kissed her then, pouring everything he had into that single moment, telling her without words how badly everything inside him was hurting.

This kiss was a branding. A violation of the boundaries she'd set between them. He tore them down and marked her soul, refused to let her breathe or think or protest.

He threaded his fingers through her hair, his other hand on her back, holding her tightly to him. He nibbled on her bottom lip. "I want you so much," he murmured.

She gasped against his mouth, the sweetest pleasure in that sound. He kissed her gently then, his tongue playing over her lips, teasing her, loving her.

He cupped her cheek with his hand, stroking her hair out of her eyes.

"Trent—"

"I miss you, Laura," he whispered right before he kissed her again, drowning out thoughts of anything but him. There was pure heat in his touch. "I miss us."

He sucked on her bottom lip, loving the feel of her mouth beneath his. Everything about her was soft and sensual, this woman who filled the dead space inside him. The stone where his heart used to be was a little softer, a little less solid.

"I don't know how to be home, Laura," he whispered, resting his forehead against hers. "But I'm trying."

Her only response was the slight shift of her nose against his. Her lips, swollen from his brutal kiss, curled slightly. His fingers just skimmed over her cheek, teasing her with the promise of more. "I know." The words scraped past a dry throat. He leaned closer, and their mouths were just a hint apart.

She opened her mouth like she wanted to speak. And part of him wanted to hear her out. But the other part of him was so tired of fighting. All he wanted to do was hold her, take her mouth in sweet nibbling kisses.

He couldn't remember the last time he'd made love to his wife but his campaign to win her back called for patience. He had no doubt he could get her into bed right now but the moment the sexual haze faded, she'd regret what they'd done.

Instead he pressed his lips to hers, hesitant, questioning, letting her control the pace, letting the trust and the love that still lived inside of her bloom. She tipped her head and opened her mouth beneath his. His tongue stroked hers and with that simple touch, brilliant heat exploded inside him. Still he yanked it back. This had to be under her control, on her terms.

His fingers pressed into her hair and angled her head so that their mouths could join completely. She gasped as his jaw scraped against hers and liquid need slid between them. Every touch reminded her of why she loved him, of why she'd waited so long for him to come back to her. And every touch brought with it a renewed intensity that refused to be ignored.

This was Trent. Trent who kissed her. Trent who brought this heat to life inside her and reminded her of all the reasons she loved him. Trent, who'd held her as she cried the last time he told her he was leaving.

Trent who was holding her now, making her crazy, one slow, sipping kiss at a time. She did the only thing a woman who loved a man could do when there were children running around in the house.

She leaned back, brushing his bottom lip with her thumb. "Tonight?"

She didn't want to wait. But she also didn't want the first time she touched her husband in almost two years to be interrupted by a child or two beating on the bedroom door. "We have to wait until the kids go to bed," she said against his mouth.

"Can't we tie them up in the bathroom or something?" His words were light. Teasing. Pained and heavy with arousal.

She laughed, then buried her face in his neck.

Chapter Thirteen

Laura set the bowl of broccoli on the table. "Ethan, I thought I told you no hamsters at the dinner table."

Ethan puffed out his bottom lip, a sure sign that he was about to cry. She was getting ready to intervene when Trent crouched down to look his son in the eye. "Fluffy needs to get put away for dinner, tiny man. She needs her own dinner."

"But Daddy, Fluffy hasn't been acting right all day. See!" Trent flinched as the hamster was thrust into his face.

He grabbed Ethan's wrist and gently pushed the animal back to where he could see it. Picking the rodent up, he turned her around in a circle like he was doing a detailed inspection. The hamster just hung there, her fuzzy belly exposed, looking at him as if to say, *are you done yet?* "Fluffy is fine. Go put her away, okay? And wash your hands."

Ethan sighed dramatically and walked out of the room, his footsteps just barely shy of a stomp. Trent straightened and walked to the sink to wash his own hands. "Does that thing always smell so bad?"

"Hamsters go into heat every four days."

"Dear lord, that's terrible."

Laura grinned as she finished slicing the top off of a loaf

of bread before sliding it into the oven. "You're the one who bought them."

"I had no clue they smelled that bad."

"They're not usually this bad. We keep the cages pretty clean." She turned to find that he'd snuck up behind her.

"I kind of left you in the lurch with them, didn't I?"

"Hello, captain obvious. You bought two rodents, then left the next day for a training exercise." She smiled to take the sting out of her words. "But the kids love them so I'll tolerate them." She turned back to stir the potatoes she had boiling on the stove. "Has Patrick said anything else about the case?"

A long silence stretched between them. She glanced over her shoulder at Trent, whose strain was showing in his eyes. Laura breathed out deeply. She wanted to ask him to talk to her. Wanted to help carry the burden of his war, but she was terrified he would turn away again, leaving her with more unanswered questions.

"Funny you should mention that," he said, and there was bitterness in his voice. "Turns out Story knew what was going on."

"What?"

"Yeah. Turns out my lieutenant wasn't the only one I shouldn't have trusted." She glanced over her shoulder to see him rub his hand over his mouth. "But he's apparently sent a statement home to Patrick admitting to what he knew and testifying against Randall."

"I still don't see how Randall is going to beat this by dragging you into it," Laura said. She knew enough about the case to know it was a disaster. Patrick had mentioned there was a flow chart somewhere outlining who they thought knew what and when they'd known it.

"Randall is going to testify that I knew he was selling weapons. I signed off on his reports without verifying them, so he's going to use that against me," he said quietly. Out of the corner of her eye, she watched him pull a beer from the fridge.

She set the spoon down on the counter. "How are you going to fight him on it?"

"My brigade commander taught me back in OIF 2 that commanders must only focus on the command. All else must be delegated. So Patrick and I are going to turn it back on Randall. He was my executive officer. He was supposed to be running the company so I could command it. I shouldn't have needed to double-check his work. It will shred his argument." He took a pull from his beer. "At least I hope it will."

"It sounds good to me," she said, offering a faint smile. A long moment passed before she sighed softly. "I know you're pissed at him right now but I think Rebecca is cheating on him again."

Silence greeted her. She wasn't sure what kind of response she expected from him, especially not now after Story's call. "I'm not surprised," he admitted.

She frowned, watching him closely, well aware that this conversation danced a little too close to their personal situation. "Why not?"

"Story has been gone even more than I have. And Rebecca isn't the kind of woman who does well on her own."

Laura turned back to dinner. "What's that mean?"

"It means some women need a man in their lives. Any man will do."

"Just like there are some guys who need a woman in their bed," she whispered, hating herself for dragging the rumors into their kitchen. But they could no more deny them than ignore them. It was better to lance the wound, draining the poison so that it had a chance to heal rather than fester.

He stepped into her space, cupping her face and stopping her need to be in motion. "Laura, I meant it when I said that I've never cheated on you. I've never even thought about it."

"I know," she whispered. She turned away before he could see everything that she could not hide. The agony of those rumors had burrowed deep, whispering a horrible explanation in her ear for every moment of silence on the other end of the phone.

"Laura."

She closed her eyes, steeling her heart against the agony in his voice. She sucked in a deep breath and plunged ahead.

"The first time Rebecca hinted around that something was going on downrange, I didn't believe her." Her voice was raw, the emotion ragged. "But the rumors kept getting worse and worse. And you barely talked to me for months."

She was ashamed of her lack of trust. She wasn't by nature an untrusting person. But she'd failed. Failed at trusting her husband, failed at standing strong for him when he needed her most. His actions, his silence, had destroyed her faith not only in him but in herself, too. She'd walked away when things had gotten too tough and that single action had decimated the person she'd thought she was. "It chipped away at my faith in you."

She saw it now, everything she'd done to help break up their marriage. She'd been cold on the phone when he'd needed her support. She hadn't looked beyond the rumors. She'd focused on her own hurt, her own sadness, letting the silence on the phone widen the fractures between them. She closed her eyes, unable to let him see the depth of her shame.

His hands on her shoulders were gentle as he urged her to turn toward him. The heat from the stove warmed her back as his hands stroked her. His eyes were dark, rimmed with sadness. "I'm so sorry I wasn't man enough for you to believe in," he whispered.

Of all the things he could have said, an apology was the most unexpected.

There it was again. The quiet admission of everything

that was wrong between them. The world tilted beneath her feet as her husband's hands caressed her, bringing to life all of the emotions she'd locked away.

She leaned into him then, letting go of a little piece of the hurt, another weight that bore down on her. He was home. He was working on things, a little bit at a time.

It was enough.

The kids were asleep. Tucked away in their beds, all hamsters accounted for; evening quiet settled over their home as Laura padded into their bedroom. Trent had been quiet since his phone call with Story, quiet but not unreachable. He did not pull away this time like he would have in the past.

She stood in front of her dresser in their bedroom and pulled her rings from the small jewelry box. Her fingers hesitated now over the cold golden rings, which stood for everything they'd once meant to each other. Everything about this evening had been so achingly normal. So beautiful and twisted.

She toyed with the rings, stopping just short of putting them on.

The significance of something so simple terrified her. She held them in the palm of her hand, remembering the first time Trent had slid them on her finger. She'd been terrified and excited and a thousand other emotions. She remembered looking into his eyes and seeing love looking back.

She'd believed then that they could make it through anything.

The bathroom door opened. Trent stood there in the doorway, watching her. His gaze flicked down to her hand. The muscle in his jaw jumped.

Then he walked toward her. Slowly, until he stood behind her in the mirror, their reflections close, their bodies closer. The scar over his heart stood out in stark relief against the crisp dark hair that dusted his chest. A starburst of damaged skin and bloodred memories.

She closed her eyes, remembering that horrible day.

On behalf of a grateful nation…

His chest radiated warmth and she shifted, leaning back into him. Just a little but it was enough. His arms came around her, his hands sliding down her forearms to cup her hands. His eyes darkened and warmed, but he said nothing. Instead he traced his index finger over her knuckles, their gazes locked in the mirror. He ran the tip of his finger roughly against her hand, circling the rings she held there.

Her breath jammed in her throat as he lifted the rings, then turned her hand over. His body surrounded her, his heat penetrating her skin.

He slid her wedding band over her finger. A slight pop over her knuckle and then it was in its place. He lifted her hand until he could press his lips to her palm, then slid her engagement ring, a single solitary diamond, back where it belonged.

He held her then, his arms wrapped around hers, his eyes holding hers in the mirror. Slowly, he started to sway. His hips moved against hers, reminding her of an old familiar rhythm that had once been a normal part of their lives. He traced his hands over her skin. Her arms. Her collarbone. The pulse in her throat. All the while she watched him in the mirror. Watched her body as though it belonged to someone else.

He dragged his thumb over her bottom lip, nudging her lips to part. She stood there, unable to move, wanting so badly to surrender to the racing need inside her, knowing that if she did, she'd be sacrificing everything she'd fought so hard to retain.

Instead she simply stood and basked in the warmth from his bare skin so close to her own. He scraped his teeth over the sensitive skin of her earlobe. She felt him, thick and hard against her buttocks. She arched into him, needing the intimate pressure.

Trent could not believe his wife was in his arms. Wearing her rings. He simply stood and held her, unwilling to do anything to break the spell that floated around them. An easy, erotic haze built between them as he watched her beautiful body sway with his in the mirror.

This woman awed him. Every day she stood with him, she taught him something beautiful about the world.

He slid his hands down her arms, threading his fingers with hers, loving the feel of her body arching into his. Slowly, so slowly, he lifted her arms, wrapping them around his neck until she was arched in front of him. Her breasts were heavy and full against the thin tank she'd put on after her shower. He slipped his fingers down her ribs, marveling at the shudder that ran through her body.

With one index finger, he traced the exposed strip of skin on her belly. A tiny expanse but one begging to be explored. Hooking his finger, he dragged the soft cotton higher, higher until the soft scoop of her breasts was barely exposed. "You're so beautiful," he whispered, tracing his tongue over her ear. She trembled in his arms but didn't lower her own. Her fingers tensed on the back of his neck.

He skimmed his fingers over the exposed underside of her breasts. Watched her nipples pearl beneath the thin cotton. Ached to taste her.

He slid the tank a little higher, flicking it over one nipple until the pink bud was puckered and exposed. Her breath tumbled from her lungs as he traced his thumb over the sensitive skin.

"I could do this for hours," he whispered. "Just watching your body respond to my touch. I've missed you so much."

She closed her eyes as he pushed her pants off her hips,

then lifted her arms enough to slip the tank over her head. "Laura." His voice a whisper. An erotic command. She opened her eyes.

She was naked. Exposed in his arms. He nudged her arms back around his neck, his hands skimming her waist to cradle her hips. He traced his thumb over her hipbone, his touch dancing closer and closer to where she ached for him.

"I want to touch you," he whispered. She couldn't look away from the intensity of his gaze. His hands were sure, familiar and strange all at once. "Can I touch you there?" he asked. He skimmed a single finger over the seam of her sex. Moisture spread beneath his touch. "Please, Laura. Let me touch you." He scraped his teeth along her jaw. "Open for me," he urged. "Just a little."

He knew how to make her body sing. She knew it. He knew it. This was more than just sex. This was about power. About desire.

About healing.

She parted her thighs, just a little bit. Moisture glistened on the soft hair. She watched, entranced, as his fingers slipped over her body, caressing. Urging. Stroking her lightly until her thighs spread farther. She was completely open and completely lost to his touch. Desire spiraled wide inside her as his fingers danced over her swollen sex, tracing the lines of her body until she thought she'd snap if he didn't give her what she needed. She arched mindlessly against him, begging with her body what she could not speak. She needed this man. Wanted him inside her, filling her. Completing the erotic dance with her.

Reminding her of all the reasons she loved him.

He slipped a finger inside her and she exploded. Her entire world shook as he stroked her, drawing out her pleasure until her body hummed and she felt boneless.

He laid her gently on the bed, amazed by the power of her

release. She lifted her thighs, wrapping them around his hips as he found the place he'd missed more than anything: the loving sanctuary of her arms. He threaded his fingers in hers and dragged her arms over her head once more.

Waited until she met his gaze. Needing her to know, to be sure that this was what she wanted. "No regrets, Laura?"

He paused then, his blood pounding in his veins, needing to slide into the warm welcome she offered. But he wouldn't. Not like this. Not until he knew she was sure.

She freed one of her hands, tracing it around his neck. "I need you," she whispered, arching her hips to slide her body over the tip of his erection.

Trent was lost. That simple sensation, that slightest touch and he buried himself inside her. Her gasp was beautiful against his mouth, her taste the sweetest pleasure. He lifted her hips as she matched his rhythm, their bodies immediately seeking the synchronicity that came with loving the same person for so long.

Her heart might have forgotten what it was like to love this man but her body had not.

And when he shattered inside her, everything in her world was right for a brief, blinding moment.

Chapter Fourteen

✥

"Where are the kids today?" Shane asked as Trent climbed into his truck.

"With our neighbors." He slammed the door shut. "Laura figured it would be easier to pay for a babysitter than drag the kids around Austin all day."

"Probably a good plan," Carponti said from the backseat, where he was fiddling with his iPod. "If Nicole has her way with me, I'm going to end up in a furniture store for half the afternoon." He glanced up, plugging an ear bud into his ear. "Though I suppose it's better than picking out flowers and decorations after we go to the dress shop. Man, I never thought I'd see you emasculated like this. Did you forget to get your balls out of Jen's purse? Oh wait, I forgot you had them rewired. Never mind."

Shane didn't respond to Carponti's taunt. Instead, he turned the radio to the heavy metal station out of Austin. "First Sarn't Story e-mailed me yesterday," he said to Trent.

"Yeah, I talked to him," Trent said. Just like that, the anger and the betrayal were back. He didn't know how to tell Carponti and Garrison what Story had done so he kept it to himself. They'd find out soon enough.

"He's at Camp Cooke in Taji," Shane said. "He didn't sound too happy. Man, some bad shit is happening there."

Trent looked out the window, memories from the Triangle of Death rising up to torment him.

"Laura told me she thinks Rebecca is cheating on him," Trent said quietly. "Do you think he knows?"

"Probably."

"Why did he e-mail you?"

"To say he was sorry he can't be here for the wedding." Shane glanced over at him. "Did he get in touch to ask you about the hearing?"

"Yeah." Trent frowned, rubbing the bridge of his nose with his index finger and smothering the anger. "I hate that all of you are being dragged through this."

Since Story had been Trent's first sergeant when he was in command, he'd worked hand in hand with Trent to ensure that their troopers were prepared each and every time they went out in sector. In theory, he'd also worked closely with Lieutenant Randall. If Randall testified that Trent knew about the missing weapons, Story's counter-testimony would hold a lot of weight.

As the hearing to determine whether or not Trent's case would go to court-martial drew closer, a feeling of deep unease took up more and more space in his belly. It wrestled with his nightmares and the general anxiety he felt about being at home, pushing away the goodness from his night with Laura.

The fear he still struggled with had blossomed inside of him the day he woke up in the hospital bay, unable to hear, unable to move because of the wicked wound that had ripped his flesh from his bones. He'd fought to get back out with his boys, refusing to leave them in the thick of the battle without him. Maybe if he hadn't been so stupid, the wound would have healed better. The scar over his heart had long since healed but the relentless fear had woven itself into his skin as it knitted back together.

That fear was a permanent companion now. He didn't believe Emily when she said it would fade but he wondered if he would ever live another day without the constant terror that he would lose those who mattered most to him. And while he was pissed and hurt that Story had known about Randall, he still wanted his old friend to be out of combat.

He understood what drove Story. The same urges had driven him to combat again and again. And now that Story was back downrange and Trent was not, a new, unfamiliar feeling twisted in his guts. Guilt sliced at him for letting his friend go back to war without him.

Shane cleared his throat. "So listen, this ah, wedding is kind of a big deal to Jen."

Carponti leaned between the front seats of the car, his iPod cradled in his prosthetic hand. "And it's not to you?"

"Don't be an ass. Of course it is. But this is . . . I need to do this right for her."

"And you need us because . . . ?" Carponti said.

"Because I have no idea how to be married. Not in a normal marriage where I actually love my wife."

"You loved Tatiana once," Trent pointed out.

"I loved the idea of Tatiana more than I loved her. I know that's a callous thing to say but it's true." He swallowed and dragged one hand over his face. "I haven't told Jen about the deployment. I don't know how to tell her."

"You're assuming you're going," Trent said.

"You're still gimped up from getting blown up last year," Carponti shifted and sat back in his seat. "I qualified expert last week on my M4. The commander was amazed."

Trent grinned. "How hard was it to learn to shoot left-handed?"

"Pretty fucking tough. It's really weird but I figured it out. I spent a week with a shooting coach from the Ranger Regiment out at Benning. Helped a ton."

"That's awesome. Guess the commander is going to let you deploy?"

"Hell yeah. Plus, I threatened to call the division sergeant major if he didn't. And we all know that Sergeant Major Giles is part of my fan club. He'd put in a good word for me."

Trent choked back a laugh. "He is no such thing. He hates you."

"He just acts that way. He told me he was going to shove my prosthetic up my ass if I didn't get it out of his face two weeks ago. But he said it in the most loving way."

Trent laughed and shook his head, turning to look at Shane. "When are you going to tell Jen that you might be on this deployment?"

"I have to tell her soon. Like before we get married. I need to give her that out."

"Wait, what the hell?" Carponti leaned over the seats again. "You think she won't marry you if she knows you're deploying?"

"I have no right to ask her to wait for me like this. We're already six years into this war and eight into Afghanistan and we don't know how long the war will be. I asked her to marry me when I was still hurt. There was a good chance I was getting out of the military. If I get to stay in...She deserves to make that choice. Before I marry her." His voice grated rough with emotion.

"She's not going to walk away over this," Trent said. He sucked in a deep breath. Once he'd thought the same thing about Laura and he'd damn near lost her. He wasn't going to feed into Shane's fears about Jen but he wouldn't disagree that he needed to be honest with her.

But Jen knew what she was getting into by marrying the

big sergeant. She was marrying a man who would leave and go back to war. When Laura had married Trent, the war hadn't started yet. They hadn't yet known what half a decade at war would feel like, what it would do to them.

He rubbed the scar over his heart. He'd gotten a second chance with her. He didn't know how but he had. And no matter what he did, he refused to screw it up.

Because having her back filled the dead space inside of him with something good, something he would do anything to hold onto.

"I'm not coming out."

Laura leaned against the wall of the changing room as Nicole and Jen laughed hysterically outside the curtain.

"Jen, this isn't funny. This dress makes me look like a fat cupcake with sprinkles. Why would you do this to someone you call a friend?"

The dress was worse than horrid. Bright silver with sparkling red jewels draped over her breasts. The bust was the only redeeming part. Right below her ribs, the fabric exploded into a ruffle of fabric and fluff that made her look like an overdone...cupcake.

"Oh come on, you have to let us see."

"No. Pick a different dress. I love you like a sister but I'm not wearing this."

Nicole finally stopped laughing for long enough to make a threat. "Either come out or we're coming in."

Laura took another look in the mirror and decided that she even hated the bust. "How come you're not wearing this monstrosity?" she asked Nicole.

"Because I wanted to see how it looked on you first."

"Not funny."

Jen giggled and the sound of her friends' laughter bloomed in Laura's heart. Once upon a time, she'd worried

Jen would never laugh or smile again. The cancer had taken its toll on her but she'd fought back, refusing to let it beat her. "Yes it is. Come on, let us see it."

"Laura, do you have the car keys?" Laura closed her eyes as Trent's voice broke through the hysterical laughter outside the curtain. She could not let him see her in this. "What's wrong?"

"Laura won't come out and show us one of the bridesmaid's dresses that Jen asked us to model," Nicole said. "Go in and get her."

"No!" She hadn't been able to get the dress done up in the back. It was gaping open, a giant flapping maw of material.

But the curtain was already moving as her husband stepped into the tiny changing room, filling the space.

He still had on the tuxedo pants and crisp white shirt that he'd tried on in another part of the store. The shirt was open at the neck, revealing a sprinkling of dark hair at the edge of his collar. She lifted her gaze from the hard lines of his chest to his face. His lips curled with a teasing smile that flattened when his eyes flicked down her body and back up again.

A quiet look passed between them and the world faded away for a moment. It was just him and just her. Like they used to be. When she'd still loved him unconditionally.

Loving him was not the problem, she thought as his gaze swept down her body encased in the horrid dress. It never had been. The sleeves of his shirt were rolled, exposing the corded muscles of his forearms. Veins stood out against his skin. She lifted her gaze to his face, his expression unreadable.

"What did you need the car keys for?" she asked softly.

"I needed to get the cell phone charger out of the car." His eyes darkened as he watched her.

She offered a faint smile, trying to ignore the heat that burned in her belly. "Tell them this dress is horrendous."

He glanced down, his nostrils flaring slightly as he studied her. Her blood warmed beneath his scrutiny and then he lifted his eyes to hers. He flicked his tongue over his bottom lip before scraping his teeth over it. Memories from loving him last night blossomed inside her, like a flower reaching toward the sunlight.

"It is pretty bad." His throat moved as he swallowed. He didn't smile.

"You look hungry." His expression was tense. "Maybe looking like a cupcake wasn't such a bad thing," she whispered.

"I can help you out of it if you want."

She suddenly became aware of the silence from the other side of the curtain. "I think I've seen this movie," she whispered, her voice sounding husky even to her own ears. "Is this the part where we have hot make-up sex in the changing room?"

"We haven't fought lately," he murmured, stepping as close as the dress would allow.

"No, not lately." She kept her voice low as she ran her finger along the cool fabric of his shirt. The collar was sharp against the tip of her finger, warmed by his skin. "You look nice."

She tipped her chin to study the man of her dreams. The man she'd loved since the ninth grade. And she felt like the luckiest woman alive.

He smiled warmly. "I'd say the same but..."

Laura laughed. She couldn't help it. "I know. I look like a red velvet cupcake."

It was all so achingly normal. He brushed a strand of hair from her eyes.

"What would you say if I admitted to thinking inappropriate thoughts right now?" he whispered, his breath hot on her ear.

"What kind of inappropriate?" It felt good, teasing him.

This play of words dancing between them, twining their bodies together like velvet ropes.

He licked his bottom lip, drawing her gaze to his mouth. "The kind of inappropriate that involves you wearing a lot less than this dress."

She lifted her hand, her palm resting over the scars that covered his still beating heart. Her mouth was dry, her blood heated. Arousal, that's what this was. Arousal caused not by her own hand but by the proximity of her husband.

"Hey, no getting naked in the bridal shop!" Carponti's voice was close to the curtain—too close.

"Go away, Carponti," Trent growled. He moved, shifting his body so that she'd be blocked from view if Carponti ripped back the curtain, which wasn't outside the realm of possibility.

Yards of fabric separated them, but he was so close that the heat from his body radiated off him and into her. She lifted her face to his.

"I'm kind of stuck in this dress," she admitted, lifting her gaze to meet his, the question laced with suggestion. "Can you get the rest of the zipper for me?"

He knew it for what it was. A simple, loaded request. A lesser man would have walked away, avoiding the torment of seeing his wife's naked back without being able to do anything about it. But after the other night, after feeling the pleasure of her body beneath his, he was like a dying man gasping for air. He couldn't turn away from her. Not now. Not ever. How had he ever run from this? From her?

From them?

But Trent was not a lesser man. Trent was hungry. Starving for his wife's body beneath his lips. He breathed in deeply, unable to speak as she turned, offering him the sensitive skin of her back.

He met her gaze in the full-length mirror. He wanted her now. His blood pounded in his ears as he lifted his hand to her shoulders, unable to resist the temptation of her bare skin. The ruffles of the dress kept him from stepping closer.

She lifted her arms, tucking her golden hair beneath her palms and raising them up, exposing the soft curve of her neck. The swell of her breasts was barely contained in the bodice.

Almost afraid to touch her, he finally traced the pad of his finger down her neck, down the centerline of her back.

She shivered visibly, arching beneath his touch. Her lips parted and the only sound he heard was the quiet gasp of her breath.

He shifted his erection away from the painful zipper of the tuxedo pants, then focused his erotic attention on the delicate curve of her spine beneath the black of her strapless bra. Slowly, so slowly, he met her gaze as he traced his thumb down her spine. Her mouth was beautiful, her lips parted and flushed. But her eyes, heavy with arousal, were what held him captive as he pushed the offending zipper lower, lower as he sought to free her from this monstrosity of a dress.

She moved to pull the dress off, but he cupped her upper arms to stop her. "Let me?" he whispered. He nuzzled her ear, her skin hot beneath his touch. "I can't get enough of touching you, Laura."

Touching her now, her response was a gasp, a silent huff of breath against his cheek as she turned her face to his, her mouth asking for his taste.

Slowly he traced his fingers up her arms, and over her shoulders. They skimmed the swell of her breasts in that sexy strapless bra and the dress fell in a pool at their feet, forgotten.

He watched her reaction in the mirror. Watched as her

eyes closed to the barest slits, and she arched her hips against his. While he was fully clothed behind her, she wore nothing but the strapless bra and panties. He loved how small she looked in his embrace, felt a thrill of power spike through him as she surrendered to his touch.

He could take her then. Right there in the dressing room. If he slipped his hand into her panties, he knew he would find her wet and supple and swollen, so ready for his touch. It would be fast and intense.

It would barely scratch the surface of what he wanted to do with her. He urged her back against him, felt the heat of her skin penetrate the clothing he wore. Felt the soft curve of her ass against his erection, the sweetest friction of softness and fabric. It was torture touching her, loving her and not feeling her body wrapped around his.

He skimmed his hands down her belly, skirting closer to the heat that drew him. He wanted so badly to touch her. To feel her arousal coat his fingers. He could watch her face contort as he stroked her, the risk of getting caught adding to the erotic thrill of having his nearly naked wife in his arms.

"God you're beautiful," he whispered against her ear. He cradled her hips, framing them in the mirror, loving the gentle swell of her belly and the curves that she'd always hated. But she was a woman, a woman who'd given him two beautiful children. Her body was no longer flawless but watching her skin flush beneath his touch, he knew he would never find greater perfection. Even if he went to the ends of the earth, his wife would still be the only woman who did it for him.

He traced the edge of her panties with his index finger, loving the thrill of pleasure that shivered over her skin.

This. This was what he'd missed. The beauty of his wife's arousal. The soft cries she made when she was coming apart in his arms. This was the memory he had carried with him into battle.

The fear came from out of nowhere, stealing up from a dark place in his soul, raw and primal, ripping through him like a beast. Promising the loss of the thing he loved more than anything else in the world.

He wrapped her tight in his arms, pulling her flush against him, burying his face in her throat. Inhaling her scent, the warmth from her skin. Feeling her body shudder in response as she wrapped her arms over his and simply stood. Letting him lean on her.

Letting him hold her. A simple embrace laced with unspoken things, twining them together.

Chapter Fifteen

So I was called in yesterday by the prosecution's team of lawyers," Shane said as he flipped through a book of candles and flowers. It was a strange sight to behold: a big bald man with black tattoos threaded down both arms and yet, there he was, flipping through a book of pink and white and delicate.

Trent would have smiled if not for his comment. "And?"

"Well, she asked me about the paperwork and routine crap. Then things got a little interesting," Shane said. He looked up. "She asked me if I'd ever seen you lose your temper." Shane shrugged. "Said nothing came to mind."

Carponti smiled. "Yeah, it was funny how nothing came to mind when I was asked either." He paused. "But why is that relevant at all anyway? I mean, we all argue and fight. So what?"

Trent looked down at his hands. "I don't know. But Patrick has me seeing a counselor, working to build a clean bill of mental health for this case."

Shane swore quietly. "This isn't about you deploying too much. It can't be."

"Maybe it can be," Trent said. "Maybe they're going to paint me as stressed out, et cetera and use it to show my judgment was questionable. Makes it easier to believe I would forge paperwork to sell parts to buy off Iraqis and keep them from blowing us up, doesn't it?"

"Not really," Carponti said. "I mean that's a pretty convoluted fucking theory. Why isn't it easier to believe that Randall just did some illegal shit for money?"

Trent smiled. "That's the point, actually. The simple answer to the problem is the easiest. This case they're trying to build against me is complex and difficult. Makes it harder." He looked at Shane. Trent shook his head as they headed out of the bridal shop and he wound his way back through the racks and hangers of a thousand different wedding dresses.

Jen had staunchly refused to show her wedding gown to the men in the room but that hadn't stopped Laura and Nicole from modeling dresses. After Laura's disastrous cupcake dress, they'd summoned all of the men over to look at what seemed to be dozens of other dresses, each worse than the last. All of them looked like they had been made by mad wolverines. On acid.

Carponti had declared that he loved his wife but if he had to sit through one more dress, he was going to kill himself, a comment that had earned him a slap on the back of the head from Shane and an elbow in the ribs from his wife. The physical abuse had done nothing to keep him from laughing, and he had still been cracking up as the three men started for the coffee shop next door. Trent had peeled off from the others not only because he needed his phone, but also because he wanted one last look at Laura.

He was eager to get his wife alone. The memory of her nearly naked, encased in his arms in the dressing room earlier, was driving him out of his mind as the afternoon had progressed with mind-numbingly painful slowness. All the things that had gone wrong between them no longer seemed important.

He walked back toward the fitting rooms, hoping to catch her before she tried on the next monstrosity.

"Jen, I think this might be the one," Laura called from behind the curtain.

He paused near the opening to the fitting rooms, unwilling to interrupt them. He held his breath as the curtain moved aside. Nicole stepped out first, followed closely by Laura.

He didn't even see Nicole.

In that moment everything in his world centered on his wife, her body draped in shimmering silver that hugged her curves and made his palms ache to touch her. The gown pooled at her feet, a cascade of fabric that looked like it had been made just for her.

He shifted then, his skin feeling too tight. The movement caught Laura's eye and she met his gaze. He swallowed and lifted his hand to push his glasses back up.

She offered a hesitant smile, the barest turn of her lips.

Hope soared inside him again. Maybe, just maybe, they'd find their way through the darkness. Together.

"So are you going to spill or are we going to have to pry it out of you?" Nicole asked. She handed the delicate silver dress to the clerk, who had just rung up Laura's purchase.

"Spill about what?" Laura asked.

"We'd have to be blind to miss the sparks between you and Trent," Jen said. Her wedding gown was already sealed in a black fabric zippered bag, protected from the elements and prying eyes. "You two are getting along."

Laura smiled, more to herself than to either of her friends. "Yeah."

She looked up to find Jen studying her. "This is a good thing, right?"

Laura lifted her shoulder. "It's not a bad thing, if that's what you mean."

"But?" Nicole prompted.

"But nothing." She paused. Her body tightened as she remembered the feel of his hands on her skin, his breath on her ear. "Things are good."

"That's really great, hon." Jen squeezed her hand. "Are you okay with everything?"

"Yeah. I am. I'm just...things haven't been this good in a long time." She bit her lips. "I'm afraid I'm going to wake up tomorrow and it's all going to be over."

Nicole accepted her receipt from the cashier and lifted the sleek black garment back over the counter. "Look, I love you and I love your husband. You can't live like the rug is going to get yanked out from under you tomorrow."

"But it could," Laura said. "All of this could end tomorrow."

"Then you'll have had today. No one knows what tomorrow is going to bring," Nicole said. "But enjoy today while you have it. Hold on to these good memories because there will be plenty of dark times when you'll need them."

Laura smiled, lifting her own dress. "I know."

"It takes a strong person to do what you've done," Jen said. "Trent's a fool if he throws this away."

She walked outside, her thoughts drifting back to the feel of her husband's hands on her body. The feel of him inside her. The drape of his arm over her waist as they'd fallen into sleep.

She looked up as the men stepped out of the coffee shop. Her gaze landed on her husband's broad shoulders. His hands.

"Hey," she said as he approached.

"Hey." He slipped the dress from her hands and fell into step with her. Nicole and Carponti and Shane and Jen paired off and headed to their respective vehicles. "You're being awful quiet," he said.

She smiled over at him, unwilling or maybe unable to give voice to the needs swirling inside her. She didn't know how to ask him for what she wanted, what she needed.

"We've still got a couple of hours before we have to pick up the kids," she said. Her lips were dry. She traced her tongue over her bottom lip, entranced by his gaze dropping down to her mouth. "We should take the long way home."

"Are you okay?"

She offered him a smile. And let an idea take hold. "Yeah. I think I am."

Laura was being quiet. She hadn't said a thing since they had picked up his truck at Jen's house and turned toward home. Every so often, he would catch her watching him.

"You looked beautiful today," he said after the silence grew too heavy.

"Hmmm." She shifted, a lithe tension running through her. He didn't dare hope that he was reading her body language right. She looked like she was getting ready to explore a dark erotic fantasy.

But that couldn't be. Right? His blood hummed as he watched her out of the corner of his eye. The subtle part of her thighs. The slight arch of her back. The barest parting of her lips.

Everything about her made his body ache with sexual awareness. He'd wanted this woman for so long and touching her earlier, watching his hands move over her body today, he ached. Wanted things fixed between them. Back to a normal that would have involved him pulling the car over and taking her fast and hard in the backseat.

"Is something wrong?" he finally asked.

Laura looked at him for a long moment, her golden eyes dark with promise.

Then she unbuckled her seatbelt as Trent attempted to

hold onto the fragile remnants of his sanity, as all the blood rushed out of his brain to somewhere decidedly more primitive. He had to be dreaming. Had to be.

Trent stilled, his blood hammering through his veins at the sight of the heat in his wife's eyes. He swallowed, his lips curling into a faint smile as he tried to focus on watching the road. "What are you doing?" His voice was thick. Tense.

"Communicating?" Laura leaned close, pressing her lips to the edge of his jaw. Her thumb traced the line of the scar there, scorching the sensitive flesh.

"Ah..." There were no words for the force of the arousal that slammed into him at the brush of her lips against his skin.

She didn't kiss him. Her lips curled like a cat drinking fresh cream as she urged his free hand onto her thigh, then higher to where she was... "Holy shit."

He yanked the car into the wooded turnoff of an unsold plot of land. Away from the country road and anyone who might happen by.

He cleared his throat, his fingers sliding into naked, hot, wet heat. "When did you take your panties off?"

"Do you like it?"

He glanced at her, his mouth dry.

"Do you like it?" she repeated. Before things had gone terribly wrong between them, they had always been passionate lovers, but this was new and exciting. The risk of getting caught thrummed through his veins, wrestling with his arousal, sharp and deep and primitive. He didn't know when she'd gotten the idea for this, but he wasn't about to argue. The way she was looking at him was driving him wild.

"Ah, yes. Yes, I do." His voice was rough.

"Then don't ask questions. Just touch me." She pushed her skirt higher up her thighs, giving him access to her intimate flesh. His hands fisted in the material and she shifted, opening for his touch. There was no hesitation as his fingers stroked her slick heat. She moaned deep in her throat, igniting a brilliant, liquid fire that coursed through his veins.

Trent savored the moment, simply touching his wife. Freely. With no restrictions. She made beautiful sounds as she writhed against his fingers, driving him slightly insane with the tiny movements of her hips. Her sweetness slipped over his fingers and he wanted so badly to be inside her. He drank in this intense rush, this violent passion here and now. He would not question the severity of her response or the force of his own arousal.

He reached across her, tipping her seat back as far as it would go. He leaned over, pressing his lips to her thigh, grateful that the design of the car didn't impede his access to her secret swollen flesh. He slipped his hand beneath her hips, urging her to lift, just a little.

And then she was there, her swollen sex exposed and open, glistening with arousal. He looked up to find her watching him, her eyes heavy-lidded, her lips parted. Her breath a quiet gasp as she waited for his touch.

He slipped his tongue over her and savored the sound of her ragged gasp. In the back of his mind, he wondered what would happen if they were caught. If a policeman happened by. The risk added a sinful urgency to his touch. He stroked his tongue over her sweet center until she arched her back, coating his fingers with slick wet heat. He slid a single finger inside her as he suckled her and she was lost, twisting and vibrating as the orgasm ripped through her and tore her to shreds.

Trent was lost in her pleasure. He could never feel better than now, at this moment. He could spend a lifetime feeling her coming beneath his fingers, his tongue. He had so much to atone for. She made sexy, mewling sounds deep in her throat as he slipped his fingers from her body, kissing her fiercely, needing her more than he'd ever needed her.

Laura gave everything she was to him in that kiss. She wanted her confidence with him back. Wanted to feel the power of his arousal under her touch.

She leaned over, sliding her hand down to stroke the hard ridge of his erection through his pants. Trent went absolutely still, his body tight. "Laura."

"Hmm. Shhh. Watch for cars?"

"Laura..." His voice held a plea.

"Not another word," she whispered, squeezing him gently.

He held his breath as her fingers found his zipper, freeing him from the confines of his pants. Watched her eyes darken as she stroked him, slowly, slowly, until his breath was nothing more than a harsh gasp and he had to fight the urge to close his eyes.

Trent could die a happy man. He glanced down to see his wife's beautiful fingers wrapped around him, bringing to life every fantasy he'd carried with him over the long dark nights he'd spent without her. When she leaned over close enough that her breath floated across his erection, his cock went impossibly hard.

"Laura—" He slid his hand through her hair, wanting what he dared not ask for.

Her fingers were soft and cool on his skin. She squeezed him, her breath flitting over the swollen head, a vicious tease. He was hard as stone, and it felt like every ounce of blood in his body throbbed in his cock. The blood pounding in his ears guaranteed he wouldn't hear a damn thing until it was too late.

"Hmmm. I dreamed about doing this," she murmured.

"Right now?" He could barely speak.

"Yeah." She rubbed her lips softly against the tip and he flinched at the gentle torment. "I've had a long time alone to dream things up."

Trent barked out a laugh, but the sound strangled in his throat when her soft mouth closed over the tip of him. She slowly slid her mouth down the hard length of his cock, caressing him like he'd dreamed about a thousand times before. He threw his head back and fought the urge to fist his fingers in her hair. Her hand stroked him while she used her mouth on him and damn him, he wasn't going to last. Pleasure built deep in his belly and he went infinitely still, praying he'd hold off.

And then he glanced down at his beautiful wife with her mouth on him and his entire world exploded.

Chapter Sixteen

Laura wasn't sure what she'd expected to happen when they got home, but a quick tumble in the bedroom had been high on her list of priorities.

Instead, they paid the babysitter, checked on the sleeping kids, and made sure the rodents hadn't escaped again. Then she went to the bathroom to get washed up. When she came back to the living room, he was sitting in a chair, his eyes glued to the TV screen as he rubbed the scar on his chest.

He didn't see her. He couldn't.

Trent was watching the news. Images of a battle that had been raging for three days north of Baghdad flashed through their living room. Explosions punctuated the silence of their home.

Sweat broke out on his forehead, and stress was visible in the rigid set of his jaw and the harsh dark line of his mouth. She stepped into his view, the movement catching his attention, breaking the spell. Trent's eyes focused on her face even as an acute sadness creased his lips.

He closed his eyes and forced himself to take a long inhale. He winced and she wondered if it physically hurt when he expanded his lungs. His jaw and his shoulders tensed, and his hand flexed as though he were cradling the barrel of his weapon.

Fear licked at her soul. He'd said it himself—he didn't really know why he felt compelled to leave home again and again. But he couldn't help it. And the next time he left, everything they'd rebuilt together would be destroyed.

She did not speak, did not dare to voice the unspoken question jammed in her throat. Instead, she walked over to the arm of the chair where he sat, and leaned down until she was spread across his lap. "Are you okay?" she whispered.

He clicked the television off. Silence wrapped around them once more.

It was a long moment before his arms came around her shoulders.

And when he spoke, he opened part of his soul to her.

"I was just remembering the feel of the fifty-cal machine gun when my gunner laid down covering fire."

"Would you deploy again?" she whispered, terrified of the answer.

Laura's fingers twined with his and she looked up just as he opened his eyes. The emotion she saw there was ragged and raw, the fear a relentless, writhing thing. "I don't know," he said.

His honesty hurt but she shut it down, needing more to talk to him, to hear what he was saying instead of only hearing what she wanted to.

"I used to think it was where I belonged," he said. He leaned forward, slipping his glasses off and setting them on the coffee table. "But I look at everything I've given up, everything I've lost..." He looked over at her, his eyes tortured. "It wasn't worth it. It wasn't worth nearly losing you, it wasn't worth missing all the time with the kids." He scrubbed his hand over his mouth. "I gave the army everything I had and now I'm being court-martialed."

"Was that so hard?" she whispered, hating the hope that blossomed inside her, knowing that it could be crushed so easily. He had never shared with her before. Tonight? It was simply enough that he hadn't pushed her away.

He squeezed her hand, threading his fingers with hers. He couldn't meet her gaze. "You have no idea."

A lump blocked her throat, and it felt like a weight had lifted, just a little, from around her heart. His hands slid up her arms, stopping to stroke her neck. His palms were hot against her skin, his thumbs tender where he stroked beneath her ear.

"This isn't easy for me, Laura. Talking about it doesn't make it any better." His voice was harsh. Ragged. She wondered if there would ever come a time when he wouldn't get angry when he talked about the war.

"Avoiding it—avoiding your family—doesn't make it any better either." She pressed a gentle kiss to his shoulder. "I can't help you if you're not here."

She met his gaze and the legion of dark emotions churning in his midnight black eyes. "Maybe I don't want to poison your life with the war."

"It's too late for that." Heat from his skin pulsed against her palm. "I'm not saying that to make you feel guilty," she added quickly. "I'm just saying that the war has been in our lives since the day you died. Not being here has only made it harder on all of us."

"For what it's worth, I'm sorry." He licked his bottom lip a moment before he swallowed.

"I know," she whispered.

A sliver of heat drifted through her blood as she remembered how much she loved him. Oh God, but she remembered. Being with him made her feel so good—like a flower reaching for the sunlight after a long, dark winter. The knowledge hit her again with increased certainty.

She still loved this man.

The war had done nothing to change that.

His kiss was hesitant as he touched his tongue to her lips, a feather light caress. A burst of pleasure rushed through her as his tongue slid across her lips.

His fingers threaded through her hair and angled her mouth to open for him. Desire seared through her veins like a fire banked too long and suddenly exposed to fuel. She felt his breath, warm and soft against her skin. She closed her eyes and felt the ragged vibration of his breathing as he lifted her easily, carrying her to their bedroom.

"I can't do this right now, Laura," he whispered as he nestled against her body. His chest moved against her back, his breathing slow and easy, belying the thick emotion in his voice.

Tears blocked her throat as she lay with him. His quiet words didn't surprise her but they still hurt.

He shifted her until she was beneath him, then he kissed her so fiercely that her body begged for his touch. Instead, he merely framed her face with his hands, his body rough against hers. "I want to." One thumb stroked at her temple. "But I can't do it right if I still hear the war in my head." He nuzzled her nose with his.

She smiled then because she couldn't stop herself. "Your noble notions of sacrifice were strangely missing in the car earlier."

He laughed and she felt it rumble deep in her belly before he lowered his forehead to hers. She cupped his face, needing to chase away the shadows she saw creeping back into his eyes. "It's okay." She waited until he met her gaze once more.

"Really?"

"No." She kissed him then to show him what she could not say. She understood his racing thoughts. Understood that

there were times when he couldn't turn the war off in his
head. She wanted to push him onto his back and make him
forget forever everything about Iraq.

Instead, she simply curled into his body, her soul at ease
for the moment, content that they were together—that her
husband was back in her bed.

"Incoming!"

Laura opened her eyes abruptly, her body shaking. The
darkness around her echoed with the sounds of a scuffle.

Laura flicked on the bedside lamp, sending pale light
casting into the darkness. Trent had tossed one arm over
his head, his fists bunched around an invisible weapon. His
brow was drawn into a tense frown, his features twisted with
hate and violence.

Common sense held her back when instinct urged her to
wrap her arms around him and pull him from the nightmare
that haunted him. He shouted again and rolled to his side,
his arms rising up like he was holding a weapon only he
could see.

"Trent?" She jostled his shoulder gently. "Wake up. It's
just a dream."

He didn't stop or stiffen. He showed no signs of hearing
her. The nightmare pressed on and he grunted like he'd been
shoved against a wall. She pushed harder against his shoulder, a clawing, writhing terror ripping at her heart.

She never saw him move.

She landed with a thud on the floor before she knew what
had happened and she had a brief moment to be grateful for
the thick carpet. He'd pulled her down to the floor and covered her body with his. "Stay down."

His hands swept down her body in a decidedly nonsexual
way. His voice was different. Raw. Ragged. Like he'd been
shouting over the thunder of machine guns.

Laura shoved at his shoulder, all two hundred pounds of him crushing the air from her lungs. She fought the panic that he wasn't really there with her in their bedroom. He was somewhere far away, some place she could not reach him. "Trent, wake up!"

He twitched and buried his face in her neck. "Story! Come on, buddy, don't do this."

Laura froze. Story was deployed. He wasn't dead.

"Goddamn it, Top, get up!"

His elbows were on either side of her head and the heat from his body pressed into hers. He scanned the darkness, searching for an enemy that only he could see. She felt trapped, pinned beneath a man who could not see her. She shoved desperately at his shoulder, the heel of her palm pushing against the scar over his heart. Fear danced down her spine, twisting in her belly. "Trent!"

He grunted and looked down at her. He wasn't seeing her. He wasn't there. His eyes were empty, unseeing. But it was the pain, the pain and the horror in his eyes made her soul cry out. She had no idea what this man had gone through. All this time she'd just wanted him home and he was facing things she'd never see and could never hope to understand.

How had she hoped he would share this with her?

He looked lost. And more than that. Afraid. Of things she could not see and would never understand. She panicked, tears streaking down her cheeks as she shoved and shoved and shoved. "Wake up. Trent, wake up!"

He jerked once, his breath sucking into his body with a massive gasp. He blinked, looking around, finally seeing her in the dim bedroom light.

"Jesus, Laura." He scrambled off her, pulling her upright. "Oh fuck, did I hurt you?"

She shook her head and rubbed the back of her neck and sat up. Her body protested the too fast movement, but otherwise everything seemed okay. "No." She turned her face and looked into his dark eyes. "Are you okay?"

"I think I should probably ask you the same question." His eyes scanned her body, new panic warring with the old nightmares. "Are you sure you're not hurt?"

"I'm fine." She reached for him, threading her fingers with his. She rested their hands on her thigh. "You said Story's name," she said quietly, watching him.

He sat next to her, his back propped against the frame of the bed. She was amazed he didn't pull away. "It was just a bad dream. I have them all the time."

Disappointment clutched at her heart. No matter how many times she tried to walk through the darkness with him, it was one thing he never shared with her. He'd never let her stand with him against the abyss of the war—what he'd seen, what he'd lived through.

She had no idea the things he'd done, the friends he'd lost. She didn't know and God knew she wasn't strong enough to go through what he'd gone through. But she wanted to be there with him. Wanted to be there to help him when the darkness got too heavy.

Their thighs touched where they sat on the floor. Laura fidgeted with the drawstring on the waist of her pajama pants, trying to keep the tears from spilling down her cheeks. She was so tired of crying for him. Each moment that passed took with it the fragile hope that tonight would be different. That he would let her stand with him even when she couldn't know the pain he'd lived through. The silence spread between them, a gulf that was more than physical. A gulf that shattered everything they'd done to try and rebuild the fragile trust between them.

Every so often, she'd catch bits of the conversations between him and the men who'd been there with him. A joke about a dud grenade. A comment about the heat or the night vision goggles freezing in the extreme cold. But he always clammed up and stopped talking when he realized she was listening.

Whatever hell he'd gone through, he'd kept it—and himself—from her. Whenever the war reared its ugly head, brutal silence always filled the room.

She sniffed and swiped at her cheeks, hoping he wouldn't notice. The disappointment lodged in her throat. She wondered if he would sleep on the couch tonight, further cementing the chasm that had reappeared between them. How long would it be before he was gone again, leaving her for the war he could never leave behind?

She bit her lips, refusing to cry again. She'd known better than to do this, to trust him with her heart one more time. She'd known better and she'd been a goddamned fool.

He was going to leave her again. He was going to walk out that front door with his duffle bag and his assault pack and head back to the war.

Leaving her alone, just like always.

He broke her. And she was a goddamned fool for letting him.

The silence stretched between them. Laura couldn't move beneath the weight of the devastation.

Then he shifted, the sound of cotton sliding against cotton in the dark. His arm slipped around her shoulders and urged her close, until her cheek was rested in the pocket of his shoulder. She tensed, not wanting the hollow gesture but he refused to relent, forcing her to either walk away or relax against him. He pressed his cheek against her hair and they sat in silence, Laura's need to tend his unseen wounds unmet and unanswered.

He tensed a moment before he spoke, his whisper barely penetrating the silence. "I don't mean to shut you out." A ragged admission.

He shifted and she felt his lips press to her forehead. She slid her hand onto his lap, resting her palm against his thigh. The silence hung between them thick and heavy and filled with hurt. And in the hushed darkness, she waited, unable to speak past the block in her throat.

When he spoke, his words shattered more than the silence.

"Story and I were leading a clearing mission. A buddy of mine was inside the village, searching these houses that were little more than mud huts." His chest rose as he took a deep breath.

Laura didn't dare move, afraid she would break the fragile moment into a hundred thousand pieces. She had no idea what this was costing him, could not imagine what he'd gone through.

"There were a few buildings with tunnels beneath them. Story took a couple guys into them after two fighters who'd attacked our patrol with an RPG."

She closed her eyes, imagining a building made of mud and dirt, a tunnel pulling all the light from the room. "The tunnel was narrow and cramped. I tried to get Story to listen to me but he was determined to get the fuckers."

He shifted, rubbing his eyes. His voice sounded far away, like the memory came from a place deep inside him. The ragged pain cut at her, tearing her heart to shreds. "I should have maintained our position when the fighting started." His breath shuddered through him. "I could hear Story screaming on the radio." A pause. "I gave the order to collapse in, to try to get to our boys."

His breath trembled when he blew it out. She shifted, resting her hand on the scar over his heart. He reached up, cupping her face. "I know it was just a fucking nightmare but Story died because of me."

A sob broke free before she could stop it. What had he

lived through that he dreamed about his friends dying? "It was just a bad dream."

He didn't notice. His body was tense, restraining violence and motion. He was hurting. Goddamn it, he was hurting. She wanted to help but nothing she'd ever done had prepared her to deal with this ragged grief and blame and all the fucked-up memories from the war.

"But it wasn't. That was a real mission. Except it wasn't Story who died. My guys collapsed in instead of maintaining security. Two of our boys would probably still be alive if they'd been airlifted out in time. But we had to secure a hot landing zone for the MEDEVAC flight three clicks away."

She twisted until she sat facing him on the soft carpet of their bedroom floor. She cupped his face, waited for him to lift his gaze to hers. This was just one twisted memory, just one bad thing that had happened during the war that had driven him away from his home. To try to atone for sins, real and imagined, that he'd committed during war.

Her heart broke for him. But damn it, she was not going to sit there and cry while her husband's heart bled out. "Story isn't dead," she whispered. "And you didn't kill your men."

He tried to look away. "Trent." He met her gaze again. "You made a mistake. You can't fix it. Running away, leaving us doesn't fix this." His cheeks were wet beneath her fingers. "It doesn't fix *you*."

"Story told me that once." He looked at her. "When I got the papers from you downrange. He sat with me that whole first night. Smoking a cigar while I tried to figure out how to unfuck our marriage." He paused, remembering that far off night. "Said that if I didn't get my sorry ass home to you, I was going to end up like him, bitter and alone."

He reached for her then, threading his hands in her hair and pulling her close, until her face was buried in his neck. She wrapped her arms tight around him and simply sat, breathing in the warm, real scent of her husband. For the first time since he'd left all those years ago, she'd been given a glimpse at the life he'd lived without her. The life he'd tried to protect her from.

There were no words she could speak that weren't empty platitudes, spoken by a wife who had not lived through the war and the chaos and the hell. Anything she said would only make it worse, expanding the differences between them.

She couldn't tell him she understood because it was infinitely different to comfort the grieving spouse of a fallen soldier than it was to hold one of your boys as he died.

Her heart ached and her soul bled for the man next to her. And she wished more than anything she had some way to take the hurt away.

He shifted then, a rustle of fabric against skin. She reached for him, finding his hand in the near darkness, and threaded her fingers with his.

It was the only thing she could think to do.

"Please don't leave me." He rested his cheek against the top of her head again, hugging her body against his. "I can't do this alone."

Chapter Seventeen

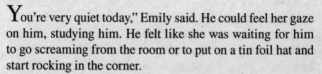

You're very quiet today," Emily said. He could feel her gaze on him, studying him. He felt like she was waiting for him to go screaming from the room or to put on a tin foil hat and start rocking in the corner.

He released a hard breath. "I had a pretty bad nightmare last night." He swallowed. "It was a mix of one of my buddies dying and a real mission." He looked up at her. "How fucked up is it that I'm dreaming about my friends—who are not dead, by the way—dying at war?"

He shifted and pushed his glasses up onto the top of his head.

It was a long time before Emily spoke. "I think it's reasonable for you to expect more nightmares in the coming months," she said gently.

He looked over sharply. "I can't do that. I think I threw my wife out of bed because of incoming rounds last night."

"Was she hurt?"

He closed his eyes, hearing again Laura's quiet sniffle in the darkness. "Maybe not physically, but yeah, I hurt her."

"I'm sorry. Was she okay?"

"I think so." He remembered falling asleep with her in

his arms. It was not a gentle sleep, not a restful one. But he'd woken with her body twined with his, her hand resting over the scars on his heart.

"Has anyone ever talked to you about your emotional rucksack?" Emily asked, interrupting his thoughts.

"No?"

"It means that we all have the capacity to deal with bad news. And when the first piece of bad news hits, we can stuff it down and keep going. But eventually, our bags get too heavy and there's no more room to stuff things down anymore." She looked at him, her expression filled with compassion. "And sometimes we keep stuffing anyway because we don't think we have time to deal with things. What happens to a bag you stuffed too full when you open the top?"

"The laundry pops out of the top."

"Trent, you've been stuffing things for so long, your body and your mind are probably in shock at the fact that you're starting to unpack things. The nightmare felt real because it was real, at least part of it."

Trent looked at the young doctor. "What if I hurt my wife?" he asked. His voice was thick, filled with things he couldn't say. What if he hit her? Or threw her out of bed? Or hurt one of the kids? Thank God they didn't have any guns in the house.

He flinched from the nightmare thought that could too easily come true.

"I can't promise that you won't have more nightmares. But there are things you can do to avoid them. Avoiding certain foods at bedtime. Turning the TV off."

"That stuff really works?"

"We think it helps. Will it work completely? Probably not. But if you lessen the likelihood, as you continue to unpack and start to heal some of the hurt you've done to yourself, maybe you'll start to see them taper off." She scribbled a note in her file. "How are things with Laura? Any more troubles with the kids?"

Trent leaned back, uncrossing his legs. "Things are good, actually. Better than I thought they'd be in a couple short weeks."

Emily's smile lit up her face. "That's wonderful to hear. How's the medication working?"

"It's okay. I don't take it that often but knowing it's there helps, if that makes sense."

"It makes perfect sense," she said. "We've known for a long time that the placebo effect is a statistically significant result. Sometimes, just having the medication makes a difference."

He sat for a moment, listening to her as she described some new therapy she wanted him to try.

He'd come here because of the court-martial, because Patrick had told him to get a clean bill of health. "Can I ask you something?" he said abruptly.

"Sure."

"Have you already written the report for the court-martial?"

"Of course. I wrote that after your first visit."

Trent ran his tongue over his teeth. "So why am I still here?"

Emily's expression was carefully blank. "Why don't you tell me that?"

He was still there because he loved his family. Because this had helped to at least start him on the road to somewhere approaching normal. He smiled, realizing that if Patrick had planned this, it had worked out.

"Did Patrick put you up to keeping me in therapy?"

"No. But I did get a note from your old first sergeant, telling me that if I could help you be less crazy, he'd buy me a beer when he got home from Iraq." Emily shrugged. "I don't drink and I normally don't try to keep clients here under false pretenses. But Story told me about your kids and your wife and how much you love her. I figured if I could get a couple visits out of you, maybe I could make a difference." She crossed her legs. "I hope you're not upset?"

Trent's smile started slowly then spread beyond his mouth to the empty space in his heart that was not so empty anymore. "No. In fact, I think I owe my first sergeant that beer when he gets home."

"Yeah, you probably do. You have a lot of people in your life looking out for you. You need to take care of yourself so you can take care of them." She paused. "Will I see you next Thursday?"

He looked down at his hands. At the wedding band around his left ring finger. He never thought he'd be the guy that would go and let someone crawl around inside his head.

He looked up at her. "Yeah. You will."

Trent walked through the chapel, unable to concentrate on anything to do with Shane's wedding. His thoughts were distracted and raw, a hangover from the ragged memories that had risen up and tormented him. The war was doing it again. Demanding he leave, that he go back to doing what he was good at. Fighting.

But somehow, the war felt very far away. The whispers were there but their seductive promise of adrenaline and power were...diminished. His mind drifted from memory to memory, focusing on home, on ignoring the siren's call of the war. On his family that still loved him.

Emma giggling as he blew a raspberry on her tummy.

Ethan squealing with laughter as Trent dangled him upside down.

Laura's eyes filling with tears as she watched him walk from that crowded gym one more time.

Emotions twisted around inside him, filling the dead space. He wasn't afraid of feeling anymore. There was a time when being around the guys, around Shane and Carponti and Story, would have been the only slice of normal in his life. That being around the guys would have fit better than being around his family.

But the pieces were fitting back together now, better than they had before.

"You're thinking way too hard," Carponti said, leaning on the altar. "We're supposed to be plotting a way to get Mr. Cranky Pants to the church on time and you look like you just stepped in a pile of dog shit."

"Hamster shit, more likely," Trent mumbled.

Carponti laughed. "Yeah, well, you were the one who bought them. I'm still shocked Laura let the kids keep them."

Shane walked up and joined them. He'd been off looking for the chaplain's assistant. "Where did everyone go?"

"Bride's room."

"What are they doing in there, anyway?" Carponti asked, glancing down the hallway.

"Painting each other's toenails. How the hell should I know?" Trent asked.

"Quit bickering like an old married couple and help me. I still need to find the chaplain's assistant to confirm that everything's in order for the ceremony. The little shit's nowhere to be found."

Trent stuffed his hands in his pockets and raised both eyebrows. "Did you really just refer to a chaplain's assistant as a little shit?"

"Isn't that like a speed pass straight to hell?" Carponti said.

Shane shot them both a deadpan look. "I have met some really great chaplain's assistants over the years. This kid? Not even close to the same quality. My calibrated NCO Spidey senses tell me he's using drugs."

Trent sobered. "What makes you say that?"

"Just a hunch. You've been an officer for too long. You're not as finely in tune with the stupid shit our boys are still doing."

"I'll go see if he's in the back office." Carponti wandered off, leaving Trent and Shane alone in the chapel. The silence of the worship center was sterile. Clean. It felt light, somehow untouched by the darkness of the people who walked through it.

"You doing okay?" Shane asked after a moment.

"Yeah. Actually I am." Last night had been hard, so goddamned hard. But this morning, Laura had lain in bed with him for a few minutes between waking up and having to get the kids going for school and he'd felt something strange—a sense of peace.

It was something he'd never thought he'd ever feel again.

"Do you worry about screwing things up with Jen?" Trent asked.

Shane shifted and folded his arms over his chest. He cleared his throat. "It took me a long time to realize I was a large part of the reason why my first marriage failed. And I am determined not to repeat those same mistakes with Jen."

"Are you going to deploy again?"

Shane sighed. "Probably. I've only got a few more years to go before I can retire. I'll stay in, do this last rotation then go try to find a desk job somewhere."

"You? At a desk?" Trent shook his head.

"You need to do the same damn thing," Shane said.

"I'm working on it," Trent said. "I honestly didn't think I had a second chance."

"Laura loves you. She's always loved you. You were just too stupid to see that she was right here, waiting for you to get your head out of your ass and come home to her."

Regret twisted against Trent's heart. He'd given up so

much, chasing an elusive master that would never let him go. The army didn't need his sacrifice. It didn't need his blood.

He was one of the lucky ones. He had a beautiful family, a family he'd avoided because he couldn't confront the magnitude of changes the war had wrought in him.

It was time to face the life he had.

Something warm swelled and burst inside him, shocking him with the overwhelming simplicity of being...home. He rounded the corner to find Laura reading a pamphlet. She smiled as he approached.

"Where are the kids?" Trent asked her.

She motioned over her shoulder, then slipped the pamphlet back into its slot. "Ethan took Emma to the bathroom."

"You let them go alone?"

She smiled. Obviously he hadn't hidden the shock in his voice very well. "Yes. It's good for him to learn to watch over his little sister."

"That means that either she's going in the men's room or he's going in the women's room." Trent sounded horrified and Laura couldn't suppress her smile.

"He's six. He's fine in the women's restroom for a little while longer." She shrugged, a smile teasing her lips. "Besides, it's Thursday afternoon during family time. No one is here right now anyway."

"Oh."

Shane stalked around the corner, fury radiating off him in palpable waves. "We don't have a church."

Just like that everyone appeared in the little hallway.

"What do you mean, we don't have a church?" Jen said. "What happened?"

"The little shithead stoner chaplain's assistant didn't schedule it," Shane snapped. "The chaplain's free to marry us, but some officers' wives' club meeting is going to be here in the chapel that day."

Carponti scowled. "They should just move the meeting. Why do they get priority?"

"Because it's the post commander's wife's pet project," Shane said. He sighed heavily, covering Jen's hand with his. "We'll figure something out," he said softly.

"Why don't you just get married at your place?" Trent asked. "You've got enough space for it."

"Sure," Shane snorted. "We can get married on the back porch."

"We could build a gazebo. Or one of those pergola thingies that have the slating over the top?" This from Carponti, who suddenly looked serious. As if a light bulb had been turned on inside her head, Nicole instantly whipped out her smartphone and started typing.

"We could set it up this weekend. There's an unfinished furniture place in Temple. We could check there," Laura said, brightening at the idea. "And I could get some sheer drapes. It would be beautiful."

Jen didn't look convinced. "That's a lot of work to get done in a weekend," she said. "We could just go to the Justice of the Peace." She lifted her chin, looking up at Shane. "I don't really care where we get married."

"It matters." Shane cupped her cheek and stroked his thumb over it before he looked over at them. "Let's do this."

Laura shooed Carponti and Nicole out, and she and Trent followed right behind them.

"I think building the pergola is a perfect idea," Trent said, after they had shut the door.

"I've already found one," Nicole said, holding up her smartphone. "We can pick up the materials today and start building."

"We'll need gravel to level the ground out," Laura said.

Trent looked over at her. "How do you know all this?"

She smiled up at him. "I've kept myself amused with

home improvement projects while you've been gone," she said. "How much money are we talking about?"

"We're looking at about $500." Nicole held the phone out so Laura could see. "Trent, we'll need your truck."

"Done. We can go pick up the material now if they like the looks of it." He glanced at Laura.

"We'll need to feed the kids on the way, but yeah." Laura grinned. "This is awesome."

Carponti looked down at his prosthetic. "I wonder if they make a hammer attachment for the Nub."

Laura choked back a laugh as Trent groaned and shook his head. The kids came running toward them from down the hall, and Emma collided with Laura's leg.

"Hey, kiddos, we need to take a little trip."

"Aww! Mommy, I wanted to go to the lake today," Ethan said, stomping his foot. Laura narrowed her eyes, wondering if it was possible for her son to have PMS. Most of the time he was such a great kid. But sometimes? She wanted to volunteer for a deployment.

Trent knelt down to Ethan's level. "We've got to do something really important for Shane's wedding. I'm going to need your help, though, okay? Because I'm out of practice with building stuff."

"Mommy's really good at building stuff," Emma said.

Ethan's eyes went wide. "What are we building?"

"A place for Shane and Jen to get married," Trent said.

"Do I get to nail anything with my hammer?" Ethan asked.

"Can I help, too?" Emma asked.

He glanced up at Laura, unsure about what the age limits were for hammers. She stood there, watching him, her hand over her mouth, her eyes shimmering. He held his breath thinking he'd gone too far, that he'd undermined her somehow. But then she nodded, a hesitant smile on her lips. He was sure she already had a plan to keep them entertained while the adults worked.

"Sure you can. But you've got to be really careful with the hammers and stuff. We've got to head out now to get the supplies we need. Can you and your sister be good for us?"

Ethan nodded solemnly. "Sure, Daddy."

"Promise, Daddy," Emma said.

Laura watched the interchange between her son and her husband. It was such a simple exchange, yet so significant. He'd come so far. She knew there were still long days and nights ahead of them but watching him with their kids, watching him smile and feel at ease, she knew they had a chance. A small chance, one that could easily be destroyed by a careless gesture or thoughtless word, but a chance nonetheless.

The little things were what mattered most to two people building a life together. Not the big grand gestures. It was Shane telling Jen he wanted their wedding day to be perfect—not because Jen demanded it but because he wanted it to be special for her.

It was Nicole, staying strong while her husband recovered from his injuries.

It was Trent, kneeling in front of their son and daughter and talking them into helping him build something for their friends.

In that moment, she looked at her husband and her son and her daughter and her heart was open and vulnerable. Her soul was stripped bare.

There was no protecting her heart from her love for this man. He could very well leave her again but at that moment, she loved him with everything she had.

Chapter Eighteen

❧

Laura wasn't planning on staying at work long today. The entire unit was back from NTC and Laura had planned on taking a day off to finish some of the prep work for the building project this weekend. She was trying to get a few e-mails sent that absolutely had to be sent and then she was going to make herself scarce, because the longer she stayed at the office, the more she risked getting pulled into something she didn't have the time to deal with today.

So of course, Patrick knocked on her door right as she was finishing her last e-mail. Because karma hated her.

"You have a sec?" he asked.

She hadn't honestly expected to be left alone to actually get some work done. "Sure, what's up?"

"So this is going to sound like a really jacked-up request but do you have LT Randall's wife's address?"

Laura rocked back in her chair, folding her arms over her chest. "Seriously?"

"Yes, seriously. The company doesn't have her address and her husband isn't answering his phone and we need to find her."

"Why isn't she at work?"

"That's what we need to find out. Apparently, she's been unaccounted for for three days."

Laura leaned forward. "Are you kidding me?"

"No." Patrick leaned on her door. "So can you help me out?"

"Sure. Give me a sec." It actually took her less than a minute to pull the soldier's address. "Now what?"

"Now I'm going to her house." There was bitterness in Patrick's voice.

"I'm not exactly sure that's a good idea," Laura said. "Why are you going? And don't we usually go in pairs to soldiers' houses?"

"I'm going because most of the unit isn't here today because of the training holiday. It's a long drawn-out story that starts with Colonel Richter telling me to get my ass out there and get her here no matter what before close of business today." He paused. "So are you volunteering? I mean, I know she's a soldier and all but technically, she is a spouse."

Laura sighed and resigned herself to not getting out of there early because Patrick was right. It was part of her job description to do home visits. They were by far her least favorite part of the job because you never knew what you'd find. "Sure," she said and grabbed her purse along with a log form, so that she could keep detailed notes of everything that happened today.

Adorno lived less than a mile away but a few minutes later, when she opened the door, Laura was reminded of exactly why she hated home visits.

Randall's wife was a walking disaster. Her eyes were red and swollen. Her hair hadn't been washed in at least three days and Laura could see what looked like two boxes of half-eaten pizza on the kitchen counter behind her. There was evidence of a crime against Ben & Jerry's on the kitchen table behind her. "What?" Adorno said.

Patrick released a deep breath. "I need you to get dressed. The brigade commander wants to see you."

"I'm on quarters." She thrust a piece of paper at him. Laura frowned as Patrick's face flushed deep scarlet as he read the sick call slip. Laura looked at him and waited for an explanation. What the hell was on that slip to make him blush?

He handed it to her and Laura read it once, then again, then looked back at the soldier, a deep sympathy twisting beneath her heart. She should hate the girl but what was on that slip was enough to make her feel nothing but compassion for the young woman.

Her husband had given her an STD. It didn't get much worse than that.

"The brigade commander wants to see you," Patrick said again. "This isn't really optional."

Her bottom lip quivered. "But what about…?" She motioned to the paper in Laura's hand.

"The colonel will clear it up with the docs, I'm sure."

Laura looked at the young woman. "For what it's worth, I'm sorry."

Adorno's eyes flashed angrily. "Thank you but don't be sorry for me. I want to cut my cheating, lying husband's balls off. I'll be much better then."

Beside her, Patrick cleared his throat. "Yes, well, please don't do any of that around me. I'd rather not be involved in any assault cases."

Adorno laughed but it was a harsh, strangled sound. "Can I meet you at brigade?"

Patrick shook his head. "Sorry. You need to ride with myself and Mrs. Davila. No one has seen you for three days."

Her lip quivered again. "My asshole husband won't be there, will he?"

"Not that I'm aware of," Patrick said.

Adorno sighed and it reminded Laura of one of Ethan's

sulks. She almost smiled but figured the young soldier wouldn't do well with that. She'd think Laura was laughing at her when she was doing no such thing.

Adorno stepped back and invited them into the house. "Fine," she said. "I have to take a shower."

As she retreated to her bedroom, Patrick and Laura stood in the foyer. Laura briefly noticed that there was no cat and no kittens, either. Looked like she'd been lying about the cat the other day at the office. Nice.

Neither of them was willing to cross any farther into the house. It wasn't dirty. It was messy and had clearly not been cleaned in a few days. But Laura wasn't in any place to judge.

There was a crash from the bedroom and Laura and Patrick rushed back.

Adorno knelt on the floor, her small body wracked by great, heaving sobs as she tried to pick up ragged pieces of broken glass.

"Here, stop. You're going to cut yourself." Laura eased her away from the glass but she was practically incoherent.

"I…can't…believe…he cheated on me."

Laura had seen far too many young wives devastated by one of the ugly truths of the army life: Men often strayed. It could be because of the war, the strain, or simply too much distance between them and their spouse.

Adorno had learned this lesson early in life. Still, it came with a price tag because her husband's cheating had come with an STD. One that could be cured, but still. It sucked, and no matter how much Laura had hated this soldier at one time, she felt nothing but sympathy for her right then.

"Want me to call Trent and tell him you'll be late?" Patrick said, picking up the last of the broken glass.

Laura glanced at her watch. She was supposed to meet everyone in half an hour. There was no way she'd make it. "Yes, please."

Adorno looked at her like she'd grown three heads. "Trent? Trent Davila is your husband?"

Laura leaned back. "You didn't put that together with my name and his being the same?" she asked.

Adorno shook her head slowly. "Oh ma'am, you must hate me." Her voice was the barest whisper.

Laura said nothing. What could she possibly say that wasn't a lie? She did hate this soldier at one point. Maybe not at that exact moment, but there was bitter resentment toward a soldier who would lie to save her own skin and ruin Laura's husband's life.

"You do hate me," Adorno said when Laura didn't respond.

"I think you've made some poor choices," Laura said finally, seeking the only pragmatic thing she could say.

Adorno's eyes filled once more and she covered her face with her hands. "I hate him," she whispered. "He ruined my life." She swiped angrily at her cheeks. "I believed him when he said he was working late." She looked at Laura. "I feel so stupid."

"We all make stupid choices when it comes to love," Laura said. "Did you ever love him?"

"I thought I did," she said sadly. "Now? Now I'm not sure." She paused. "I am so sorry for what he's done to Captain Davila."

Laura swallowed the lump in her throat. "It's not just what he did to my husband," she said gently. "What he's done has affected our entire family." She could have said what *you've* done but she didn't. If anything, this young woman needed her support right now. She'd been married, involved in a big news army scandal, cheated on, and now, it looked like, left. Laura didn't need to add anything else to the baggage this young woman was going to carry around with her. But she looked at the young soldier quizzically. "How did you not put two and two together and not know he was my husband? I've been to the FRG meetings."

Adorno flushed. "Davila is a really common name. And I thought you were just there because it was your job," she said. Her cheeks flamed red. "I ruined your life and you're still being kind to me. You knew all along who I was?"

Laura nodded.

"How could you be nice to me?"

"Well, I did want to choke you when you demanded I call the brigade commander over kittens." Adorno flushed and covered her mouth with her hand and Laura wasn't sure if she was smothering a laugh or a sob. "But we were all young once. We all did stupid things in the name of love." She waved one hand. "I generally try to limit my stupid things to ruining my own life and not other people's, but you get the idea."

"How can you sit here and make jokes? Why don't you hate me?" Such a tragic insecurity in her voice.

"Part of me did for a little while." Laura sighed gently. "You've made some mistakes but you can't change those. All you can do is try to learn from them."

Adorno nodded, her eyes filling again. "Thanks for sitting with me," she said.

"You're welcome," Laura said. "Now we really need to get going. The brigade commander is waiting on you and last I checked, soldiers didn't keep colonels waiting."

"What's he want to talk to me about?"

"Probably what's going on with your husband."

Anger clouded Adorno's eyes once more as she pushed to her feet. Her smile was bitter cold. "Oh, I can't wait."

"Pass me the level?" Trent said from up on the ladder.

Laura handed it up, still bracing the pole in case it needed more adjustments. "Is it good?"

Trent paused, watching as the bubble sought equilibrium in the liquid. After a moment, it settled exactly where it needed to be. "Perfect."

He handed her the level and climbed down, tugging off his gloves. He surveyed the construction site. "Not bad for six hours of work," he said, stuffing the gloves in his back pocket.

Laura grabbed a broom and swept over the fine sand coating the paving stones. He watched her work, awed by her abilities with a hammer for most of the afternoon.

"So the plan is to meet up at first light tomorrow?" Carponti asked.

One side of Jen's porch was now covered with a stack of lumber, and just below the porch four poles were curing in quick-drying concrete. A ten-by-ten space was covered with paving stones, interlocked and held into place by special sand.

"I'll have breakfast and coffee ready to go," Jen said, still looking shocked that they had managed to get the foundation set and the poles in the ground before complete darkness had fallen.

Shane grinned and wrapped one arm around her shoulders. "Stop looking so surprised. This is what we do."

"You guys kick in doors, last time I checked," Laura said. "Masonry and basic carpentry aren't in that duty description."

Trent glanced over at Ethan, who was busy still pounding away on a plank with a toy hammer. Emma looked far too serious with her little blue plastic saw. Her hair was sticking out over her head in a fuzzy black halo.

"The kids are going to sleep well tonight," Laura said, stepping closer to him as Nicole and Carponti finished stacking the tools on the back porch.

"They will?" He looked down at his wife in the waning daylight. Her face was covered in dust, her skin damp with sweat.

"Oh, they're going to be little monsters right before bedtime, but once they're in bed, they'll be out cold. They might even sleep in tomorrow morning."

"I doubt that."

Laura laughed and the sound did something to his insides. "Yeah, me too."

"They had fun today."

Laura lifted one shoulder and tucked her hands into her pockets. The motion stretched the old blue t-shirt over her breasts. Sweat ringed the collar of her shirt.

She looked beautiful. Sweaty and sexy all rolled into one.

"I liked working with you today," she said softly. "I miss how well we work together on stuff."

He swallowed and shifted, angling his body toward her. "Yeah, we've always done stuff like this well."

She did not pull away or increase the space between them. Her gaze slipped down his body, to the dusty t-shirt that clung to his chest.

He reached for her then, brushing a spot of dust from her cheek. "I think we need to get the kids home," he murmured.

"Yeah." Her tongue flicked out, wetting her bottom lip. The light from the back porch glistened on the moisture.

There was commotion and activity all around them but it felt like a blanket of silence shielded them from the rest of the world. Her scent wrapped around him, sending arousal swelling through his veins.

He gave in to the temptation and leaned closer, intent on brushing his lips against hers.

Time hung suspended as their lips touched, a hesitant kiss. The sweetest pleasure gasped from her mouth, filling a void in his heart.

His hand threaded in her hair almost before he knew what he was doing and he shifted until her chest bumped against his. Her lips parted beneath his and the kiss abruptly turned sensual.

Her tongue slipped between his lips and gently touched his. His wife was kissing him. This was the taste of love he'd been missing. The simplest, most potent pleasure.

He drank from her like he was a dying man. Her arms slid around his back, her nails digging into his flesh through the thin fabric of his shirt. Her body was soft and supple beneath his and he wished with all his heart that they were alone.

"You two should get a room!" Of course it was Carponti.

Trent broke the kiss but he refused to act like it was something he should be ashamed of. He stroked his thumb over Laura's bottom lip. No words passed between them.

There was nothing that needed to be said that hadn't already been acknowledged in the wicked heat of that single kiss.

"I cannot believe Emma spent a whole hour screaming," Trent said, closing the bathroom door behind him and clicking the lock into place.

Laura sighed and stripped off her dirty pants, intensely aware that her husband was in the small bathroom with her.

"I can. I expected worse from both of them," she said, reaching into the shower to turn it to full blast.

"Worse than that?"

"Oh, when they go supernova, it's a nightmare." She turned her back to him, unfastening her bra beneath her t-shirt.

"How do you cope with that?" Trent dragged his sweat-stained shirt over his head and Laura took in the lean strength of his chest as he leaned down to take off his socks. Another moment and he stood in their bathroom wearing nothing but dirty jeans and a smile.

Laura's insides melted a little as her gaze dropped to the trail of dark hair that disappeared beneath the waistband of his jeans.

She turned away, testing the water temperature and wondering if he was going to follow her into the shower.

"On the really bad days I sometimes sneak a glass of wine after they go to bed."

He slipped his glasses off and set them on the counter. His dog tags bounced against his ribs.

It was far too tempting to pretend that everything in their lives was normal. Instead she reached inside the shower and tested the temperature again. "It's been a long day," she murmured.

He didn't say anything as she ducked into the walk-in closet to strip off her clothing. When she was undressed, she quickly stepped into the shower, closing her eyes as the steaming water sluiced over her head—the pressure of it pounding at the tension in her shoulders. She'd always enjoyed home improvement projects, but that didn't mean her body didn't protest at the end of a long day.

"Ah, Laura? What the hell is this?"

She wiped the water from her face and stuck her head out from behind the shower curtain.

And wanted to die of embarrassment.

Trent stood in the middle of their bathroom, holding a red plastic penis in one hand. He flicked a switch and a low buzzing filled the whole room, audible even over the sound of the shower. Laura cleared her throat, positive her face was redder than the vibrator Trent was holding.

"Well, ah," she blew out a breath, searching for some words to explain. Heat crawled across her cheeks that had nothing to do with the hot water. "You've been gone a lot."

His eyes widened dramatically. "Yes, but it still hurts to meet my replacement in person. What's this model called, the Drill Sergeant?"

She stifled a horrified laugh. She couldn't help it. "Would you please turn that thing off and put it away?" She pulled the shower curtain shut again, praying that the next time she stuck her head out, the offending vibrator would be back in its box where it belonged. Damn it, she should have hidden it

better. But the top shelf of the closet was the perfect place to **keep** the kids from finding it. Her husband?

Apparently not.

She turned off the shower and wrapped her body in a fluffy towel. Her husband was no longer standing in the middle of the bathroom but his silence made her suspicious. She was afraid to go looking for him because he might have more embarrassing questions about her, ah, deployment boyfriend.

She shook her head and reached for her toothbrush just as he emerged from the closet. She glanced down and choked. He'd stuffed the vibrator between the buttons of his jeans. The plastic penis hung out of his pants, and she burst out laughing. "That's not funny! Put it away!"

"Hey, baby, why don't we..."

"Trent! Give me that!"

She couldn't remember the last time they'd laughed like this but damn it felt good. She whirled and lunged for it, not missing the fact that she was reaching for his groin and had her vibrator not been there, she might have gotten a handful of something else. She pulled the vibrator from his pants and stuffed it behind her back as he made a grab for it.

Her breath caught in her throat as her awareness of this man struck her, reminding her of how much she'd once loved him.

She still did.

He bunched his fists at his sides like he was fighting the urge to reach out to her. Then suddenly he moved, skimming his fingertips across her forehead, brushing her hair behind her ears. Her breath caught in her lungs as she dropped the vibrator in the sink behind her. Trent took advantage of her position and backed her up against the counter. They breathed in quiet gasps, the only sound over the rapid-fire beating of her heart. His fingers splayed across her hips and she shifted beneath him, spreading her thighs to hook them around his hips. But he held himself back, sliding his palm up her thigh and cupping her slick heat.

"It's a shame," he murmured.

She stilled. "What is?"

His thumb slid over her exposed hipbone—a light, teasing caress. "That you never sent me another video."

"Video of what?" Her breath hitched as he leaned in, nibbling on the edge of her jaw. His fingers danced over her belly, sliding closer to where she was wet and aching for him.

Her fingers clenched on his shoulders, spasming as he traced her collarbone with the tip of his tongue. His breath was hot on her skin, teasing the moisture from her shower.

He nuzzled her ear while he slid the tip of one finger over the seam of her slick heat. "Another one of you touching yourself," he whispered.

In some dim part of her brain not lost to the intense pleasure of his touch, she recognized that she was completely naked beneath her towel while he was still wearing his jeans. "You're wearing too many clothes," she murmured, nipping at his ear lobe.

He tensed as she dragged her hands down the crisp dark hair of his chest and reached for his pants. Her fingers trembled over the zipper momentarily before she quickly pulled it down and tugged his boxers and his jeans to the floor, freeing his erection.

He turned her so that she was facing the mirror. Then he stood behind her, his lean, strong body molded against hers as his hands drifted down her sides and over the towel that was the last barrier between them. She dropped her head back against his shoulder, closing her eyes as intense sensations overwhelmed her. He scraped his teeth over her neck, then something cool and soft dragged up her thigh.

She glanced down to see him sliding her vibrator against

her skin, tracing it beneath the edge of her towel. She held her breath even as her face flushed.

He nipped at her ear, his breath warm against her damp skin. "So how often did you, ah, use this?"

She gasped as he traced it over her damp skin. "Why? Jealous?"

He tugged at her earlobe with his teeth. "You have no idea."

"Trent—"

He slid one hand up her throat, turning her mouth until he claimed her lips. The tip of the vibrator teased the edge of her intimate flesh. The idea of him doing this to her...

She didn't want it. Not right now. At this moment, she wanted her husband's hands on her body, her husband's flesh filling her. Tonight, she wanted this man—the only one she had ever dreamed of.

She turned in his arms, tugged the vibrator out of his hand and dropped it back into the sink.

Then she dragged her fingers through his hair and pulled him closer to her. He tugged her towel out of the way and leaned against her body until the counter dug into her lower back, a delicious swipe of pain mixing with the thrill of his hands on her.

Slowly, slowly, he pushed his hands over her thighs, urging her to part for him. She arched and tried to shift, but he stopped her, holding her between his strong hands, his eyes darkening as he leaned back and simply took her in.

Her arms were braced against the counter, her breasts heavy and full. Her back arched, her intimate flesh exposed. She was more than beautiful.

She was the center of his world. She balanced him, kept him grounded. And he'd been running from the one person he needed more than anyone else.

He kissed her lips, her collarbone, the gentle swell of her

breast. He kissed a trail down her neck, moving ever lower until he reached the apex of her thighs, giving a gentle press of his lips to the warm, wet sanctuary he craved.

He sank to his knees in front of her and nuzzled the inside of her thigh. Her sex was the deepest swollen pink, liquid glistening on her skin, her soft curls. Arousal shot, hard and fast, through his blood at the scent of her, warm and musky and inviting.

He kissed her then, gently, tracing his lips and tongue down her soft skin, licking at the moisture that still dripped over her flesh from her shower.

Her gasp was the sweetest pleasure. And then he parted her with his tongue and her response was beautiful and it shoved aside the darkness in his soul. She arched gently beneath his mouth, her hips hesitantly rocking as he slid his tongue through her soft sex.

When he suckled her, she cried out, his name on her lips, her hips jerking from his grip. Trent went absolutely still except for the movement of his mouth over her body as he savored the taste and feel of her beneath his tongue. He angled his head until she opened completely for him, surrendering in body as well as spirit. She was here. She was his. And by God, he was going to remind her of everything good between them.

Laura didn't dare open her eyes. She knew what she would see. Her husband's mouth where only her own fingers had been for so long. His tongue traced over her swollen sex and an urgency built inside of her. Finally she looked down at him.

The sight of his mouth on her was more powerful than she could have imagined. His hands spanned her hips, holding her in place on the edge of the counter. One of her calves was draped over one of his strong, wide shoulders. And his mouth moved, sliding through her heat and drawing out her pleasure.

She threaded a hand through his hair.

He looked up, their eyes meeting as he pressed his lips again to her most swollen heat. His gaze locked on hers, he traced his tongue over the swollen core of her body. A hot, possessive pleasure swept over her as he slipped one finger inside her, teasing her with the lightest friction while his tongue drove her wild. She fisted her hand in his hair, rocking against his mouth, her release there, just there. She closed her eyes, dropping her head back, and let the pleasure come, hard and fast through everything that she was until she thought she'd come apart in his arms.

Pleasure still shuddered through her when he carried her to the bed. His skin was slick with sweat. He laid her down on the bed, needing just to feel her with him, but she smiled and urged him onto his back.

Everything felt right and good and *real* between them. As though their separation had been nothing more than a nightmare, still lingering, still trying to crawl into the bed with them.

Feeling mischievous, she crawled into his lap. Bracing her hands against him, he smiled up at her in the dim light, his eyes dark and serious in the shadows. She arched against him, the apex of her heat brushing against the hair on his thighs. The sharp scrape of pleasure at her core made her body melt with new arousal.

He made a sound deep in his throat and it rumbled through his chest. His palms skimmed her thighs, coming to rest on her hips. They were twined together, already naked. A slight shift of her hips and he would be inside her warm, slick heat.

He tried to lift her hips but she arched away from him. He scowled. "Games, Laura?"

"Now it's my turn."

His throat moved as he swallowed, his body tense and oh so ready. "So what do I have to do?"

Her laugh was husky and sensual. Throaty and filled with feminine power. He'd always loved that about his wife. He loved how they'd grown together, learning to pleasure each other's bodies. He could still remember the first time they'd made love. It was a hot, sultry night. He'd brought sleeping bags for the back of his truck. Somehow, he'd made her come that night and he'd gotten hooked on watching her. He loved seeing her lips part, her breath come in quick, harsh gasps.

He'd loved watching her come earlier. She'd been spread open and gorgeous and when her orgasm had spilled across his lips, his fingers, he'd damn near exploded without a single touch to his cock.

Now? Now she rose naked above his body and Trent was lost in a sea of memories that mixed potently with the reality of her touch.

Her hips filled his palms but he didn't try to guide her to his cock. He wanted to let her take the lead.

They'd played this game before. So many times. He loved letting her have her way with him. There was something so beautiful in the way her body rose over his, the way her sweet sex slid down onto his erection.

This was everything that was right between them. Everything that had not been twisted and ruined by the war. She dipped her hips lower and he held his breath in anticipation. Waiting for that first caress of her sex against his cock.

There. Smooth, warm silk spread over his erection, embracing him gently as she slid against his length, not yet taking him in. Her lips parted, her eyes closed. Her gasp was pure pleasure.

She was still his. Her heart knew it. Her body knew it.

She shifted again, slipping her slick, wet heat against his erection, caressing him, teasing him. His eyes shot open the moment she nudged him closer, until his cock was poised at the opening of her sex.

He clung desperately to the ability to think as she twisted her hips on the tip of his cock.

His breath lodged in his throat as she slid the barest fraction of a movement, sucking the tip inside her, teasing him with the warmest, wettest heat. He clenched his fingers into her hips and her answering gasp rocked his world.

Another movement and she slid slowly, fully onto him, taking everything deep, deep inside her.

This was more than just sex. This was more than arousal or a quick screw.

This was coming home. This was coming back to the place where he belonged. His wife's loving embrace. His wife's beautiful pleasure as she lifted her hips from his before sliding down his length once more.

He let her control the pace. Let her take her own pleasure from him. Because watching desire paint her features and slick over her skin was its own reward. Her nails dug into his chest as she rode him, her gasps coming quick and fast and matching her pace.

He gripped her hips as she rocked against him, drawing out the sweetest pleasure, the harshest pain. He opened his mouth to speak but no words could break past the powerful lump lodged in his throat.

He rode the wave of loving her as long as he could, until she trembled and exploded and vibrated in his arms once more.

He rolled them over, lifting her legs around his hips and sinking so, so deep inside her. Her hair spread out on the pillow, framing her in a soft, golden halo. Her body vibrated beneath his, the wave of her orgasm riding over his cock as he surrendered to the darkest need and drove home.

Afterward, he rested his forehead against hers and the damp sting of tears coated his cheek. He would never know if they'd been his or hers.

Chapter Nineteen

Somebody got lucky last night." Nicole looked up from where she was cracking open eggs.

Laura's face heated as she herded the kids into Jen's living room, armed with snacks, games, and crayons. Somehow she doubted they were going to be satisfied with anything less than power tools but she was still hoping they'd opt for a safer distraction.

Ethan was convinced he was helping Daddy build the deck, as he called it.

The kids raced to the back porch where Trent was already powwowing with Carponti. Laura busied herself near the stove, flipping pancakes to add to the already massive stack on the center island.

"None of your business," Laura said with a smile.

Jen walked into the kitchen and Laura knew instantly that something was wrong. "Whoa. What happened?"

"Nothing. I just didn't sleep well last night," she said, more sharply than usual.

Laura glanced at Nicole, who shrugged. Walking over to stand next to Jen, Laura put a hand on her shoulder. "You okay?"

Jen's movements were jerky as she flipped the next pancake on the griddle. There were dark circles under her eyes, and they were so prominent that concealer wasn't doing much to hide them.

Silence fell over the kitchen like a shroud. And Laura felt a tiny curdle of panic take hold in her belly.

"Jen?" She dared to reach for her friend, her hand gentle on her shoulder. Fear clutched at her, twisting in her belly like a toxic, living thing. "Are...are you sick again?"

The last pancake came off the griddle and Jen set the spatula down, her eyes fixed on the black cooktop of the stove.

Her bottom lip trembled and the dam broke.

"Where the hell is the gimp?" Carponti asked, standing on the back porch, holding a stainless steel coffee mug.

"Haven't seen him yet," Trent said, eyeing the cup of coffee enviously.

"You look like you had a hell of a night," Carponti said. "Your wife finally take your dick off the no-contact order?"

Trent laughed. "Something like that." He cleared his throat. "Things are going good." Too good. A goodness that he feared would slip through his fingers no matter how tightly he held on to it.

Nicole stepped onto the back porch, her expression somber. "Shane's upstairs. Go talk to him."

"What's wrong?" Carponti asked.

"Just go. He needs you both right now. And no smart-ass remarks."

Trent was up the stairs in an instant, Carponti right behind him.

They found Shane sitting on the edge of his bed. He was bent forward, his elbows on his knees.

Never in all the years he'd known the man had Trent

seen him look so bleak, so drained of hope. His mouth was pressed flat, his eyes damp.

"Oh shit," Carponti whispered, for once serious.

Fear slithered in, dragging the c-word back with it. Jen was a survivor. She was young.

She'd sacrificed one breast to beat the cancer that had ravaged her body. It couldn't be back. Not now. Not so soon after she and Shane had found each other.

They stood in simple, heavy silence. It was a long moment before Shane shifted, dragging his hand over his mouth. The words, when he spoke, came from a voice ravaged and raw.

"Jen's pregnant."

The air shifted around them. The news wasn't so dark after all. But based on Shane's reaction, it was clearly still terrifying.

Trent searched for anything to say that would ease the ragged grief in his friend's voice.

"So," Carponti said slowly, "your sperm are experts at escape and evasion, huh?"

Shane's expression broke, and he gave a sharp laugh that sounded suspiciously like a sob. Trent shook his head and elbowed Carponti in the ribs.

"Ow!" he rubbed his side. "What the hell was that for? It's true, isn't it? How the hell else do you explain how they made it past the vasectomy?"

Shane scrubbed his hands over his face. "I don't know." His voice was pained.

But the tension had snapped, broken a little beneath the irreverence of Carponti's joke. Trent stepped into the room, leaning on the high dresser.

"This is not a good thing, is it?" He had no idea if getting pregnant after breast cancer was advisable. Judging by Shane's expression and obvious distress, it was not.

"No, it's not a fucking good thing," Shane snapped, rubbing his hand roughly over the back of his neck. "I'm freaked the hell out about her cancer coming back and she's busy flipping through baby books." Shane scrubbed his hands over his face.

"Wait. She wanted this?" Carponti said, stepping in and leaning against the open doorway.

"Yeah. She was really upset with me about the vasectomy. I thought we'd taken care of everything. I—fuck."

"Guess your dick overruled you, huh?" Carponti said.

"Not funny."

"It's a little funny. You can picture your sperm in full body armor, trying to batter their little way through the gap to capture the flag—er, egg." Carponti frowned. "I am going to have to go look up exactly how a vasectomy fails now. Call it my morbid curiosity." He turned his attention back to Shane, his expression suddenly sober. "Jen's a nurse. She wouldn't do this if she thought it would make her sick, would she?"

Shane's expression darkened again. "I love that woman so much it terrifies me. And I refuse to risk her life to have a baby. Pregnancy could kill her. The cancer could come back and she wouldn't be able to have chemo or anything." His voice thickened and he cleared his throat roughly.

His voice broke and he covered his face in his hands, scrubbing roughly.

Trent had never faced a burden like this one. Laura's pregnancies had been healthy and normal, except for the first one. The first time she had gotten pregnant, she miscarried. He still remembered finding her sobbing on the bathroom floor after they'd come home from the doctor's office.

He'd picked her up and carried her to their bed, then he'd held her until the pain medicine kicked in and she fell asleep. He'd held her until the pain had stopped. Until she'd accepted that this baby wasn't meant to be. That they could try again. Soon after, she had wanted to try again, even though she knew he was leaving for war and she would need to go through the pregnancy alone.

He'd loved her strength. He'd loved her determination to shove the grief of that first pregnancy behind her. He remembered lying there that first night in their new home, her fingers dancing over his where he'd rested his palm on her belly.

But never had he worried that one of his wife's pregnancies might kill her.

"Shane?"

Everyone turned at Jen's quiet voice. She'd snuck upstairs, padding quietly up the steps without anyone hearing her.

Shane said nothing. He simply straightened and opened his arms. Jen walked into his embrace, and he wrapped his arms tight around her waist, resting his head against her belly.

"I'm afraid," he whispered as Carponti and Trent left the room.

"Me, too."

Trent walked downstairs, followed by an unusually silent Carponti. Laura looked up from where she stood near the island. He said nothing, merely went to her, wrapping his arms around her and holding her close. He'd come so damn close to losing her. He had her back. For this moment and hopefully a hundred thousand more, he had her back. He kissed her forehead and pulled her close, unable to think of ever letting her go.

"This is definitely not a death sentence," Nicole said after a while.

Laura was serving the kids breakfast on the back porch while the adults ate in the kitchen, where they could talk privately while keeping an eye on Ethan and Emma through the sliding glass door. Shane and Jen had not come downstairs yet. Almost an hour had passed and the house was eerily silent. Even the kids had picked up on the fact that something was wrong.

"I take it you've been asking Dr. Google," Carponti said, munching on a piece of scorched bacon.

"Of course. Look." Nicole held her phone out. "There have been huge advances in this field. And a recent clinical trial showed that there was no greater risk of cancer for pregnant women who have had it and those who haven't."

"Then what is Shane afraid of?" Carponti asked.

"The risk," Trent said quietly. "The risk that he's going to lose her." He glanced at his wife out on the back porch, scooping yogurt onto the kids' plates. "It's nothing he can control."

Carponti smiled but it was a distant and unfocused expression. Finally he glanced at his wife, his expression suddenly serious. "You're not allowed to get cancer, okay? And no dying, either."

Nicole offered a strangled laugh and kissed the top of his head in a quiet, intimate gesture. Nicole and Carponti were both so gruff and sarcastic, but they were deeply committed to each other. After everything Carponti had gone through, after surviving the war and his injuries, their bond remained strong.

Strangely, he wasn't jealous. Laura stepped back through the sliding glass door and put the yogurt back in the fridge.

"They still haven't come down?"

Trent shook his head. "You don't think they're going to cancel the wedding?"

Laura smiled sadly. "No. They'll figure this out. Maybe we should go out there and get started before it warms up?"

"That's a good idea. Shane's probably going to need therapy to get through this one. Maybe we should call the chaplain?" Carponti asked.

"He'll be fine," Trent said. "Think you can wield a hammer today without hitting yourself?"

"Ha ha fuck you ha ha." Nicole elbowed her husband in the ribs. "What? The kids can't hear me."

Shaking her head, she pulled him to his feet and led him onto the back porch and out to the building project. Trent turned to look at Laura, who was struggling to keep herself busy.

"You okay?" he asked softly.

She turned away, busying herself with the breakfast dishes. "Yeah."

"Hey?" He stepped in front of her, gently grasping her shoulders. She seemed so small and fragile. Damaged and wary. "Talk to me?"

The weight of that single question bore down on him. He was asking her for something he'd been unable to give her. But he hoped that maybe, maybe she would trust him enough to lay her burdens on his shoulders for once. She'd been carrying all of his for so long.

She looked up at him, her gaze filled with anxiety. She smiled tremulously and lifted one hand, sliding one finger over the edge of his glasses. "You were gone when she was sick," she whispered. Her voice was thick. Heavy. "Ethan was just a baby and I was pregnant with Emma." She blinked rapidly and he reached out, cradling her neck, offering his silent support. "I spent a lot of nights on her couch. Helping her to the bathroom when she was too sick to walk." Her voice cracked a little beneath the memory. "She was not a good patient."

Trent urged her closer and she stepped into his embrace, resting her cheek against the scars on his. He cradled her face, felt the wetness on her cheeks and wished he could take the fear from her. Of all the things in life he feared, cancer had never been one of them. He had no idea what Laura had gone through with Jen.

"I don't want to lose her," she whispered.

Trent pressed his lips to the top of her head. "You won't." But his promise felt empty and hollow and beyond the scope of things he could control.

It was a long time before Jen stepped onto the back porch, followed closely by Shane.

All work came to an abrupt, anxious halt. Shane stood behind his fiancé, his hands framing her shoulders, his expression tight. No, they hadn't figured this out yet. Her eyes were no longer rimmed with red, her face was no longer swollen from crying, but she watched him worriedly as he moved toward Trent and Carponti.

Laura hung the hammer she'd been using in her tool belt and waited as Jen descended the steps. Her friend put on a brave smile. "I'm not sick," she said. "I'm pregnant."

Laura laughed and pulled her into a hug. "I hope you don't have morning sickness as bad as I did with Emma. It was awful."

Nicole wrapped her arms around them both, joining the group hug. "Guess this means the next shower we do is a baby shower."

Jen laughed with her friends as Shane moved around them to join Trent and Carponti, who were standing with a plank propped between them.

"At least we don't have to get you a different dress," Laura said. "Your boobs won't swell that much in two weeks."

"Boob. Singular."

Nicole laughed. "Guess we're going to have to get you a pregnancy prosthetic. Do they make ones for that?"

Jen offered a horrified laugh. "I'm sure we can figure something out."

"When do you go to the doctor's?"

"I have to see someone who specializes in cancer in pregnant women."

"But you're in remission," Nicole said.

"And I have been given a direct order to stay that way," she said, glancing at Shane. A warm smile played over her lips. "But we're going to take it cautious and slow."

"Is the big guy ready to start drinking?"

Jen smiled softly at Laura's question. "He's thought about it."

Laura pulled her gloves back on. "Okay then, we have a construction project to finish because I need to go to the store to find draperies for this thing. I swear, if I end up having to sew curtains…"

Chapter Twenty

"Ethan, put the hamster away."

"Dad-dy!"

"Ethan, your mother told you to get in the tub."

"But Daddy, we haven't gotten to play with the hamsters all day!"

Trent crouched down to his son's level, fully aware that he was being glared at by both a six-year-old human and a hamster that was surely one of the four horsemen of the Apocalypse. "Ethan, I'm not even going to argue about this," he said, fighting the urge to threaten to donate the hamster to Goodwill. "Put the hamster away and get in the tub."

Trent was tired and every bone in his body ached from the day's work. It hadn't been nearly as backbreaking as patrolling on foot in full body armor in the middle of Baghdad in August, but his body was used to those things. It wasn't so used to climbing and hammering.

Ethan sighed dramatically and stomped off. Trent stretched and walked into the kitchen, scanning the fridge and trying to decide what to prepare for an evening snack.

They'd barbecued at Shane and Jen's house, so the kids wouldn't need to eat again before they were tucked into bed.

Judging from the sounds coming from the bathroom, that might be a while. His son seemed to be trying to set a new record for tantrums.

He gathered a few stray dishes and then started up the dishwasher, listening to the distant sounds of his wife preparing to bathe his children. He pulled out lunch meat for sandwiches, figuring they would be an easy dinner before everyone collapsed from exhaustion. It was a good exhaustion.

Suddenly a naked little boy streaked out of the bathroom and ran down the hallway, ducking into one of the bedrooms.

"Ethan?" Laura called out to him. "Trent, can you grab him for me? He still needs to take his bath!" Her voice was tired but not stressed.

Following Ethan's giggles, Trent went off in search of his son.

His son.

His heart tightened. There were other sons whose daddies weren't coming home. And some of them weren't coming home because of decisions Trent had made. He'd made his choice when he'd pledged to become a soldier. He'd never imagined the weight of the ghosts that would one day haunt him.

He walked into Ethan's room and the stone in his chest softened a little more. He loved how Laura had made it into a classic little boy's room—midnight blue with red furniture. She'd given their son his own space. Room to be a little boy, instead of being taken over by his baby sister.

"Ethan?"

The giggling came from under the bed and Trent knelt down to peer beneath it. Ethan was wedged into the far corner, as far away as he could get from Trent's reach. Suddenly he was struck with the vision of another child, tucked beneath a bed like this one, but cringing instead of laughing.

The flashback punched him in the gut, catching him off guard as he was suddenly transported to another room in a dirty, bombed-out house.

"I escaped, Daddy. You can't reach me!"

Trent sucked in a hard breath and shook himself mentally. He was home. His kids were safe.

He smiled and reached beneath the bed. He snagged a little foot and gave it a tug. Ethan giggled and kicked but Trent managed to drag the naked boy out from under the bed.

Ethan squealed as Trent carried him from the bedroom by his foot. He rounded the corner to the bathroom, his son hanging upside down in front of him, laughing hysterically.

Laura was washing Emma's face when Trent walked into the bathroom. She flashed him a grateful smile as their son continued to squeal and squirm.

Her smile touched his soul. "I caught this for you. I think it's a rare breed of naked fish."

"I'm not a fish, Daddy!"

Ethan hung over Trent's forearm, giggling like mad and looking at his father with absolute adoration in his eyes. Like Trent wasn't a complete stranger. Trent stopped suddenly, overcome with the realization that his son actually loved him, the father who'd been absent for almost his entire life. He clutched Ethan to him and inhaled the warm scent of his son.

Ethan wrapped his arms around Trent's neck and his little hand patted his father's shoulder. "Don't be sad, Daddy. Mommy will make everything all right."

Trent swallowed and blinked rapidly. What could he say? He set Ethan down and knelt down to the boy's level. "Yeah. Mommy always makes things all right."

Ethan's little black-haired head nodded and he wrapped his hand around Trent's index finger, looking at Trent like he was some kind of hero. It struck Trent how small and innocent his son—his children—were. Trent wasn't a hero. He rubbed his eyes beneath his glasses and swallowed. Again. He sucked in a hard breath, trying to keep the weight that settled on his chest from crushing his lungs. He needed to step back, needed to get outside.

A little hand pushed on his shoulder. "Daddy?" It was his daughter's voice.

He opened his eyes, only now realizing that he'd squeezed them shut. He stared into little Emma's golden eyes. He marveled again about how much she looked like a miniature version of Laura. "I love you, Daddy."

His vision blurred, and he pulled his daughter and son close. Their tiny arms came around him, their little hands so small on his back. They were so fragile. Vulnerable. But they were safe. There were no bombs for his children. No men with guns to steal their dreams or send them down a dirt-strewn alley as human shields.

He stayed absolutely still and drank in their innocence, so completely grateful that they'd had Laura to raise them well. She had done that and so much more.

Alone.

The floor creaked and Trent looked up to see Laura step into the hallway. Her eyes were dark and filled with worry as she looked down at him holding their kids.

"Mommy, Daddy's sad. Will you make him feel better?"

Trent smiled as his gaze met his wife's. He couldn't help it. His son's innocent question had sent his mind to a less than innocent place. Laura blushed and Trent saw that he wasn't the only one with a wandering mind.

"Daddy will be fine. Come on. Ethan, it's time to wash up."

"Daddy, will you read to me?" Emma asked. She thrust a book with a disgruntled cat on the cover.

He tipped the book back so he could read the cover. "Bad Kitty Gets a Bath?"

Emma nodded. "Bad Kitty is a bad, bad kitty," she said solemnly. "She hates taking baths."

He glanced at Laura, who stood watching from the door. There was a look of easy contentment on her face, as though tonight were just another normal night. As though this wasn't the first time he had sat and done something so blessedly normal as read his children a bedtime story.

"Sure."

Ethan washed in record time, joining them on Emma's bed. Laura moved a blanket and sat on the opposite side of Emma. Ethan was pressed to Trent's other side and Emma nestled between her mother and father. For once, there was no fighting. Only quiet snuggles at the end of a long day.

He paused for a moment, savoring the intensity of the love bursting inside him. This. This was what he'd missed out on.

He released a quiet breath. Then opened the book.

"This is how Kitty cleans herself," he read. A smile spread across his face as he continued reading about how Kitty licked and licked and licked herself clean. Emma giggled when he got to the suit of armor needed for the bath.

The sound warmed something inside of him. He glanced over at Laura, his throat suddenly thick. She met his gaze as she stroked one hand over Emma's head. "I think it's time for bed, guys," she said gently.

For once, they didn't argue. Emma snuggled down in her blankets and Trent leaned down, kissing the top of her head. "Night night, Daddy," she whispered sleepily.

"Night night, baby girl."

He followed Laura into Ethan's room. Their son lay on his back, and his arms went tight around his mother's neck. "Night, Mommy."

"Night, sweetheart." Laura kissed him on his forehead, then stepped back to give Trent some room.

Ethan's arms came around his neck and squeezed tight. "I love you, Daddy."

"I love you, too." He leaned back, brushing Ethan's hair out of his face. He clicked off the light and closed the door.

And stood in the hallway for a long moment with his wife, unsettled by the power of his own emotions.

He loved this woman. This woman who gasped his name when his fingers slid through her hair. This woman whose fingers traced down his ribs to dig into the small of his back as he walked her backward toward their bedroom.

Trent traced her body with his hands until she arched against him. He cradled her face in his palms, stroking his thumbs over her cheeks. Slowly he lowered his lips to hers, teasing, tasting. He traced his tongue over her bottom lip and savored the shiver that ran through her and into him.

He wanted to hear his name on her lips when he teased her nipples between his teeth, when he kissed her swollen flesh and made her squirm with his tongue. He wanted to look in her eyes as she came apart in his arms.

She met his gaze and an urgency burned between them, all golden fire and brilliant desire.

"Laura." Her name was a whisper on his lips, a hesitant question.

She surprised him. She didn't look away. She didn't tremble or hesitate. Her hands slipped up his chest, twining with his arms until her fingers framed his cheeks. "I want this." She swallowed, then met his gaze once more. "I want you. I've always wanted you."

Triumph soared within him and he kissed her, drowning in the taste and touch and feel of his wife. He breathed her in, devoured her, claiming her with every ounce of passion and pain he carried inside him.

The lifetime he'd lived before the war seemed like it had

happened to someone else. There were two chapters of his existence: before the war and after. But there was one constant, one person who had always helped him. One person who kept the light in his soul from snuffing out beneath the darkness of war and pain and death.

As long as his wife was in the world, waiting for him, loving him, he had the strength, the will to go on. To come home, back to her.

Now, he guided her into their room and lowered her to their bed. He slid her top off her shoulders, revealing her soft skin, then moved her pants down, down, over her hips, dragging her panties with them until she was bare and exposed and swollen, then tugged until she straddled his lap, her entire body exposed for his every whim. He looked up into her eyes while he slipped his fingers over her sensitive skin. Her nipples pearled beneath his thumbs and he pinched her lightly, reveling in her quick gasp.

He looked up at her as she straddled him, loving the feel of her body against his. Slowly, she dragged her nails from the twisting sinew of his forearms down, lower down his sides. He shuddered beneath her touch and a thrill of desire shot straight through him.

"God but I love your chest." She leaned forward and pressed a tender kiss on the scar over his heart. He flinched as she dragged her tongue over the jagged red starburst that should have killed him. She paused, and kissed the center of the scar. "All of you," she whispered.

His body tightened beneath hers and she shifted, sliding against his erection. He gasped and arched, trying to tug his hands out of his shirt. She wiggled in his lap until he was poised at the very center of her, her most intimate flesh just out of his reach.

"Not fair." His voice was a grunt. But when he tried to thrust deep, she lifted her hips.

He swallowed and his eyes narrowed in the dim bedroom light. She traced her thumb back and forth over the scar on his chest. "It's just a scar, Laura."

She shook her head. "It almost took you from me," she whispered.

"But it didn't."

She leaned down, tracing her tongue over the scar. Cold fire trailed over his skin as she blew on it and he shivered with barely restrained need.

In a single moment, he pulled his hands free and dug them into her hips, rolling her over until she was beneath him, and he pushed fully, deeply inside her. She shivered and wrapped her legs tightly around his hips even as she tugged him down, claiming his mouth.

She pressed her lips to his heart once more. "I'm glad you came home," she whispered.

Slowly, he began to move, sinking deep inside her warm, welcoming embrace, his breath a groan as their pleasure built. A riot built inside her as she buried her face in his neck and bit back the passion that threatened to overwhelm her.

And when her release came, it was so intense, so full of pleasure and passion and hope, it stunned her. But it was the feel of her husband's cheek pressed against hers in the aftermath of their loving that touched her soul.

In the hazy aftermath, they lay together, wrapped in the comforter on their bed. She shifted to study him in the dusky light. She leaned toward him and traced her index finger over the pale scar that lined his jaw.

"What?" he whispered.

"Tell me more about how you got this one."

He tensed at her question and a quick bolt of fear shot through her that he would walk away, shutting her out like he had done before. Her hand rested on his shoulder, her fingertips pressed to his pulse. She felt his breath catch, his body tighten.

It was a long time before he spoke.

"Our Bradley got hit by a deeply buried IED outside Basra." He sucked in a deep breath. His palm on her back tensed, his fingers digging into her back with the memory. "I got bounced out of the commander's seat and knocked into my driver." He closed his eyes and Laura's heart broke for the pain in his voice. "I cut my jaw on the manual turret control."

His brow knit together. He looked like he'd cracked the seal on a thousand bad memories and might never be able to banish them. She slid her fingers up to cup his jaw, tracing the scar once more. What could she say to that? What were the right words to say when he'd lived through something she could not even imagine. She pressed her lips to his heart. "I'm glad you were okay."

He turned his face and kissed her forehead quickly. His breathing slowed but his words remained tight. "My gunner died that day."

His Adam's apple bobbed beneath her fingers where they'd drifted down to rest on his throat. "I'm sorry, Trent."

He scrubbed his hand over his mouth. But he didn't pull away. Laura didn't dare move, afraid to break the moment and leave him alone and vulnerable. "Garanji was a good kid. His parents immigrated to the U.S. from Iran. He had a little sister, and he was always worried she was going to date an American boy instead of an Iranian." He grinned. "One of my platoon sergeants used to give him so much shit."

"Iaconelli?"

"Yeah. Reza's Iranian, too. Part, anyway." Trent's eyes shimmered and reflected the glow from the fading sun. "He was pretty busted up when Garanji died." He cleared his throat. "We all were."

She didn't say anything. What could she say? She'd been

crying about being alone while Trent had been burying young soldiers in far off corners of the globe.

She suddenly felt selfish and petty, ashamed that she hadn't understood—hadn't known—the full story behind a simple scar on her husband's body.

She closed her eyes. He'd chosen this, she reminded herself. He'd chosen not to share the roughest facts of his deployed life with her. What he'd gone through was hard but he hadn't needed to walk that road alone.

She could never do what he did. His life was so different from hers, and her daily stresses and worries suddenly seemed so trivial.

They lay together in silence. Neither of them moved for a long time.

He shifted then, a rustle of fabric in the quiet evening. He pulled his arms around her and drew her closer. "Thank you," he whispered.

"What are you thanking me for?" She found the words, but they barely slid past her lips.

He leaned closer, and their mouths were just a hint apart. His breath brushed against her lips. "For giving us a second chance."

She wanted to speak. Wanted to tell him about everything she was feeling—her love, her fear, her uncertainty— but his lips pressed against hers, hesitant and questioning. She tipped her head and opened her mouth beneath his. His tongue stroked hers and with that simple touch, brilliant heat unfurled inside her.

His fingers pressed into her hair and angled her head so that their mouths could join more completely. She gasped as his jaw scraped against hers and need sparked between her thighs.

This was Trent. Trent who kissed her. Trent who made her feel this languid heat inside her. Trent who was holding her now, making love to her with his mouth, making her crazy—one slow, agonizing kiss at a time. She did the only thing a woman who loved a man could do.

She surrendered to the need and the heat and the joy and kissed him back.

Chapter Twenty-One

Laura walked into the headquarters on Monday sore and stiff and achingly happy for the first time in a long time. She was almost able to believe that they would make it, that things between them would continue to get better. That they were somehow stronger now than they'd been a few weeks before.

But the weight of the court-martial hung around her shoulders, a sobering reminder that just as things were starting to turn around in her marriage, they might be ripped apart once more.

She swallowed hard, trying to ignore the resurgent fear that squeezed around her heart.

She could lose him again. Just when she'd finally gotten him back.

Trent was supposed to meet her there in a few minutes. They were supposed to sit down with Patrick and go over the last bit of her testimony before the hearing in a few days. She was nervous. So much depended on the officers in that hearing having more faith in her husband than she'd had in him.

She walked down the hall toward her office, lost in thought. She rounded the corner and stopped short, nearly colliding with Lieutenant Randall.

Instantly, she took a step backward, needing space between herself and a thick-necked man who radiated violence. "What the hell did you say to my wife," he spat.

"Good morning, lieutenant," she said, emphasizing his rank.

"Don't 'good morning' me," he said. "What the fuck did you say to my wife?"

She took another step back, hating herself for backing down in the face of his anger. But then again, she wasn't an idiot. He was a stocky man and if he chose to lose his damn mind and take a swing at her, it wasn't going to be because she was an idiot and refused to back away.

"You mean the wife that you cheated on and gave an STD to? That wife?" Laura asked.

"She left me. She fucking left me." He paced the small space like a caged thing.

Laura was grateful for the sounds of soldiers arriving for work in the ops office.

"And how exactly is that my fault?" she asked.

"She said you talked to her." He rounded on her. "That you made her feel bad for fucking lying about your piece of shit husband." A deep flush crawled up Randall's neck, and he ground his teeth until she thought his jaw might fracture from the pressure. "Bitch, you ruined everything. Just like your husband. Always ruining a good thing," he ground out.

"My husband is a better man than you'll ever be," Laura said quietly. "Now get the hell away from me."

Randall stared down at her and for a flicker of a moment she thought he might actually hit her. Laura opened her mouth to speak but before she could get any words out Randall was yanked backward, slammed up against the wall. There was a sudden commotion as Trent pressed his elbow to Randall's throat, twisted his fist in the man's collar. "Watch your mouth around my wife, you little shit."

"Trent, I'm thinking this is not a good way to get the

charges dropped," Patrick said lightly, glancing over his shoulder as a full colonel Laura didn't recognize stepped out of the conference room. "I'm sure officers at the hearing would much rather see you two discussing your differences of opinion in a more calm, loving way."

Trent's nostrils flared. For a moment, Laura thought she saw his elbow press harder into Randall's skin.

He released his grip and the LT coughed, rubbing his throat.

"Apologize to my wife," Trent said, his words clipped.

"Sorry, ma'am."

"Stay the fuck away from my family," Trent hissed. He released him and Randall stalked off, his expression a hard mask of fury.

Patrick grabbed Trent when he made to follow Randall down the hall. "Unless you want to get deeply acquainted with prison sex, keep your damn hands off him."

Trent shrugged Patrick off, irritation vibrating from him in waves. "Got it."

Laura turned, her fingers twining with his, squeezing gently. She smiled up at him, painfully aware of the strength and power of this man. It had twisted up her insides to see evidence of what he was capable of right in front of her. Her hand trembled when he squeezed it back.

"Are you okay?" His voice grated.

"Yes." He couldn't spend the rest of the day this angry. It was bound to go badly for him.

She took a single step closer. Her lips curled into a soft smile. "That was, um," she glanced around, "really sexy."

His expression faltered. "What was?"

She slipped her arms around his waist, not caring that they were in the middle of the hallway. "You threatening him to protect me. I don't usually go for the whole Cro-Magnon man thing. But I liked it."

"Yeah?"

"Yeah." She flicked her tongue over her bottom lip, followed by a quick scrape of her teeth. "It's lunchtime."

"It's not even close to lunchtime." Trent raised both eyebrows, his jaw tight. She loved that she could still get to him, still see that desire light up his eyes. "What did you have in mind?"

"I was thinking we could sneak out to Belton Dam."

"That might be risky in the middle of the day. There are Blackhawks flying around." His voice sounded harsh. Tight. Erotic.

"When did that ever matter before?"

Trent walked into the ops office. Things were good with Laura. Too good.

He couldn't let himself relax. Couldn't allow the fantasy that they might actually have a chance at beating this thing take hold. There were a few more days until the hearing that would decide his fate, but now, knowing that Randall had lost a key piece of his defense by alienating his wife?

Trent felt hopeful for the first time in a long time.

He was a few minutes early and the office was still empty from lunch. Iaconelli, though, sat at his desk. His shoulders were slumped, his elbows resting on his knees.

"Hey," Trent said, walking over. "You okay?"

Iaconelli looked up, his eyes bleak. There was a Gatorade bottle in one hand that probably didn't have Gatorade in it. He swayed a little in his chair. "Story." He swallowed a long pull from the bottle. "We lost Story."

Trent's skin went cold. He sank into a chair next to Iaconelli. Took the proffered bottle and took a long pull off it himself. The straight vodka burned all the way down and made his eyes water.

At least that's what he told himself.

* * *

The bedroom was pitch black but for the light from the television. Trent laid in bed, the bottle held loosely in one hand, staring unseeing at the screen. The blankets were tangled around his legs. He hadn't slept.

"Sir, what is it going to take for me to get new body armor? It screws with the guys' heads to wear bloody gear."

Trent looked up from cleaning his weapon. His own body armor had blood near the groin protector. "Well, I could give the logistics guy a hand job, see if that helps?"

"It might," Story said, *his face twisted into a concerned frown.* "Sir, you okay?"

"Laura is leaving me."

Story closed the door then and sat across from him. "That sucks." *He paused.* "I'm sorry."

"How do I fix this? How do I get her to understand that I have to be here?"

Story shook his head. "It doesn't work that way. The old saying that if the army wanted you to have a family, it would have issued you one . . . it's a cliché but it's true. And you've chosen the army a hell of a lot more than you've chosen her lately."

Trent tossed his glasses on the desk, staring at the stark words on the divorce papers in front of him. Reality squeezed around his heart, cutting off his air.

He'd done this. He'd ruined everything with his wife. He'd left her alone to raise the kids, to run their home.

"The wives never understand why we have to go," Story said quietly. *"Rebecca won't leave me but we don't have a real marriage. You had that with Laura."*

Trent heard what his friend hadn't said. You fucked that up.

"I need to go home," he said, looking at his first sergeant.

Story nodded. "Well, that's about to get a lot easier. We

have an appointment with the colonel and sergeant major in an hour." He paused. "We're getting fired."

He shook his head, trying to shake off the memory. Trying to shut down the pain. But it ripped through him, tearing and slashing and slicing. The alcohol did nothing to numb it. Trent took a long pull off the bottle, his throat numb, the rest of his soul not following fast enough. He wanted his heart to stop. Anything to stop the searing pain that threatened to consume him. He stared into the darkness.

He remembered bits and pieces, flashes. Horrible, dark thoughts. An explosion of glass and violence.

Grief filled him. Smothered him.

He started to rise, but her arms tightened around his waist.

He looked down.

He hadn't realized she was sitting with him, his body tucked against her. Warm wetness soaked his thin t-shirt. They were not her tears. He closed his eyes, unable to look at her, unable to pull away, to keep her from seeing this side of him. This terrible grief that made him want to do violence, to rush back to the war and exact vengeance for his friend's death.

Laura's fingers tightened on his waist. He buried his face in her neck and let the grief tear from him.

No words could encompass the emotions surging through his soul. She wrapped him in her arms and simply held him. In the silence, he wept. For every lost soldier. For Story. For Doc. For Ripley and Bull. For Naseem, his terp who'd lost his whole family to Saddam. For Garanji.

He didn't speak. He couldn't. But finally, he wept for the friend he'd lost. And this time, Laura held him when he shattered.

It was a long time before he spoke, his speech slurred. "Did you know that Story saved my life?" he whispered into the darkness.

"No," she said softly.

"It was that day back in '04." He breathed deeply, the sound echoing in his ears. He felt empty, hollowed out. "When I got blown up, he dragged me out of the fight. He thought I was dead, too." He grunted. "We were so inexperienced back in '04. The round got between my body armor and my chest and my heart stopped on impact."

"I'll never forget what it felt like to hear that you'd been killed," she whispered. "It was like the world dropped from underneath me." Her fingers drew gently down his chest. "I didn't know how I was going to go on with my life without you out there in the world somewhere."

Slowly the force of his grief ebbed, no more a tempest but a trickle. He didn't move, he couldn't. And his wife, his wife was still there.

"You stayed with me," Trent murmured, his voice sore. He cradled her face in his hands.

She sniffed, her hands fluttering over his chest, like she didn't know what to do with them. He lowered his forehead to hers, tears leaking out from behind his closed eyes once more. She simply wrapped her arms around his neck, pressing her body to his.

He paused before speaking again, and when he did it was a whisper more powerful than the loudest shout.

"I was wrong . . . so goddamned fucking wrong."

Her arms tightened around his neck. "About what?"

"About the war, the army, fucking everything. Every choice I've made has been wrong. Terribly fucking wrong." He cupped her cheek. "Except the one to come back to you." He lowered his forehead to hers. "I was coming home before I got fired. I was going to figure out how to fix this and then I was going to go back to my boys. But I was wrong about that, too. You're the only thing in the entire world that I've ever gotten right." He ran his fingers over her cheeks. "Regardless of how the hearing turns out, I'm quitting."

"Quitting what?" There was a wariness in her voice. A fear.

"Everything. The army. The war. I want to stay home and be a dad." His brows drew into another frown. "I want to be here for you."

"I'm not asking you to do that." Her voice was thick with emotion. He hated that he was hurting her all over again.

"You should. You should demand the world from me. You deserve so much better than what I've ever given you." He scraped his fingers over her cheek. "I can't give you your husband back and I can't give you back the time I've spent away from you."

He stroked his thumbs over her cheeks until she opened her eyes and looked at him. He needed her to see him, the truth of the man he was. He couldn't hide that from her. Not any more. And the truth wasn't something shiny and new. It was badly damaged. It was flawed and broken.

Trent cradled his wife's face in his palms, savoring the soft feel of her skin beneath his fingertips.

"You would really give it all up?" she asked.

Doubt crept in, whispering around his heart. Could he walk away from his troops and the uniform that he'd worn for so long in exchange for runny noses and muddy shoes and PTA meetings? He closed his eyes and felt the little heads resting on his shoulders when he'd read to them at bedtime.

His arms tightened around her. "How did we get to this point?" he asked, brushing his lips over her forehead.

"A lot of reasons." She closed her eyes, wishing the war hadn't chipped away at the foundation of their marriage. Wishing they hadn't spent so much time apart.

Wishing that things weren't so goddamned fragile between them.

Even at that moment, lying in bed, she felt the cloying, clinging fear that the honeymoon was going to end soon. That the strain and the stress were going to slink back into their bed and start chipping the frail thing building between them.

She pressed her lips to his chest, pushing away the worry and the fear and the doubt and deciding for now that she would lie in her husband's arms and simply be.

He shifted so that he was lying between her thighs, and framed her face in his palms. In the pale light, she looked up at him. His eyes were dark and for once uncovered by his glasses. She lifted her knees, resting them against his sides.

"I know ... I know the court-martial is a large part of how we ended up here." His voice was a serrated blade. Rusty and dangerous. "But maybe ..." He closed his eyes. "Maybe if it forced us together ... to be in the same space ... maybe it's a good thing?"

Her lips twisted into a wry smile. "So we needed a court-martial to push us back together? Seems a little extreme."

He nibbled on the corner of her mouth before lifting his gaze to hers once more. "I don't want to waste this. This isn't about the court-martial for me anymore, Laura. This isn't just about making things easier for the kids." His thumb stroked her temple. "This is about us now. Maybe it always has been."

She blinked rapidly. He opened his mouth but she pressed her index finger to his lips. "You've been a good soldier. You've gone to war. You should have had a loving wife holding down the home front. And I tried to do that for so long." She stroked his face gently between her fingers. "But you crushed me. You left me alone and empty and I just couldn't do it anymore. I never understood when other wives said they couldn't handle the loneliness anymore." She bit her lips together, needing the pain to ground her. To help her get the words exactly right. "I needed to know you still loved me enough to come back to me. I needed something to hold onto. I had nothing but a memory." Her voice broke. "I'm so sorry it wasn't enough. That I wasn't strong enough to keep waiting."

She swiped at her cheeks, refusing to look at him. She swallowed. "I wasn't strong enough to wait for you." She tried to move away. He panicked. She was leaving him. He was going to have to face this world alone, without her.

He reached for her then, pulling her back, dragging her close and holding her with a quiet urgency that spoke all the things he could not say.

"I left you," she whispered.

"I deserved it." He rested his cheek against her head, holding her. "I never deserved your faith in me."

"I lost it, Trent. I wasn't strong enough to hold on."

He captured her left hand in his. Stroked his thumb over her rings. "This isn't about being strong enough, Laura."

"Then what is it? Failure? Dishonesty? What is it that destroyed us?"

He kissed her gently. "We did. I did. Because I forgot that you were my wife. You needed a husband... You needed me. And I haven't been here for a long time."

The hush fell over them again. A pitch black, deep, abiding calm.

"Are you really getting out of the army?" she whispered.

"Yes." There was no ambiguity in his voice. "There's nothing left for me. I can't lie to the boys. I can't tell them they're fighting the good fight. I just can't do it anymore." He cleared his throat. "I have to step aside. Let someone who still cares do this."

"It's not that simple." She shook her head. "The army is part of who you are."

"And it always will be. But you're part of who I am, too."

This was not an argument she wanted to have. She wanted him home with her. She wanted all of this over and done with. But he needed to come to that decision for his own reasons. Not in a moment of grief.

"I'm half a man without you in my life," Trent said after a long moment. "I need you. I need to know you're out there in the world for me to come back to." And at that moment—her mouth beneath his, her fingers brushing the edge of his scar—one more crack was healed, one more wound bandaged.

"I'm afraid, Laura. I'm afraid of what I've become. Of what I've brought into our home." He traced the curve of her cheek with the pad of his thumb. "But I still want another chance."

She closed her eyes and Trent felt his fate hanging by the barest thread. He had no hint of how she felt. He didn't know but he had to try. He'd crossed one too many lines in his life that hadn't been worth it. This one was.

She looked up at him, her eyes shining brightly. "I love you. And it took me all of this to remember that 'I love you' doesn't come with a 'but.' Forgiving someone else is easy. Forgiving yourself?" She brushed her lips against his. "That's much harder." She rubbed her cheek against his. "I can't do that for you. But I can walk with you while you work on it."

He rested his cheek against the top of her head. "I haven't been a good husband. I'm not a good man."

She cupped his cheek. "You're wrong." She offered a watery smile. "Well, you're right about the not-being-a-good-husband thing. But you are a good man. You always have been."

He licked his lips and stroked his thumb over her cheek. He kissed her because he was terrified of losing her again.

Terrified because he'd come so close to destroying the one person in his life worth living for. He'd nearly broken her. He could see that clearly now. And while his faith in the system he'd sacrificed everything for was far from restored, his faith in his wife, in their family, was a little more patched up. And lost himself in the taste and touch and love of his wife.

"Daddy."

Something poked Trent in the soft spot between his shoulder and his chest. He frowned but tried to ignore it, desperate for a few more minutes of sleep.

"Daddy."

The whisper was more urgent now. A little hand on his shoulder, shoving him from the warm nest of blankets and his wife's soft body.

"Hnnngh." He blinked and opened his eyes. Ethan's face blurred then came back into focus. Trent sat up, the concern etched on Ethan's tiny face cutting through the fog of sleep. "What's wrong?"

"Fluffy's missing." His little voice broke.

"Tell him to go back to bed and we'll find Fluffy in the morning," Laura said, her voice thick with sleep. Then she rolled over and instantly went back to sleep. Trent was envious, but he couldn't shake the idea that he might accidentally squish Fluffy as he stumbled to the bathroom in a couple of hours.

He rubbed his eyes before he reached for his glasses, then slid out of bed and crouched down in front of Ethan. "Okay, buddy. Where does Fluffy usually escape to?"

Ethan shrugged and looked lost and helpless and sad, as though he might never see Fluffy again. Trent brushed his hair out of his face. "Okay, well, let's let Mommy sleep and we'll go find him."

"Her, Daddy. Fluffy's a girl."

Trent frowned, wondering why it mattered. At three

in the morning, very little seemed to matter. All that was important at the moment was getting Ethan back to bed.

And, apparently, that involved finding Fluffy. Ethan wrapped his little hand in Trent's and pulled him toward his bedroom. For a moment, the feeling of his son's fingers wrapped around his overwhelmed him. A lump rose in his throat and he brushed his thumb over Ethan's fingers.

He bent and cupped Ethan's face. "Let's go find that rodent."

Forty-five minutes later, Trent was reasonably certain he did not care if Fluffy spent the night in Alcatraz being stalked by a hungry cat. He'd torn apart the back bedroom where the hamsters lived, moved every piece of furniture, lifted every last box, and still there was no Fluffy.

He'd set a trap of peanut butter in the middle of the floor.

No Fluffy.

He'd briefly contemplated a mousetrap, but then remembered his aim wasn't to scar his son for life.

Leaning against the couch in the back bedroom, his arm slung around Ethan's shoulders, Trent looked down at the sleepy boy. "Hey, buddy, why don't we call it a night and we'll find Fluffy in the morning?"

"No, Daddy." Ethan yawned. "If we don't find her tonight, she'll fall asleep during the day and we'll never find her."

"I don't know where else to look."

"The printer! Daddy, I think I just saw her in the printer."

Trent frowned and glanced at the ancient inkjet printer. It looked like something that had come out of the late 1990s. It was actually being used as a stand for the smaller laser printer Laura had bought.

"There's nowhere for a hamster to hide in there."

"Uh huh, Daddy. Fluffy can get into really small spaces."

He looked down at his son. "Define 'really small.'"

"Paper towel tube."

There was a tiny hole in the front of the printer, no more than an inch wide. He peered in and could just barely make out her beady black eyes and whiskers. "No way."

It turned out that extracting a hamster from a printer was a delicate operation. More delicate than Trent figured he had the patience for at past-four a.m., but the desire to not drag a bloody mess out of the printer instead of a live rodent gave him a miraculous reserve of patience.

Twenty minutes and twelve pieces of the printer later, Fluffy was successfully extracted from her prison and secured back in her cage with excessive amounts of duct tape sealing any openings and a small suitcase lock securing the door.

Ethan studied Fluffy for a moment, then looked up at Trent like he'd hung the moon. He threw his arms around his father's neck, his breath a huff in Trent's ear. "You're the best daddy in the whole wide world," he whispered.

Trent's heart swelled in his chest as he hugged his son tightly. After a long moment, he eased him back. "I think it's time for you to get back in bed, don't you think?"

Ethan chose that moment to yawn mightily and rub both eyes. Getting him back to sleep turned out to be as much of a production as getting the hamster out of the printer. He had to brush Ethan's teeth again, get him a drink of water, help him go potty, and find his stuffed bear.

It was approaching dawn by the time Trent finally crawled back into bed. Laura made a sleepy sound and he eased in beside her, shifting until her body was nestled against his. He buried his face against her hair and breathed the scent of her in.

She sighed and snuggled closer, pulling his hand up to rest near her heart. "Did you find the rodent?" she mumbled.

"Mmmhmm."

"My hero." Her words were a whisper against his forearm.

He kissed her shoulder and closed his eyes. An overwhelming sense of the rightness of things nailed him center mass. He felt. He felt the fear of losing his family, he felt the fatigue of five a.m., he felt the stress of combat that weighed him down. He felt love—an overwhelming love for his wife, for his family.

He felt all of it and the power of the emotions nearly crushed him with their rightness.

He was home. He had a second chance.

Chapter Twenty-Two

T rent stood in the courtroom at the First Cavalry Division headquarters, his hand clasped in his wife's. There was a stubborn set to Laura's jaw as she swiped a piece of lint from his collar. As always, her eyes were what gave away her worry.

He captured her hand in his. "It'll be fine, Laura. Stop fidgeting."

"I can't."

He smiled tightly. "I know."

Patrick walked into the courtroom, a file tucked beneath one arm. Like Trent, he wore his Blues, a sharp dress uniform used for formal occasions. Trent had been to other Article 32 hearings and they'd all been held in the duty uniform of ACUs. Trent assumed that the formal uniforms they were wearing today had been decided by the location.

"You need to pull your shit together," Patrick said by way of greeting.

Trent frowned. "What are you talking about?" His voice was flat.

Patrick gripped his shoulder. "Look, I know Story's death is hitting you hard but you need to put all of that emotion away. I need you to be fully present. Don't bring any baggage into this courtroom."

Trent swallowed and breathed deeply. "Roger."

"I'm serious, Trent. They're going to try to get you to react. You need to dial it back. Just sit there and let me handle this for you."

Laura would help him do that—she was the only person who could. Her silent, supportive presence wrapped around him like a warm blanket.

She was not just here for show. The rings on her finger meant something. He squeezed her hand tightly.

Laura had dressed sharply today: a neat pencil skirt and a crisp white blouse. Her hair was tied back in a perfect bun. All she was missing was a pair of wire-rimmed glasses and she'd looked like a sexy librarian. It dawned on him that he should have told her that.

It wasn't like he was going to jail at the end of the day. But he could have told her how beautiful she looked when they were alone, and he'd missed the opportunity. It was such a little thing, but right now the oversight weighed on him. He squeezed her hand again and then had to let her go so that he could take his seat.

The court started to fill up. Shane and Carponti flanked Laura as everyone filed into their seats. They led her to the row directly behind where Trent would be sitting. They'd only be separated from him by a low wooden wall.

Trent kept his expression carefully blank as Adorno walked into the courtroom. She looked harder than he remembered. Stiffer.

She did not sit with her husband. She didn't even look at him. She stood close to another lawyer, who was having a hushed, intense conversation with Lieutenant Randall. Trent glanced at Patrick, who was watching the interchange with interest.

"What's going on?" he asked as he took a seat next to Patrick.

"I have no idea, but whatever it is, Lieutenant Randall is not happy about it. He's killing that poor piece of gum."

Patrick was right. Randall was doing violence on the gum in his mouth and glaring daggers at his wife, who refused to look at him.

A major walked into the courtroom and leaned across the low barrier separating the counselors from the crowd. He whispered something in Lieutenant Randall's ear, then they both motioned for Patrick. Together, the two majors and the colonel walked into a small room next to the judge's bench.

Trent felt Laura lean in behind him. "What's going on?" she whispered.

He turned around. "No idea."

"Do we want to take bets on whether this is a good thing or a bad thing?" Carponti asked, leaning across the low wall.

"Not particularly a fan of knowing the odds," Trent muttered.

Trent caught his wife staring at the door beyond which Patrick had disappeared with Colonel Pritchard and the unidentified major.

"Sure wish I knew what was going on," Laura said quietly.

"Yeah." Trent leaned one arm on the low wall, capturing her hand in his, needing the comfort of her touch.

An uneasy silence had settled in the courtroom. A stray cough. A rustle of fabric.

The door opened. Patrick stepped through, followed by the other two men.

His friend's expression was polished and unexpressive. But in his eyes Trent saw a glimmer of victory.

He held his breath as Patrick took his seat, turning to talk to him. But he didn't get the chance—he was interrupted by Randall's shout.

"Oh, bullshit!"

"Watch it, lieutenant."

"Fuck you, sir. You were supposed to take care of this."

Randall's lawyer's face flushed. "And you were supposed to keep your dick in your pants. But instead, you went and pissed off the key witness."

The major was standing next to Adorno. He was clearly her lawyer. She lifted her chin, glaring at her spouse. "The only person I'm willing to testify against is my husband." Her voice was high-pitched and grating but her words were some of the most beautiful words Trent had ever heard.

"You realize I can make her testify about Captain Davila's actions," Randall's lawyer said harshly.

"You could, but that puts your client at risk as well," the major said, leaning against the low wooden wall. "Or you could cut your losses and we could all just recommend that the charges are dropped given the, ah, recent developments and the witness's unwillingness to cooperate." He grinned. "Unless of course you're so vested in this case you want to try the young commander over there without any real evidence."

"Goddamn it, this is bullshit!" Randall exclaimed, his face bright red.

"Lieutenant, one more outburst and I'm going to resign as your attorney."

"You can't do that. The only reason you're still a lawyer is because of my father."

"Yeah, well, putting up with you for the last few months has made me reconsider my debt," his lawyer said calmly. "There's nothing I can do. Even you have to see that."

Adorno leaned forward, barely a foot away from her husband. "I hate you. I hate what you made me become. I lied because of you."

"I didn't make you do anything." He looked down at her with disgust.

Her bottom lip quivered. "I lied because I loved you and you convinced me that Captain Davila was ruining your career." She glanced from Trent to her husband. "Well, I'm done. You'll have the divorce papers tomorrow. And if you really want to move forward with this sham, I'll gladly testify about everything." She smiled coldly. "With proof." She turned to her lawyer. "Sir, can I go? I need to go."

The major grabbed his briefcase. "Call me and we'll figure out how to war game this with the division commander."

When Lieutenant Randall opened his mouth, his lawyer held up his hand. "Not one more word, lieutenant. Go. Now."

The court cleared. Patrick whistled, smiling at his friend. "I think that's a first in my career," he said lightly. "You were onto something when you said the army has something in common with *Days of Our Lives.* Maybe more in common with the *Springer* show, though."

Trent held his breath as Laura spoke from behind him. "Does that mean what I think it means?" she asked.

"Yeah. Yeah, I think it does." Patrick's cell phone vibrated on the desk. He glanced at the text message then looked over at Trent. "Colonel Richter has made some adjustments to the case."

"That was fast," Trent said. "What does that mean?"

"You'll have to talk to him." Patrick's expression revealed nothing.

Trent glanced at his wife, his heart slamming against his ribs. She reached for him, squeezing his fingers gently. "I'll see you in a little bit."

Trent wiped his palms on his uniform pants and took a deep breath before knocking on the door of his brigade commander's office.

His pulse pounded in his ears, blocking out all other sound. Laura had wanted to come with him, to hear firsthand what Colonel Richter had decided to do about the charges against him, but one did not take one's spouse to a meeting with the brigade commander. No matter how much he might have wanted her there, it simply wasn't done.

Colonel Richter looked up from where he was placing picture frames in a small box. The big colonel had been a centerpiece of Trent's life for as long as he could remember. The man had even been his battalion commander the first time he deployed.

Now he stood in his commander's office, unanswered questions on the tip of his tongue. Did Richter think Trent deserved a court-martial? Why hadn't he intervened? As the brigade commander, he had the choice to continue the process started by his battalion commander or stop it.

Trent had chosen not to walk into his commander's office to ask for help. He'd waited, patiently, for a leader he'd trusted to act.

Apparently now that the evidence against Trent had crumbled, the waiting was over. He had no idea what to expect as he stood on the carpet in front of his brigade commander's desk.

And waited.

"You always think you're ready to change command," Colonel Richter said by way of greeting. "But there are always things you leave undone."

Trent swallowed and said nothing, standing at the position of attention, even as his glasses slid down the bridge of his nose.

"It's hard to believe it's been two years since I took charge of the brigade. But it's time for me to go." Colonel Richter wrapped the photos in an old brown t-shirt and lowered them into the box. Finally, he paused and stared into the box of photographs.

"All charges against you have been dismissed."

Seven simple words that could have been said at any point

in the last year and a half. Seven small words that changed
Trent's life, lifting the burden from his shoulders.

Why now? He clenched his fists by his sides, anger and
frustration clawing at him. *Why did you wait until my life
was almost completely destroyed?*

But there were things one simply could not say to a full
colonel. Trent cleared his throat and breathed deeply, trying
to rein in his churning emotions.

The charges that had been hanging over his head for the
last year were gone. It was over.

Relief, palpable and damn near crushing, washed over
him. Absently, he rubbed the aching scar over his heart. It
always ached, but lately it didn't seem to be keeping him up
at night like it used to.

"You want to ask me why, don't you?" Colonel Richter
said, pausing to look at Trent before placing another picture
in the box.

"It crossed my mind, sir."

Colonel Richter studied him quietly. "It's purely selfish
on my part. I didn't want to leave this unfinished. The new
commander has no ties to anyone in this brigade. He doesn't
have to live with the decisions you and I have made during
this war. He's a Pentagon man." Another picture into the box.
The office looked barren, devoid of the passion and intensity
Colonel Richter had brought to the brigade. At one time Trent
would have followed him anywhere. He was that kind of
leader. One of the few real warriors among the senior ranks.

"Have a seat." Colonel Richter paused and moved to the
small couch. He rubbed his hand over his mouth, his gaze
distant and unfocused for a moment. "I had to let this situation develop the way it did for a lot of reasons, none of
them good. I know you felt like I left you out in the cold and
I'm sorry for that." He cleared his throat. "But the truth is, I
could not have acted before now."

"Sir, if I may: What changed?" It was as close to demanding an answer to the question of why as Trent dared to dance.

"Lieutenant Randall's father has been stepping on my neck since this whole thing started. He's a sneaky old bastard, I'll give him that. He had his boss call the division commander and when the chief of staff of the army calls a division commander, the commander tends to listen." Colonel Richter leaned forward. "I had to play this out the right way or it could have been taken out of my hands. Once Randall's wife changed her story, the case fell apart and I could dismiss the charges."

Trent's career had been sacrificed to placate a spoiled lieutenant's father. He'd known that, of course, but somehow hearing it from Colonel Richter made it sound more calculated.

The brigade commander's expression was grim. "Division is deploying to Afghanistan next spring. I could use a few officers with Afghanistan experience. It's a different fight than Iraq."

Trent had been there almost a decade ago, when special forces was fighting the war from horseback and the conventional forces were attempting to remove a mountain range from the face of the earth at Tora Bora. His first taste of combat had slammed into him like the main gun on his tank. The need for adrenaline had hardwired itself into his bloodstream on that first tour in hell.

He could go back. Back to war. Back to the heady mix of combat and terror.

Away from his family. Away from Laura.

Story had died because he hadn't been able to keep away from the fight.

His blood burned with the futility of it all. Everything he'd sacrificed—all the time he'd missed with his family—

all of it had been for nothing. He had a long way to go before
the grief would not be raw and cutting.

It was a battle he would no longer fight.

Trent swallowed, clenching his fists by his sides.

"I can't go with you, sir." He summoned the energy to
meet his commander's gaze, which was filled with resigned
disappointment.

"Think about that answer, son."

"Sir, I'm not your son," he said, quietly crossing the line.
"I appreciate you dismissing the charges, sir. But my time in
the army is done."

Colonel Richter stood and Trent rose to his feet. "I understand you're upset. Think about this before you make any
irrevocable decisions."

Trent bit down on the inside of his cheeks to keep from
saying anything else. It took what felt like an act of God, but
all he said was, "Roger, sir. But I've given the army enough.
I've done my time in hell." He looked into Colonel Richter's
eyes, seeing the disappointment there. It was a terrible thing,
to let down someone you admired.

But it was worse, so much worse, to consider his life without his wife and family.

"Are you sure about that?" Colonel Richter asked.

Trent didn't hesitate. He nodded once. And ended his
career.

Laura looked up as her husband stepped into her office, closing the door behind him. An odd expression was twisting his
features. Not victory. Not defeat. Fatigue. As if everything
over the last few months had slammed into him all at once.
She stood, crossing the small space to meet him.

"Okay, you've got to tell me something before I go crazy,"
she said, a hitch in her voice.

Trent rested his hands on her shoulders, his eyes dark and

shadowed behind his glasses. "The charges have been dismissed," he said softly. "He offered me a chance to salvage my career by deploying with division in the spring."

He looked down at her hands where they rested on his chest. "I'm not going." His voice was thick. She said nothing while she listened to him describe his conversation with the colonel. She listened and her heart broke at the stunning lack of loyalty that had been shown to her husband.

The loyalty Trent had given the army had nearly destroyed their marriage.

She brushed her lips over his as he captured her hands, his big palms rough against hers.

"I screwed up everything with us, Laura." He rubbed his thumbs over the flesh of her knuckles and the sensitive skin near her wedding ring. He sounded so broken. The words were so raw, ripe with his still-fresh grief and the betrayal of the army, for which he'd sacrificed everything.

"Because you're not a perfect man," she whispered, "but you're a good man." She rubbed the material of his uniform over the scar on his heart. "And you're mine."

She slid her arms around his neck and drew him close. He felt deflated, somehow defeated. She simply held him. It was a long moment before he relaxed and let himself be held. His arms slowly came around her waist.

With a shuddering breath, he exhaled, like he'd been depending on the air in his lungs to keep himself upright. After a long moment, he leaned back. "So I'm going to need some help writing a resumé," he said with a twisted smile on his lips.

"You're not making any major life choices right now."

"This is what I want."

"I know you do. But I also want you to make this decision when you're not grieving for a friend."

"Nothing will change my mind. I can't do this anymore. You deserve better."

"So do you."

"No, I don't."

She smiled then, and the sight lit the darkest corners of his soul. "You're going to argue with me now?"

His answering smile was sad. "Maybe."

"I need you to hear what I'm about to say." Her fingers stroked over the skin of his cheeks, his forehead. Her eyes filled with relief. "I've wanted you home for so long." She rested her forehead against his, savoring the feel and touch of having her husband close enough to touch. "The war almost broke us. But it didn't. It didn't. Now we need to take some time for us. We need to figure out who we are without the war hanging over our heads."

"Laura, I'm—"

"I'm not actually finished." She pressed her finger over his lips. His eyes were dark with unspoken emotion. "You came home but that's just a start. We've got a long way to go. But we're going to work on that together."

He smiled against her finger. "Can I talk now?"

She closed her eyes, terrified that he would back out, that he would decide to deploy again. And if he did? She would wait. She knew that now. Because these last few weeks had refilled her well. She was no longer empty, no longer pining after a man who didn't know how to be home. It would hurt, but if he decided to stay in the army, she could do this. She would do this.

But there was fear in her voice when she said, "Depends on what you're going to say."

He brushed his nose against hers. "I don't deserve you." He crushed her to him then, pushing the air from her lungs with the intensity of his embrace. A moment more and he kissed her, pouring a thousand unsaid things into that kiss, that single moment. Her heart blossomed beneath his touch, opening and expanding and making room to love this man again. Not the man who'd left her and gone to war. This man. The man who had come home, a little bit broken, a little bit different, but still the man she loved.

It had taken nearly losing him to see that. She closed her eyes and savored this single moment. Needing it. Needing him.

"I love you." The words tore from his lips, ragged and harsh against her ear. "I'm sorry it took me so long to come home."

The swell of emotion crested and broke and she leaned back, swiping beneath her eyes. "You came back. That's all that matters."

"I'm not the same man I was," he said gently. "I've got a lot of work to do to rewire my normal."

She stroked her hands over his cheeks. "You're right. You are different. But you came back to me. That's all that matters."

He pulled her against him again, wrapping her tight in his arms. "I was always coming back to you. It just took me a while to get here."

Epilogue

❦

Are you ready for this?" Trent asked, brushing lint from Shane's lapel.

"Honestly?" Shane asked roughly. The crisp blue of their uniforms looked sharp in the setting Texas sun. The warm Sunday afternoon was not oppressively hot and the breeze flowed through the sheer curtains Laura and Nicole had finished hanging that morning. "Yes," he said softly.

"How's Jen feeling?" Trent buffed the U.S. insignia on Shane's collar.

"She's not sick yet. So that's a positive."

Carponti adjusted his sleeve. "So what do you want, a boy or a girl?"

"I just want Jen and the baby to be healthy." Shane's voice thickened and he cleared his throat. "I don't care either way."

"I felt the same way," Trent said.

"Oh, I think having a girl would be worse," Carponti said. "I think being sent to the store for tampons at midnight has got to be harder than being sent to the store for a box of condoms."

Trent laughed and shook his head. "There's something wrong with you."

"Come on. You're not going to be embarrassed to go to the store for tampons?"

"I've been married for more than a decade. I've bought tampons before."

"Really? Regular or super?"

Trent laughed and pinched the bridge of his nose before he excused himself and headed toward the house. "None of your damn business."

Trent took in a deep breath and headed into the small bedroom on the first floor, where Shane had spent much of his time recovering from his battle wounds. This was good. Things felt right.

He dug through the small bag he'd brought with him, his hand wrapping around the small orange pill bottle. None of the usual anxiety had started squeezing his heart or shortening his temper but he'd been wary of trying to do too much. He stared down at the bottle, trying to decide if he should take the anxiety med or run the gauntlet and see what the day brought.

A quiet knock on the door made him tighten his grip on the bottle. He was almost tempted to hide it. Laura slipped in, a warm smile on her face. Her gown looked like it was painted on her body, and her caramel-colored hair was piled high on her head, with just a few stray ringlets dusting over her bare shoulders.

Trent's mouth went dry as she approached him.

"You okay?" Her fingers slid over his where he held the bottle, warm and soft and strong.

He swallowed, looking down at their joined hands. "I was, ah, debating whether or not I should take one. Just in case."

Her fingers tightened around his. "Whatever you decide, it's what's best for you. It's a temporary thing. We'll get you through this." She brought her other hand up to cover their hands. "Normal takes time. We'll get you there."

Her smile was brilliant, casting light into the lingering dark corners of his soul. "I didn't think you'd understand."

"I don't," she said honestly. "But that doesn't make it any less real to you. I want you home. The rest will take care of itself." She lifted her chin, meeting his gaze. "And I'll be here to walk through whatever darkness you go through as long as you'll let me."

He pushed his glasses to the top of his head, then lowered his forehead to hers. "Thank you."

"You're welcome." She brushed her lips across his. "Now we've got a wedding to attend." She met his gaze. "Are you ready?"

"Yeah. I think I am."

He tucked the pills back into his hygiene bag. They were there if he needed them. For now, that was enough.

Laura stuck her head out of the back door and made a motion with her hands.

"Okay, here we go," Shane said roughly from the pergola.

"Take your seats!" Carponti shouted over the crowd.

"This isn't a formation," Trent said. "You don't have to pretend you're the sergeant major."

Carponti adjusted the sleeve of his uniform over his prosthetic hand, his voice unusually gruff. "Yes, I do. Sarn't Major Giles told me to make sure that no one shows their asses today."

The intimate crowd settled into their seats, then silence fell over the small gathering. A light breeze wafted through the sheer curtains around the pergola. Another moment passed and the back door opened.

Ethan and Emma stepped out onto the porch together. Emma wore a tiny silver dress similar to Laura's and Nicole's and carried a tiny basket of flowers. She wasn't quite able to master the duties of a flower girl because instead of dropping a few petals here and there, she dropped clumps at random intervals. Ethan carried a small pillow and Trent wondered how Laura had managed to get the rings attached securely enough to keep their son from spilling them.

His son and daughter made their way down the porch steps together, both of them looking far too serious. Trent's heart swelled in his chest as they approached. His little girl looked at him with big eyes filled with trust and love, and his tiny man was trying hard to look grown up and serious. He pointed his little sister toward the chair she was supposed to sit in and then sat in the one next to it. Trent's eyes watered.

Nicole emerged next and Carponti straightened his posture as his wife made her way down the aisle. Nicole looked glamorous as always, but there was something about the way she looked at Carponti that made Trent's heart settle into place. They joked about sex and nothing ever seemed serious between them but when it mattered, she was there for him.

Then the world tipped beneath his feet as his wife stepped onto the back porch. He'd already seen her in the silver gown, but the light shimmered off her now, making her glow. Seeing her take that first step off the back porch and down the aisle toward him, he felt like he was watching his bride approach all over again. She was more beautiful now, more whole.

More precious. Because they almost hadn't had this day. Or any other days. His mouth went dry and he cleared his throat roughly.

Laura smiled at him like he was the only man in the world, and a fierce swell of emotion ran through him. He swallowed as she stepped onto the pergola. The sunset glinted over her shoulders, framing her in a silver and golden glow. His blood warmed and he wondered how long it would be before he could steal her away for a moment alone.

Then everything stopped as Jen stepped onto the back porch.

Trent felt his throat close as he looked at his best friend's future wife.

She wore no veil, just a simple headband sparkling with sparkling stones. Her gown swept over her shoulders with the tiniest capped sleeves and sloped gently over her breasts. There was no trace of her scar, no visible proof that she was anything less than perfect. Because she was.

Next to him, Shane cleared his throat. Then coughed and did it again. Trent and Carponti leaned over at the same time.

"Are you crying?" Carponti whispered.

"Fuck off, both of you," Shane mumbled beneath his breath. He exhaled with a rush as she stepped onto the pergola. "Hey."

"Hi." She smiled up at him, her eyes glittering brightly.

"If you go through with this, you're never getting rid of me," he said quietly.

"Chaplain, would you do the honors before he chickens out?" Jen asked.

Chaplain Hobbes smiled. "Of course."

As the ceremony started a strange sound that faintly resembled a sniffle came from behind him, but he did not turn around. He wasn't sure he could survive seeing Carponti cry. He was pretty sure the world would end if he did.

He met Laura's gaze as Shane took Jen's hands.

And as his long-time friend married the woman of his dreams, Trent stared at the woman of his. There was still a long journey ahead. Many dark nights. Coming home from war was not a single event. It was a process. A journey.

Trent was one of the lucky ones. He'd had a family to come back to. A woman he'd almost lost.

As Shane kissed his wife, Trent swallowed the hard lump of emotion in his own throat. So many friends lost.

But Shane had made it. So had Carponti.

They'd come home. They'd come home. Back to the families that had waited for them. Back to the families that made it all worthwhile.

It was a start.

**Jessica Scott's Coming Home series
continues...**

The last thing Sergeant First Class
Reza Iaconelli wants is to deal with the
army psych docs. But when one of his
soldiers causes trouble, he finds himself
face-to-face with beautiful Captain Emily
Lindberg. Army regulation pulls them
apart but desire brings them together in...

All for You.

**Please see the next page for
a preview.**

Prologue

☙

Camp Taji, Iraq

2007

Sergeant First Class Reza Iaconelli had seen better days. He closed his eyes, wishing he was anywhere but curled up on the latrine floor in the middle of some dirty, shitty desert. The cold linoleum caressed his cheek, soothing the sensation of a billion spiders creeping over his skin. He had to get up, to get back to his platoon before someone came looking for him. Running patrols through the middle of Sadr City was so much better than being balled up on the bathroom floor, puking his guts out.

He'd sacrificed his dignity at the altar of the porcelain god two days ago when they'd arrived in northern Baghdad. It was going to be a rough deployment; that was for damn sure. Dear Lord, he'd give anything for a drink. Anything to stop the madness of detox. Why the fuck was he doing this to himself? Why did he pick up that godforsaken bottle every single time he made it home from this goddamned war?

The walls of the latrine echoed as someone pounded on

the door. It felt like a mallet on the inside of a kettle drum inside his skull. "Sarn't Ike!"

Reza groaned and pushed up to his hands and knees. He couldn't let Foster see him like this. Couldn't let any of his guys see him like this. "You about ready? The patrol is gearing up to roll."

Holy hell. He dry heaved again, unable to breathe until the sensation of ripping his guts out through his throat passed. After a moment, he pushed himself upright and rinsed out his mouth. He'd definitely seen better days.

He wet his brown-black hair down and tucked the grey Army combat t-shirt into his uniform pants. Satisfied that no one would know he'd just been reduced to a quivering ball of misery a few moments before, he headed out to formation, a five- to seven-hour patrol through the shit hole known as Sadr City in his immediate future.

He was a goddamned sergeant first class and he had troops rolling into combat. They counted on him to do more than show up. They counted on him to lead them. Every single day.

Maybe by the time he reached thirty days in-country, he'd stop heaving his guts up every morning. But sick or not, he was going out on patrol with his boys.

The best he could hope for was that he wouldn't puke in the tank.

Chapter One

❦

Fort Hood, Texas

Spring 2009

Where the hell is Wisniak?" Reza hooked his thumbs in his belt loops and glared at Foster.

Sergeant Dean Foster rolled his eyes and spat into the dirt, unfazed by Reza's glare. Foster had the lean, wiry body of a runner and the weathered lines of an infantryman carved into his face, though at twenty-five he was still a puppy. To Reza, he'd always be that skinny private who'd had his cherry popped on that first run up to Baghdad. "Sarn't Ike, I already told you. I tried calling him this morning but he's not answering. His phone is going straight to voicemail."

Reza sighed and rocked back on his heels, trying to rein in his temper. They'd managed to be home from the war for more than a year and somehow, soldiers like Wisniak were taking up the bulk of Reza's time. "Have you checked the R&R Center?"

"Nope. But I bet you're right." Foster pulled out his phone before Reza finished his sentence and started walking a short distance away to make the call.

"I know I am. He's been twitchy all week," he mumbled, more to himself than to Foster. Reza glanced at his watch. The commander was going to have kittens if Reza didn't have his personnel report turned in soon, because herding cats was all noncommissioned officers were good for in the eyes of Captain James T. Marshall the Third, resident pain in Reza's ass.

Foster turned away, holding up a finger as he started arguing with whoever just answered the phone. Reza swore quietly, then again when the company commander started walking toward him from the opposite end of the formation. Reza straightened and saluted.

It was mostly sincere.

"Sarn't Iaconelli, do you have accountability of your troops?"

"Sir, one hundred and thirty assigned, one hundred and twenty-four present. Three on appointment, one failure to report, and one at the R&R center. One in rehab."

"When is that shitbird Sloban going to get out of rehab?" Captain Marshall glanced down at his notepad.

"Sloban isn't a shitbird," Reza said quietly, daring Marshall to argue. "Sir."

Marshall looked like he wanted to slap Reza but as was normally the way with cowards and blowhards, he simply snapped his mouth shut. "Who's gone to the funny farm today?"

The Rest and Resiliency Center was supposed to be a place that helped combat veterans heal from the mental wounds of war. Instead, it had become the new generation's stress card, a place to go when their sergeant was making them work too hard. Guys like Wisniak who had never deployed but who for some reason couldn't manage to wipe their own asses without someone holding their hands abused the system, taking up valuable resources from the warriors who needed it. But to say that out loud would mean agreeing with Captain Marshall. Reza would drop dead before that ever happened.

Luckily Captain Ben Teague approached, saving Reza the need to punch the commander in the face. The sergeant major would not be happy with him if that happened. Reza was already on thin ice as it was and there was no reason to give the sergeant major an extra excuse to dig into his fourth point of contact.

He was doing just fine. One day at a time, and all that.

Too bad guys like Marshall tested his willpower on a daily basis.

"So you don't have accountability of the entire company?" Marshall asked. Behind him Teague made a crude motion with his hand.

Reza rubbed his hand over his mouth, smothering a grin. "Sir, I know where everyone is. I'm heading to the R&R Center after formation to verify that Wisniak is there and see about getting a status update from the docs."

Marshall sighed heavily and the sound was laced with blame, as though Wisniak being at the R&R Center was Reza's personal failing. Behind him Teague mimed riding a horse and slapping it. Reza coughed into his hand as Marshall turned an alarming shade of puce. "I'm getting tired of someone always being unaccounted for, Sergeant."

"That makes two of us." Reza breathed deeply. "Sir."

"What are you planning on doing about it?"

He raised both eyebrows, his temper lashing at its frayed restraints. His mouth would be the death of him someday. That or his temper.

Right then, he didn't really care.

He started ticking off items on his fingers. "Well, sir, since you asked, first, I'm going to stop by the shoppette for coffee, then take a ride around post to break in my new truck. I'll probably stop out at Engineer Lake and smoke a cigar and consider whether or not to come back to work at all. Around noon, I'm going to swing into the R&R Center to make sure that Wisniak actually showed up and was seen. Then I'll spend the rest of the day hunting said sorry excuse for—"

"That's enough, sergeant," Marshall snapped and Teague mimed him behind his back. "I don't appreciate your insubordinate attitude. Accountability is the most important thing we do."

"I thought kicking in doors and killing bad guys was the most important thing we did?" Reza asked, doing his damnedest not to smirk. Damn but the man tried his patience and made him want to crack open a cold one and kick his boots up on his desk.

Except that he'd given up drinking. Again. And this time, it had to stick. At least, it had to if he wanted to take his boys downrange again.

The sergeant major had left him no wiggle room. No more drinking. Period.

"Sergeant—"

"Sir, I got it. I'll head to the R&R Center right after formation. I'll text you…" He glanced at Foster, who gave him a thumbs-up. Whatever the hell that was supposed to mean. Wisniak was at the R&R Center, Reza supposed?

"You'll call. I don't know when texting became the army's preferred technique for communications between seniors and subordinates. I don't text."

Reza saluted sharply. It was effectively a fuck off but Marshall was either too stupid or too arrogant to grasp the difference. "Roger, sir."

"Ben," Marshall mumbled.

"Jimmy." Which earned him a snarl from Marshall as he stalked off. Teague grinned. "He hates being called Jimmy."

"Which is why you've called him that every day since Infantry Officer Basic Course?"

"Of course," Teague said solemnly. "It is my sacred duty to screw with him whenever I can. He was potty trained at gunpoint."

"Considering he's a fifth generation army officer, probably," Reza mumbled. Foster walked back up, shaking his head and mumbling creative profanity beneath his breath. "They won't even tell you if Wisniak has checked in?"

"I practically gave the lady on the phone a hand job to get her to tell me anything and she pretty much told me to kiss her ass. Damn HIPAA laws. How is it protecting the patient's privacy when all I'm asking is if the jackass is there or not?"

Reza sighed. "I'll go find out if he's there. I need you to make sure the weapons training is good to go." Still swearing, Foster nodded and limped off. Too bad Foster wasn't a better ass kisser; he'd have already made staff sergeant.

But Marshall didn't like him and had denied his promotion for the last three months because Foster was nursing a bum leg. Granted, he'd jammed it up playing sports, but the commander was being a total prick about it. It would have been better if Foster had been shot.

"Damn civilians," Reza mumbled, glancing at Teague. "I get that the docs are only supposed to talk to commanders but they make my life so damn difficult sometimes."

"They talk to you," Teague said, pushing his sunglasses up on his nose and shoving his hands into his pockets.

"That's because they're afraid of me. I look like every stereotype jihadi they can think of. All I have to do is say *drka drka Mohammed jihad* and I get whatever I want out of them."

"A Team America: World Police reference at six-fifteen a.m.? My day is complete." Teague laughed. "That's so fucking wrong. Just because you're brown?"

Reza shrugged. Growing up with a name like Reza Iaconelli had taught him how to fight. Young. With more than just the asshole kids on the street. He'd learned the hard way that little kids needed a whole lot more than attitude when standing up to a grown man.

"What can I say? No one knows what to think of the brown guy. Half the time, people think I'm Mexican." He started to walk off, still irritated by Marshall and the unrelenting douche baggery of the officer corps today. They cared more about stats than soldiers. It was total bullshit. The war wasn't even over yet and it was already all the way back to the garrison army bullshit that had gotten their asses handed to them from 2003 on.

"Where are you heading?" Teague asked.

"R&R. Need to check up on the resident crazy kid and make sure he's not going to off himself." He palmed his keys from his front pocket. Reza slammed the door of his truck and took a sip of his coffee, wishing it had a hell of a lot more in it than straight caffeine.

He ground his teeth. Things would have been different for Sloban if they'd gotten things right. If *he'd* gotten sober sooner. But no. He'd dropped the ball and Slo had paid the price.

He'd rather have his balls crushed with a ball peen hammer than deal with the R&R Center. He hated the psych docs. They were worse than the bleeding heart officers he seemed to find himself surrounded with these days. Just how he wanted to start off his seventy-fourth day sober: arguing with the shrinks.

Good times.

"I don't really think you understand the gravity of the situation, Captain."

Captain Emily Lindberg bristled at the use of her rank.

The fact that a fellow captain used it to intimidate her only irritated her further.

Add in that he was standing in front of—no, he was leaning over—her desk trying to back up his words with a little threat of physical intimidation and Emily's temper snapped. Captain Jenkowski was built like a snake—tall and solid and mean—and he was clearly used to bullying his way through docs to get what he wanted.

Well not today.

She inhaled a calming breath through her nose and spoke softly, deliberately attempting to keep her composure. "I'm sorry, Captain, but I'm afraid you're the one who doesn't understand. Your soldier has experienced significant trauma since joining the military and his recurrent nightmares, excessive use of alcohol to self-medicate, and inability to effectively manage his stress are all indicators of serious psychological illness. He needs your compassion, not your wrath."

"Specialist Henderson needs my size ten boot in his ass. He sat on the damned base last deployment and we only got mortared a few times. He's a candy pants wuss who has a serious case of *I do what I want-itis* and now he's come crying to you, expecting you to bail his sorry ass out of a drug charge." Emily could practically see smoke coming out of the big captain's ears.

Once upon a time she would have flinched away from his anger and done anything to placate him. It was abusive jerks like this who thought the army was all about their ability to accomplish their mission. The mouth breather in front of her didn't care about his soldiers.

It was up to folks like Emily to hold the line and keep the army from ruining yet another life. There had already been more than fifty suicides in the army this year and it was only April. "What Henderson needs, Captain Jenkowski, is a break from you pressuring him to perform day in and day out. My duty-limiting profile is not going to change. He gets eight hours of sleep a night to give the Ambien a chance to work. And if you don't like it, file a complaint with my boss. He's the officer in charge of the hospital."

"You fucking bitch," he said. His voice was low and threatening. "I'm trying to throw this little motherfucker out of the army for smoking spice and you're making sure that we're stuck babysitting his sorry ass. Way to take care of the real soldiers who have to waste their time on this little weasel instead of training."

The door slammed behind him with a bang and Emily sank into her chair. It wasn't even nine a.m. and she'd already had her first go round with a commander. Good times.

A quick rap on her door pulled her out of her momentary shock. "You okay?"

She looked into the face of her first friend here at Fort Hood, Major Olivia Hale. "Yeah, sure. I just…"

"You get used to it after a while, you know," Olivia said, brushing her bangs out of her eyes.

"The rampant hostility or the incessant chest beating?" Emily tried to keep the frustration out of her voice and failed.

"Both?"

Emily smiled grimly. "Well that's helpful."

Moments like this made her seriously reconsider her life in the army. Of course, her parents would be more than happy for her to take the rank off her chest and return home to their Cape Cod family practice. The last thing she wanted to do was run home to a therapy session in waiting. Who wanted to work for parents who ran a business together but had gotten divorced fifteen years ago? At least here she was making a difference, instead of listening to spoiled rich kids complain about how hard their lives were or beg her for a prescription for Adderall so they could stay up for two days and prepare for their next exam.

Here she could make a difference. Do something that mattered.

Her family wouldn't understand.

Then again, they never had.

"Can I just say that I never imagined that I'd be going toe-to-toe with men who had egos the size of pro football linebackers? Where does the army find these guys?"

"Some of them aren't raging asshats," Olivia said. "There are a lot of commanders who actually care about their soldiers."

An Outlook reminder chimed, notifying her that she had two minutes. Emily frowned then clicked it off. "It must be something special about this office then that attracts all the ones who don't care."

She'd recently moved to Fort Hood because it was the place deemed most in need of psychiatric services. They had the unit with the highest active-duty suicide rate in the army. She was trying her damnedest to make a difference but the tidal wave of soldiers needing care was relentless.

Add in her administrative duties on mental health evaluations and sometimes, she didn't know which day of the week it was.

"Does it ever end?" she whispered, suddenly feeling overwhelmed at the stack of files on her desk. Each one represented a person. A soldier. A life under pressure.

Lives she did everything she could to save.

Olivia shrugged. "Not really." She glanced at her watch. "I've got a nine o'clock legal brief with the boss. You okay?"

She offered a weak smile. "Yeah. Have to be, right?"

Olivia didn't look convinced but didn't have time to dig in further. In the brief moment she had alone, Emily covered her face with her hands.

Every single day, Emily's faith in the system she'd wanted to help weakened. When officers like Jenkowski were threatening kids who just needed to take a break and pull themselves together to find some way of dealing with the trauma in their lives, it crushed part of her spirit. She'd never imagined that confrontation would be a daily part of her life as an army doc. She'd signed up to help people. She wasn't a commander, not a leader of soldiers. She was here to provide medical services. She'd barely stepped outside her office so all she knew was the inside of the clinic's walls.

She'd had no idea how much of a fight she'd have on a daily basis. Three months in and she was still shocked. Every single day brought something new.

She wasn't used to it. She doubted she would ever get used to it. It drained her.

But every day she got up and put on her boots to do it all over again.

She was here to make a difference.

A sharp knock on her door had her looking up. Her breath caught in her throat at the sight of the single most beautiful man she'd ever seen. His skin was deep bronze, his features carved perfection. There was a harshness around the edge of his wide full mouth that could have been from laughing too much or yelling too often. Maybe both.

And his shoulders filled the doorway. Dear Lord, men actually came put together like this? She'd never met a man who embodied the fantasy man in uniform like this one. The real military man was just as likely to be a pimply-faced nineteen-year-old as he was to be this... this warrior god.

A god who looked ready for battle. It took Emily all of six-tenths of a second to realize that this man was not here for her phone number or to strip her naked and have his way with her. Well, he might want to have his way with her but she imagined it was in a strictly professional way. Not a hot and sweaty way, the thought of which made her insides clench and tighten.

She stood. This man looked like he was itching for a fight and darn it, if that's what he wanted, then Emily would give it to him.

It was just another day at the office, after all.

"Can I help you, Sergeant?"

Reza glanced at the little captain, who looked braced for battle. She was cute in a Reese Witherspoon kind of way, complete with dimples, except for her rich dark hair and silver blue eyes. If Reza hadn't been nursing one hell of a bad attitude and a serious case of the ass, he would've considered flirting with her.

Except that the sergeant major's warning of *don't fuck up* beat a cadence in his brain, so he wouldn't be flirting anytime soon. Besides, something about the stubborn set of her jaw warned him that she wasn't someone to tangle with. She didn't look tough enough to crumble a cookie, and yet she'd squared off with him like she might just try to knock him down a peg or two. This ought to at least make the day interesting.

Reza straightened. She was the enemy for leaders like him, who were doing their damnedest to put bad troops out of the army. People like her ignored the warning signs from warriors like Sloban and let spineless cowards like Wisniak piss on her leg about how his mommy didn't love him enough.

This wasn't about Sloban. He couldn't help him now and that fact burned on a fundamental level. He released a deep breath. Then sucked in another one. "I need to know if Sergeant Chuck Wisniak signed in to the clinic."

"I'm sorry but unless you're the first sergeant or the commander, I can't tell you that."

Reza breathed hard through his nose. "I'm the first sergeant."

Her gaze flicked to the sergeant first class rank on his chest. He wasn't wearing the rank of the first sergeant, so his insignia was missing the rocker and the diamond that distinguished first sergeants from the soldiers that they led. Sergeants First Class were first sergeants all the time, though.

Her eyes narrowed. "Do you have orders?"

Reza's gaze dropped to the pen in her hand and the rhythmic way she flicked the cap on and off. He swallowed, pulling his gaze away from the distracting sound, and struggled to hold on to his patience.

"First sergeants are not commanders. We don't have assumption of command orders." He pinched the bridge of his nose and sighed. "Ma'am, I just need to know if he's here. Why is this such a big deal?"

"Because Sergeant Wisniak has told this clinic on multiple occasions that his chain of command is targeting him, looking for an excuse to take his rank."

"Well, maybe if he was at work once in a while he wouldn't feel so persecuted."

The small captain lifted her chin. "Sergeant, do you have any idea what it feels like to be looked at like you're suspect every time you walk into a room?"

Something cold slithered across Reza's skin, sidling up to his heart and squeezing tightly. "Do you have any idea what it feels like to send soldiers back to combat knowing they lost training days chasing after a sissy-ass soldier who can't get to work on time?"

A shadow flickered across her pretty face but then it was gone, replaced by steel. "My job is to keep soldiers from killing themselves."

"And my job is to keep soldiers from dying in combat."

"They're not mutually exclusive."

Silence hung between them, battle lines drawn.

"I'm not leaving here without a status on Sarn't Wisniak," Reza said.

Captain Lindberg folded her arms over her chest. A flicker in her eyes, nothing more, then she spoke. "Sergeant Wisniak is in triage."

"I need to speak with him."

Lindberg shook her head. "No. I'm not letting anyone see him until he's stable. He's probably going to be admitted to the fifth floor. He's extremely high risk. And you're part of his problem, Sergeant."

Reza's temper snapped, breaking free before he could lash it back. "Don't put that on me, sweetheart. That trooper came in the army weak. I had nothing to do with his lack of a backbone." Reza turned to go before he lost his military bearing and started swearing. She'd already elevated his blood pressure to need-a-drink levels and it wasn't even nine a.m.

He could do this. He breathed deeply, running through creative profanity in his mind to keep the urge to drink at bay.

Her words stopped him at the door, slicing at his soul.

"How can you call yourself a leader? You're supposed to care about all your soldiers," she said, so softly he almost didn't hear her.

He turned slowly. Studied her, standing straight and stiff and pissed. "How can I call myself a leader? Honey, until you've bled in combat, don't talk to me about leadership. But go ahead. Keep protecting this shitbird and tie up all the counselors so that warriors who genuinely need help can't get it. He doesn't belong in the army." He swept his gaze down her body deliberately. Trying to provoke her. Her face flushed as he met her eyes coldly. "Neither do you."

Emily sucked in a sharp breath at Iaconelli's verbal slap. In one sentence, he'd struck her at the heart of her deepest fear.

It took everything she had to keep her hands from trembling.

Her boss Colonel Zavisca appeared in the doorway, saving her from embarrassing herself.

"Is there a problem, Sergeant?"

Sergeant Iaconelli turned and nearly collided with the full-bird colonel, who looked remarkably like an older version of Johnny Cash.

Sergeant Iaconelli straightened and his fists bunched at his sides. "You don't want me to answer that. Sir."

"I don't think I appreciate what you're insinuating."

"I don't really give a flying fuck what you think I'm insinuating. Maybe if your doctors did their jobs instead of actively trying to make my life more difficult, we wouldn't have this problem."

"What brigade are you in, Sergeant?" her boss demanded.

She watched the exchange, her breath locked in her throat. The big sergeant's hands clenched by his sides. "None of your damn business."

Colonel Zavisca might be a medical doctor but he was still the senior officer in charge of the hospital. Emily had never seen an enlisted man so flagrantly flout regulations.

"You can leave now, Sergeant. Don't come back on this property without your commander."

The big sergeant swore and stalked off.

Emily wondered if he'd obey the order. She suspected she already knew the answer.

Her boss turned to her. "Are you okay?" he asked. Colonel Zavisca's voice was deep and calming, the perfect voice for a psych doctor. It was more than his voice, though. His entire demeanor was something soothing, a balm on ragged wounds. His quiet power and authority stood in such stark contrast to Sergeant Iaconelli.

Men like Sergeant Iaconelli were energy and motion and hard angles. And he was rude. Colonel Zavisca was more like some of the men at her father's country club except without the stench of sophisticated asshole. He was familiar.

"I'm fine, sir. Rough morning, that's all."

Emily stood for a long moment, Sergeant Iaconelli's words still ringing in her ears. He had no idea how much his comment hurt. She didn't know him from Adam but his words had found her weakness and stabbed it viciously.

In one single sentence, he'd shredded every hope she'd held on to since joining the army. She'd wanted to belong. To be part of something. To make a difference. He'd struck dead on without even knowing it. Her family had told her she'd never fit into the military. She fought the urge to sink into her chair and cover her face with her hands. She just needed a few minutes. She could do this.

The big sergeant didn't know her. His opinion did not matter. Her parents' opinions did not matter.

If she kept repeating this often enough, it would be true.

Her boss glanced at the clock on her wall. "It's too early for this."

She smiled thinly. "I know. Shaping up to be one heck of a Monday. Is triage already booked?"

He nodded. "Yes. I need you in there to help screen patients. We need to clear out the folks who can wait for appointments and identify those who are at risk right now of harming themselves or others."

"Roger, sir. I can do that. I need to e-mail two company commanders and I'll be right out there."

"Okay. Don't forget we have the staff sync at lunch."

Even this early, the day showed no sign of slowing down and all she wanted to do was go home and take a steaming hot bath. She'd been trying to work out a knot behind her left shoulder blade for days now and things just kept piling up. She needed a good soak and a massage. Not that she dared schedule one. She'd probably end up cancelling it anyway.

"There's that smile. Relax. You're going to die of a heart attack before you're thirty. The army is a marathon, not a sprint."

"Roger, sir." She waited until he closed the door before she covered her face in her hands once more. She could do this. She just needed to find her battle rhythm. She'd get into the swing of things. She wasn't about to quit just because things got a little rough.

Her cell phone vibrated on her desk. Oh, perfect. Her mother was calling. Not that she was about to answer that phone call. She couldn't deal with the passive-aggressive jabs her mother was so skilled at. Besides, she was probably just going to press Emily to give up on—as she put it—slumming in the army and come home.

She'd worked too hard to get where she was and she damn sure wasn't about to go limping home. How could she? Her parents had looked at her like she was an alien when she'd told them about Bentley. As though she had somehow been in the wrong for her fiancé's betrayal. As though, if she'd been woman enough, he never would have strayed.

If she ever went home again, and that was a really big if, she would do it on her own terms. She'd walked away from everything in her life that had been hollow and empty.

She was rebuilding, doing something that mattered for the first time in her life. Every day that she avoided calling home or being the person her father and his friends wanted her to be was a victory. No one in her family had supported her when she'd needed them. She might not have found her place yet in the army but just being here was a start. It was something new and she wasn't about to give up, no matter how much Monday threw at her.

Tuesday really needed to hurry up and get here, though, because as Mondays went, this one was already shot all to hell.

Captain Ben Teague hates the administrative B.S. of company command, until a legal case puts him up against Major Olivia Hale. She is as by the book as a lawyer gets, but there's something simmering beneath that icy reserve—and Ben just can't resist turning up the heat...

Please see the next page for a preview of

It's Always Been You.

Prologue

❧

Northern Baghdad

FOB War Eagle 2005

Is this hell? Because it feels like hell." Second Lieutenant Ben Teague swiped his sleeve across his forehead and accomplished absolutely nothing. Sweat still dripped steadily down his forehead as he walked the perimeter of their tiny combat outpost with his platoon sergeant.

"Don't start complaining about the air conditioner again." Next to him, SFC Escoberra scowled at him.

Ben smirked and patted Sarn't Escoberra on his shoulder. It was so easy to get his platoon sergeant irritated. "I was not going to mention the a/c. What makes you think I'd do such a thing?"

"Fuck off, LT." Escoberra looked down the alley toward the city that hated them. It was a shit position, as shit positions went. Nothing quite like being alone and unafraid on the battlefield.

"Easy there, big fella. Didn't mean to get your PTSD all riled up."

Escoberra snarled and Ben grinned. "You're in a lovely mood. Don't tell me you're cranky about this lovely little mission, too?"

"Don't start, LT."

"What? We can barely defend our position, we don't have enough ammo, and we're not serving any purpose other than to hold some piece of real estate down. The commander can't even give me a good reason for us to be out here."

Beside him, Escoberra sighed heavily and lifted his weapon, checking the field of fire. "LT, you need to quit pissing and moaning about this. The men are going to hear you."

Ben sobered and snapped his mouth closed. His platoon sergeant was right. It wasn't good to let the boys hear the leadership arguing about the mission. "Let's change the subject to something less depressing. How's the family?"

Escoberra's eyes crinkled at the edges. "My wife seems to think our almost twelve-year-old daughter needs a personal trainer."

Ben coughed, trying to hide a laugh. "Yeah, 'cause that's all you need is to think about your daughter getting smoking hot while you're deployed."

"Not funny. I'm not ready for her to grow up yet and she's not even mine," Escoberra said quietly. "I love that little kid. I swear to God if some raging hard-on hurts her…"

"No boy is going to dare come around with you there."

"That's the problem. I'm not there," Escoberra said. "I'm stuck here."

Ben adjusted the strap on his weapon then toed the concertina wire strung across a low concrete barrier. "Does her dad ever come into the picture?"

"Nah. He's out of the picture. I'm not complaining, though. She might not be mine by blood but she's family by every other way that matters." Escoberra glanced down the road. "And speaking of the commander, guess who's coming to the family dinner for a site visit later tonight?"

Ben rubbed his eyes beneath his sunglasses and let out a hard sigh of frustration. "I don't want to deal with the fucking commander. I'd rather deal with my mother."

Escoberra snorted. "What's wrong with your mother now?"

"The Almighty Colonel Diane Teague called the battalion commander and tried to get me moved to go take an executive officer job. Fuck that, man. I don't want to count pens and toilet paper." Ben wiped his gloved hand over his forehead, looking out over the edge of the barrier on the roof. Their single building stronghold wasn't exactly an impenetrable fortress but at least it provided a nice view of the city. When things were getting blown all to hell around them.

"She's just trying to look out for your career."

"My mom needs to worry about her part of the war and let me worry about mine." Grit scraped over his skin. "Fuck, man, moms are supposed to bake cookies and kiss your booboo when it hurts. Mine eats napalm and pisses razor wire."

"You never struck me as the kind of guy who had mommy issues," Escoberra said.

"Screw you, man. I don't. I was just saying I'd rather deal with her than the commander. The commander is a pain in my ass that can get me killed as opposed to just a pain in the ass. See the difference?" Ben spat into the dirt, not actually wanting to delve into talking about his mother. He shouldn't have brought it up. "We need to get ready to head out on patrol. Maybe I can avoid the commander if I'm too busy getting shot at."

"Play nice, LT. I'm tired of the first sergeant running a wire brush over my ass because of you constantly fighting with the commander. You're a lieutenant, he's your boss. You don't get to tell him how you really feel about things,"

Escoberra said. His words were mild but beneath the calm was a temper. Ben knew this firsthand, and as much as he liked screwing with Escoberra, he also knew his limits.

He wasn't entirely sure that Escoberra wouldn't take his head off if given the right provocation. "Think of it as an exfoliation treatment," Ben said after a while.

After an impossible silence, Escoberra finally glanced at him, then looked back out toward the endless, dusty city. It was too quiet out there. "The sun is getting to you. You should drink water."

Ben bit his bottom lip where it had split some time during their last firefight. It opened again with the movement and warm, coppery blood coated his tongue. He spat into the dirt. "It's a hundred and twenty-six degrees. Of course the sun is getting to me." He adjusted his body armor, itching to go out on patrol and *do* something. "Tell me again why we're hanging out here?"

"Waiting for the bad guys to drive right by." Escoberra pointed at a white pickup that zipped by the end of the road, then stopped. Two faces peered out at them.

Ben's stomach flipped beneath his ribs. His heart started racing in his chest. "You're really fucking scary sometimes with that warrior intuition shit you've got going on."

Escoberra palmed the butt stock of his weapon. "Call it in. Get air support en route. This could get ugly."

But Ben didn't get the chance. A brilliant flash of heat seared across his skin a second before the boom knocked him on his ass.

And then all hell broke loose.

Chapter One

❦

Fort Hood, 2009

Four years later

Captain Ben Teague prayed to the caffeine gods and waited for the espresso machine to dispense the morning sacrifice. He'd never really considered why an infantry battalion had an espresso machine in the middle of the battalion operations office but right then, he wanted to kiss the man who'd had the foresight to buy it and keep it well-stocked with beans.

Somehow, he didn't think that Sergeant Major Cox would appreciate the gesture.

It was four-thirty in the morning on a Monday and someone had had the good idea to call an alert. Which meant that instead of getting to sleep like a normal person, Ben and everyone else in this clusterfuck of a battalion had dragged their carcasses on post at the ass crack of dawn.

Ben was liable to stab someone if he didn't get coffee stat.

Funny, he'd actually thought he was going to finally get some sleep when he'd actually nodded off. But as usual, it had all been a tease. The phone had yanked him out of that fog between sleep and waking. Damn it, he was getting caffeine before the morning briefing.

He kicked his New Kids on the Block trucker hat higher up on his head and counted to ten while the espresso machine ground the beans, then dispensed the precious liquid.

The warning light flashed red and the steady stream of espresso dripped to a halt. Ben wanted to cry.

"It needs water, sir."

"Thank you, Captain Obvious." Ben shot Sergeant Dean Foster a baleful look then jerked his thumb toward the espresso machine, saying nothing further. He wasn't in the mood to deal with Foster's smart-ass comments this morning. Not when Ben's sense of irony was still hung over from the night before.

"Did someone wake up on the wrong side of the bed?" Foster asked, taking the lid off the reservoir. "Do you need a hug?"

"No jokes before caffeine. Off with you, minion." Ben narrowed his eyes then waved his hands. "Now to figure out why the hell we're here at this ungodly hour," Ben muttered.

Not that it mattered. Ben had long ago given up trying to change things. And to think, once upon a time, he'd thought he could make a difference.

What a miserable joke.

"Teague, I don't give a flying fuck how much you were abused as a child, if you don't get that goddamned hat off in my building..."

"Good morning to you, too, sunshine," Ben said to the battalion sergeant major. Any day he could get the sergeant major's goat was a good day. It was one of life's few pleasures.

"Teague, one of these days..."

Someday, that would backfire on him. Until then, though... "We'll go take a long hot shower together and you can tell me your childhood traumas?"

Sarn't Major swung at him but Teague ducked. His hat wasn't so lucky. Cox grabbed it and tore the thin white mesh in half. Sarn't Major Cox was five and a half feet tall and about as wide, and none of it was fat.

"Oh come on!" Ben threw his arms up in mock disgust. "It took me at least four hours of surfing the Internet to find that hat."

Cox held up a single finger then balled his hand into a fist around Ben's hat. Cox balled up the hat and threw it at Ben's chest. "We've got brothers and sisters who died in this uniform. How about you start treating it with some fucking honor?" he growled as he stormed by. "Get your sorry ass in the conference room. You've got a meeting with the boss in twenty minutes."

Ben ground his teeth looking down at the rank on his grey uniform. Honor?

Ben knew all about it. It didn't get you anywhere.

Foster walked back in, carefully carrying the water. "Mission accomplished?"

"Yep. Right on target. And I even did it before coffee." Ben sighed. "What's going on?"

Foster shrugged. "No clue but there's a line of dudes outside the battalion commander's office right now."

Ben frowned. "Huh?"

"'Bout fifteen dudes lined up in the hallway." Foster said, jerking his thumb over his shoulder.

"No shit?"

Ben walked out of the office and turned down the hall toward the conference room. Foster wasn't kidding. There were sergeants and officers from every company in the battalion. Ben couldn't remember the last time he'd seen a line like this outside the boss's office.

Ben stopped short, his breath caught in his throat. Escoberra stood near the front. His arms were folded at parade rest, his palms resting at the small of his back. He stood solid and unmoving. Ben stood there, frozen. Escoberra shifted. For a moment their eyes locked and for a the briefest flicker, Ben saw the warrior he'd admired and looked up to when he'd been a scrappy, smart-assed lieutenant. Before he'd failed to defend a man he'd have followed to hell and back again.

Escoberra was still a warrior. It was Ben who had changed. Ben who had let the time and the bad memories drive him away from a man who'd been as close to a father figure as Ben could have asked for.

There were shadows in his former platoon sergeant's eyes now. Deep and dark.

Ben took a deep breath. A single step toward a man he admired and looked up to. Heat crawled up the back of Ben's neck. He wanted to speak, to say something to the man who'd saved his ass more times than he could remember.

"Escoberra!" The sergeant major's voice rang out. Escoberra ground his teeth and looked away, before he snapped to the position of attention and disappeared into the sergeant major's office.

It took everything Ben had to stand there while Escoberra walked away. He wanted to ask how the family was. How he was doing since the last deployment.

But Ben let him go. Because to say anything would be to acknowledge that the man in that hallway had changed. Ben didn't know if it was the war, if it was some fucked-up trauma, but the war had changed him, changed them all.

And Ben no longer knew the man in that hallway. Shame burned on his neck, the weight of his failure heavy around his shoulders.

Ben broke into a wide grin as he walked into the conference room and saw an old familiar face. "Holy shitballs!"

Captain Sean Nichols looked up from his BlackBerry, his dark expression going from guarded to grinning the moment he recognized Ben. "Holy shit, you're not in jail?"

"Very funny." Ben gripped his old friend's hand and pulled him into a one-armed man hug. "Some things never change. What are you doing here?"

"Looking for a job, apparently," Sean said.

Ben frowned. "Huh?"

"Supposedly there's some command positions opening up soon." Nichols ran his hand over the back of his neck. "I'm supposed to interview today but there's some massive shitstorm going on."

"Yeah, I saw that. Where have you been?"

"Iraq, Afghanistan, and back again." Sean nodded toward the other officers in the room. There was a big dude in one corner who looked like a professional wrestler, talking with one of the first sergeants. "These all your guys?"

"Nope. Never seen any of them before," Ben said.

The battalion commander, Lieutenant Colonel Gilliad, walked in, followed by Sarn't Major Cox and a small brunette major Ben had never seen before. She walked stiff and straight, and her hair was pulled back sharply from her face. Her right sleeve was missing a combat patch. Ben found himself wondering how she had been in the army long enough to be a major but had somehow managed to miss the war.

He didn't look away as she scanned the room, her eyes cool and appraising.

Ben wasn't fooled. He'd seen that look far too many times.

She was a woman on a mission. Just what they needed: a lawyer on crusade. Ben didn't do crusades.

They all snapped to attention as the commander walked to the center of the room.

"Gentlemen, welcome to Death Dealer Battalion.

Congratulations. Every one of you in this room will take command in less than a month," Gilliad said.

Silence hung in the heavens for half a moment. No one moved. No one spoke.

Ben breathed in deep and slow, keeping the ragged edge of his emotions in check. "Uh, sir, I think there's a mistake."

Gilliad pinned him with a hard look. Next to him, the major looked down at her paperwork, shaking her head, disapproval written on her pretty face.

"Teague, I'll see you in my office." Gilliad turned back to the other captains. "Bello, you and First Sarn't Delgado have Diablo Company. Martini, you and First Sarn't Tellhouse have Assassin Company. Teague, your first sergeant will be here before the week is out. You're taking Bandit Company. Navarro, you and First Sarn't Sagarian are taking Headquarters Company. Nichols, you and First Sarn't Morgan are taking Chaos Company."

"Sir—"

"Let the commander finish, Captain Teague," Sarn't Major Cox warned quietly.

Ben ground his teeth and fought the anxiety twisting in his guts.

Gilliad cleared his throat. "Every company command team in this battalion has been relieved of their duties effective immediately. You all are the new team. Major Hale is going to help with transition on the legal side of the house. We have our hands full, gentlemen, and I expect you to clean house and get this unit back to fully mission ready."

Ben blew out a low whistle. He'd never heard of something like this. Not in his entire life as a military brat or his own career. One commander, maybe two in rapid succession, but an entire battalion worth of company leadership fired on the spot?

And Gilliad expected Ben to be one of the new commanders?

Not in this lifetime.

Gilliad continued. "The forward support company leadership is changing out as well. That new command team will be on the ground shortly as soon as the support battalion figures out who that will be." He glanced over at the small major. "Major Hale has my guidance. Your number one priority for the next forty-five days is getting rid of the shitbag soldiers running this unit into the ground. I want the druggies gone. I want the dealers and the gangbangers gone. I want the fucking criminals out of my army. Am I clear?"

A murmured *hooah* went through the gathered men.

Ben couldn't speak.

His lungs had stopped working.

Command.

He didn't want this. He couldn't do it.

There had to be a mistake. The boss could find someone else.

He had to.

Because to command, you still had to believe what you did mattered. He released a shuddering breath.

And Ben hadn't believed that in a long, long time.

Major Olivia Hale watched the captain at the edge of the room. His back was stiff and straight and he radiated unspent fury. She wondered at the tired lines beneath his eyes, the hard set of his jaw.

He was so furious at being told he was taking command. The rest of the men had stiffened with awareness. Excitement. Command was the greatest reward for an officer's hard work—a chance to lead soldiers and make a difference. Olivia would command in a heartbeat if she could. Successful commanders made their units better places.

Why didn't this dark and angry captain want the job?

She lifted her chin. Whether or not the pissed off captain

took the job wasn't her problem. Her job was to help clean up this unit. She'd been asked personally to assist by the division commander—she'd been on his staff many moons ago when she'd been a brand new shiny lieutenant and she'd loved working for him. He'd been decisive. He'd been a mentor.

She hadn't been able to say no when he'd asked her to help this battalion.

"Gentlemen, I need time with each of you to go over the current status of your legal situations." She pointed to the stacks of folders in front of her. "I've got each company's information here. Please take your files and look them over before you come see me."

Gilliad nodded once in her direction. "Olivia is the best at what she does. We are going to clean this battalion up."

The angry captain shifted and she saw his nametag. Teague.

"Motherfucker," he muttered, loud enough for the entire room to hear.

"Teague!" Sarn't Major Cox exploded but LTC Gilliad held up his hand.

"In my office. Now, captain."

Teague shoved off the wall and stalked out of the conference room, followed closely by the battalion commander.

She watched him go, her gaze hanging on the man struggling with such fierce resentment at being given a great honor. What kind of man interrupted his battalion commander?

What kind of man was so angry at the chance to be a leader?

She pushed her thoughts away. He was not her problem. She focused on the men in front of her as they stopped by the conference room table.

A tall, lean captain with dark hair and green eyes stopped

near the table. "Sean Nichols, ma'am. Do we have any discretion in these cases?"

"What kind of discretion are you talking about, Captain Nichols?"

"In general. Do we get to say this kid did a dumb thing and he deserves a second chance?"

There was nothing Olivia could say. She knew there was a difference between the right answer and the legal answer, and even the army answer. "That's going to be a conversation between you and the battalion commander."

The tall captain nodded once and left, and after another moment, Olivia was alone in the conference room with the sergeant major.

She didn't quite know what to think of Sergeant Major Cox. He was her height but stocky and he looked mean as hell. She definitely wasn't used to his kind outside of the hospital headquarters where she used to work.

"Things are going to get rough around here, ma'am," he said after a long silence. His voice sounded like gravel and rocks.

"I'm not sure I understand what you mean."

"You start taking away people's livelihoods and things start getting tense. So while I have no doubt that the new command teams can handle things, just watch yourself around here. Don't hesitate to let me know if you're having problems with any soldier."

"Thank you for the warning," she said, not wanting to alienate the command sergeant major. "I've seen the misconduct you have down in this battalion, Sergeant Major. The quantity doesn't even come close to some of the terrible things I've seen."

"I hope you're right." Cox rubbed his hand over his mouth. "One more thing. You see that?"

He pointed toward a black cowboy hat with gold cord

wrapped around the base that he'd carried in with him. "Yes?"

"Get one. You can't be assigned here without it."

She smiled flatly. "I'll add it to my to-do list."

She couldn't care less about the silly hat, but she just smiled and nodded and headed to her next meeting.

She was here to do a job, not buy a hat and the swagger that went along with it.

THE DISH

Where Authors Give You the Inside Scoop

❤ ❤ ❤ ❤ ❤ ❤ ❤ ❤ ❤ ❤ ❤ ❤ ❤ ❤

From the desk of Kristen Ashley

Dear Reader,

When the idea for LADY LUCK came to me, it was after watching the Dwayne Johnson film *Faster*.

I thought that movie was marvelous, and not just simply because I was watching all the beauty that is Dwayne Johnson on the screen.

What I enjoyed about it was that he played against his normal *The Game Plan/Gridiron Gang* funny guy/good guy type and shocked me by being an antihero. What made it even better was that he had very little dialogue. Now I enjoy watching Mr. Johnson do just about anything, including speak. What was so amazing about this is that his character in *Faster* should have been difficult to like, to root for, especially since he gave us very few words as to *why* we should do that. But he made me like him, root for him. Completely.

It was his face. It was his eyes. It was the way he could express himself with those—*not* his actions—that made us want him to get the vengeance he sought.

Therefore, when I was formulating Ty Walker and Alexa "Lexie" Berry from LADY LUCK in my head, I was building Ty as an antihero focused on revenge—a man who would do absolutely anything to get it. As for

Lexie, I was shoehorning her into this cold, seen-it-all/done-it-all/had-nothing-left-to-give woman who was cold as ice.

I was quite excited about the prospect of what would happen with these two. A silent man with the fire of vengeance in place of his heart. A closed-off woman with a block of ice in place of hers.

Imagine my surprise as I wrote the first chapter of this book and the Ty and Lexie I was creating in my head were blown to smithereens so the real Ty and Lexie could come out, not one thing like I'd been making them in my head.

This happens, not often, but it happens. And it happens when I "make up" characters. Normally, my characters come to me as they are, who they are, the way they look, and all the rest. If I try to create them from nothing, force them into what I want them to be, they fight back.

By the time I got to writing Ty and Lexie, I learned not to engage in a battle I never win. I just let go of who I thought they should be and where I thought they were going and took their ride.

And what a ride.

I'm so pleased I didn't battle them and got to know them just as they are because their love story was a pleasure to watch unfold. There were times that were tough, very tough, and I would say perhaps the toughest I've ever written. But that just made their happy ending one that tasted unbelievably sweet.

Of course, Ty did retain some of that silent angry man, but he never became the antihero I expected him to be, though he did do a few non-heroic things in dealing with his intense issues. And I reckon one day I'll have my antihero set on a course of vengeance who finds a woman who has a heart of ice. Those concepts never go away. They just have to come to me naturally.

But I had to give Ty and Lexie their story as it came to me naturally.

And I loved every second of it.

Kristen Ashley

♥ ♥ ♥ ♥ ♥ ♥ ♥ ♥ ♥ ♥ ♥ ♥ ♥ ♥

From the desk of Anna Sullivan

Dear Reader,

There's a lot more to being a writer than sitting at a computer and turning my imagination into reality. Of course I love creating characters, deciding on their personal foibles, inventing a series of events to not only test their character but also to help them grow. And that's where everything begins: with the story.

But every writer does her share of book signings and interviews. As with every profession, there are some questions that crop up more often than others. Here are some examples—and the answers that run through my mind in my more irreverent moments:

Q: Why did you become a writer?
A: Because I like to control the people in my life and the only way I can do that is to invent them. (And

unfortunately, I still don't have much control; it's regrettable how often they don't listen to me and get into trouble anyway.)

Q: Those sex scenes, huh? (This invariably comes along with a smirk, waggling eyebrows, or a wink.)
A: I have three kids, you do the math. And please don't wink; it's almost never cute.

Q: Where do you get these ideas?
A: I used to ask my children that after they did something…unexpected. They'd usually come up blank. So do I, so I'll just say I don't know where the characters come from, but they won't leave me alone until I write them. I think there may be a clinical diagnosis and prescription meds for my affliction, but what kind of fun would that be?

But seriously, I hope you enjoy my second Windfall Island novel, HIDEAWAY COVE, as the search for Eugenia Stanhope, kidnapped almost a century before, continues.

Now Holden Abbot is joining the quest for truth, justice, and the American way…Wait, that's Superman. Well, Holden Abbot may not be the man of steel, but he's tall and handsome, and his smooth Southern accent doesn't hurt either. And even if he can't leap tall buildings in a single bound, Jessi Randal is falling head over heels in love with him. She may be Eugenia Stanhope's long-lost descendant, though, and that puts her life in danger, along with her seven year-old son, Benji. Holden may have to do the superhero thing after all. Or he may only be able to save one of them.

I had a great time finding out how this story ended. I hope you do, too.

Anna Sullivan

www.AnnaSulivanBooks.com
Twitter @ASullivanBooks
Facebook.com/AnnaSullivanBooks

♥ ♥ ♥ ♥ ♥ ♥ ♥ ♥ ♥ ♥ ♥ ♥ ♥ ♥ ♥ ♥

From the desk of Rochelle Alers

Dear Reader,

Writers hear it over and over again: Write about what you know. I believe I adhered to this rule when continuing the Cavanaugh Island series with MAGNOLIA DRIVE. This time you get to read about a young Gullah woman and her gift to discern the future. As I completed the character dossier for the heroine, I could hear my dearly departed mother whisper in my ear not to tell too much, because like her, my mother also had the gift of sight.

Growing up in New York City didn't lend itself to connecting with my Gullah roots until I was old enough to understand why my mother and other Gullah held to certain traditions that were a litany of don'ts: Don't put your hat on the bed, don't throw out what you sweep up after dark, don't put up a new calendar before the beginning of a new year, et cetera, et cetera, et cetera. The don'ts go on and on, too numerous to list here.

I'd believed the superstitions were silly until as an adult

I wanted to know why my grandfather, although born in Savannah, spoke English with a distinctive accent. However, it was the womenfolk in my family who taught me what it meant to be Gullah and the significance of the traditions passed down through generations of griots.

In MAGNOLIA DRIVE, red-haired, green-eyed Francine Tanner is Gullah and a modern-day griot and psychic. She is able to see everyone's future, though not her own. But when a handsome stranger sits in her chair at the Beauty Box asking for a haircut and a shave, the former actress turned hairstylist could never have predicted the effect he would have on her life and her future.

The first time Keaton Grace saw up-and-coming actress Francine Tanner perform in an off-Broadway show he found himself spellbound by her incredible talent. So much so that he wrote a movie script with her in mind. Then it was as if she dropped off the earth when she abruptly left the stage. The independent filmmaker didn't know their paths would cross again when he made plans to set up his movie studio, Grace Lowcountry Productions, on Cavanaugh Island. Keaton believes they were destined to meet again, while Francine fears reopening a chapter in her life she closed eight years ago.

MAGNOLIA DRIVE returns to Sanctuary Cove, where the customers at the Beauty Box will keep you laughing and wanting more, while the residents of the Cove are in rare form once they take sides in an upcoming local election. Many of the familiar characters are back to give you a glimpse into what has been going on in their lives. And for those of you who've asked if David Sullivan will ever find a love that promises forever—the answer is yes. Look for David and the woman who will tug at his heart and make him reassess his priorities in *Cherry Lane*.

Happy Reading!

Rochelle Alers

ralersbooks@aol.com
www.rochellealers.org

♥ ♥ ♥ ♥ ♥ ♥ ♥ ♥ ♥ ♥ ♥ ♥ ♥ ♥ ♥

From the desk of Jessica Scott

Dear Reader,

The first time I got the idea for my hero and heroine in BACK TO YOU, Trent and Laura, I was a brand-new lieutenant with no idea what deployment would entail. I remember sitting in my office, listening to one of the captains telling his wife he'd be home as soon as he could—and right after he hung up the phone, he promptly went back to work. He always talked about how much he loved her, and I wondered how he could tell her one thing and do something so different. And even more so, I was deeply curious about what his wife was like.

I was curious about the kind of woman who would love a man no matter how much war changed him. About the kind of woman with so much strength that she could hold their family together no matter what. But also, a woman who was *tired*. Who was starting to lose her faith in the man she'd married.

Having been the spouse left at home to hold the family together, I know intimately the struggles Laura has faced. I also know what it feels like to deploy and leave my family, and how hard it is to come home.

I absolutely love writing stories of redemption, and at the heart of it, this is a story of redemption. It takes a strong love to make it through the dark times.

I hope you enjoy reading Trent and Laura's story in BACK TO YOU as much as I enjoyed bringing their story to life.

Xoxo

Jessica Scott

www.JessicaScott.net
Twitter @JessicaScott09
Facebook.com/JessicaScottAuthor

♥ ♥ ♥ ♥ ♥ ♥ ♥ ♥ ♥ ♥ ♥ ♥ ♥ ♥ ♥

From the desk of Shannon Richard

Dear Reader,

So UNSTOPPABLE had originally been planned for the fourth book, but after certain plot developments, Bennett and Mel's story needed to be moved in the lineup to third place. When I dove into their story I knew very little about where I was going, but once I started there was no turning back.

Bennett Hart was another character who walked onto the page out of nowhere and the second I met him I knew he *needed* to have his story told. I mean, how could he not when he's named after one of my favorite heroines? Yup, Bennett is named after Elizabeth Bennett from Jane Austen's *Pride and Prejudice*. Don't scoff, she's awesome and I love her dearly. And *hello*, she ends up with a certain Mr. Fitzwilliam Darcy...he's my ultimate literary crush. I mean really, I swoon just thinking about him.

And I'm not the only one swooning over here. A certain Ms. Melanie O'Bryan is hard-core dreaming/fantasizing/drooling (just a little bit) over Bennett. Mel was definitely an unexpected character for me. It took me a little while to see that she had a story to tell, and I always like to say it was Bennett who realized her potential before I did.

Both characters have their guards up at the beginning of UNSTOPPABLE. Bennett is still dealing with the trauma he experienced when he was in Afghanistan, and Mel is dealing with getting shot a couple of months ago. Mel is a very sweet girl and she appears to be just a little bit unassuming...to those who don't know her, that is. As it turns out, she has a wild side and she lets Bennett see it in full force. Bennett and Mel were a different writing experience for me. I was discovering them as they discovered each other, and sometimes they surprised me beyond words. They taught me a lot about myself and I will be forever grateful that they shared their story with me.

Cheers,

♥ ♥ ♥ ♥ ♥ ♥ ♥ ♥ ♥ ♥ ♥ ♥ ♥ ♥

From the desk of Lauren Layne

Dear Reader,

I am a hopeless romantic. For as long as I can remember, I've been stalking happy endings. It started with skimming Nancy Drew and Sweet Valley Twins books for the parts about boys. From there, it was sneaking into the Young Adult section of the library way before my time to get at the Sweet Valley High books—because there was kissing in those.

By my mid-teens, I'd discovered that there was an entire genre of books devoted to giving romantics like me a guaranteed happily ever after. It was the start of a lifetime affair with romance novels.

So it shouldn't come as a surprise that as I was stockpiling my book boyfriends, I also did a fair amount of thinking about the future hero of my own love story. I had it all figured out by junior high. My future husband would have brown hair. He'd be a lawyer. Maybe a doctor, but probably a lawyer. He'd be the strong, silent type. Very stoic. He'd be a conservative dresser, and it would be strange to see him out of his classic black suit, except on weekends when he'd wear khakis and pressed polos. We'd meet when I was in my mid-to-late twenties, and he'd realize instantly that my power suits and classic pumps were his perfect match. Did I mention that in this vision I, too, was a lawyer?

Fast forward a few (okay, many) years. How'd I do?

Well…my husband has brown hair. *That's the only part I got right.* He's an extroverted charmer and wouldn't be caught dead in a standard-issue suit. He's not a lawyer, and I've never seen him wear khakis. Oh, and we started dating in high school, and were married by twenty-three.

I couldn't have been more wrong, and yet…I couldn't be more happy. Although I am a "planner" in every sense of the word, I've learned that love doesn't care one bit about the person you *think* is your perfect mate.

In my Best Mistake series, the heroines learn exactly that. They have a pretty clear idea of the type of person they're supposed to be with. And they couldn't be more wrong.

Whether it's the cocktail waitress falling for the uptight CEO, or the rigid perfectionist who wins the heart of a dedicated playboy, these women learn that being wrong has never felt so right.

I had a wonderful time wreaking havoc on the lives of Sophie and Brynn Dalton, and I hope you have as much fun reading about the best mistakes these women ever made.

Here's to the best of plans going awry—because that's when the fun starts.

Lauren Layne

www.laurenlayne.com